SIOUXSIE
AND
THE
BANSHEES

1980-1987

Into
The
Light

Laurence Hedges

SIOUXSIE
AND
THE
BANSHEES
1980-1987

Into
The
Light

Laurence Hedges

WP
WYMER
PUBLISHING
Bedford, England

First published in 2024 by Wymer Publishing
Bedford, England www.wymerpublishing.co.uk Tel: 01234 326691
Wymer Publishing is a trading name of Wymer (UK) Ltd

Print edition (fully illustrated): **ISBN: 978-1-915246-58-5**

Edited by Jerry Bloom.

Printed and bound in Great Britain by
CMP, Dorset.

A catalogue record for this book is available from the British Library.

Typeset/Design by Andy Bishop / Tusseheia Creative
Cover design by Tusseheia Creative
Front cover photo © David Arnoff

Contents

Prologue

Latitude Festival, Henham Park, Suffolk.
10:00pm, Sunday 23 July, 2023.

I am mesmerised by the 'revolving door' equipment removal for Black Midi, the penultimate band of the night to play before the headlining act graces the BBC Sounds stage, watching starry eyed as road crew, guitar, drum and assorted 'other' electronic paraphernalia techs meticulously install equipment with military precision.

Everything is checked and re-checked: monitor levels, guitar tunings, even the perfunctory proliferation of black gaffer tape that one of the crew lovingly double and triple checks to ensure set lists are firmly secured to the stage.

There is a particular frisson of excitement when a blue Vox Teardrop guitar appears. We, the audience, in our thousands, are 'packed in like sardines'.[1]

I have positioned myself as near to the stage as possible and am centred enough so I can savour every moment of the protagonist's performance, selfishly unencumbered by no one in front taller than me.

The house lights go down and Camille Saint-Saëns' ethereally beautiful *The Carnival Of The Animals* (VII Aquarium)[2] ushers firstly the band and then a spectacularly mysterious cloaked and hooded figure. A tumultuous cheer raises the roof. The cloak is shed, the Pam Hogg[3] designed silver jumpsuit hood taken down, and the evocative first six bass guitar notes of 'Night Shift'[4] make the hairs stand up on the back of my neck.

Siouxsie is here.

Chapter One
Israel

London, May 2023.

"…it's not about religion as such, it's more general. A disillusioned person, or whole race who've ceased to understand or believe in what they held to be the truth. It tries to put across, you shouldn't cover what you feel inside by teaching or attitudes imposed on you. It emphasises the strength of the individual". [5]

Siouxsie Sioux

"We need to do one of those Christmas songs. That's what we should do".[6]

Budgie

The ethereal sound of John McGeoch's gorgeous overlayed guitar solo is running through my head, two minutes and one second into 'Israel'[7]. Although fleeting, this moment of blissful transcendence heralds a new era for Siouxsie and The Banshees', especially creatively. McGeoch was now a fully-fledged member of the band, leaving Magazine after *The Correct Use Of Soap* was released in May 1980. He also wrote and played on Visage's[8] debut album, which was dispatched the same month as 'Israel' and *Kaleidoscope* in November 1980.

Just as McGeoch's ten or so seconds of sublime finger picking segues effortlessly into 'Israel's' bridge, perhaps more symbolically it represents a coming of age for a band, just over four years after stepping into the breach at The 100 Club on 20 September 1976.

'Israel' came to fruition after Siouxsie and The Banshees had weathered the temporary setback of the sudden departure of drummer Kenny Morris and guitarist John McKay in Aberdeen on 7 September 1979, the same day as the band's second album *Join Hands* was released, fourteen dates into a thirty-four-date European tour to promote the new album, and a few hours before the band were due to go on stage at the Capitol Theatre.

Support band The Cure played an extended set, and Siouxsie Sioux, after apologising to the audience and offering them their money back for the cancelled gig, took to the stage with The Cure and Steve Severin to play an improvised version of 'The Lord's Prayer'.

An ensuing ten-day hiatus, during which time Sioux and Severin 'went through the horrors of trying to find new band members'[9], the Banshees recruited drummer Peter Clarke aka Budgie from The Slits. Robert Smith would do a set with The Cure before assuming guitar duties with Siouxsie and The Banshees for the remaining nineteen dates of the tour.

'Israel' was the band's first twelve-inch single, reaching number 41 on the UK singles chart, sandwiched between 'The call up' by The Clash and 'Girls Can Get It' by Dr Hook. As Rory Sullivan-Burke, John McGeoch's biographer, states, "Israel' 'would lay down a significant marker the band were about to take with the new album.

Siouxsie recognises the significance of 'Israel', not just at the time, but throughout the band's career. "Israel', I think, probably was the first song that started it, with us starting from scratch as it were. Again, a lot of guitarists just love 'Israel' – any guitarist since, whether with the Banshees or anyone, just wants to be able to play it and loves being able to play it'.[10]

Written in a hotel room in Amsterdam on 11–12 October 1980, at the tail end of the band's first major UK and American tour with McGeoch in 1980, the plan was to release 'Israel' as a Christmas single. Steve Severin recalls that the song 'came together very quickly at the sound checks'.[11]

Adopting the Star of David for the single was another significant milestone for the band; an atonement for Siouxsie's adoption of the swastika several years earlier, the tipping point of which had been the appearance of 'a lot of National Front skinheads turning up to gigs.

They used to piss me off so much'.[12]

Siouxsie endeavoured to stop the skinheads coming to gigs, 'drawing attention to them and slagging them off, even stopping the gig and beating the shit out of them a few times. But they just wouldn't fuck off'.[13]

The antidote to the unwanted audience members culminated in the band leaving the stage and coming back on, wearing the 'Israel' Star of David tee shirts, playing 'Drop Dead' with the searing glare of the spotlights on the skinheads at a gig in Derby on 23 February 1981. 'It was fantastic. The whole audience felt empowered and turned on them'.[14]

'Israel' begins with the melodic austerity of both Steve Severin's flanged bass and Budgie's metronomic bass drum, before Siouxsie's falsetto and John McGeoch's haunting minor-chord four-note arpeggiated guitar motif are ushered in, the latter gorgeously, harmonically flange soaked.

These four notes are conceivably just as iconic as those played by David Gilmour on 'Shine On You Crazy Diamond', the first track on *Wish You Were Here*[15] by Pink Floyd: ethereally resonant, a feast for the ears. The song has a beautiful simplicity about it, underpinned by the almost jazz-like syncopation of Budgie's gentle, nonchalant tapping on the ride cymbal, exemplifying creative restraint, as well as Siouxsie's dislike of the sound of the high hat, describing it as the sound of 'hairspray'[16].

Instead, the two cymbals become a mechanism for the tambourine 'to get more emphasis and more colour'[17] to accompany Siouxsie's 'Little orphans in the snow'[18] sleigh bells; after all, this was their Christmas song.

Budgie's polyrhythmic virtuosity serves the filmic narrative of 'Israel', and the synergistic virtuosity of Budgie and John McGeoch come to the fore when, two minutes and twenty-seven seconds into the song, Budgie's tom-tom isometrics and McGeoch's four-note refrain are joined by the overdubbing of shimmering guitar chords, acoustic sounding but played on McGeoch's beloved Yamaha SG guitar.

Both lyrics and instrumentation have a powerfully discernible confidence. There is a pictorial romance in Siouxsie's delivery, a yearning for a simpler, gentler time, conceivably the antithesis of Israel's complex history. John McGeoch's seven-second short-delay guitar solo, using a deftly executed hammer on technique, takes the song into the realms of the sublime: short and beautifully executed.

A marker has been laid down, and McGeoch's playing on 'Israel' heralded 'a phase of unbridled creativity, something that could only be beneficial for the band and the chilling yet beautiful new sound that was to define the coming album'.[19]

The yearning evoked in Siouxsie's voice is supplemented by a thirty-strong Welsh choir, which is also a barometer of the band's continued, all-encompassing, creative vision. They had previously adopted a similar layering of voices on 'Premature Burial' from *Join Hands*, released in 1979, through studio jiggery pokery using, as co-producer Mike Stavrou recalls, 'double tracking'.[20]

It is also noteworthy that 'Israel' was co-produced by Nigel Gray, who would also share co-production duties with the band on *Juju*, who had previously used three different producers for *The Scream* (Steve Lillywhite) and *Join Hands* (Mike Stavrou and Nils Stevenson).

'Israel' reflects a period of galvanised lucidity for Siouxsie and The Banshees. The album *Kaleidoscope* marked a transitionally fragmented period for the band; a time of limbo before John McGeoch became a permanent member.

The Clive Richardson-directed video for 'Israel' includes all four members of the band, whereas 'Happy House' and 'Christine', despite McGeoch's playing on both songs, as well as the majority of *Kaleidoscope*, sees the band as a threesome, reflective of McGeoch's last hurrah with Magazine.

Never before had the band looked so confident, at ease and resolute than in this four minutes and fifty-four seconds. Filmed at the Brixton Academy[21] while the band were rehearsing for their extensive UK and North America tour, which took place between 16 February 1981 and 14 November 1981, Richardson, adopting Caravaggio-like chiaroscuro, uses a plethora of individual shots of Siouxsie, Budgie, Severin and McGeoch, while also utilising the auditorium space to capture them as an ensemble.

There is no Banshees' 'uniform'. Instead, this is a group of individuals: a besuited beatnik-like Steve Severin in his beret, sunglasses and skinny tie, replete with his Ernie Ball Music Man Stingray bass guitar, stage right; John McGeoch wearing a chunky Native American choker necklace, magenta tee shirt ripped at the neck and leather biker jacket, in deep immersive revery with his SG; Budgie powers away like an athlete on his drum kit, wearing a pink sleeveless shirt; and then there is Siouxsie, bedecked all in black from head to toe with the first outing for her iconic thigh-length boots and Star of David tee shirt.

The artwork for the 45rpm single is a Rob O'Connor[22] designed die-cut gold sleeve with a gradated blue, white and orange Star of David, to reflect aspects of land and sky, on a plain black background on the A-side label. The B-side label is italicised gold and white text. The flip side of the single 'Red Over White', sees Siouxsie and The Banshees delve further into the realms of sonic experimentation, which began on the polygonal *Kaleidoscope*.

The lyric's focal point evokes Hans Christian Andersen's 'The Snow Queen'[23], with its allusions to transfiguration, the parable of good versus evil, and the otherworldliness of altered states, both literal and metaphorical. There is also 'The Tale Of The Juniper Tree'[24] by the Brothers Grimm,[25] laden with folkloric bloodlust, as well as both symbol and metaphor surrounding themes of fertility, biblical allegory, child-abuse, cannibalism, revenge and re-birth.

'The wife prayed for a child day and night, but they did not get one. In front of their house there was a yard where a juniper tree grew, and one day in winter the wife was standing beneath it peeling an apple, and as she was peeling the apple she cut her finger and the blood fell on to the snow. "Oh," said the wife, sighing deeply as she saw the blood before her on the snow, and she grew so downcast, "if only I had a child as red as blood and as white as snow"'.[26] The ensuing narrative is one of spiralling aberration, told with mischievous comity.

Whether lifting net curtains in suburbia or poking beneath the canopy of snow within the realms of a fairytale, Siouxsie's filmic world, articulated through a breathy, haunting delivery, ushers us into a beguiling, auricular hall of mirrors. The band stretches out, especially Budgie, whose percussive, multilayered cross-rhythms underpin the song.

He uses tom toms across the whole drum kit to create a pattern for the vocal, as well as effecting a bass line, a throwback to working with Ian Broudie in Big In Japan during a spell where there was no bass player, which is testament to Budgie's musicality and desire to contribute more to the band than the standard four-to-the-floor beat.

The damascene moment, which remained with Budgie in perpetuity, was watching an interview with Ginger Baker from 1968 and realising that, as a double bass drum player, Baker was putting his left foot to use throughout his playing, keeping time with his right foot and creating patterns with his left, creating a greater range, depth and colour to the percussive sounds.

The first instance of Budgie's use of this technique for Siouxsie and The Banshees can be discerned on 'Hybrid' from the 1980s *Kaleidoscope*. Budgie also cites the mentoring and nurturing of Dennis Bovell, bringing in elements of Dub Reggae when Budgie joined The Slits as well as a legion of other influences including early John Bonham (Led Zeppelin), John "Drumbo" French (Captain Beefheart And His Magic Band), The Glitter Band, Topper Headon (The Clash), 1970s Disco, Bill Legend (T. Rex), Terry Chambers (XTC), Bill Ward (Black Sabbath) and Ian Paice (Deep Purple).[27]

On 'Red Over White', the high hat has been reinstated, splicing, punctuating and searing through the polyrhythmic rumble while Steve Severn's austere but efficacious bass playing runs in parallel, with the occasional flanged perceptible note. At three minutes eighteen seconds, a cacophonous, splenetic and deranged wall of feedback comes to the fore courtesy of John McGeoch, akin to the frenetic playing of Lou Reed on The Velvet Underground's 'I Heard Her Call My Name' from the band's second album *White Light/White Heat*[28].

It is unsurprising that guitarists such as Jonny Greenwood[29] cite McGeoch as a huge influence, using the instrument as a conduit for cogent expression. At four minutes and twenty-six seconds, the outro is a reprise of 'Israel'. 'Red Over White' was entirely incomparable to any other previous Siouxsie and The Banshees song.

Both 'Israel' and the ensuing album *Juju* reflect Steve Severin's mushrooming songwriting abilities. With Siouxsie at the helm lyrically and vocally, Budgie and John McGeoch providing unparalleled musical virtuosity, and Steve Severin's adroitness as a songwriter, this was a world-beating combination.

Footage of the band playing 'Israel' live on *Something Else*[30], their second outing on the television programme, attests to their closeness, confidence, resolve and musicality. There is also a mesmeric version of 'Tenant' from *Kaleidoscope*, replete with McGeoch's use of the

MXR Flanger[31], mounted on a microphone stand.

Live, and with John McGeoch fully on board the Siouxsie and The Banshees bus, the band had a formidable array of songs to choose from. Set lists throughout the 1980 tour are eclectic, and the order in which songs are played varies from gig to gig, with the inclusion of B-sides such as 'Pulled To Bits', 'Red Over White', 'Drop Dead/Celebration' and 'Eve White/Eve Black', alongside a variation of 'Christine', 'Happy House', 'Tenant', 'Trophy', 'Red Light', 'Paradise Place', 'Hong Kong Garden', 'The Staircase (Mystery), 'Switch', 'Icon', 'Regal Zone', 'Playground Twist', 'Helter Skelter', 'Metal Postcard (Mittageisen)' and the newly written 'Voodoo Dolly', which debuted at Brady's Club in Liverpool on 9 September 1980, and 'Into The Light', which was inaugurated live alongside 'Congo Conga'[32] at the Hammersmith Palais on 30 December 1980, the last performance of the 1980 tour, after a sixteen-date stint in North America that included eight appearances at the Whiskey A Go Go in Los Angeles, where Siouxsie and The Banshees played two sets per night: one at 7pm and the other at 11:00pm.

The 1980 tour was a milestone for the band. Four redoubtable, creatively ambitious musicians playing at what would become the 'top of the Banshees'[33] game. Online recordings from the tour reflect a no no-nonsense approach, with an expedience of patter between songs, excepting Siouxsie's mindfulness of audience members being crushed at the front of the stage and the occasional laconic riposte to an audience member's request for 'Hong Kong Garden'.

The documentary 'Girls Bite Back (AKA Women In Rock)'[34], directed by Wolfgang Blud, includes both live footage and interviews with Nina Hagen, The Slits, Girlschool and Siouxsie and The Banshees.

The three Banshees' songs captured during their 3 October 1980 gig are blistering versions of 'Paradise Place', 'Christine' and 'Jigsaw Feeling', interspersed with (mainly) a deadpan Siouxsie holding court in interview on themes of Siouxsie and The Banshees: 'If I was four years younger now, I wouldn't be in a band'[35], plans for the future: 'get married, settle down and have children'[36], and Berlin: 'I wouldn't like to live here'[37], balanced by Steve Severin's observation, 'I think the town's gorgeous'[38], echoed by a thumbs up by John McGeoch.

Contextually, a snapshot of the musical landscape is a festival gig Siouxsie and The Banshees played at the Futurama Festival[39] at Queen's Hall in Leeds on 13 September 1980, alongside Robert Fripp, Echo & the Bunnymen, U2, Altered Images, Clock DVA and Soft Cell.

All bands on the bill were formed at more or less the same time as the Banshees, excepting Robert Fripp, who had disbanded King Crimson in 1974, latterly contributing to the song 'Heroes'[40] by David Bowie and albums by Peter Gabriel[41] (Third album[42] or 'Melt!' as it is often referred to), Blondie[43] (*Parallel Lines*[44]), Talking Heads (*Fear Of Music*[45]) and sessions for Bowie's *Scary Monsters (And Super Creeps)*[46].

Futurama Festival was reviewed by Paul Morley for the *NME*, proclaiming Siouxsie and The Banshees to be 'the most positive thing that happened all day'[47] and 'the weekend's major attraction'[48].

Clearly not much of a festival cheerleader, or at least in this instance, Morley nonetheless eulogises Siouxsie and The Banshees' performance as 'lavish and emphatic, they had the best light show, the largest number of known songs, and they were even things like 'tight' and 'smooth''.[49]

By 16 February 1981, Siouxsie and The Banshees were out on the road again, embarking on a ninety-date world tour that included the UK, Europe, Australia, North America and Canada. Before that, the band road tested[50] four new songs for the band's fourth BBC Radio 1 John Peel Session[51] on 10 February 1981 at Langham One Studios[52], three of which will appear on *Juju*, including 'Halloween', 'Voodoo Dolly' and 'Into The Light'. 'But Not Them'[53] featured in *Juju* rehearsals, was released as part of 'The Creatures'[54] EP, recorded 25 to 27 May 1981 and released 25 September 1981.

The Peel Session crystallises the Banshees' paroxysm of creativity, fuelled in equal measure by determination, relentless gigging and perhaps a soupçon of lingering awareness that the band could have so readily imploded on 7 September 1979.

There is a darker edge to the new songs, an extraordinary transfiguration that evinces a peerless band progressively swimming in their own stream. Previously explored domestic Hitchcockian psychodrama is augmented by facets of the supernatural; a multicoloured phantasmagoria amplified by scintillas of macabre folkloric incantation, all fortified by the musical synergy of all four band members. There is also an echo of themes explored in 'Premature Burial'[55] from 'Join Hands'.

Chapter Two
Juju

Let The Ceremony Begin...

'There are more things in Heaven and Earth, Horatio, than are dreamt of in your philosophy'.[56]

'Hamlet', William Shakespeare

'We felt like a really strong working unit again and were determined to make up the lost time from the fallout of the 1979 split. John (McGeoch) would come round my place and we started working up ideas for Juju*'.*[57]

Steve Severin

Siouxsie and The Banshees' polychromatic musical palette, despite the tenebrosity that would become associated with *Juju*, is set against an era of political and economic strife in the UK. Unemployment was in excess of 2.5 million in April, and there was the perpetual fulmination of public-sector strikes.

The fallacy of social cohesion in cities was writ large in a series of incendiary riots in Brixton in London between 10 and 12 April, prompted by a pileup of grievances including recession, racial tensions and provocation by police and other bureaucratic bodies.

In July, there were riots in Liverpool (Toxteth), Birmingham (Handsworth), Manchester (Moss Side) and Leeds (Chapeltown), as well as other towns and cities across England. The Arab sphere had entered a period of uncertainty and any esprit de corps between the

UK and its European partners had hit its nadir. A vestige of light relief was supplied by the wedding of Prince Charles and Lady Diana Spencer on 29 July, and Bucks Fizz victory in the Eurovision Song Contest with 'Making Your Mind Up'.

Juju
'In certain West African religious or spiritual traditions: an object revered for its magical powers or ability to influence the material world or human affairs, esp. one used as a charm or means of protection'[58]

The title of the album was 'based on a television programme about the growth of esoteric cults in the Western world as an antidote to the bland, dreary nature of most people's lives'.[59]

'Juju was the first time we'd made a "concept" album that drew on darker elements. It wasn't pre-planned, but, as we were writing, we saw a definite thread running through the songs, almost a narrative to the album as a whole'.[60]

Steve Severin

Recording the album began 16 March 1981 at Surrey Sound studios in Leatherhead, the same venue as *Kaleidoscope*.

'Spellbound'
Where to begin…

'It's the perfect Banshees' song; a combination of pop sensibility, with a kind of otherness as well, and it's just musically brilliant'.[61]

Rory Sullivan-Burke

'The magic that we want is not textbook magic. We use words like voodoo and spellbound but they're not to be taken literally. The best magic is when something good happens and you don't plan it, it's not in your control. To an extent it's in your control, but to be totally in control of everything then would be boring, life would be boring. If nothing went "something magic's happened", but it's not like that, it's just a feeling'.[62]

Siouxsie Sioux

Billy 'Chainsaw' Houlston writes, 'On that first day they wasted no time, and immediately set to work on the track already chosen for release as their next single 'Spellbound'. The lyrics of the song were penned by Steve, a while back, who then took the process one step further by setting it to music on the piano. He taped the piano accompaniment and played the results to John, and they worked on it together from there; the song finally coming together with contributions from the rest of the band'.[63]

Recorded at Surrey Sound studios on 16 March 1981 and released as a single on 22 May 1981, before the release of *Juju*[64], 'Spellbound' heralds the Siouxsie and The Banshees transition into full flight. From the opening flanged twinning of John McGeoch's guitar and Steve Severin's bass, not dissimilar in some respects to his introspective playing on 'Pulled To Bits'[65], to Siouxsie's opening vocal, fourteen seconds into the song, accompanied by Budgie's tambourine and high hat, the song enters into canter mode, brim-full of overlaid instrumental textures, with McGeoch's twelve-string acoustic leading the charge, underscored by the venerated finger picking of the Yamaha SG.

Budgie's pounding rhythm, utilising the floor tom, creates a colossal sound with echoes of Kenny Morris' playing, peaking thunderously at one minute and forty-one seconds, congruent with Siouxsie's visceral urging to take one's elders by the legs and fling them down the stairs, lifted from the nursery rhyme 'Goosey Goosey Gander'[66], of which there have been several interpretations including the 'left leg' being derogatory slang for Catholics during the English Civil War 1642–51.

This derives from a traditional distinction between left- and right-handed spades in Irish agriculture, which was adopted as a figure of speech and subsequently bastardised as a term of abuse to discern between Protestants and Catholics, as in someone digging with the wrong foot. The 'Goosey Goosey Gander' is thought to directly reference the goose-stepping of Oliver Cromwell's soldiers as they searched for Catholic priests, hidden in the houses of Catholic dignitaries and other upper-class families.

Goosey goosey gander,
Whither shall I wander?
Upstairs and downstairs
And in my lady's chamber.
There I met an old man
Who wouldn't say his prayers,
So I took him by his left leg
And threw him down the stairs.

Although the lyrics were penned by Steve Severin, Siouxsie's interpretive disdain for any entity representing a semblance of authority is deftly dealt with, as illustrated in earlier songs such as 'Switch', which proffers the thesis that, whether doctor or vicar, both creeds prescribe 'medicine'.

By the same token, the Alfred Hitchcock film *Spellbound*[67], one of the first films to deal with Freudian psychoanalysis, also explores aspects of psychiatry; the 'spell' in question manifest in a multiplicity of scenarios, the foremost being the instant attraction between the two protagonists, Ingrid Bergman[68] as the psychiatrist Dr Constance Peterson and Gregory Peck[69] as the amnesiac patient Dr Anthony Edwardes.

The latter is revealed as John Ballantyne, whose initial charm and ease of manner is overwhelmed by a guilt complex triggered initially when Dr Peterson uses the prongs of her fork to delineate the shape of a swimming pool.

The dark furrows she makes elicit a sudden outburst from Peterson at the unlimited supply of linen at Green Manors[70]. There are several other instances, when seeking refuge at the residence of Dr Peterson's one-time supervisor Dr Brulov, that Ballantyne's mania, including the sight of train tracks and the pattern on Dr Peterson's dressing gown and bedspread, precipitate his anxiety.

It comes to a head when he is overwhelmed by the blinding whiteness of the en-suite bathroom. It transpires that the recurring, monochromatic optical triggers relate to a childhood memory when Ballantyne was sliding down an outdoor bannister and accidentally knocked his brother off, causing him to be fatally impaled on a fence, the root cause of his guilt complex.

The film explores the working of the human psyche in relation to both real and imagined entities, and the power of the mind to entertain the most fantastical of ideas. One of the most spectacular scenes in the film is the Salvador Dali[71] designed 'dream' sequence, which sees Ballantyne recalling an elaborate vision, which is dissected and analysed by Dr Peterson and her mentor Dr Brulov, to ascertain whether his unconscious vision is mere chimaera or can solve the conundrum of Ballantyne's true identity, and whether or not he were responsible for the murder of the real Dr Edwardes.

Originally conceived as a twenty-minute segment, subsequently distilled to under three minutes due to financial constraints, the sequence is overflowing with psychoanalytic symbolism, including a multitude of eyes, curtains, scissors, playing cards, a man with a stocking-covered face, a figure falling off a building wearing skis, someone ensconced behind a chimney, holding and subsequently dropping a bent-out-of-shape wheel, and Ballantyne himself being pursued by large wings as he is running down a colossal slipway.

The scene is replete with perspectival distortion and long shadows, entirely in keeping with the visual tenor of Dali's painting.

Hitchcock subsequently stated that 'What I was after was the vividness of dreams. As you know, all Dali's work is very solid, very sharp, with very long perspectives, black shadows. This was again the avoidance of the cliché: all dreams in movies are blurred. It isn't true – Dalí was the best man to do the dreams because that's what dreams should be'.[72]

Hitchcock's film, festooned with rich symbolism, parallels the 'otherness' of the human psyche explored in Siouxsie and The Banshees' oeuvre, specifically 'Christine' and 'Eve White/Eve Black'.[73]

The video accompanying 'Spellbound', again directed by stalwart Clive Richardson, is the band's most adventurous and cinematic to date. Shot primarily in the Burnham Beeches[74] woodland, where a myriad of *Hammer Horror*[75] films were filmed due to its proximity to Pinewood, Shepperton and Bray studios, the video begins with the multi-layered slow-motion juxtaposition of a black and white cat, Siouxsie, adorned in black, on her hands and knees, a solitary lit candle and burning violet curtains.

This segues into a further agglomeration of imagery, including 'spinning' images of individual band members including Siouxsie in a yellow and black polka dot dress, the same colours as her eye makeup. Budgie's shirt bears the same black and white striations that so agitate John Ballantyne in Hitchcock's 'Spellbound', as the pivotal motif of firstly Siouxsie, then Severin, Budgie and McGeoch hurtle through the woodland.

As the song progresses, there are further overlays of imagery, including some impressive gymnastic agility from Siouxsie, wearing a black carnivalesque Venetian mask, and Budgie, both holding a sizeable red drape (Siouxsie can also be seen clutching a viridian green drape in the video), which re-appears when the band are plagued by a shrouded, Oni-wearing[76] apparition 'not unlike the one that can be found in the Japanese film *Onibaba*[77], directed by Kaneto Shindo[78], which was one of Siouxsie's favourite films at the time of recording'[79].

She commented, "There's a great Japanese film, *Onibaba*, about a woman who kills a Samurai warrior and steals his mask. In the end the mask sticks to her face and when they rip it off, it tears away her flesh so that her own face is a mask".[80]

Shindo took inspiration for *Onibaba* from a Shin Buddhist[81] parable read to him as a child, about a woman donning a terrifying mask that cements itself to her face. Shindo was also deeply affected 'by the ravages of Hiroshima and Nagasaki, and the disfiguring legacy of the atomic bomb attacks'.[82]

In mythology, Onibaba translates as 'Demon Hag', women who have transmuted into Oni, their karmic senescence a result of resentment. The Hikaru Hayashi-composed theme, not entirely dissimilar in style to Alfred Hitchcock's go-to composer Bernard Hermann (conspicuous by his absence for the 'Spellbound' soundtrack), utilises Taiko[83] drumming, the influence of which can be discerned in Budgie's playing, latterly recording with renowned Taiko drummer Leonard Eto[84], who appears on The Creatures' *Hái!* album, and is accompanied and punctuated by both brass and strings and the blood-curdling screech as someone is run through with a sword, reflecting the grotesque violence of the film.

In the film, a woman, played by Nobuko Otowa[85] and her daughter in-law, the actor Jitsuko Yoshimura[86], live in a satoyama[87] region near Kyoto during the Onin[88] war during the Sengoku[89] period in 15th-century Japan.

The two principal characters, hidden in swampland among the seven-foot-high blade-like Suzuki grass fields, trade the possessions of the warriors they ambush and kill. They inhabit a myopic world where Shindo renders everything as metaphor or symbol, focusing on the paramountcy of certain aspects of human nature such as sexuality and the will to survive. The two women's obdurateness sees them in the thick of their own battle; to be extant, while men are absent, at war.

The two women live in a hut nestled in the tall reeds, seemingly sheltered from the rest of the world, and the main action of the film, at least initially, concentrates on the humdrum of their domestic life, except for the occasional bounty, resulting in carcasses to be unceremoniously dumped in a deep pit. Their spoils are bartered for food from a hard-hearted merchant.

The narrative intensifies when the women's neighbour Hachi, played by the actor Kei Satō[90], returns from the war in an almost hallucinatory state to tell the women that their son and husband has been killed in battle.

Hachi's presence and his sexual desire for the daughter, which is eventually reciprocated, is seen as a betrayal of the mother-in-law's dead son. She warns the younger woman of the sin of her sexual desire, citing that her 'infidelity' to her dead son is sinful and will be punished in the realms of purgatory.

After encountering a lost, masked Samurai, the mother, under the guise of leading him to the nearest road, takes him to the makeshift mausoleum, deftly jumping over it while the Samurai falls to his death. Stripped of all his other possessions, the removal of the Oni mask proves a near impossible task, as it is seemingly welded to the Samurai's face.

When the woman prises it off, the warrior's face reveals a

disfigurement at odds with his self-proclaimed beauty, his stated reason for the disguise. The mask is subsequently worn by the mother-in-law, transforming her into a hovering, terrifying, demonic apparition to frighten her daughter-in-law as she makes her way to see Hachi, who happenstances an interloper in his hut eating Hachi's food, only to be gored by one of Hachi's spears.

The denouement of the film is Shakespearian in its misadventure. The mother-in-law, owning up to her duplicity, begs for the mask to be removed as it has become unyieldingly clamped to her face and needs to be shattered before it can be prised off to reveal, as with the Samurai, a mutilated face.

Free of the mask, the older woman screams, "I am not a demon. I am a human being," as both women flee their hut and bound into the night, with the final scene seeing them leaping across the pit of death.

While fanciful, one can see direct corollaries between *Onibaba* and the video for 'Spellbound'. For instance, the abundance of running in *Onibaba*, whether the characters are being pursued or are in pursuit, characterises the pivotal motif of 'Spellbound'.

The Oni mask, which is worn by a cloaked Steve Severin in the Banshees' video, in *Onibaba* proves the macabre vanquishing of both Samurai and older woman.

Both Shindo's film and Richardson's video navigate and narrate elemental themes of light and dark, with a plethora of night-time scenes in *Onibaba*, especially the full-screen close ups of excoriated faces, rendered visible by the cinematic chiaroscuro reminiscent of the paintings of Caravaggio[91].

The night-time woodland scene in 'Spellbound' proves problematic for Siouxsie and The Banshees; they clearly run with greater trepidation compared to the daytime, culminating in John McGeoch losing his footing two minutes twenty-nine seconds into the video.

Onibaba's DNA can be seen in William Friedkin's *The Exorcist*[92]; the Oni mask providing the impetus when Friedkin created the 'Captain Howdy' white-faced demon in the film. Friedkin also cited *Onibaba* as one of the most frightening films ever made, calling it 'a masterpiece of horror and suspense'[93].

Steve Severin's recollection of the 'Spellbound' video shoot is less than effusive, recalling '…it was Cup Final day. Spurs were playing Man City and I had to spend the whole day up a fucking tree! I was so glad it was a draw. It meant that I could watch the replay'.[94]

The B-side of 'Spellbound' reflects the band's further deep-diving sonic experimental deconstruction, with two songs, 'Follow The Sun'[95] and 'Slap Dash Snap'.

'Follow The Sun', like the percussive intensity of 'But Not Them', moves at a languid pace, evoking a not dissimilar landscape to that of *Onibaba*, except that the Suzuki grasses have been replaced by fields of corn and the 'Oni' now appears as a scarecrow.

The three-dimensional, filmic feel of the song is heightened by a miscellany of backward guitar, sounding like an Ektara[96], austerely effective bass guitar, xylophone, triangle and wood block. The tambourine that kicks in at fifty-five seconds conjures up the rhythmical buzz of cicadas.

It is not beyond the realms of possibility that the 'children of the corn' Siouxsie sings of were inspired by the Stephen King[97] story of the same name, the synopsis of which involves a couple, Burt and Vicky, on the brink of divorce, driving through Nebraska, en route to California for a vacation, when they accidentally run over a young boy who has had his throat cut and been hurled into the road.

Burt opens the boy's suitcase to discover a crucifix made of tangled corn husks. The couple agree to report the incident to the police, place the body in the boot of their car and drive to the nearest town, a small, remote community called Gatlin, to ask for help.

It transpires that the backwater is populated by a cult of murderous children who deify a demon that inhabits the local cornfields. As the story unfolds, it transpires that, twelve years previously, the children of Gatlin massacred the town's adults and have decreed that members of their community are forbidden to live past their nineteenth birthday.

The Stephen King story shares some obvious folkloric elements with *The Wicker Man*,[98] and more latterly the Ari Aster[99] directed *Midsommar*.[100] All three stories explore the consequences of crossing a threshold from the quotidian world into the gloaming microcosm of transgressive pagan ritual, sacrifice and hedonistic amorality.

'Slash Dash Snap' is a disassembled vignette of electronica that reflects the early-1980s' vogue for Fairlight[101] sampling, but the song is much more than that. Nearly five years on from their 100 Club debut, and after more than two hundred live performances, plus the imminent release of the band's fourth album, 'Slash Dash Snap' mirrors the Banshees' trajectory of burgeoning creativity, allowing them to take risks and stretch out.

Great artists evolve. Piet Mondrian[102] acquired academic rigour through his formal Fine Art training in the Netherlands but, like Siouxsie and The Banshees, there was always an element of discordant abstraction, even when painting landscapes approximating the style of Post/Neo-Impressionist painters including Georges Seurat[103] and Paul Signac,[104] themselves pioneers of the science of colour-oriented Pointillism[105] and Divisionism.[106]

Just as Mondrian distilled the mainstay of pictorial elements down to their primacy: red, yellow, blue, black and white, horizontal and vertical planes within the parameters of a square or rectilinear format, which in turn could yield infinite abstract possibilities, Siouxsie and The Banshees were using the B-side to create their own unique sonic parallel universe. 'Slap Dash Snap' is also redolent of the William S. Burroughs[107] 'Cut Up' technique, although this can actually be traced further back to the Dadaists[108] of the 1920s.

The technique was subsequently adopted by David Bowie and was also how the Bonzo Dog Doo-Dah Band[109] established their name. Burroughs' method was literally to cut up passages of his own and other writers' prose with scissors and then paste them back together.

The author and visual artist also used this collage technique in other media, transcribing taped cutups that involved several analogue tapes spliced into each other, film montages and an array of mixed-media experiments that coalesced tapes with television, movies, or actual occurrences.

The opaque acerbity of Siouxsie's lyrics and overlayed bickering, reverberating vocal, referring to castles, parcels and shiny razors, reflect the compelling dissonance of fragmented instrumentation.

Aspects of 'Slap Dash Slap' can readily be discerned in Radiohead's 'Kid A'[110], where everything is stripped back, deconstructed and less becomes distinguishably more.

'Spellbound' reached 22 in the UK Official Singles Chart and stayed in the Top 40 for seven weeks. It was also the band's breakthrough single in the USA, peaking at 64 in the US Dance Chart.[111]

The Banshees' *Top Of The Pops* appearance to promote the single on 4 June 1981 and subsequently 18 June 1981, sees the band squeezed onto a stingy, awkwardly shaped studio stage – a diamond-shaped platform that echoes its geometric sculptural backdrop. The band, as ever, appear nonchalant and as though from a preternatural realm: entirely felicitous considering the nature of the song being performed. Siouxsie, ever beguiling, 'owns' the stage and there is a perfect visual symmetry to the band.

There is cohesion and orderliness without the straightjacket of a generic style. Perhaps the Banshees realised that dogmatic adherence to any style or fashion would curtail their ambition to be truly phenomenal.

Of course, Siouxsie has become synonymous with an unequivocal 'look'. However, this, I feel, rather preserves an artist who was forever moving forward in aspic.

During Pablo Picasso's well-documented Rose Period when he was living in Paris between 1904 and 1907, he and his girlfriend Fernande Olivier used to consume opium and hashish at a friend's place.

Eating hashish pills meant that 'Picasso had a wretched trip – it came to him that he had come to a dead end, painting the same thing over and over again'.[112]

Sartorially and musically, there is no definitive Siouxsie, just as there is no categorical Siouxsie and The Banshees. It is, perhaps, not an overstatement to say that Siouxsie and The Banshees invented 'Goth'[113] as a musical genre because, in truth, they did; much to Siouxsie's chagrin, asserting 'Gothic in its purest sense is actually a very powerful, twisted genre, but the way it was being used by journalists – "goff" with a double "f" – always seemed to be to be about tacky harum scarum horror and I find that anything but scary. That wasn't what we were about at all'.[114]

Steve Severin also points out that 'We'd actually described *Join Hands* as "gothic" at the time of its release but journalists hadn't picked up on it'.[115]

John McGeoch expands on the theme, 'The sound to *Juju* had more of a rock feel to it and, in some ways, harks back to *The Scream*. We were always more thriller than horror, that Hitchcockian juxtaposition of two unlikely elements. More blood dripping on a daisy than scary beast sinking its fangs into its victim'.[116]

Fittingly, 'Spellbound's far-reaching brilliance captured a new audience when it was used for the closing credits of the Netflix[117] series *Stranger Things*[118] season 4, episode 9 finale.

In-house Polydor graphic designer Rob O'Connor recalls the process of designing the artwork for the single: 'Regarding illustrators and photographers, particularly designers, you wouldn't give them the time of day because that's what we all did in the department. I did, however, take a lot of notice of the work of Lars Hokanson[119] and Lois Hokanson, two woodcut artists.[120] I showed their work to the band, and they liked it, so I commissioned the artists to create an African-looking tribal scene which depicted aspects of ritual and dancing, which was very much in keeping with the theme of the *Juju* album'.

The monochromatic woodcuts, used for both front and back single cover, evoke the work of German Expressionist[121] artist Emil Nolde[122], especially the work 'Candle Dancers (Kerzentänzerinnen)' 1917[123], a motif explored through a Nolde painting of the same name from 1912, which depicts two women dancing with uninhibited abandon.

The nature of black and white woodcut printmaking allows the artist directness of expression, and the Hokansons' designs use the positive/negative characteristics of the medium to depict a vortex of shapes, from which one can discern a configuration of masks, figures and limbs, all colluding to create an efficacious design.

The back cover design depicts a hybridised therianthrope, part bird, part human, hovering as it looks down towards the animated and ominous human figure below.

Rob O'Connor, in interview, emphasised the unique position of Siouxsie and The Banshees in being signed to a major record label, yet being able to maintain complete artistic autonomy, free of interference.

Every facet of the band's output was directed, choreographed and mandated according to what they desired, and O'Connor, the Banshees' go-to record sleeve designer since *Join Hands*, understood what the band were trying to accomplish and how this didn't always coalesce with Polydor: 'As I remember it, I had already started working for Siouxsie with the other albums and we had a little bit of a relationship. When I started working on the designs for *Juju*, I was still at Polydor. By the time the artwork was delivered, I had set up Stylorouge[124], so *Juju* was bridging the gap for me.

Siouxsie and The Banshees were one of the first punk bands to sign to a major label who had creative control written into their contract; not many had. The band were very quick to be critical of the record company. In those days, a lot of the bigger record companies had lost their way and weren't prepared for punk. So they had to relearn the rules almost about how music was working. It was sort of growing from the ground up, much more subterranean. The band and I had learned through the previous two album releases that we needed to insist on what we wanted'.[125]

'Life is just like a cut up'.

Billy 'Chainsaw' Houlston[126]

O'Connor came up with an initial design, which he then presented to the band: 'I started putting visuals together. One of them was based on a Victorian anatomical drawing idea, which I wanted to suggest to them as a pastiche. It was like a naked man's body, which I presume was originally drawn from life. It'd be like a cadaver that had been sliced open and then pulled apart. And then you can see the inside of someone's chest and all the organs. I found the exact reference of a drawing like this; the corpse hands pulling their chest open. The idea was to redraw it, not me personally, but to get someone who really knew about anatomical drawing, using scraper board, so it looked authentically Victorian, and had little people hidden inside, as well as organs, tubes, guts, and all the rest of it. To cut a long story short, the band didn't like the idea, dismissing it very quickly'.[127]

O'Connor needed to go back to the drawing board to implement another idea. 'The thing I really liked about the anatomical concept was the typography, which had a kind of Victorian textbook feel to it, with Roman fonts that said fig 1. the ventricles, or whatever it might have been, and it was just that nice mix of Roman and italic typography. That's what I really wanted to retain, and the band then suggested a picture of what they wanted us to investigate: an African talisman, some kind of mask. And I found something in the recently opened Museum of Mankind,[128] which, if I remember correctly, we visited and saw all these quite boring objects, more useful perhaps to a scholar or academic. We were told that there were a lot more artefacts behind the scenes which we could access if we could be more specific about what we wanted to see. Subsequently, I sent a photographer back to the museum and it was his photograph that ended up on the album cover. I don't know if you'd call the object he captured an actual Juju, I suppose it is, but Juju's tend to be much more like jewellery or something. But it's a genuine thing, probably 150 years old and made of ebony.'[129]

Regarding the Juju itself, 'The photograph of the object was really dark, surrounded by vines and hair. Because it was so dark and black, we were a bit underwhelmed. We tried, just as an experiment, to give it a slightly blue printed tint and then reversed it as a negative. So anything that was black and blue went white to gold, so it looked a bit more unusual, and a bit more 'horror', really. The other reference that came up in conversation with the band was the possibility of having all of the lyrics cut up, but this would have involved a lot of typography, and we didn't have all the lyrics at the time. So, we got some very abstract music, just scales or something, and the guy who I worked with on this was doing a record cover for a single for a band called The Wall[130] who were an arty northern punk band. I liked what he did with post-production. I got him involved and he started put together the background for the *Juju* album cover. The torn-up aesthetic we tried initially looked too real. It was a slightly yellowed music sheet paper with annotations, with different coloured paint and pencil and all over it. It just looked a bit childish, but as soon as we flipped it and made it a negative, it felt like the conjoining of the statue and the music worked really nicely together. We reinstated the typography at the top, which was a mixture of a Roman typeface and italic. And then I split the overall design down the middle, with the Juju on the right-hand side. Everything sort of fell into place. And the band really liked it'.[131]

'Into The Light'

'Into The Light's debut live outing was at the Hammersmith Palais[132] on 30 December 1980, and it was recorded for the *Juju* album on 20 March 1981 at Surrey Sound studios. It is a song that demonstrates perfectly how confident the band had become in their use of multifaceted orchestration to create sonorous mosaics.

Both Steve Severin's bass and Budgie's drums synchronous initiation of the song preludes the powerful single chord jangle, seven seconds in, of John McGeoch's MXR flanged, Gizmotron-fuelled guitar, aided and abetted by his faithful twin setup of Roland Jazz Chorus and Marshall JCM800 amplifiers.

It's conceivable that producer Nigel Gray's musical aesthetic introduced more space into the Banshees' sound, especially on *Juju*, and McGeoch's playing on 'Into The Light' is not entirely dissimilar to that of Andy Summers[133], especially on a song like 'Walking On The Moon'[134] (the catalyst for McGeoch's initial suggestion that Siouxsie and The Banshees use Gray as a producer), where Summers employs chord fragments, leaving the lower range of notes to the rhythm section, the net result of which is the guitar providing a sort of polychromatic burst.

McGeoch's intransigent creativity, aided and abetted by what would become his characteristic sound, especially on *Kaleidoscope* and *Juju*, would resonate with producer Nigel Godrich,[135] especially the guitar playing on Radiohead's 'There, There'.[136]

Goodrich also credits the influence of Nigel Gray, recalling, 'As a kid, I was obsessed with *Regatta de Blanc* by the Police, and saw it was produced by Nigel Gray. A lightbulb went off that there was someone called Nigel doing this stuff'.[137]

McGeoch's official biographer Rory Sullivan-Burke surmises that it's possible that a Fairlight is used on aspects of 'Into The Light', but it is more likely that the sound is due to the guitarist's pioneering inventiveness with sound.

Lyrically, 'Into The Light' projects an apologue of a different type of conjuration, with liaison as its key trope. It isn't beyond the realms of possibility that the two hearts entwining and the bleaching into white (alluding to Budgie's peroxide white hair, perhaps), and clandestine orientation of being kept out of sight, pertain to Siouxsie and Budgie, whose side project 'The Creatures' eventuated with the beginning of some initially sequestrated assignations.

Siouxsie improvised the lyrics as she sang them, accompanying Budgie and Severin as they bounced some ideas around during a live soundcheck. There is a bewitching essence to Siouxsie's lovestruck libretto and operatic declamation, which plays with juxtaposed imagery, light and dark, with the adroitness of a poet, invoking 'He wishes for the cloths of heaven'[138] by W.B.Yeats[139] with its allusions to lambency, crepuscularity and darkness.

> Had I the heavens' embroidered cloths,
> Enwrought with golden and silver light,
> The blue and the dim and the dark cloths
> Of night and light and the half-light,
> I would spread the cloths under your feet:
> But I, being poor, have only my dreams;
> I have spread my dreams under your feet;
> Tread softly because you tread on my dreams.

Siouxsie and Budgie's relationship remained unknown to John McGeoch throughout his tenure as a Banshee: 'I honestly didn't know that Siouxsie and Budgie had started a relationship. I still had no idea the day I left the band. I suppose the thought had crossed my mind when they started working as The Creatures... I can only assume there was a lot of creeping around in hotel corridors late at night'.[140]

Siouxsie attributes at least part of the attraction to Budgie to her love of 'big drums'[141] and 'That's what was great about The Glitter Band – two drummers!'[142]

For Budgie's part, he views playing music and coalescing with other musicians as having a coruscating effect on him, citing 'Jayne from Big In Japan' and Ari from The Slits'.[143]

Budgie also describes the dynamic between vocalist and drummer thus: 'There is definitely a special link between drummers and vocalists, and that link is imperative if the music is going to be good. The singer and the drummer play the roles of conductor and interpreter and everything else in the music revolves around that'.[144]

The galvanisation of Siouxsie and Budgie's relationship, both personally and professionally, manifested itself through the introduction of 'But Not Them' from the outset of the 'Juju' tour, which they started playing 'together as a duo in the middle of the set'.[145]

'But Not Them' was the perfect vehicle for drums and voice, and both Steve Severin and John McGeoch encouraged Siouxsie and Budgie 'to try doing some stuff together. That said, they were probably sniggering, expecting us to trip up'.[146]

With no room left on *Juju* for additional material, Siouxsie and Budgie used a fortuitous window of time while Steve Severin and John McGeoch took a break from 'teasing the arrangement of 'Arabian Knights' out of its original 3/4 waltz time'[147] during the sessions for *Juju* at the Ritz Rehearsal Studios[148] in Putney in London.

Siouxsie and Budgie enlisted the help of producer Mike Hedges[149] for their side project, spending three days at London's Playground Studio[150], between 25 May and 27 May 1981, recording the *Wild Things* EP,[151] taken from the Maurice Sendak[152] book *Where The Wild Things Are*,[153] which centres around Max, a young boy, who, after dressing in his wolf suit, wreaks mayhem throughout his house and is subsequently sent to bed without his supper.

Max's bedroom mutates into a jungle, and he sails to an island inhabited by monsters, simply called the Wild Things, which try to frighten Max. This proves futile, and, after terrorising the creatures, Max is acclaimed as the king of the Wild Things and cavorts with his underlings.

After a while, Max ends the festivities and orders them to bed without their supper. However, to the Wild Things' chagrin, Max starts to feel lonely and decides to give up being king and return home. The creatures take umbrage, not wanting Max to go, and throw themselves into paroxysms of anger as Max tranquilly sails home. On returning to his bedroom, Max discovers a hot supper waiting for him.

The Creatures' name was suggested by Steve Severin to Siouxsie at one of the regular parties he used to hold with his flatmate Richard Jobson[154] in West Hampstead, and she 'loved it'.[155]

The five songs recorded for the *Wild Things* EP were 'Mad Eyed Screamer', 'So Unreal',[156] 'But Not Them', 'Wild Thing'[157] and 'Thumb'.

The artwork for The Creatures' *Wild Things* EP captures Siouxsie and Budgie's ardour through two photographs taken by Adrian Boot[158] in a hotel where Siouxsie and The Banshees were staying after a gig they played in Newcastle on 10 August 1981 to celebrate the 'Handicapped Olympics' (sic).[159]

Siouxsie recalls being 'asked to do a special gig for an invited audience of kids, so we did all our singles. It was one of the greatest gigs we ever played'.[160] After the gig, Siouxsie remembers, 'Fuelled by a lot of champagne, Budgie and I let Adrian Boot, a photographer we'd known for ages, take shots of us in the shower in one of the hotel rooms. It was my obsession with Hitchcock's shower scene in *Psycho* again. I wanted the ambiguity of sex and murder for the shot and, of course, in black and white. For the label photos, I wanted the spirit of (Millais') pre-Raphaelite painting of Ophelia underwater, and covered in flowers, and wanted it to look as if I was nude. Because it was going to be a head and shoulders shot, I wasn't too bothered. There were a lot of flowers'.[161]

Rob O'Connor muses that Siouxsie 'may have overlooked the photographs that a couple of gay fans from the USA had sent to her of themselves in a shower. Either that or the band may have made this story up to get me going! I don't remember the *Psycho* reference, although I guess it's an obvious one in retrospect. What I loved about the images was that the subject matter dealt with raw, spontaneous desire and the shoot was carried out in an appropriately last-minute fashion. It really captured the stripped-back sensuality of the EP. I still find the Creatures projects very exciting musically.[162]'

'Arabian Knights'

Recorded at Surrey Sound studios on 17 March 1981, 'Arabian Knights', the second single from *Juju*, was released 24 July 1981. It was written in 3/4 time, like 'The Staircase (Mystery)', and subsequently changed to 4/4 time.

'Arabian Knights' was recorded for the BBC Radio 1 Richard Skinner Studio Session[163] show at Langham House, recorded on 4 June 1981, first transmitted on 16 June 1981 and first played live on 16 June at the Hammersmith Palais.

Conceivably 'Desert Kisses' more obstreperous twin, Siouxsie's 'Arabian Knights' lyric has been described as a critique of gender equality. However, this conjecture runs counter to Siouxsie's intentions: 'It's nothing to do with a 'feminist' thing, it's like a humane thing. Like how the Muslim women cope, I don't know. The way women are treated in some religions, if it was a race being treated like that and not a sex, there would be uproar about it.'[164]

At the time, Siouxsie was listening to a lot of The Doors[165] and one can detect parallels between 'Arabian Knights' and 'Riders On The Storm'. What typifies both songs is the deftness of instrumental and vocal conveyance, fashioning an enveloping, captivating, cinematic narrative.

'Arabian Knights', putatively, borrows its theme from the story or series of stories of the same name. Included in *One Thousand and One Nights*[166], a collection of Middle Eastern folktales set in the Middle Ages, 'Arabian Knights' is the story of Shahryār,[167] whom the narrator, his wife Scheherazade, describes as a Sasanian king, ruling in India and China.

Shahryār is dismayed to discover that his brother's wife is an adulterer. Subsequently, unveiling his own wife's infidelity, Shahryār has her killed. His resentment and mournfulness are such that he decides that all women are unfaithful, and he marries a series of aristocratic virgins, procured by his Vizier[168], only to behead each one the next morning before they have a chance to humiliate him.

Scheherazade, much to her father's chagrin, volunteers to marry Shahryār. Scheherazade is well versed in the legends of preceding kings, having collected a thousand volumes relating to bygone races and dead rulers, as well as the arts, philosophy and science. Knowing her probable fate, Scheherazade asks that she might say goodbye to her younger sibling Dunyazad, who suggests that Scheherazade tell Shahryār a story that night.

Shahryār is enraptured by the tale, but Scheherazade stops in the middle, conscious that dawn is about to break. Shahryār grants Scheherazade a reprieve so she can finish the story the next night, and she begins another, more thrilling tale. She, again, stops halfway through, meaning her life is spared once more. After one thousand and one nights, and one thousand stories, Scheherazade announces to the king that she has no more tales to tell and asks to say goodbye Shahryār and Scheherazade's three sons. However, Shahryār is so enamoured with Scheherazade's thousand stories, he falls in love with her, and she is absolved.

Siouxsie's enthusiasm for film means it is likely that she was familiar with the 1942 Hollywood film version, a substantially sanitised adaptation of the original story. In the film, the overseer at a harem tells the story of Haroun-Al-Raschid, the caliph of Baghdad. Kamar, Haroun's brother, is infatuated with Scheherazade, a dancer at Ahmad's circus. Scheherazade has been assured that she will marry the ruler of the land, so Kamar instigates a coup and Haroun is forced to flee.

During the rebellion, Haroun is wounded and found in the street by Scheherazade, who takes him to the circus where he is concealed. Kamar, assuming Haroun is dead, seizes the title of caliph and orders Sherazade to marry him. Kamar's commander perceives Scheherazade as a threat and decrees that she be sold as a slave. The film ends with Haroun freeing Scheherazade and falling in love with her.

Wittingly or otherwise, Siouxsie remained resolutely unafraid to explore themes and motifs that would prove inflammatory, and, in the case of 'Arabian Knights', it was one singular noun, as Siouxsie explained in 1986, 'To think, some of our records might end up with an 'X' certificate. Like all the fuss over our 'Arabian Knights' single with the line about 'orifices'. It was only a new way of describing something... something natural, physical. It wasn't smutty or rude. Just imagery... but they don't like that'.[169]

Further reflection in 1989 elicited a quintessentially Siouxie remark, 'With 'Arabian Knights' it was quite a thrill to get the word 'orifices' on the radio'.[170]

The lyric of 'Arabian Knights' comprises a wealth of juxtaposed imagery that ostensibly serves as critique of the extreme end of the spectrum of Middle Eastern cultural mores. The genius of 'Arabian Knights' is that the listener is blindsided by the overwhelming romanticism of the song; the riches promised by gorgeous, sweltering instrumentation and luxuriant vocal delivery accompanied by a superfluity of barbed, disquieting imagery including allusions to abduction, oil spills, and acquired culinary appetites.

John McGeoch's tremulous flanged, single-chord introduction is joined by the admonitory rumble of Steve Severin's bass, Budgie's percussive thumping, evocative of the bass-drum-heavy introduction to the Shangri-Las'[171] 'Leader Of The Pack'[172], and Siouxsie's vocal, and there the melody takes full flight. It is at one minute and fifty-nine seconds when 'Arabian Knights' reaches its sonic climax, heralding Siouxsie's acerbic libretto alluding to women serving the sole purpose of producing babies while their husbands indulge in some sordid extra-marital activities. The outro of the song regains its initial serenity, with the patter of Zills[173] replacing the tambourine for added frisson.

'Arabian Knights' peaked at number 32 on the UK Singles Chart. Two videos were shot for the song, both directed by Clive Richardson. The original promo aired on *Top Of The Pops* on 20 August 1981 and was subsequently not seen until over twenty years later when it resurfaced on the *The Best Of Siouxsie And The Banshees (Sound & Vision)* DVD[174].

The plot involves Siouxsie being unrolled from a carpet at the beginning of the video by the other band members, conceivably alluding to the iconic scene in the 1963 film 'Cleopatra',[175] superimposed against a backdrop of undulating sand dunes, as a snake winds its way across the desert, waves crash against precipitous cliffs and Steve Severin, Budgie and John McGeoch play backgammon.

Siouxsie, for part of the video, is dressed in a purple velvet and gold-embroidered Moroccan kaftan, golden headscarf topped off by a wide rimmed sorceress' hat draped with black chiffon, as she flies through the air on a magic carpet. Sword fighting ensues between Severin, Budgie and McGeoch against the backdrop of a magnificent Iranian Iwan[176], while Siouxsie brandishes her own foil.

The second video[177] for the song is a less lavish affair, set against the precipitous backdrop of the Marseille[178] coastline, the opening sequence featuring a far more casually dressed Siouxsie, not quite hitting her acting cue when the first chorus kicks in; however, this is entirely in keeping with the overall tenor of the video, which is more an assemblage of juxtaposed and not entirely cogent vignettes. The swordfight scene that coincides with the instrumental section of 'Arabian Knights' is a cleverly edited sepia-toned sequence; every sword strike and blow is spliced to coincide with the 'Gated reverb'[179] effect of Budgie's drumming. The anchor for both videos is Siouxsie as majestic sorceress. The video ends with a series of Banshees' silhouettes against a crepuscular backdrop.

In journalist Alex Petridis' article '100 Albums To Hear Before You Die'[180], he describes 'Arabian Knights', along with 'Spellbound' as 'poised, peerless exercises in magic realism that you could dance to'.[181] Smashing Pumpkins singer and guitarist Billy Corgan chose 'Arabian Knights' as one of the songs on his BBC6 Music Playlist.[182]

The B-side of 'Arabian Knights' comprises two songs: 'Congo Conga' and 'Supernatural Thing'. 'Congo Conga' could be considered Siouxsie And The Banshees' creative apogee, a conglomeration of everything happening at once.

Ushered in by a single electronic pulse courtesy of a Jew's Harp,[183] the song then employs Siouxsie's plethora of 'Ohs', which is in turn accompanied by some pioneering funk-oriented bass, dramatic percussion and a powerful three-note guitar Blondie-like 'poppy' refrain from John McGeoch.

As with so many Banshees' songs, particularly B-sides, 'Congo Conga's' precociousness is predicated on every facet of instrumentation serving the song, in turn rendering it a masterclass of restraint. Eliminating the superfluous has become the band's raison d'être.

At two minutes and one second, 'Congo Conga' accelerates into overdrive with the whirling dervish timbre of a tin whistle, chaperoning in voice, guitar, bass and drums. Siouxsie's vocal exudes exultation, although this euphoria belies a not insignificant reference to the Mau Mau movement, a nationalist and anti-colonial insurrection in Kenya during the 1950s.

Primarily directed by the Kikuyu[184], the movement also involved members of other ethnic groups in Kenya, all of whom were opposed to British colonial rule and the impounding of their land.

The 'Congo' in the song is conceivably an allusion to the Belgian Congo[185] where Siouxsie's parents met, and her brother and sister were born. The 'Conga', a dance that was believed to have migrated from Africa with West Indian slaves, subsequently became a popular street dance in Cuba, appropriated by politicians during the early years of its republic as a pre-election appeal to the population.

In tandem with its dance antecedents, the conga drum, also known as tumbadora, is an elevated, narrow, single-headed drum from Cuba, having been developed by Cubans of African descent during the latter part of the nineteenth century. The drum is staved, akin to wooden barrels, and categorised into three groups: quinto (tallest lead drum), tres dos or tres golpes (middle drum), and tumba or salidor (lowest drum).

'Congo Conga' has a similar rapturous disposition to its Cab Calloway[186] jazz-oriented namesake, albeit through a glass darkly.

'Supernatural Thing', originally written by Haras Fyre,[187] otherwise known as Patrick Grant and Gwen Guthrie,[188] was recorded by Ben. E. King in 1974 and released in 1975, where it became a top five hit on the Billboard Hot 100.[189]

Budgie's introduction to the song is not a million miles away from the Ian Paice[190] jazz swing he so venerated. One need only listen to the first thirteen seconds of 'Living Wreck' from the album *In Rock*[191] to discern percussive parallels, including a similar method of using the high-hat as a mechanical armature for the tambourine.

The song is jam-like and extemporised in its playfulness and exemplifies a band entirely in its own stream, eluding categorisation. One of the facets which makes the song distinctive are the myriad seductive vocal overdubs that add to its multi-layered nature. 'Supernatural Thing' could be seen as the 'poppier' constituent of Siouxsie and The Banshees, the 'supernatural' suggesting Siouxsie and Budgie' relationship, as well as befitting the 'Juju' leitmotif.

The design for the 'Arabian Knights' single sleeve followed a similar modus operandi to 'Spellbound'. However, this time it was Rob O'Connor's illustrations providing the basis for what was intended to be turned into woodcuts by Lars and Lois Hokanson.

Siouxsie and The Banshees approved these initial drawings, but Polydor kiboshed the woodcut proposal because outsourcing the work to a third party would, as far as they were concerned, prove too costly. O'Connor subsequently embellished his initial designs using felt tip pen so they would have the appearance of authentic woodcuts based on the Hokanson blueprint.

The front cover, black on red, is an imposing figurative composition, evoking the resolutely bold work of German artist Kathe Kollwitz.[192] The back cover, black on green, portrays the striking, dynamic silhouette of a dancer, while another figure crouches over two drums. Both front and back covers use the same gold Roman font with 'Siouxsie and The Banshees' above the images and 'Arabian Knights' below.

'Halloween'

> *The night was dark, no father was there,*
> *The child was wet with dew;*
> *The mire was deep, and the child did weep,*
> *And away the vapour flew*[193]

William Blake

Four songs into side one of *Juju* and recorded on 18 March 1981 at Surrey Sound studios, the ebullience of the album continues to accelerate with 'Halloween'. The kernel of the song originates with a bass line Steve Severin was toying with when John McKay and Kenny Morris were still in the band, and lyrically, at least in part, 'Halloween' is an exploration of the moment when one becomes cognisant of the self, as Steve Severin recalls, 'My source for that ('Halloween') is something that happened to me when I was very young, understanding reality for the first time... I suddenly realised when I was about six that I was a separate person. Suddenly I knew I was around instead of just being a part of things. And once that happens you realise that you've lost something like an innocence'.[194]

John McGeoch ushers in the song with a teasing, shivering guitar introduction and is then joined by the melodious cadence of Steve Severin's bass, accompanied by a shimmering cymbal. A countless number of Banshees' songs possess an intoxicating gyring, due in no small part to Severin's panoply of musical references that include, among countless others, Bernard Hermann, as well as, one would surmise, Camille Saint-Saëns' carnivalesque 'Danse Macabre',[195] Aram Khachaturian's 'Sabre Dance',[196] which one can readily discern in John McGeoch's playing one minute thirty-eight seconds into 'Halloween', Julius Fucik's 'Entry Of The Gladiators',[197] Gioachino Rossini's 'William Tell Overture'[198] and, with a considerable leap of imagination, Sol Bloom's 'The Streets Of Cairo'.[199]

The 'Sturm und Drang'[200] of 'Halloween' is beholden to the congruous 'narration' of the song by all four band members. Contentiously and subjectively, 'Halloween' could wear the exalted 'perfect Siouxsie and The Banshees song crown', or at least approximate the band's appetency to create frisson in perpetuity.

It would be lazy to make parallels with John Carpenter's film 'Halloween'[201] just for the sake of it, other than its cinematic iconography and the Hitchcockian trope of suburban dissonance explored on *The Scream*. Siouxsie's lyrics meditate on Severin's preliminary idea of innocence lost – part joyous reminiscence, part acerbic grisly chimaera.

'Halloween' is the wide-eyed preserve of children, dressing up as ghouls, demons and ghosts to claim their bounty from unsuspecting neighbours: ostensibly (more or less) repercussion-free extortion. It wouldn't have been lost on Siouxsie that Halloween lore developed out of Celtic harvest festivals, in particular the Gaelic festival Samhain,[202] which is regarded as having pagan roots.

There is also a theory that Samhain may have transformed eventually into the Christian All Hallow's Day[203], along with All Hallow's Eve. The addition of Vibraslap[204], a percussion instrument formerly made from the jawbone of a donkey, horse, mule, or cow, that produces a vigorous buzzing sound and in most of Latin America, including Mexico, Peru, El Salvador, Ecuador and Cuba, enhances the psychodrama of the song.

'Monitor'

'Break on through to the other side'.[205]

Jim Morrison

Curtain-twitching gets a facelift…

'Section 4 of the 1824 Vagrancy Act gave police officers the discretionary power to arrest anyone they suspected of loitering with intent to commit an arrestable offence. A survival from a much earlier period of social upheaval, following the mass demobilisation of soldiers after the Napoleonic Wars, it was redeployed intensively from the sixties onward against young black men in Britain. They could be arrested, charged and convicted simply for walking down the street'.[206]

Deemed to be a significant contributory factor in the race riots of 1981 and its associated abuse of power, the Sus law[207] was repealed on 27 August 1981. In a turn of events straight from the pages of J.G.Ballard,[208]however, a proliferation of surveillance systems at residential parking garages and housing estates owned by local authorities was put into operation.

Some of the first remote CCTV systems such as the Robot Slow Scan 500 would 'monitor' activity and authorise the transmission to an alarm receiving centre, using a standard telephone landline or PSTN.[209] The introduction of CCTV across the UK prompted much heated discourse about encroachment on civil liberties. Its application from the mid-1960s in sport, including automobile racing, wrestling and boxing, would subsequently be remodelled as pay-per-view[210] television, all of which was grist to Siouxsie and The Banshees' mill for 'Monitor', the lyrical crux of which centres around '… the advent of Closed-Circuit TV and the idea of real violence as entertainment'.[211]

As an adjunct, there was also the phenomenon of 'snuff films'[212], which professed to show scenes of actual murder. The concept of snuff films came to light during the 1970s, when an urban myth emerged that a secret industry was making such films for profit. These rumours were amplified in 1976 with the release of a film called *Snuff*[213], which exploited the myth in its marketing campaign.

However, *Snuff* the film relied solely on special effects to mimic murder. The subterranean snuff genre entered the mainstream with the advent of *Videodrome*,[214] written and directed by the 'King of Venereal Horror'[215] David Cronenberg.[216]

The narrative of the film pivots around CIVIC-TV television station, which specialises in sensationalist programming. Harlan, the operator of CIVIC-TV's unauthorised satellite dish, shows the station's president, Max Renn, *Videodrome*, a sprawling production allegedly being broadcast from Malaysia, depicting anonymous victims being violently tortured and subsequently brutally murdered. Presuming this to be the future of television, Max directs Harlan to begin unofficial use of the show. Cronenberg's film is also a prophetic glimpse into what would become the cumulative indistinctness between viewer and viewed, courtesy of webcam[217] technology, whereby the mantilla of demarcation has evolved further into the realms of often lurid, monetised transaction.

'A story was related to Siouxsie of how, when CCTV was installed in a tower block in an attempt to curtail vandalism and crime, it instead resulted in the tenants deriving more pleasure from watching the 'real life' crime on CCTV than watching fictionalised accounts on their own televisions'.[218]

This embryonic modus operandi of surveyed exclusivity has become the ubiquitous viewing median with the advent of multiple internet platforms offering a never-ending repository of satiating, algorithmically effectuated imagery.

In response to this escalating all-pervasive organism, filmmaker Adam Curtis[219] remarked, regarding the rise of social media platforms and the 'attention economy'[220], 'I know that social media corporations like what they call high arousal emotions, because it keeps people online longer'.[221] Curtis' counter argument is the consumer's steadfast desire for blockbuster movies, many of which are three hours long.

A voltaic John McGeoch riff kickstarts 'Monitor' and, nine seconds in, simpatico with drums, bass and then vocal. The drumbeat, somewhat uncharacteristically on *Juju*, is forthrightly four-on-the-floor and more akin to a disco thump, while also allowing Budgie to go full John Bonham[222], with Steve Severin's pummelling bass guitar providing the scaffold that underpins the crescendo urgency of the song as McGeoch's ferocious guitar playing goes into overdrive.

Live versions of 'Monitor' during the 1981 tour have even more frenzied attack, with all four band members accelerating the melodrama into hyperdrive. The urgency of both lyrics and instrumentation capture the zeitgeist of how technologies were moving during the 1980s and not necessarily into the realms of Arcadia.[223]

'Monitor' was recorded at Surrey Sound studios on 20 March 1981 and debuted live on 20 January 1981 at the Portsmouth Guildhall,[224] and was played a total of eighteen times during the 'Juju' tour.

'Night Shift'

'Night Shift' is the song I always go back to, especially living in Yorkshire, on a winter's night walking around in the dark, with the howling wind and the rain, blaring out of my headphones. It's a really amazing, frightening, powerhouse of a tune'.[225]

Rory Sullivan-Burke

If art acts as a barometer of the times in which it is made, 'Night Shift', track number six on *Juju*, sees the mercury rising to white heat. A song that pulls no punches, the listener is escorted from the world of the prurient into the murk and mire of the serial killer.

On 5 January 1981, Peter Sutcliffe,[226] more notoriously known as the Yorkshire Ripper[227], was arrested and charged with the murder of thirteen women and the brutal assault of seven others in the Manchester and Leeds areas.

It is alleged that an estimated 2.5 million police hours were spent trying to trace and capture Sutcliffe, scuppered by the perfect storm of their attitude towards the victims, many of whom were sex workers, along with the inability to process the information gathered, as well as a hoax contrived by Wearside Jack.[228]

The 'Night Shift' of the Banshees' song makes dual allusions to one of Sutcliffe's many stints of employment in the 1970s, as well as his predominantly nocturnal activities. Cumulatively and incrementally, the shadows have lengthened on *Juju* and Siouxsie's lyrics on 'Night Shift' weave a narrative rich in metaphor and symbolism, alluding to Sutcliffe's own marriage and the model of perfection he deemed his mother, until Sutcliffe's abusive father, posing as his wife's lover so he could lure her to a local hotel, took Sutcliffe and two of his siblings to witness her adultery.

When Sutcliffe's mother arrived, his father produced a negligee from his mother's bag as her children looked on. This incident has been deemed the tipping point for Sutcliffe, mangling his perception of flawlessness, which he had associated with his mother, and turning women into a scourge that, in his febrile mind, needed to be destroyed. The marble slab and cold flesh of the lyric observes, perhaps, the near surgical and calculated methods Sutcliffe employed to attack and maim his victims, utilising a Ball-peen hammer[229], knife, screwdriver and rope, as though the women were cadavers braced for dissection.

'Siouxsie already had a set of lyrics for this track, a fact which Steve and Budgie were unaware of when they created the music. Upon hearing the results of their collaboration, Siouxsie saw it as the opportunity she'd been waiting for and coupled it with her lyrics. No longer novices in the recording studio, the band proved their prowess and precision by recording the track in one take'.[230]

'Night Shift's' doleful minor, McGeoch and Severin's flanged introduction, demonstrates all the poignancy and pathos one would associate with Russian composer Sergei Prokofiev's 'Romeo and Juliet'.[231]

Budgie's drumbeat, suggesting furtive footsteps, is a low-key pulsating rumble replete with all the ominousness audible on Led Zeppelin's 'Kashmir'.[232] Siouxsie's initial vocal delivery comes across as lullaby-like, reflecting the initial deadly charm of the perpetrator, adopting the role of benign confidant.

It's at one minute and eighteen seconds that the 'Fuck the mothers kill the others' elegy sees the song fulminate with ferocity. If 'Night Shift' were a painting, it would be the righthand panel of Hieronymus Bosch's 'The Garden Of Earthly Delights' (1490–1500). The panel portrays Hell and is considered Bosch's most striking representation of the subject.

There are instances when the panel is referred to as the Musical Hell, owing to the instruments used to inflict pain on sinners who have devoted their time to secular music.[233] While lust abounds after the expulsion of Adam and Eve from Paradise in the centre panel, in the scene of Hell, all the Seven Deadly Sins[234] are castigated.

An example of this is the punishment of the avaricious, who are gorged on and immediately evacuated from the anus of a theriomorphic[235] creature with what appears to be an owl's head, sitting on a type of child's commode.

The song becomes an aural onslaught, aided by the tempestuous, unremitting wall of feedback provided by John McGeoch, and the twin bludgeoning of Budgie's bass drum and Steve Severin's grumbling bass underpinning it with an inauspicious death rattle, suggesting the carnivorous plant in the film version of *Day Of The Triffids*.[236]

'Night Shift' was recorded at Surrey Sound studios on 18 March 1981 and first played and heard live on the inaugural date of the 1981 tour, 16 February 1981 at the Hammersmith Palais.

'Sin In My Heart'

Replete with the yearning sounding John McGeoch Siren-like E-Bow[237] and with Siouxsie's blue Vox Mark VI Teardrop electric guitar (on which Siouxsie wrote the song) providing accentuation, 'Sin In My Heart' originally ran at ten minutes but was significantly edited for the album.

Steve Severin's doleful reverb-ridden three bass notes are soon accompanied by Siouxsie's guitar and the stealthy pitter-patter of Budgie's snare drum as McGeoch's E-Bowed guitar comes into focus. The initial lugubrious tension is ruptured by the sound of breaking glass thirty-one seconds into the song (reprised at three minutes twenty-eight seconds), which then transmutes into a steady beat.

At one minute thirteen seconds, this is a longer than usual instrumental introduction for a Banshees' song, creating a build up to the arrival of Siouxsie's rapturous vocal, bolstered by the clangorous sound of tom toms, which, as 'Sin In My Heart' builds, become even more palpitating.

Siouxsie's lyrics and the essence of the song carry the denigratory baton forward from 'Night Shift' with allusions to subservience, cowering and deceit. It is a bilious, claustrophobic confessional with all the obstreperous, inflammatory, alcohol-fuelled rhetoric observed between the two main characters Martha and George in Edward Albee's 'Who's Afraid Of Virginia Woolf',[238] which sees the warring couple's dysfunctional marriage self-immolate during the early hours of one morning after a party. It is played out in front of their two invited younger guests, Nick and Honey, both of whom become entangled in Martha and George's psychodrama.

'You talkin' to me?'[239]

'We sound very strong together, live, so I don't think the fact that they're watching me will affect the rest of the group. They're taking it all in through their ears'.[240]

Siouxsie Sioux

Siouxsie adorned the covers of at least ten journals and magazines in 1981 including *Sounds*, *Rolling Stone*, *Vague*, *Rockin'On*, *RAM*, *The Bob*, *New Music News*, *OOR* and *Rockerilla*, with all magazines and journals running features about the band. Further articles and interviews, coinciding with the 1981 tour and subsequent release of *Juju*, appeared in *Smash Hits*, *Trax*, *Sounds*, *Zigzag*, *Record Mirror*, *NME* and *Flexipop*.

The interviews offer a glimpse into the machinations of the band, their dissimilarities predicated on the nature of questions asked. Some journalists refer to the band's reputation for contrarianism and recalcitrance; others allude to Siouxsie's self-anointing as the 'Ice Queen'. However, a constant was capriciousness, conceivably provoked by the nature of questions asked, as *Sounds* journalist Valac Van der Veene[241] records, 'I'd been warned of 'ice', 'no reaction', 'the usual answers' and (of course) 'they hate the Press'. Instead – warmth, fun, joy and honesty from Siouxsie. Steve Severin merely mouthed into my microphone, leaving me to guess intuitive answers. His sneer said 'go home and work it out'. He talks quietly and leads you up cul-de-sacs. This reticence conceals the 'grandeur' of a collection of individuals who market pure emotion'.[242]

Some enquiry is sacked as puerile, while other interrogation is met more favourably, or with appreciable affirmation, especially when the core of the band, Siouxsie and Severin, are probed about literary, cinematic and musical influences, as Siouxsie expounded: 'I loved Bette Davis in *Whatever Happened To Baby Jane?* I enjoy frightening films. They're quite safe, like fairy stories. Tension is important. I like the humour in *Psycho*, the way the bloke talked to his dead mother. *Eraserhead* was very funny. I hate cynical people who shout out and make jokes at the scary bits'.[243]

Regarding name-checking other bands and musicians, Siouxsie and Severin enthuse about Suicide[244], The Cramps[245] and their esteemed Velvet Underground and The Doors, while also saying 'I think most groups who are talked about in comparison with the Velvets or the Doors, they lack somewhat in imagination, or are just being totally derivative of those groups. Which I despise, to be quite honest... all those people are influences plus, I dunno, James Brown or Aretha Franklin, the Jackson Five!'[246]

Attitudes towards sex, death and religion are also touched on, the latter of which, in relation to Siouxsie being asked about the Banshees' adaptation of 'The Lord's Prayer' and whether she was admonishing any particular religious precepts, Siouxsie recalls, 'I remember my sister was sent to a convent... how cruelly they treated her, how cruel and cold they were. Religion's fine if it brings people together, if it can stop them feeling alone. The warmth in people should be brought out. When dogma is included, that's when I've no use for admiring anything religious'.[247]

There is a distinct volte face when certain smouldering coals are being raked over, the departure of Kenny Morris and John McKay being one of them, and questions about 'older' material from previous albums. While Budgie seems perfectly content to talk about stepping into the fray on 18 September 1979 during the 'Join Hands' tour, '… it was very weird – it was like a challenge. There was a very vacant drumkit. That was the time when I decided I was gonna be a… banshee. On that 'Join Hands' tour I had to adopt those beats from Kenny, like with Palmolive with the Slits. I had to adapt and change and eventually re-arrange and re-write!'[248]

Steve Severin, however, makes his feelings clear on the perennial interview standard about 'the split', venturing 'There's so many quotes on that particular subject I just don't want to talk about it'.[249]

Severin's disposition also switches to disdain if there is too little focus on the new *Juju* material. *Record Mirror* journalist Mark Cooper's studied interview with the band in 1981 offers greater exposition of *Juju*, interspersing the interview transcript with excerpts from the album's song lyrics. Cooper ventures that '*Juju* is a dark world, a complete atmosphere and the whole record works as a style, a form of hypnosis. And as an examination of control, of the power of performance when the band transfixes the audience and themselves and works a dance-dark magic. A magic in which the audience becomes the band's puppet and sometimes the band belongs to the audience, becomes their puppet. A great metaphor for the band's hypnotism'.[250]

Cooper's empathy extracts more revealing responses from Siouxsie and Severin; on the theme of necromancy, Severin explains, 'I'm always intrigued by those things that you really have to delve into… if you got totally into black magic or something you'd have to become a totally different person; you could"t live the same way. You'd just have to cut yourself off and maybe it's because you have to have such commitment that people consider you evil'.[251]

Siouxsie warms to the theme of the outsider, venturing, 'It's like going back to the Dark Ages; witches were the ones who kept themselves to themselves apart, nothing to do with anything, being a bit eccentric. It's just their character wasn't as bland and open as everyone else's and so they were branded as something unsavoury and punished for it'.[252]

Regarding interviews as a whole band, it would be inaccurate to assert that Budgie and John McGeoch's voices remained silent. It was probably more a case of strategic demarcation. Siouxsie and Severin were becoming seasoned, albeit occasionally weary interviewees, fielding inevitable questions concerning past, present and future Banshee incarnations, trying to disentangle half-truths, speculation and rumour, including the 'Juju' tour being Siouxsie and The Banshees' last.[253] It wasn't.

'Head Cut'

'I'd like to be rich enough to collect masks, head masks – Japanese and African busts and heads. My brother and sister were born in the Congo and they've these fantastic ebony tribal masks collected by my mother'.[254]

Siouxsie Sioux

'Head Cut' takes the listener back to the fervid and fevered landscape of *Onibaba* with its carnivalesque, skiffle-like introduction. Twenty-four seconds into the song, with the slightest of perhaps unwitting nods to the Sex Pistols' 'Anarchy In The UK', 'Head Cut' crashes into the discordant hall of mirrors and weaves through a flickering stroboscopic and mutilated series of unnerving, lustful and fetishist images, which appear to be anchored in the setting of a hallucinatory museum, with the narrator ensconced in one of the galleries, observing the target of their predation.

The dissonant sounds of John McGeoch's guitar, mewling and crying like the mutant baby in David Lynch's *Eraserhead*[255] are braced by the steadfast oscillation of drums and bass, and the discernible resonance of handclapping, all adding to the illusion of chaotic bedlam.

The unsuspecting victim forms part of a familial scene in one of the museum's galleries, as they are contemplated being coagulated into butchered fragments; a torso and a face with the eyes and mouth cut out. The coveted is deemed predatory and not irreproachable as the licentious lurker descries the obverse: a compatible deviant whose conservative outward appearance belies a profligate inner self.

Siouxsie's lyric is a reticulation of pyretic amalgamation of surreal juxtapositions. Visitors have become museum exhibits, replete with masks fashioned from wood or plaster facsimiles. The 'wood cut' alluded to also suggests the medium employed for the 'Spellbound' single sleeve. Our concupiscent scopophiliac in 'Head Cut', now in the full throes of delirium, yearns to take the severed head (the best part) of their heart's desire back home, where it will be adorned with bright red lipstick, fed with bread and placed in the freezer.

Siouxsie's lyrics also allude to shrunken heads (under the bed) or tsantsa,[256] severed human heads that were used by tribal for a variety of purposes. Some were war souvenirs or served a ceremonial purpose. In other cases, tribes might employ them to intimidate their enemies, using the heads as a threat. The heads were also used in religious rituals and, even in recent times, for trade purposes.

Although headhunting was commonplace among many ancient tribes, the act of shrinking heads was practised throughout the Pacific and northwestern Amazonian regions of South America.

Shrunken heads were a feature of the Pitt Rivers Museum[257] collection in Oxford until 2020, when they were withdrawn from public view as it was felt that the way they were displayed didn't explain adequately the cultural norms related to their making and instead led people to think in stereotypical and racist ways about Shuar culture.[258]

This Cocytus[259] of the absurd endures with the sacrificial corpse of the victim being gyrated, roasted and burnt on a spit, enveloped by ritualistic, convulsed flames as they imbibe the spectacle; pored over by ricocheting shadows and colluding with Siouxsie's libidinous taunting cooing, chirruping and yowling; a demented master of ceremonies.

'Head Cut' is dispatched with a degree of nonchalance, confuting its subject matter, like a hybrid of John Cale's deadpan, matter-of-fact narration of The Velvet Underground's 'The Gift', with its egregious denouement, and the ear-cutting torture scene in Quentin Tarantino's *Reservoir Dogs* accompanied by Stealers Wheel's 'Stuck In The Middle With You'.[260]

'Head Cut', recorded at Surrey Sound studios on 26 March 1981, was also part of the Richard Skinner BBC Radio 1 show recorded on 4 June 1981 and first broadcast on 16 June 1981: its first live jaunt.

'Voodoo Dolly'

Voodoo (noun): 'A religion, influenced by traditional African religions, that involves magic and attempts to communicate with spirit and dead people, common in parts of the Caribbean, especially Haiti, and in parts of the southern United States'.[261]

'I suppose everyone has their own personal voodoo dolly which is capable of destroying them. A bad habit, or something they like but shouldn't. A vice, most vices; one that's hard to control, hard to kick. The same for men with certain girlfriends, they're like voodoo dollies, always winding them up and they destroy them'.[262]

Siouxsie Sioux

Track number nine brings us to the final act of *Juju*, the John McGeoch and Steve Severin opening of which is the sonic correlation of finding the key to the forbidden cellar, unlocking the door, turning the handle and standing at the top of the wooden stairs looking down into the damp, tenebrous catacomb of forsaken, cobweb-strewn, rotting furniture and junk. You know that the ravaged wicker highchair sitting at the bottom of the stairwell, dimly lit by a solitary light bulb, is both superfluous and inanimate. But the prying, inquisitive self wants a closer look. Just a peek...

In the 1975 Dan Curtis[263] made-for-television horror film *Trilogy Of Terror*,[264] all three cinematographic monographs are based on short stories by writer Richard Matheson[265], with actor Karen Black[266] the protagonist throughout. The first episode, 'Julie', concerns a college professor who manipulates, drugs and seduces her students; the second chapter focuses on the dysfunctional, rivalrous relationship of twin sisters Millicent and Therese, who transpire to be the same person afflicted by multiple personality disorder, the result of an inverse Oedipal relationship, with Therese sleeping with her father and subsequently killing her mother.

The other 'Millicent' personality possesses a subjugated sexuality to cope with her revulsion at her deeds and concludes that Therese is planning to use a voodoo doll to kill her. The cataclysmic finale is not the vitiation of Therese but the suicide of one person inhabited by both entities, discovered by the family doctor with the voodoo doll beside her.

The third instalment, 'Amelia', was remodelled by Matheson himself, and focuses on a woman terrorised by a Zuni[267] fetish doll in her high-rise sub-let apartment.

Returning home after buying the Zuni hunting fetish at a curio shop for a man she has been seeing, an anthropology teacher at the local college, Amelia unboxes her trophy, which is accompanied by a scroll that claims the doll embodies the spirit of a Zuni hunter named 'He Who Kills' and that the gold chain adorning the effigy's waist keeps the evil spirit trapped within.

A call to Amelia's mother, breaking with their regular Friday evening routine so Amelia can be with her male companion, meets with an emotionally manipulative response. When Amelia leaves the room to run a bath, the Zuni doll's golden chain suddenly drops off. Mayhem ensues, with the doll pursuing Amelia unrelentingly, brandishing a kitchen knife. Amelia barricades herself behind numerous doors, attempts to drown the doll and shuts it in a suitcase, all without success.

As the doll sinks its teeth into her neck, Amelia wrenches the doll away and throws it into the oven where her supper has been cooking. The Zuni doll shrieks and burns, emitting a cloud of acrid smog. Thinking it safe, Amelia opens the oven only to breathe in the untethered spirit of the doll. The final scene of the film, following a serene phone call to her mother to make amends and invite her to the apartment, reveals Amelia has now taken on the mantle of the Zuni, replete with razor-sharp teeth, as she sits, cross-legged on the floor, making downward stabbing motions with a kitchen knife.

It is not too fanciful to imagine Siouxsie singing the opening couple of lines to 'Head Cut' in an intimate jazz club, simulating the role of shamanistic chanteuse with the vocal allure of Nina Simone,[268] Jim Morrison and the 'lady in the radiator'[269] from David Lynch's *Eraserhead*, all with the augmentation of portentous substratum.

'Voodoo Dolly' was the result of a band 'jam' during rehearsals for the Futurama 2 festival in 1980,[270] with Siouxsie providing the lyrics.

'Voodoo Dolly' was recorded live at Surrey Sound studios on 30 March 1981, ostensibly the only way to do the instinctual nature of the song due rectitude. Done and dusted in two takes, the second take of the song is the one that can be heard on *Juju*.

At three minutes seven seconds, there is a palpable change to the rhythmic timbre of the song as it starts to hurtle with glacial sheets of white noise provided by John McGeoch's wailing guitar, sounding like the illegitimate offspring of Jimi Hendrix's wall of feedback on 'Wild Thing' at the 1967 Monterey Pop Festival[271] and Lou Reed's blitzkrieg on The Velvet Underground's 'I Heard Her Call My Name'.[272]

Masters of cinematographic psychodrama, Siouxsie and The Banshees do not disappoint with the grand finale of 'Voodoo Dolly'. The band's second-longest song to date after 'The Lord's Prayer', 'Voodoo Dolly' embodies and captures the intrinsic nature of the band; a coalescing of dissonance and the mellifluous, the loving embrace and the sucker punch.

At around five minutes and thirty seconds, 'Voodoo Dolly' languidly transfigures from sonic psychosis to consummated lucidity. The 'Juju' has woven its concluding hex. Pop trivia enthusiasts might like to spot the similarities between the remaining seventeen seconds of 'Voodoo Dolly' and the final twenty seconds of Radiohead's 'Karma Police'[273]; further acknowledgment of the approbation in which John McGeoch was held by Nigel Godrich, Johnny Greenwood and Ed O'Brien.[274]

Juju was to become the band's second-highest charting album in the UK, peaking at number seven, and remaining in the top one hundred for seventeen weeks.

The complexity of the Banshees' oeuvre, replete with its own tessellated substratum and delicious capriciousness, demands the listener's attention.

Alluding to the 100 Club debut, Siouxsie recalls wanting 'something apocalyptic to happen, like making people's guts fall out'.[275] The band was also acutely aware of the precarious balancing act of releasing singles that would nestle in the Chart between any array of, for the most part, unremarkable songs, yet crafting albums that were increasingly objets d'art, occupying a captivating mid-ground between the bitter and the sweet.

Of the Banshees' canon, Siouxsie remarks 'You can't listen to it as background music... it needs involvement from the listener to work properly'.[276]

There was much fanfare and no small degree of exaltation as the band continued the 1981 'Juju' tour, something which Siouxsie found increasingly incongruous, having been used to more than a modicum of confrontation from audiences during previous tours.

This was part of the package, surely? And something of a quid pro quo for Siouxsie, clearly thriving on the fractious enmity; the residuum of Punk. Of the band's ascending star, Siouxsie recalls 'Our level of success became weirder by the 'Juju' tour. All these people would come along and be nice to me and I actually got quite annoyed. If you want to make me cringe, compliment me. I was supposed to be giving everyone a hard time, but I couldn't do it if they were applauding out of genuine love for the band. I felt really awkward'.[277]

There was one instance when this unconditional adulation proved one step too far, as Siouxsie recollects, 'At the Hammersmith Odeon show, I remember berating the audience for being so nice to us. I sang one of the hit singles with my back to the audience as a childish (but at the time satisfying) show of disapproval. I know it sounds perverse, but it took a long time to get used to being liked rather than having people trying to start fights with us'.[278]

Siouxsie's antipathy was, at least in part, assuaged by the rationalisation that if the band's fans were really into their music then perhaps they were deserving of a little more latitude.

More than anything else, Siouxsie was trying to prevent the audience becoming 'an army of sycophants'.[279] First and foremost, it was the music that took centre stage, not a multitude of cartoon-like Siouxsie clones.

Whatever the intrinsic or extrinsic monologue, the band's steadfast fortitude and honesty were of pre-eminent importance, as Severin expressed, 'Even though we'd picked up more of a mainstream audience I was conscious that we'd created a strong identity of our own and, as a band, I felt we were operating outside the rest of the musical scene. Different trends came and went, but we didn't care about fitting in, trying to be like other bands. By setting ourselves apart, we built a solid foundation for what we did from then on'.[280]

Chapter Three
North America Part Two

The band's second foray across the Atlantic Ocean began at the Commodore Ballroom in Vancouver on 8 August 1981, where Siouxsie's recalcitrance found another conduit, luxuriating in heads turning when Siouxsie and The Banshees walked down the street, wondering where, exactly, the band had parked their spaceship.

Siouxsie recalled, 'North America was a completely alien world but I quite liked it because at least I had something to hate again; I could get the conflict back'.[281]

Live shows had the cumulative frisson of the band playing at the pinnacle of their power, compounded by the occasional prospect of an exciting contretemps. Siouxsie relates, 'At the show in Pasadena (14 October 1981), John tried to stop a fight by whacking someone with his guitar'.[282]

According to Severin, 'It was halfway through 'Christine', so he was only playing an acoustic, but he took it off and belted the bloke he thought was responsible. I think he got the wrong person, so he was whisked away in handcuffs after the show'.[283]

John McGeoch was summarily arrested and put in jail. Serendipitously, the gig promoter was the son of the District Attorney, so McGeoch was released on bail early next morning. Subsequently, he needed to make sure he 'didn't sign anything in case it was a summons'.[284]

The North American leg of the 1981 tour, as described by Siouxsie and Severin in Mark Paytress' 2003 *Siouxsie and The Banshees The Authorised Autobiography*, proved to be appliquéd with episodic and divergent vignettes.

When the band were in Houston to play a gig at the Babylon Club on 19 October 1981, Severin remarks 'we realised it had a gay district and we were headlining the best gay disco in town. Siouxsie made friends with the trannies who all sat on the edge of the stage, while everyone else looked like they were in Dr Hook And The Medicine Show.[285] There were Stetsons all over the place'.[286]

A day later, when the band played at Ole' Man Rivers[287] club in New Orleans, Siouxsie didn't necessarily make any new soulmates when she 'came out on stage and said, "All right, you swamp people?"'[288]

The tour's inclusion of venues in both hinterland and metropolis brought the unexpected and fortuitous. Siouxsie remarks 'with die-hard fans... the gigs would be amazing'.[289]

But the scale of touring inherently included the opposite. Siouxsie continues, 'We'd often end up at these scary truck stops after gigs in full, sweat-ruined make-up, and people would look at us with complete horror on their faces... There was one place where a woman that was a fairly well-known psycho took her top off and ran through the car park. All the truckers locked themselves in their vehicles while someone rang the police'.[290]

Towards the end of the tour and ensconced in Minneapolis on 5 November 1981 for the evening gig, Siouxsie decided to instigate her own incidental odyssey. Conceivably slightly overwhelmed and punch drunk from seemingly interminable tour bus journeys, she 'put on a Stetson and a poncho and... hit the bars[291] at 11am in the morning'.

Part mission and part possession, Siouxsie convinced herself that brandy was to be the liquor of choice and, having stumbled upon a less than salubrious locality, went into a bar 'determined to get fuelled up and beat the shit out of someone'.[292]

Siouxsie's appetite for a bar room brawl wasn't satisfyingly slaked as she 'sat in the corner scowling and giving off such a threatening vibe that everyone simply stayed away from me. You'd think that a girl on her own looking weird would be a prime target to gang up on or mug, but they weren't having any of it. I really wanted someone to pull a gun on me or something'.[293]

Whether exorcism or catharsis, presumably an amalgamation

of both, pre-gig, John McGeoch plied a drunken Siouxsie with copious amounts of black coffee, walking her around in circles to sober her up. Reflecting on her not-so-near-death experience and the subsequent Minneapolis performance, Siouxsie recalls, 'It turned out to be a great gig… I'd managed to sober up and had got rid of a lot of my frustration. In my head I'd been fighting with myself… To this day I'm astounded nothing happened, because I was dying to get shot or run over or end up in prison. I must have had some sort of force field around me'.[294]

The 1981 tour was wrapped up with two dates at the Peppermint Lounge[295] in New York City, comprising a sixteen-song set, beginning with 'Clockface' and ending with 'Helter Skelter'.

For whom the tour tolls…

'On long tours, there's always a point where it feels perfect, a point where you're all striving for the same thing. But there's also always a point where you never want to get back on that bus again. You get used to it to some extent, but it doesn't stop it happening'.[296]

Steve Severin

Between 21 March 1980 and 14 November 1981, Siouxsie and The Banshees had notched up a total of 133 dates. Live, the band were unparalleled: tight, professional, brilliant and had thrown themselves heart and soul into the Banshees' 'project', while finding the time, inclination and energy for a little extracurricular moonlighting, including Steve Severin producing Altered Images' debut single 'Dead Pop Stars'[297], which was released on 27 February 1981 and stayed in the UK Chart for two weeks from 28 March 1981 to 4 April 1981, peaking at number 67.

Conceivably because the song title hit a raw nerve after the assassination of John Lennon[298] in New York on 8 December 1980.

'Dead Pop Stars' has tangible echoes of the perturbation elicited by the Banshees' debut 'The Scream'. Altered Images' singer Clare Grogan[299] had expressed her love and admiration for Siouxsie and the band were all members of the Siouxsie and The Banshees fan club.

Altered Images landed a guest slot on the 'Kaleidoscope' tour after sending a demo tape to Billy 'Chainsaw' Houlston on finding out that the Banshees were going to play several gigs in Scotland. Severin was also chief producer of Altered Images' debut album *Happy Birthday*,[300] released in September 1981, which reached number 26 on the UK album chart.

Mike Hedges

The end of the 1981 tour meant the band could stop for breath. Siouxsie stayed in the USA, spending Christmas in Los Angeles and San Francisco with friends, even visiting Disneyland, replete with 'leather mini-skirt, leather jacket, spiky wristband, big hair and thigh-length boots'.[301]

Steve Severin was doorstepped by Lydia Lunch,[302] who was in the UK to play a handful of dates alongside The Cure and The Birthday Party, bereft of a band after having sacked them pre-flight at JFK airport. Lunch thrust her new album *13.13*[303] into Severin's hands and demanded he 'learn it and put a band together'.[304]

After his initial refusal, Severin warmed to the idea and, as Lunch was 'supporting The Cure, it seemed a great opportunity to go on the road and have a laugh with no responsibilities'.[305]

Not exactly Severin's finest musical hour, the band essentially played a wall of feedback over an album Lunch had acquired, a soundtrack of the Arab-Israeli Six-Day War,[306] which consisted of 'gunshots and Arabs and Jews screaming at each other'[307], recounting the experience as 'truly dreadful, absolutely awful'.[308]

Severin nonetheless got to hang out with Robert Smith and give himself permission to 'go on stage pretty drunk',[309] which was something Severin would never do with Siouxsie and The Banshees. Severin had also formed a close bond with John McGeoch and got to know McGeoch's circle of friends from Scottish bands, including Midge Ure[310] and Richard Jobson.

The band were all based in northwest London at the time, 'living in fairly dodgy flats'[311] around Maida Vale due to the proximity of Nils Stevenson. Despite the cumulative number of hit singles and top-selling albums, as well as being on the road exhaustively since

1977, Siouxsie and The Banshees weren't exactly millionaires, having earned a total of £1,500 each for the entire year, well and truly busting the myth of musicians being rich as Croesus[312] overnight.

The Banshees first encountered producer Mike Hedges when the band were at the Morris and McKay impasse in 1979, and Robert Smith stepped in as their guitarist so they could complete the 'Join Hands' tour.

Hedges had been working as an engineer on the Chis Parry[313] produced The Cure B-side to 'Jumping Someone Else's Train'[314] 'I'm Cold' with Siouxsie on backing vocals. Hedges had worked as an assistant engineer on an eclectic range of albums, including albums by Heatwave,[315] Bert Jansch,[316] Andrew Lloyd Webber[317] and Tim Rice,[318] and Gary Moore,[319] and had co-produced the aforementioned The Creatures' *Wild Things* EP.

Chapter Four
Lighting The Blue Touch Paper

'Fireworks'

'No one produced The Banshees. They produced themselves'.[320]

Ray Stevenson

'It was Steve who created the nucleus of the song during the group's last English tour, when he wrote the lyrics'.[321]

Billy Houlston

Although Nigel Gray had been the stalwart producer for 'Kaleidoscope' and 'Juju', and a veritable constant in terms of the Banshees' recording history to date, cracks started to appear when there was some disagreement between band and producer over the song 'Voodoo Dolly',[322] which Gray considered 'far too raucous'.[323]

It was his job to ensure that this roisterous side to the band didn't find its way out of the recording studio under his watch. This didn't play out well with the band and culminated in band and producer parting ways when Siouxsie and The Banshees came to the conclusion that recording the song 'Fireworks'[324] wasn't working with Gray on production duties.[325] They duly employed the services of Mike Hedges, who had recently been the co producer on The Cure album *Seventeen Seconds*.[326]

The Banshees began to see Hedges socially, with John McGeoch describing him as a 'huge teddy bear, a smashing guy with ginger hair and a ginger beard. He used to take me home in his Porsche 928, without doubt the fastest thing I've ever been in'.

At the time, Hedges was part owner of Playground Studios, so-called because Hedges had a penchant for experimenting with an array of sounds and techniques, including, as Siouxsie recalls, 'putting a microphone with a Durex stretched over it in a bucket of water to see what it sounded like.[327] Siouxsie had also found a producer who was enamoured of her vocals and would try a multitude of different effects and multi-layered inventive techniques. Recording sessions would start life as retsina sessions at a local Greek taverna, as Budgie recounts 'before we'd even try doing any work'.[328]

The Nigel Gray-produced version of 'Fireworks',[329] scheduled for release on 31 October 1981, is a discernibly stripped back but no less impressive version of the official single release, with what would become the classical component on the Mike Hedges version adeptly and melodiously enhanced by McGeoch, Severin, Siouxsie and Budgie.

Employing the services of musician Virginia Astley[330] to score the violin and cello ensemble, the song begins with twenty-six seconds of the string quartet[331] tuning up, replete with pre-performance cough and the tapping of the conductor's baton.

An ensuing two-second gap subsequently sets to with thirteen seconds of baroque-sounding strings, the first time Siouxsie and The Banshees used such orchestral arrangements – a lead that other bands would soon follow, including Echo And The Bunnymen's utilisation of orchestration on *Ocean Rain*[332] and The The's *Soul Mining*[333] and *Infected*.[334]

'Fireworks' reflects a new phase for the Banshees. The song is delivered with such ease, it is as though this were a song the band were destined to write and record. The band is well practised, self-assured and confident. Siouxsie remarks, "Fireworks' indicated the direction we wanted for the album. We wanted strings… John wanted a machine but Steve and I said it had to be real strings. They give a real, earthy, rich sound. You could hear the strings spitting and breathing and wheezing'.[335]

The song, Siouxsie comments, sounds 'sexual, explosive, distraught'.[336] Steve Severin also acknowledges that 'Fireworks' 'was a bit of a Scott Walker thing, but there was also a touch of *'Deep Purple In Rock* about it. We knew that strings might get up the noses of purists'.[337]

The lyrical content of 'Fireworks' postulates humankind as an entity burning and glowing brightly, fleetingly. There is also more than a hint of the notion of ritual or spectacle; a motif that is a continuum in Siouxsie and The Banshees' music. The ending sound of 'Fireworks' is the band letting off Chinese firecrackers.

In filmic terms, if 'Juju' is the black and white/sepia-toned tornado scene in *The Wizard Of Oz*[338] then 'Fireworks' is the moment Dorothy opens the door to reveal technicolour Oz.

'Fireworks' is Siouxsie and The Banshees at their bullish best; perfectly synchronised and explosive. John McGeoch's guitar metes out the unrestrained urgency of the song, all the while underpinned by the snap of Budgie's drumming, punctuated by a synthetic clap that can also be heard on 'Red Light', and the exquisite melodious 'killer'[339] bass playing of Steve Severin, whose skill is also reaching its peak.

John McGeoch does his best Jerry Lee Lewis[340] impression, pitching in with a maelstrom of unhinged piano. The Clive Richardson-directed video for 'Fireworks' starts with what looks like an atomic bomb mushroom cloud juxtaposed with a myriad nocturnal, apocalyptic explosions, and a screen star dressed to kill cool side profiles of Budgie, John McGeoch, dandyish in frock coat and Edwardian collared shirt, and Steve Severin every inch Andy Warhol's doppelgänger in black leather jacker and shades, as sparks fly all around them, segueing into the trio playing their instruments.

It moves on to a scene that sees Budgie rampaging with a lit flare in his hand, which in turn metamorphoses into a shot of the band atop a hill, each with a flare, ignited one by one.

Siouxsie appears, leading the charge, violet tinted, flare in hand, and the quartet is complete. There is a moment at three minutes thirty-three seconds when Siouxsie is clearly unnerved by the pyrotechnics, as the flare machine stage right shoots sparks directly into her orbit.

The feu d'artifice was to prove dangerous, as Rob O'Connor recounts: 'There was a very loose script for the video which involved the band performing in the middle of a manmade lake in the gardens of a private house somewhere on the Kent/Sussex border. There was a concrete slab which could be reached through a tunnel under the lake and up some steps. The band would be shot from different angles and it was basically a real rock and roll wig out; very self-indulgent because there's no audience or anything. And it all went horribly wrong. Unfortunately, there was a quite a bad accident involving the explosives and the video didn't get shot properly at all'.[341]

Apparently, 'the man responsible for the pyrotechnics ended up in hospital with three layers of skin missing from his face, due to a problem with one of the explosions'.[342]

Or, as Siouxsie, perhaps with a hint of lily gilding, states, 'the pyrotechnics blew his face off!'[343]

It seems that the superimposition of fireworks used for the video was the result of Clive Richardson secretly filming at Prince Charles and Lady Diana Spencer's wedding on 29 July 1981.

The *Top Of The Pops* appearance on 3 June 1982 sees the band in glorious polychrome, with Siouxsie, hair backcombed to perfection, adorned with snake arm bracelet, opulent feather earrings and fringed necklace, wearing black lace gloves, sarong, and a tee shirt with a playful, explosively phallic motif – a monochromatic transcription of the back cover of the 'Fireworks' single sleeve, Siouxsie amusing herself with some modest subversive insurrection.

John McGeoch plays Siouxsie's blue Mark IV Vox Teardrop guitar, and Steve Severin looks sharp wearing a decorative Nehru jacket and sunglasses.

Budgie adopts a sheer black lace tee shirt with striking androgynous make up. Against a backdrop of red, yellow, blue and green flashing illuminated square lights, like a peculiar stroboscopic Tetris,[344] the band brings their usual bohemian glamour to the party.

'Fireworks' entered the official UK singles Chart on 29 May 1981 and peaked at number 22, prompting John McGeoch to comment, 'I was amazed it didn't do better'.[345]

The 'Fireworks' B-side comprises 'We Fall' on the seven-inch version, with the addition of 'Coal Mind' on the twelve-inch. 'We Fall', the stimulus of which centres around falling and/or dying in one's sleep, is a multilayered, polyrhythmic, tantalisingly sparse expedition into the world of the unorthodox, where the band push further through the looking glass and into experimental submersion, conceivably ever so slightly aided by Siouxsie's increasingly chimerical lyrics which, on 'We Fall', could conceivably be a sequel to 'Fireworks', dealing as it does with dreamlike themes of colour, vampire torsos and kites.

The creative impetus behind 'Coal Mind' was *The Green Brain*[346] by author Frank Herbert,[347] which was lent to Siouxsie by John McGeoch. Widely thought to be one of the first novels to deal with the precariousness of ecology, 'The Green Brain' centres around an overpopulated future world where the antithetically named International Ecological Organisation has to dissolve the Mato Grosso jungle and decimate the voracious and malevolent insect life for inhabitable living space.

The insects prove impervious to the organisation's foam bombs and vibration weapons, repopulating the jungle and mutating exponentially in size, some taking on human characteristics. Siouxsie's song lyrics reflect this miasmic anti-utopia, rich with imagery evoking an adventure into the unknown.

She adopts the coal mine as a metaphor for this labyrinth, teeming with seemingly malevolent flora and fauna including triffids, aphids and earwigs, and the impending occlusion of life, as the base survival instincts of the 'Coal Mind' enter an altered state of hyperarousal. Siouxsie recalls the band's bookishness, 'We did a lot of reading... I soon grew to love Camus, Satre, JG Ballard and Samuel Beckett'.[348]

For such chthonic subject matter, the tunefulness of the song is sanguine, due in no small part to John McGeoch's guitar sound, a phased, almost inverse refrain of Jimmy Page's multi-tracked guitar on 'The Song Remains The Same'.[349]

Siouxsie says of 'Coal Mind', 'When we were recording it, I said to John that I wanted the guitar to sound like a train; he was *such* a great musician that he didn't go for an obvious chuffa-chuffa sound. John was often so easy and inspiring to work with'.[350]

Inventive rhythmic components of 'Coal Mind' add to the semblance of exhilaration; Budgie's driving military snare drum interposed with a metronomic bass drum kick and Severin's cumulative bass playing and musical adroitness are increasingly at the vanguard of the band's sound.

Siouxsie's vocal gymnastics demonstrate a mastery of nuanced cadence as she punctuates the ebb and flow between multi-layered harmonisation and dreamlike sotto voce.

Grand Designs

Of the artwork for the 'Fireworks' single, designer Rob O'Connor recollects, 'Stylorouge were asked to do the visuals for the single cover, and we hadn't even finished preparing them when we just got told by the band that they would be working with Rocking Russian[351] on a new album cover. So it was like, that was, that was the end of that… But the funny thing was, even though we (Stylorouge) got dumped, we still managed to carry on working to do The Creatures stuff'.[352]

Before the band switched their design allegiance, Stylorouge were employed to create the cover for *Once Upon A Time/The Singles*,[353] which was released on 4 December 1981, although, as Rob O'Connor explains, communicating the initial concept to the band in a pre-internet age was not so simple:

'The band had a hell of a year going. They went out touring extensively around Europe and we lost touch with them. In those days, it wasn't so easy. If someone was on tour in Yugoslavia, you couldn't just pick up the phone. There's no mobile phones and no email or whatever: you relied on messages getting sent backwards and forwards somehow. So while the design for *Juju* and the singles fell into place quite well, *Once Upon A Time* was a different story… you were trying to convey ideas by fax or something like that. We knew that Nils Stevenson was going to go out and meet the band for a few dates in Europe, and I got this idea for the cover. I didn't realise at the time the parallels between *Juju* and that cover, although I should have done I suppose, as I was listening to the album a lot at this point.

'And I absolutely love 'Spellbound' – it's probably still one of my favourite tracks ever; also, the track 'Voodoo Dolly', which is relevant because the initial visual for *Once Upon A Time* that I came up with was like a sketch from a photograph. It was a kind of a Victorian child's bedroom, sort of moonlit; very spooky and moody. And there's a cot, with shadows cast from the bars, and inside the cot was a doll but the doll was made to look like Siouxsie. It was a ragdoll but it had crazy black hair and big eye makeup and sexy black plastic leather boots. And the idea was to have this made as a prop, you know, like a built set which would then be photographed. And that detail was really important. I put a little note on the back of the sketch to emphasise that aspect.

'Nils was going to take it away with him but, at the last minute, he decided to get a print of the sketch made. He took the print and left the original with the note on the back explaining how it was all going to be done. And so, when the band saw the facsimile, I think they considered it was just a cartoon; that's what was being proposed, which, of course, it wasn't. Also, it didn't have a title. I mean, the last thing the band wanted at that stage in their career was to have a greatest hits album. You know, everyone wants the increased profile the greatest hits brings, and they also want the increased income from the greatest hits. But what they don't want is the unwritten message that it sends out, which is this band's career is over, and this is a retrospective review of everything they've done. No, they really wouldn't have wanted that. And, fortunately for them, there was *Twice Upon A Time*.[354] But it just proves how important the whole communication thing is'.[355]

Coming up with an alternative plan, O'Connor knew the band really liked the Clive Richardson-directed promos and thought 'it just made sense to take images from the videos and what pulled them all together was using black versions of the pictures. And it kind of made everything gel quite well. But then you've got that complete deficit of colour. So how do you re-inject it?'[356]

The answer was to intersperse the decolourised stills culled from the videos with rectangles of primary colours, which at their red, yellow and blue intersection would create green, violet and orange. The track listing on *Once Upon A Time/The Singles* is 'Hong Kong Garden', 'Mirage', 'The Staircase (Mystery)', 'Playground Twist', 'Love in a

Void', 'Happy House', 'Christine', 'Israel', 'Spellbound' and 'Arabian Knights'. The album peaked at number 21 on the UK Official Album Chart.

The 'Fireworks' single cover design clearly takes inspiration from the Viennese Secessionist art movement,[357] especially the Art Nouveau-oriented[358] new logo, which also bears striking parallels with the font adopted by designer Charles Rennie Mackintosh.[359]

The visual mastery of the new typesetting, as well as the song title, with the 'W' of 'Fireworks' prominently enlarged, is used to optimum effect; white against a gold background with a scattering of four black and white starbursts, also set against the gold background.

The righthand side of the cover design, taking up a third of the picture space, is a series of pastel drawn red, blue, green, yellow and black elongated rectangular shapes, punctuated by curlicues and arabesques, presumably to denote the fireworks' vapour trails, all rendered on a diagonal to create the sense of dynamism.

The back cover bears the same motif, appearing on Siouxsie's tee shirt when the band performed on *Top Of The Pops*. This is a new, opulent Siouxsie and The Banshees, whether developed through the close bond with Mike Hedges, facilitating new sounds and aural colouration, taking over production duties from Nigel Gray, or Rocking Russian reflecting the cumulative synergy and conjoining of music and art.

No longer is there an 'us and them' with Siouxsie and Severin in one camp and 'the arty ones', a slightly acerbic allusion to Kenny Morris and John McKay between 1977 to 1979, in another.

Now, they were all the arty ones and truly through the looking glass: part *La Belle et la Bête*[360], part *Orphee*[361], with a soupçon of *Citizen Kane*,[362] Machievellian[363] grandiosity as they embarked on their fifth studio album, the ostentatious *A Kiss In The Dreamhouse*.[364]

Chapter Five
A Kiss In The Dreamhouse

'The band drank a lot... Every day they came in someone would go back out and buy four or five bagfuls of wine which would then go in the fridge. That was at about five in the afternoon and we knew it would be an all-nighter. We were working fourteen-hour days, and I don't think I was drinking as much as the band, because I couldn't have done my job'.[365]

Mike Hedges

The majority of *A Kiss In The Dreamhouse* was recorded between June and August 1982, interspersed with a fifty-one-date world tour, their most ambitious and extensive to date, with gigs in Japan, Australia, Scandinavia, North America, Canada, France, Portugal, Italy, Spain and the UK.

Initial recording for the (as yet untitled) studio album began on 5 May 1982, during a break from touring between Yokohama on 2 April 1982 and Oslo on 18 May 1982, with what was to become the opening song on the album, 'Cascade'.

Overdubs were added to the backing track of the song, with John McGeoch playing clavinet.[366] Guitars and percussion were subsequently added. Early May recordings also included 'Greenfingers', with augmentation from McGeoch on guitar and Severin on organ. Siouxsie furnished the vocals for 'Greenfingers'. On 9 May, work commenced on 'Painted Bird', with Severin again playing organ.

With such an unremitting and punishing schedule, it is perhaps no surprise that, twelve shows in, after the initial Dreamhouse sessions, when playing the Gardet Sportfalt[367] venue in Stockholm, Siouxsie's voice suffered a complete meltdown.

Partying all night was out of the question, as Siouxsie had to be the lantern bearer as vocalist and front person, holding everything together while the rest of the band played, as she perceived it, a little bit the worse for wear.

As Budgie recalls, 'We were always embarrassed that we could all go off and enjoy ourselves when Siouxsie had to stay in so her voice would be alright the next day. Sometimes, we'd get the manager to sit with her at the bar of the hotel, while we all sneaked out behind her back to go to a club... Siouxsie used to give everything while she sang, which at times took its toll on her vocal cords'.[368]

Siouxsie's innate perfectionism, professionalism and drive meant that she was loth to take anything approximating doctor's orders and railed against the GP mantra 'Don't give 100 percent, give 60 or 70 percent'.[369]

Siouxsie was very much in the here and now, not concerned with saving her vocal cords for several years into the future. It was 'all or nothing'[370] as far as she was concerned, a motif that could be applied to *A Kiss In The Dreamhouse*.

Rory Sullivan-Burke maintains that this third and last album to include the virtuoso guitar playing of John McGeoch 'from a guitar point of view... it's not as vital or viscerally direct as *Juju* was; there is probably a little too much farting about. And I think that the production reflects the relationships within the band; a little bit cloudy. I find 'Dreamhouse' a difficult, sad listen because I know what's on the horizon; what's coming for John (McGeoch). It's a not dissimilar to the tension that can be discerned on *Join Hands*, but that might just be me projecting'.[371]

Sullivan-Burke also suggests that the band 'did get a little bit over-excited and carried away with the project. Sometimes, less is more, or less is enough. That's not to suggest that there isn't a lot of love for the album; some fans say it's their favourite Siouxsie and The Banshees album of all'.[372]

'*No Nils and Dave Woods, no Banshees*'.[373]

Ray Stevenson

Just before recording *A Kiss In The Dreamhouse*, the band also parted company with manager Nils Stevenson in the spring of 1982. Stevenson had been the one constant in the band's history from 1976, but he was beginning to exhibit increasingly capricious behaviour, as Siouxsie suggest, 'He became erratic and unreliable… he came out to the last show in New York at The Peppermint Lounge and just… lost it. One particular situation got out of control and John (McGeoch) pinned him against a wall and said, "Just fucking go home". He was too obsessive towards me and I felt suffocated by it. It was almost a *Play Misty For Me*[374] scenario. He'd be waiting outside my house… it was almost scary'.[375]

Billy 'Chainsaw' Houlston concurs, 'It had to get more professional. Nils was always more of a free spirit. He didn't sit behind a desk; he'd learned everything hands-on. But then again, whoever was manager, whoever was running the office, there was only one boss, and that was 'Siouxsie. As big a part as Severin played, the boss was always Siouxsie'.[376]

A Kiss In The Dreamhouse reflects the band's resolve to be disassociated from their musical contemporaries and, by 1982, had the creative autonomy to do exactly as they wanted.

The template for *A Kiss In The Dreamhouse* was The Beatles' 1968 eponymous album (that affectively became referred to as *The White Album*),[377] on repeat as the band gigged around Scandinavia.

Of the album's title, Steve Severin says it came to him 'after seeing a programme about Hollywood prostitutes in the forties who had cosmetic surgery to look like stars so they could get more clients. In effect, the *Dreamhouse* was a brothel'.[378]

The televisual allusion was to a 1976 American detective series called *City Of Angels*,[379] specifically 'The Castle Of Dreams' episode.

The intensity of Juju and its surfeit of otherness and darkness, catalysed, whether intentionally or otherwise, a move towards an album with a more prismatic configuration, with John McGeoch taking Severin to 'one side in the studio before we recorded it and saying "There was a bit too much creepy stuff on *Juju*; let's not continue in that vein"'.[380] Although Severin was a little surprised initially about

McGeoch's comment, he acknowledged that he was probably right.

The band was moving in an ever more experimental direction, with *A Kiss In The Dreamhouse* representing the Banshees' 'zenith' with regard to the outer limits of sonic exploration, but it would also be the last studio recording with the majestic John McGeoch, subsequently described by Siouxsie as her favourite Banshees' guitarist.

'Cascade'

'Can I have everything louder than everything else?'[381]

Ritchie Blackmore[382]

Siouxsie and The Banshees were navigating their way, one might surmise, through a chapter of hedonistic and celebratory revelry, reinvigorated by a new producer who shared their creative vision, as well as considerable appetite for carousing. With the floodgates well and truly open, let the party begin…

Originally demoed at Workhouse Studios[383] between 13 March and 15 March 1982, 'Cascade' begins in what might be described as classic Banshees' style. Severin's melancholic phased bass guitar accompanied by teardrops of McGeoch's subtle, understated ambient guitar, transposing into a Magazine-like refrain, melded with a scintilla of the 'James Bond Theme',[384] joined by Budgie with a flanged and phased percussive splash of cymbals and completed, twenty seconds into the song, with Siouxsie's stealthy, breathy whisper growing into a full-throated vocal, evoking luscious, lovelorn imagery with allusions to a 'chest full of eels', 'falling' and 'summer sin'.

The song's precipitating dizziness is pure Banshees' psychodrama, laced with the undertone of Baroque[385] sexual liaison, swollen by John McGeoch's sumptuous, overlayed guitar and Budgie's intense, pulsating drumbeat, as the song's bridge heralds the melodious strains of a harpsichord and the bass guitar reverberating with all the power of a seismic rumble.

This is not a song for the faint hearted and is the equivalent of the engastration[386] one might encounter at the most elaborate of medieval banquets. Siouxsie was also introduced to LSD[387] by Mike

Hedges, despite being warned off the drug by Nils Stevenson, telling Siouxsie, 'Whatever you do, don't take LSD, it's scary!'[388]

Siouxsie needed no further encouragement and, after initial recreational use, decided to have 'a night in under the influence just to see what would happen',[389] which resulted in her writing '"Cocoon' and some Creatures stuff'.[390]

The episode was all a bit foggy for Siouxsie to recollect in technicolour, excepting vignettes of songwriting, eating Neapolitan ice cream and thinking she was on a beach, which was in fact the kitchen floor. 'Cascade' was recorded as one of three new songs, the others being 'Painted Bird' and 'Green Fingers', which would be included on *A Kiss In The Dreamhouse*, for a BBC Kid Jensen Show[391] episode on 13 May 1982.

The BBC recording demonstrates effective restraint and is a less opulent, stripped-back version of the subsequent album recording, disclosing mastery in musicianship and how, cumulatively, Budgie and John McGeoch were adding creative éclat to the band.

Both members brought depth and colour, approaching each song with artistry akin to a painting, sculpture or film, catalysing the ingenious songwriting and lyrics of Severin and Siouxsie. Budgie's drumming, not a million miles away from Kenny Morris' original template, channels the dextrous intensity of his drumming gurus Ginger Baker, Terry Chambers, Ian Paice and Bill Ward driving the song forward.

'Green Fingers'

Of The Beatles' *White Album*, Steve Severin recalls, 'We were listening to it a lot, in terms of the variety of songs, the kind of instrumentation they would use. We were trying to launch ourselves into a post-psychedelic opulence, I guess. Hence the strings, hence a lot of really lush imagery. I would say something like 'Green Fingers' is our 'Savoy Truffle', our quirky little George Harrison song'.[392]

The second song on *A Kiss In The Dreamhouse* heralds the band's move into further uncharted psychedelic territory, ushered in by one solitary synthesiser note, with the first four seconds employing flexatone,[393]guitar and drumsticks. Ringo-esque snare, tom tom and recorder or flipple flute,[394] played by multi-instrumentalist John McGeoch, provide additional texture and colour, play in almost incidental isolation for a further eight seconds until the ensuing warmth of guitar, bass, keyboard and vocals, create a luscious soundscape.

One minute, thirty-six seconds into the song, McGeoch channels the 'chop chord'[395] stylings of guitarist Nile Rodgers[396], creating a hypnotic, seemingly unpremeditated groove.

The premise of the song, reflected in Siouxsie's lyrics, centres around 'Green Fingers',[397] an episode of Rod Sterling's[398] 1970 to 1973 series *Night Gallery*,[399] the plot of which involves a property developer (Michael Saunders), played by actor Cameron Mitchell[400] coveting land owned by an elderly neighbour (Lydia Bowen), played by actor Elsa Lanchester,[401] who has a particular talent for gardening.

His wealth of resources doesn't prepare him for the propagating alchemy his neighbour uses to ensure that both house and garden remain firmly in her possession, even if it means coming back from death through growing several of her own lopped off fingers in the soil of her beloved garden.

The 1980 film *Motel Hell*[402] was another filmic spur. It concerns protagonist farmer Vincent Smith and his younger sister Ida, both living on a farm next to a motel: Motel Hello.

Vincent is widely celebrated for his smoked meats which, it transpires, are human flesh. Vincent's modus operandi is setting traps on nearby roads to catch victims. One of his traps is to place full-size cardboard cutouts of cows on the highway, causing drivers to stop and allowing Vincent to abduct them. Victims are subsequently buried up to their necks in his secret garden, their vocal cords severed to prevent them from screaming.

The victims are cultivated and fed until they are ready for human sausage harvest. Both stories are entirely in keeping with the Banshees' gleeful fixation with the macabre and tragicomic, which can be traced back to songs like 'Suburban Relapse' on the 1978 album *The Scream*[403] and 'Premature Burial' on the 1979 album *Join Hands*.[404]

The song's exuberance, replete with bar chimes, has a folkloric, almost pagan, sensibility, driven by Budgie's atypical time signature in the form of a bustling shuffle, with a supplementary tambourine for an additional layer of aural dusting.

The 1982 BBC Kid Jensen session version of 'Green Fingers', as with 'Cascade', is a stripped back yet no less inventive recording, driven largely by Budgie's almost 'Frippertronic',[405]polyrhythmic playing. McGeoch again provides multi-hued flourishes, which seem to articulate the parts latterly augmented by the recorder for the actual *A Kiss In The Dreamhouse* album, as Severin's bass weaves its way through the song like a shimmering deep golden thread. Siouxsie's vocal is delivered with delicious cadence.

'Obsession'

'People are confused by the fact that we do songs like 'Tattoo' and 'Obsession,' which are wrongly classed as horror, which I hate'.[406]

Siouxsie Sioux

Siouxsie's vocal on 'Obsession' is ostensibly a call-and-response Gospel[407] delivery, and the orchestration of the song is as intensely immersive as the name suggests.

Putting the finishing touches to 'Cascade', which entailed recording the guitar tracks, as well as recording 'Obsession', 'Circle' and 'Cannibal Rose', marked the second punctuation point of the extensive 1982 tour between 17 June and 19 July. The band were only in Playground Studios for one day, as the mixing desk had been damaged when Budgie accidentally spurted an entire bottle of warm champagne over it.

There was a temporary move to Abbey Road, commencing on 19 June, where the Banshees found themselves in Studio Two, the same studio in which The Beatles had recorded almost all of their albums between 1962 and 1970. During the recording of 'Obsession', Siouxsie and Budgie found themselves confronted by a vast studio that was literally cluttered with various forms of percussion'.[408]

Both band members were not going to pass up the opportunity to investigate this Aladdin's cave of equipment, which included Siouxsie tinkering with the tubular bells, while Budgie, as if undertaking a piece of performance art, took his position on a drumkit-less drum riser and 'began banging out a beat with his feet and hands'.[409]

Fortuitously, the taping was underway in the control room and the entire performance was captured, including 'handclaps and heavy breathing by Siouxsie, and her use of a mic swung around her head to produce an eerie whooshing sound'.[410]

Although 'Obsession' has no drum or bass tracks, John McGeoch contributed a guitar track, 'at which time things started getting weird... as he was playing, what was being recorded mysteriously slowed down, then returned to its normal speed without explanation...'[411]

The resultant 'ghost in the machine' glitches were left in and can be heard in their entirety. The actual vocal for 'Obsession' was recorded later on 21 June 1982.

Siouxsie: 'The song's actual origins 'came about from the Juju tour in America... What I found most intoxicating about New York was the amazing bars and I had this amazing conversation with a tattooed sailor. He told me this story of someone who became so obsessed by their ex-lover that they'd break into their flat and leave their pubic hair on their pillow. It was like a folklore tale. Was I applying my experience with Nils to the story? Well... it's a connection. It made the story more poignant and allowed me to live in the place of the song'.[412]

With no less than fifteen Siouxsie cover shoots for the popular music press and interviews galore in 1982, the band were never far from the limelight and the associated, ever-increasing fanbase, which was deftly handled by the band's stalwart confidante and unofficial personal assistant Billy 'Chainsaw' Houlston.

Even though 'Obsession' is, according to Siouxsie, 'about a friend of a friend... It's an extreme example of what happens in more subtle ways in most people's relationships',[413] one could surmise that it also alludes to fan infatuation; when the music itself won't quite suffice and a token or gesture of greater significance is sought – a lock of hair or breaking into the hounded subject's dwelling in the instance of the song.

The lyrical compression and claustrophobia of 'Obsession' alludes to this fine line between idolisation and stalking, with the prowler's shunning only strengthening their resolve to devour the object of their fascination.

The array of otherworldly recorded sounds evoke a range of filmic imagery, from the unrelenting breathing that echoes the hissing radiators in David Lynch's *Eraserhead* to the iconic Bernard Hermann score for the Hitchcock film *Psycho*, especially with the inclusion of the string ensemble, easing into the song at one minute thirty-nine seconds, as the protagonist pleads for mercy for not understanding the victim's rejection of their unwanted, unrelenting attention.

Later, violins and cellos create the cumulatively sinister and volatile lava-like climax of 'Obsession', piercing and stinging with the potency of the iconic Hitchcock *Psycho* shower scene.

At one minute fifty-six seconds, 'Obsession' is pulled back into the realms of the febrile as it splinters and dissipates; the tubular bells redolent of the chiming of a deranged grandfather clock, rejoined by Budgie's percussive reverberation, part heartbeat, part prowler footsteps, and the stabbing sound of John McGeoch's guitar.

At two minutes and fifty-four seconds, the rain-soaked percussion and sotto voce lead us down an alleyway of desolate, echoing, stifled hisses and gurgles for the final eight seconds.

'She's A Carnival'

An antidote to its predecessor, 'She's A Carnival' sees Siouxsie and The Banshees return to a bacchanalian motif, allegedly inspired by 1980s fashion model and 'First Lady of London's fashion scene'[414] Princess Julia[415], seen in the Visage video for the 1980 single 'Fade To Grey' and a well-known figure on the Blitz scene[416], which also included Boy George[417] and Rusty Egan.[418]

On 5 July, Severin, Siouxsie and Budgie 'began recording the original backing track for the song, which originated during a soundcheck jam between Severin, Budgie and McGeoch in Karlshamn in Sweden a month earlier'. Siouxsie continued work on 'She's A Carnival' by recording a total of eight different vocal tracks.

Gregariously uptempo, the song tears along at full tilt from the beginning, where it is led by the ferocious snap of Budgie's snare drum, exuberance of John McGeoch's layered electric and acoustic guitar playing and Steve Severin's swirling bass playing and Siouxsie's vocal delivery, replete with Grito[419] yelps, interpreting the Steve Severin-penned lyrics.

'She's A Carnival' exudes the exhilaration of mardi gras, painting a picture of unrestrained gratification; amplified with cowbell and tambourine, with a killer middle section with crashing cymbals, the song reaches its zenith, then begins to regain its composure at two minutes and eight seconds when, at two minutes and fifty-one seconds, something beautifully incongruous, yet completely in keeping with sentiment of the song happens – forty-eight seconds of John McGeoch playing what sounds like a hybrid of a Wurlitzer[420] and Hammond[421] organ in a gloriously improvised, almost surreal instrumental passage, pausing at three minutes twenty-nine seconds to ask 'D'ya get that'?, pausing and giggling, then uttering, 'This is for the prize', perhaps alluding to this over the top funfair-like sequence, the resuming playing with greater voracity and accelerated tempo for the remainder of the song.

Although seemingly throwaway and unplanned, McGeoch's amusing intermission highlights the versatility of his musicianship. As Rory Sullivan-Burke reflects, 'John opened the band up to new musical possibilities. His greatest contributions were genuine musicality which extended beyond guitar playing. John was able to come up with, and play, a piano or organ part; he would also have been able to add saxophone if required... he was able to take the ideas and suggestions from Siouxsie, in particular, would have, and turn them into something really unique and timeless... there was an adaptability and world of opportunities that John could offer.

It was his readiness to experiment with sounds, effects and feedback and to almost make the guitar sound like something other... The Banshees hit the jackpot with John.[422]

'Circle'

Track five, side one of *A Kiss In The Dreamhouse*, rips the listener from the warm technicolour abandonment and warm embrace of 'She's A Carnival' jolting them into a more sobering realm: one which sees Siouxsie's demons reappear with vengeance, the lyric reflecting 'the depressing realisation that you're doomed to repeat the sins of your parents.[423]

It would perhaps be all too elementary in attributing a cause and effect scenario to 'Circle' regarding the sexual assault Siouxsie encountered as a nine year old growing up in suburban Chislehurst.

However, Siouxsie recounts "Circle' isn't linked to that. But that incident has shaped me and the way I protect myself. Seeing through the idea of pure sexual allure and understanding that it's usually a controlling thing. It can be in an extreme situation, like an older person abusing a much younger person... but most relationships can be broken down into someone being manipulated and overpowered by someone else'.[424]

The repeated, ominously discordant string motif on 'Circle' is the violin and cello passage on 'Fireworks' played backwards, creating the effect of a scratched vinyl record where the needle gets stuck. One can discern the sound of the tape switch at the beginning of the song as Siouxsie's wearisome narrative begins; an intoxicating conglomeration of tabloid headline and English nursery rhyme, in the same matter-of-fact vein as 'Solomon Grundy',[425] which abbreviates the life of its protagonist through marking his birth, christening, marriage, illness, worsening state, death and burial with the seven days of the week; and Dante's 'Divine Comedy',[426] the last book of which depicts Hell as nine concentric circles of torment located within the Earth and the 'realm... of those who have rejected spiritual values by yielding to bestial appetites or violence, or by perverting their human intellect to fraud or malice against their fellowmen'.[427]

Siouxsie's lyrical confabulation is her most acerbic to date, part riddle, part mantra, the first three lines of which tell a story of a girl of sixteen living a carefree life until pregnancy and childbirth at the same age make her indolent, and this is perpetuated in her own sixteen-year-old child, rendering both lives unfulfilled.

The yellow line of the song is to be avoided at all costs; conceivably an allusion to the looped nature of the Circle Line on the London Underground.[428]

One cannot underestimate what an empowering figure Siouxsie became for other female musicians in her categorical refusal to perpetuate lazy stereotypes. Although Siouxsie railed against labels or ideologies of any description, she was at the vanguard of a musical groundswell which saw women levelling the male-dominated playing field in the late 1970s and 1980s, along with Chrissie Hynde,[429] Pauline Black,[430] Debbie Harry,[431] Viv Albertine[432] and Poly Styrene,[433] all fronting or having a major creative input into successful bands and not relegated as backing singers. This was beautifully captured in Michael Putland's[434] 'Ladies Tea Party'[435] iconic photoshoot in August 1980.

Although on the record, both lyrically and in interviews about her distrust of any secular or non-secular doctrine, Siouxsie nonetheless supported the fight against a retrogressive bill on abortion that set out to repeal the 1967 Abortion Act[436] and was almost passed in 1980, stating 'It's a personal thing to do with women... Women have the right to decide their future. Parliament is predominantly male, so it's crazy that they should be allowed to decide on something like abortion. But of course it's a social thing; marriage is good business. Married couples buy products for their homes and for their children. They can get access to a mortgage. It's almost impossible if you're single'.[437]

The 'snap' of Budgie's snare drum plays the role of harsh disciplinarian, aided and abetted three minutes and seven seconds into the song by overlaid handclaps, which possess a similar foreboding, aggravated further by the top line of a synthesiser, compounding the sense of being trapped. At four minutes, three seconds, the pummelling reaches its apex of brutality when, towards the end of 'The Circle', the claps fade but the drumming becomes more militaristic and mechanical as the circle of hypnotic stupefaction fades yet remains sententiously ineffaceable.

'Circle' was also adopted as the recurrent motif for the Siouxsie and The Banshees-directed video 'Play At Home'[438] a Channel 4[439] special which will be considered subsequently in more detail.

The ever-present tintinnabulate in 'Circle' is the sound of John McGeoch channelling the chimes of Big Ben.[440]

'Melt!'

'The Baudelairean imagery of ‹Melt!' evokes claustrophobic scents of opium, sex and sickly flowers, and lapses into morbidity with lines like, 'You are the melting man and, as you melt, you are beheaded'.[441]

'There wasn't (a promotional video made for 'Melt!') but (if there had been) it would have involved a giant ice phallus!'[442]

Steve Severin

Influenced by the band's first visit to Japan between 29 March and 2 April 1982, where the ensemble experienced the most reverential and studious audiences to date at their gigs, the sixth track on *A Kiss In The Dreamhouse*, opening the second side of the album, changes the tempo and cinematic landscape as the listener is transported to a world of rapacious libido underpinned by Steve Severin's lyrical allusions to 'Le Petit Mort'[443] and the attendant roughness of what would appear to be a sadomasochistic tryst.

The musical arrangement isn't a million miles away, again, from the wistfulness redolent of The Shangri-Las, demonstrating that Siouxsie and The Banshees were a multi-dimensional, studied band, capable of evoking the most poignant of technicolour cinematic imagery.

One can hear that Siouxsie's vocals are tested to the most extreme, more than a little beyond where she is most comfortable, really stretching and straining for a higher octave range more associated with the acrobatics of a trained mezzo soprano singer.

Such gymnastics owe much to the encouragement of Mike Hedges, who believed that Siouxsie's voice was capable of swooping, swirling and reaching new heights of expression. It was not the best timing, it transpired, as journalist Garry Mulholland explains: 'Playground was once again ready for action, the hard work of honing the sprawling (*A Kiss In The Dreamhouse*) sessions into a focused suite of songs was completed by Sioux and Hedges alone in a week of intense editing and vocal overdubs.

'It put a dangerous strain on a voice that had gone completely in Sweden just a few months before. One doctor in Gothenburg had advised Sioux to give up singing altogether. "Sioux was struggling a bit," confirms (Mike) Hedges. "It wasn't easy for her. But Sioux's not the sort of person who would accept that if she didn't stop singing she'd lose her voice. She'd just go, "Oh – fuck off" and sing anyway. I think the vocals on that record are really brilliant'.[444]

The song is underpinned by Budgie's subtle, pulsing drumbeat, highly evocative of The Beatles' 'Tomorrow Never Knows' from the 1966 album *Revolver*, tantamount to a drum solo accompanied by the rich, overlayed instrumentation provided by Steve Severin and John McGeoch, the latter of whom can be heard playing piano, bouzouki,[445] electric and acoustic guitars, although it is not beyond the realms of possibility that McGeoch could cajole most sounds from his stalwart Yamaha SG, with the help of his MXR pedals.

The veritable choir of angels conjured up by Siouxsie's multi-tracked choral vocals, beginning at two minutes and nine seconds into the song, are Siren-like and painfully beautiful.

The melancholia of 'Melt!' and its associated allusions to a plethora of algolagnia has all the wretchedness of the final scene in Luchino Visconti's 1971 film *Death In Venice*,[446] where the protagonist, Gustave Von Aschenbach, ostensibly melting both mentally and physically on the beach of the Venice Lido as a rivulet of black hair dye trickles down his temple, watches with concern as, what begins as a provocative flicking of sand between Tadzio[447] and an older boy, degenerates into full-on wrestling.

After having his head pushed face down into shallow tide, Tadzio meanders and trudges through the sea to the beguiling strains of Gustav Mahler's 'Adagietto'.[448]

Taadzio turns and looks toward the enfeebled, dying Aschenbach, then raises his arm and points toward the distance. Aschenbach, in the last throes of exertion, endeavours to rise from his deckchair but crumples into death.

'Melt!' was released as the band's final single from *A Kiss In The Dreamhouse* on 26 November 1982 in both seven and twelve-inch formats. 'Melt!' peaked at 49 in the UK Chart, two places lower than 'Mittageisen' in 1979.

The B-side of the seven-inch is 'Il Est Né Le Divin Enfant', and the twelve-inch is 'A Sleeping Rain'. 'Il Est Né Le Divin Enfant', a traditional Christmas carol, was first published in 1862 by Jean-

Romary Grosjean,[449] Dawit Micael V and Paul Webster; organist of the Cathedral of Saint-Dié-des-Vosges,[450] in a collection of carols entitled 'Airs des Noëls Lorrains'.

The words were published initially in an anthology of ancient carols, published around 1875–76 by composer Dom G. Legeay and based on The King James Bible, Luke 2:6.

Both 'Melt!' B-sides were recorded on 23 and 24 October, Billy 'Chainsaw' Houlston recounting, 'Budgie had vague memories of the song, but Steve (Severin) and John (McGeoch) openly admitted to have never heard it before. Nonetheless they decided to give it a try. With surprising speed, they raced through their newly appointed task. Siouxsie and Budgie recorded the backing track, then John played the brass section on the keyboards, and finally Siouxsie and Budgie recorded additional percussion. So pleased were they with the results that they decided to couple it with 'Melt!' as a double a-side. But once again the record met the same fate as its predecessor and due to virtually non-existent radio airplay it failed to achieve the recognition and subsequent Chart success it rightly deserved'.[451]

Both 'Il Est Ne' Divin Enfant' and 'A Sleeping Rain' appear on the Banshees' 2004 compilation album *Downside Up*[452] and mark the time when Robert Smith joined the band after John McGeoch's sacking, having played his final gig with Siouxsie and The Banshees on 30 October 1982 at the Rock Ola Room[453] in Madrid.

Smith was initially drafted in as a hired hand so the band could complete the rest of the tour from 13 November to 29 December 1982. It would be wrong to judge the song in the canon of the Banshees' output as mere curio, although it is fairly conclusive that McGeoch wasn't that overjoyed at its recording, but by the time the single was released, he was out of the band anyway.

One month into Smith's second tenure as a touring Banshee, the band made an appearance on the French arts and culture television programme *Les Infants Du Rock*[454] on 15 December 1982.

The scene is an elaborate mock-up of a French street at night, replete with streetlights and cars, lightly dusted with fake snow. As the song starts, a camera pans in towards the band who, to all intents and purposes, look as though they have landed, rather abruptly and unexpectedly, from an entirely different realm.

For context, Siouxsie and The Banshees remain one of the only bands that ooze star quality, whether miming, live or in video form. This was not one of those occasions.

Siouxsie fronts the band, as usual, looking exquisitely composed and glamorous, not a strand of backcombed, crimped hair out of place. This is not the case for the singer's usual impeccable synchronistic miming, which hits the skids at around one minute and seven seconds. The rest of the band look vaguely bemused.

Severin, dressed in a black overcoat and trilby hat, part bohemian, part Droog,[455] feigns trumpet duties and is either too embarrassed or immersed in brass mimicry to raise his head, while Budgie does his level best to remain composed as he stares into the middle distance while playing a military drum with bass drumsticks.

Robert Smith, looking for the most part like a castigated small child, clearly trying not to laugh, holds two cymbals in mid-air, waiting for a cue when he can clang them together.

That moment never comes. Siouxsie does her best to make a rallying cry with smaller marching cymbals towards the end of the song. As the camera pans out from the band, the end shot is of an inscription above a shop doorway which reads 'A L'impecabble', loosely translated as 'To the impeccable'.

'A Sleeping Rain' is four minutes and eighteen seconds of further Banshees sonic experimentation, not a million miles away from Can,[456] a band often cited by Siouxsie and Severin as a considerable influence.

In fact, 'A Sleeping Rain' could fit pretty comfortably on the 'Ege Bamyasi'[457] with its percussion-led jazz swing on songs like 'Pinch' and 'Vitamin C', as well as the bass guitar set low in the mix.

Budgie and Severin's backbeat and pulse make it possible for an array of John McGeoch's punctuated guitar effects, as well as synthesiser, xylophone, kalimba[458] and tubular bell, to stretch out over the top; all in the form of a rich, multi-layered, improvised and extemporised jam.

The Gill Thompson artwork for the seven-inch single is a multi-coloured affair, featuring many Viennese Secession and Art Nouveau attributes. The main motifs include a red fantail goldfish and an orange and red orchid, set against a background of four delineated geometric sections, resembling a stained-glass window.

The largest of the four segments forms the predominant background to the orchid and comprises some sort of celestial purple shape, flecked with red, blue and white, set against a black background, with the section below a Hokusai-oriented[459] representation of water, flanked either side by the song's title 'Melt!' to the right and 'Il Est Ne'Divin Enfant' wrapped around a Celtic looking curlicue symbol on the left.

Above this is the new Siouxsie and The Banshees logo, electric blue against a pale green background. Symbolically, the front cover reflects the erotically charged sensuality of the musical content of 'Melt!', the back cover is perhaps even more provocative, with the central subject comprising two expressionistic figures in an embrace.

Nothing unusual about this per se. However, the visual content sees both figures pinned to a crucifix, the top of which is rounded to resemble a phallus, as they kiss; the front figure's hair, adorned with decorative circles and rectangles, cascades down their back.

It is conceivable that the crucifix in this particular erotic context, in keeping with the lyrical content of 'Melt!', acts as the ultimate symbolic representation of sadomasochism. The Fantail goldfish also makes an appearance to create visual continuity of the back and front of the sleeve. The cover of the twelve-inch single is a more elaborate composition, with the same visual ingredients as the seven-inch.

'Painted Bird'

Ratcheting up the sonic tension several notches, 'Painted Bird' must count among one of Siouxsie and The Banshees' most apocalyptic and explosive songs. Siouxsie's lyrics for the song were inspired by the 1965 book *The Painted Bird*[460] by Jerzy Kosinksi,[461] which Siouxsie describes as 'A very violent book… But there's also like an abstract theme in that this guy used to collect birds, and when he was feeling really aggressive, or frustrated, he'd paint this bird with different colours, and then throw it to its flock. And it would recognise its flock, but because it was a different colour, they would attack it'.[462]

'Painted Bird' is, to all intents and purposes, a barnstorming rock song, but very much on the Banshees' own terms. The first seven seconds set the tone, utilising both percussion and guitar and then, with as much tension and anxiety one might find if Picasso,[463] circa 'Guernica',[464] had collaborated with Edvard Munch[465] when he painted and drew multiple versions of 'The Scream',[466] John McGeoch's Gizmotron is set to overdrive, creating the sound of an avian apocalypse, and leads the charge with all the swooping sonic poignancy of Robert Fripp's playing on David Bowie's 'Heroes'; a six-stringed air raid siren.

Another exercise melding apocalypse and catharsis in equal measure, the song reflects the apex of Siouxsie and The Banshees' tight, creative cohesion, synergy and histrionics.

Budgie's drumming is a full-on stomp epic when the chorus kicks in, reverting, as do the rest of the band, to precarious delicacy, for the interceding verses. Steve Severin also has his work cut out, providing luscious, sweltering bass tones.

Demonstrating that Hitchcock is never far from Siouxsie's psyche, his name is mentioned in the lyric, undoubtedly or homage to the director's 1963 classic *The Birds*. At two minutes and one second, around halfway through, McGeoch creates a sound that temporarily slows the pace of the song, as Siouxsie, with a vocal effect evocative of The Man From Another Place's backward speaking voice in David Lynch's *Twin Peaks*[467], as she sings her Siren song, around twenty-four seconds of plaintive intonation.

It is beleaguered, disembodied incantation, as the song gathers a head of steam, with Siouxsie transmitting Patti Smith's vocal on 'Land: Horses/Land Of A Thousand Dances/La Mer(de)' from the seminal album *Horses*.[468]

The song's tearing pulse as it reaches its vertex, is juxtaposed for the run out of the song, at three minutes fifty-one seconds, by twenty-five seconds of synthesised drumming intensity, not completely unlike 'On The Run' from Pink Floyd's *Dark Side Of The Moon*.[469]

The demo for 'Painted Bird' was recorded at Workhouse Studios from 12 to 15 March 1982 and for the BBC Kid Jensen Show, broadcast 13 May 1982.

Both demo and BBC versions, although more austere regarding the *A Kiss In The Dreamhouse* final production, reflect the quartet at the vanguard of auricular euphoria, often with John McGeoch leading the charge, as Johnny Marr enthusiastically comments, 'It was like getting George Best on guitar'.[470]

It's not entirely inconceivable that Siouxsie and The Banshees were familiar with The Trashmen's proto-Punk 'Surfin' Bird'[471] which was covered in 1977 by The Ramones, and in 1978 by The Cramps.[472]

'Cocoon'

'It's no use going back to yesterday, because I was a different person then'.[473]

Lewis Carroll[474]

'I always think 'Cocoon'… sounds really happy but, again, the lyrics are a bit odd, they grate against the sound of the music. I think that's something we're good at, subverting lyrics'.[475]

Siouxsie Sioux

The making and recording of *A Kiss In The Dreamhouse* is, in many ways, the perfect Siouxsie And The Banshees storm, replete with moments of inspired genius, comedy and the ensuing fallout of John McGeoch's departure from the band, as well as that of manager Nils Stevenson.

The album's intensity reflects a work that was, creatively, the most hands on 'The Banshees had ever been involved in, and a disaster waiting to happen. The feverish desire to write, record, experiment, party and avoid sleep bore extraordinary creative fruit while taking an immense toll on each member of the band'.[476]

Siouxsie had discovered a new recreational chemical to keep her fully stoked-up for the unrelenting touring, writing and recording treadmill: LSD, in addition to cocaine and speed.

'Cocoon''s subterranean languidness 'is the result of when a drunken 5:00am studio jam produced an oddly beguiling take on cocktail jazz, led by McGeoch's atonal piano, Sioux took the tape home and proceeded to edit and write the song that would become 'Cocoon' while tripping. The lyric sees Sioux recede into childhood, lying in a cot, hugging her knees, imagining the thoughts of a caterpillar hiding "in the cotton wool cocoon" as a metaphor for infant insecurity.

"When we were doing these sessions and I first took acid, I remember thinking, 'I wonder if I should go and see my mum and just say, "Here, Mum… let's take some acid together". I remember thinking, "Is that a good idea, or could she die from it?" I really wanted to understand everything about where she came from and my childhood'.[477]

Siouxsie elaborates on the psychedelic details thus, 'Mike Hedges was the one who introduced me to LSD – California Sunshine. It was a hippie drug, but it didn't feel like that at all. I remember Nils once telling me, "Whatever you do, don't take LSD, it's scary!" I thought, "That sounds good", so I started to use it recreationally'.[478]

It was when Siouxsie decided to spend a night in on her own to see what might happen that the singer 'ended up writing 'Cocoon' and some Creatures stuff',[479] the whole episode 'a bit of a blur',[480] with Siouxsie indulging in some Neapolitan ice cream, thinking she was on a beach, when in fact she was 'actually in the kitchen on the floor'.[481]

'Cocoon' is another first for Siouxsie and The Banshees regarding experimentation and musicianship unlike any of their other recorded material to date.

The song was the result of a melange of creative input from various members of the band and some inspired intervention from Mike Hedges.

The evening of 3 July 1982 saw the band add flesh to the bones of an initial bit of messing around on the piano, recorded by Severin and Budgie, which ended up sounding not a million miles away from Mike Garson's freewheeling, maniacal playing on David Bowie's *Aladdin Sane*.

Initially, the pairing of Siouxsie's LSD-inspired lyric with a tune that Severin had come up with, had proved unsuccessful. However, it was at Hedges' suggestion that the band attempt 'something sleazy',[482]prompting Severin to suggest a jazz oriented 'walking bass line'.[483]

The initial piano part was then transposed to the bass, although the ensuing sound was completely different. Adding to the tenor of a smoke-filled jazz setting, Budgie, brushes in hand, joined forces with Severin and a session that went deep into the night resulted in 'Cocoon', recorded in two takes.

Budgie introduces the song, as Severin's double bass joins the fray and, just as the listener is lulled into what might be a slice of Thelonious Monk-type playing, John McGeoch takes the song into the realms of the abstract, with an array of seemingly improvised and extemporised atonal playing, as the song becomes increasingly disorienting and giddying.

Again, we are inside a *Twin Peaks* sequence, re-visiting The Man From Another Place, accompanied by Angelo Badalamenti's 'Dance Of The Dream Man'.[484]

Siouxsie's lyrics allude to the cocoon as protective shell, the mattresses and blankets a throwback to when she was bed-ridden with ulcerative colitis as a child, an experience that 'de-romanticised'[485] her view of humankind, 'feeling so helpless'.[486]

Lyrically, Siouxsie is at a pinnacle of inventiveness, with 'A pearl beaded lizard bathed in a Gossamer scent, With my heat detector lip-pit, pulling at the newly formed tissue'[487] reflecting her psychedelically enhanced reality.

'Cocoon' is a genuinely multi-sensory song, bathed in aural circumfluence. Herewith the Banshees' paradox: it is nothing like a Siouxsie and The Banshees' song, yet it is every bit a Siouxsie and The Banshees' song, a paradox that would not have been lost on a band encased in their own promethean fantasy.

It is clear that Mike Hedges facilitated the band to dig deeply into their collective psyche to descry what Alice discerned in Chapter One of Lewis Carroll's *Alice's Adventures In Wonderland*, 'a red-hot poker will burn you if you hold it too long; and that, if you cut your finger very deeply with a knife, it usually bleeds... if you drink much from a bottle marked "poison", it is almost certain to disagree with you, sooner or later'.[488]

Not that there was any semblance of circumspection with *A Kiss In The Dreamhouse*, an album which is 'a product of addiction, stress, old, sick love and new, dangerous love',[489] which would herald the end of the band's 'imperial phase'.[490]

'Cocoon' was recorded 7 to 26 July 1982 at Playground Studios, the latter period of which was interspersed with tour dates in Milan and Rome. 'Cocoon' was debuted live at the Manchester Apollo[491] on 22 November 1982.

'Slowdive'

Marking the end of *A Kiss In The Dreamhouse*, recorded at Playground Studios from 2 July to 5 July 1982, and released as a single on 1 October 1982, with the B-side 'Cannibal Roses' and 'Obsession II', 'Slowdive' is the musical equivalent of sexual frisson on the precipice of bursting its zip, anointed by the collaboration of alcohol, with Steve Severin commenting, 'It was just a drunken evening'.[492]

Siouxsie comments that it is 'Another sexual song, but more playful. It's very open, very relaxed, loose. I wrote it on the spot after a jam in the studio'.[493]

Utilising the violin playing of Anne Stephenson and Virginia Hewes, the process was as painful as it was pleasurable, as Stephenson recollects, 'Mike Hedges asked us to come in and play strings on a couple of songs. We did 'Slowdive' first. Siouxsie said, "I like Es, play lots of Es". So we started going "Ee, ee, ee…" My arm hurt after doing that E thing for so long, but we didn't mind. I was thrilled to be working with the band who'd made *The Scream*, which I thought was such an innovative record'.[494]

It's Stephenson who can be heard crying 'Oh my God' on 'Slowdive', elaborating 'I know it sounds like an orgasmic gasp… the best one I've ever done, I suspect'.[495]

It's clear that the song is playfully insouciant in its execution, with a lyric the conceivable result of being in the business of making music, putting it out into the world and then having to justify it or explain what you have done, as Siouxsie elucidates, 'Slowdive' was an improvised lyric... It's like, umm, if you're making music, what it amounts to is, because you're expressing something you can't say in words. So for me to explain what that is, is taking away something that you lose when you're just using speech. With music it should speak for itself'.[496]

On a first listen, one might surmise that 'Slowdive' is a rather straightforward, mid-tempo song, driven by a four-on-the-floor drumbeat with the added 1980s' staple of gated reverb[497] to create more of a colossal tone. However, nothing in Banshees' land is ever that austere or elementary.

Siouxsie's tongue in cheek, slightly stream-of-consciousness-orientented lyrics echo an inventory of dance crazes 'like 'The Locomotion': "Put your knees into your face/And see if you can race real slow"; "Taking honeysuckle sips/From your rolling hips".[498] Acknowledging the zeitgeist of emerging keep-fit videos, Siouxsie "wanted to turn the Jane Fonda Workout on its head"'.[499]

The sound is, at least in part, again evocative of Can's 'Ege Bamyasi'.

Perhaps a prescient warning of the fallout to come, John McGeoch's guitar playing is more absent than present in the mix of the song; a mere spectre at the feast. There is the chugging six-string bass guitar which pervades throughout, brought into the studio by Robert Smith, as Billy 'Chainsaw' Houlston recalls, 'Not having used one before, Steve began messing about with it, whilst Mike Hedges and Budgie listened to Steve's ramblings from the control booth. Inspired by the sounds Steve was producing, Budgie left the booth and accompanied him on drums. Siouxsie listened to the duo's performance, wrote a set of lyrics, recorded them and the whole track was completed in about two hours, all that remained to be recorded was John's guitar part (because he had been absent at the time 'Slowdive' was written and recorded)'.[500]

As Houlston alludes, McGeoch's contribution can only be discerned in the form of muted chord stabs and the occasional mimicry of an end-of-pier coin-operated laughing sailor.

As a final hurrah to *A Kiss In The Dreamhouse*, 'Slowdive' is both striking and unsettling in equal measure. On the one hand, it is reflective of the band's confidence and fearlessness to continue to push musical boundaries with the same tenacity and bloody-mindedness that took their first incarnation onto the stage of the 100 Club on 20 September 1976.

However, compared to the coup de grace on previous albums, 'Switch' (*The Scream*), 'The Lord's Prayer' (*Join Hands*), 'Skin', (*Kaleidoscope*) and 'Voodoo Dolly' (*Juju*), 'Slowdive' is, metaphorically, more opulent opiate than angst-ridden amphetamine.

'Slowdive' reached a peak of 41 in the Official UK Singles Chart, spending four weeks in the Top 100 from 9 October 1982 to 30 October 1982.

One review of the single is lavish in its admiration, venturing 'Siouxsie & The Banshees ought to be the eighth wonder of the world. Whatever they do is excellent. This starts off with an intro that sounds as if it's going to lead into the theme of *Psycho* and progresses into a steadily descending careering Banshee journey. This is not quite as immediate as some of their other stuff, or as varied, but it's as gripping as ever. The Banshees have patented their own sound, but they never reproduce it in the same mould without imaginative twists'.[501]

Another assessment is far less effusive, commenting, 'This sounds more like something the Creatures would do (the Creatures being our very own Siouxsie and Budgie of course) with prominent drumming and not a lot else. There is a violin but sadly McGeoch's guitar hardly makes its presence known'.[502]

The video for 'Slowdive', a labyrinthine, yet rather tongue-in-cheek slice of dramaturgy, again utilises the steadfast video direction of Clive Richardson. Filmed in a hangar on the Isle Of Dogs, during a period after the winding down of the shipping docks in the late 1970s and the onset of big corporate money and redevelopment, the epic setting is evocative of a hybridised circus and lofty theatre, with elaborate multi-coloured floor and ceiling lighting employed to create an array of vaudevillian effects through spotlighting, silhouette and chiaroscuro.

One can see why a lofty space of this nature was necessary: the inclusion of a trapeze swing adorned by Siouxsie for the video, teetering on the edge of Spinal Tap[503] territory but entirely in keeping with the ostentatious musical *A Kiss In The Dreamhouse* aesthetic.

In the first shot of the video, Siouxsie appears, not too at ease on the swing in motion, dressed to the nines in black latex and white lace,

94

with crimped black and white hair completing the striking ensemble, later appearing in an off-the-shoulder all-in-one black and white striped jumpsuit, viewed through an elaborate arabesque wooden frame.

Cut to the rest of the band, barefoot and wearing zoot suits,[504]their stealthy dance moves choreographed by Ginette Landray, an ex-girlfriend of Budgie's.

Both Budgie and Landray moved from Liverpool to London in 1979, and Landray became part of the *Top Of The Pops* dance troupe Zoo[505] from 1981 to 1983.

Steve Severin and Robert Smith's The Glove features Landray's lead vocals on the majority of *Blue Sunshine*.[506] As the drumbeat kicks in, we are treated to the consecutive eye-lined smiles and winks of Severin, then Budgie and finally McGeoch.

In one of the early shots, Siouxsie is seen alongside 'a wolfhound type dog, the relevance of which is a mystery'.[507]

Landray clearly put the band through their paces, especially John McGeoch, as Steve Severin recollects, '… we had this idea for Siouxsie to be in the foreground and the rest of us to move in syncopation behind her, so we went to a dance studio to work on choreography. McGeoch couldn't cope with it at all. After about ten minutes he clutched his chest, staggered to the back and lit up a fag saying. "I canna do this"'.[508] Ironically enough, this was the last video McGeoch would ever appear in as a Banshee.

The first B-side track, 'Obsession II', is the vocal-less 'Obsession' in its infancy. A spine-chilling, boiling caldron full of stalking tension, enveloped by a miasmic haze, fashioning the cinematic bastard child of Bernard Hermann and John Carpenter.

'Cannibal Roses', the second B-side track on the single release, is a lyrical revelation of Siouxsie's own 'Day Of The Triffids' encounter, replete with an enumeration of contiguous verses, divulging seamy verses from nursery rhymes, part explained in the booklet to accompany *Downside Up*, '…strange things were happening around me. I swear that a giant sunflower started to grow outside my first floor flat in Queens Park. Its head used to peer in the window at me when it thought I wasn't looking'.[509]

It is another great Siouxsie and The Banshees curio, with all the hallmarks of the band stretching out in full jam mode. The beginning of the song sounds like the moment when a needle jumps into the lead in groove of a vinyl record, giving the song a sense of the incidental and happenstance.

Siouxsie's aphrodisiac yelping shepherds the song into gorgeously overlayed instrumentation, including melancholic guitar playing, atonal piano, recalling the strains of Bryan Ferry's playing on Roxy Music's 'Virginia Plain',[510]loose percussion cowbell and Siouxsie's swooping, expressive, melodiously dissonant vocal, all driven forward by Severin's pugnacious bass.

'Cannibal Roses' was initially recorded on 11 July 1982 at Playground Studios, and subsequently re-recorded on 31 August 1982.

Employing the fine art skills of Gill Thompson for the hybridised erotic Tracey Emin[511] and Francis Bacon[512] oriented loose delineated figurative paintings on the front covers of both seven-inch and twelve-inch singles; both connoting sexual congress, set against a background of Mondrian-like black and mottled red, blue and pink blocks of colour, the design also uses three silhouetted cobalt blue divers, evoking the late cutouts of Henri Matisse.[513]

Four small, spliced orange circles against a cadmium yellow background also occupy the picture space; a motif also occurring on the B-side label for the twelve-inch version, this time white on pale turquoise, interspersed with three solid white triangles. The back cover for both formats of the single capitalises on the contoured divers, this time in black, as they flank a motif of undulating ribbons of cobalt blue and, in the centre, the icon of the split circle reappears atop turquoise rivulets set against an orange background with the three triangles superimposed over the top, while the overall composition employs a turquoise background.

The athleticism of the divers is echoed by the Olympic Games five-ringed symbol in the centre of the composition. The Charles Rennie Mackintosh-style typesetting is also retained.

Some of these lavish pictorial elements are also used on album cover, inspired, as with the singles, by Gustav Klimt's 'Danae' 1907–

08[514], as well as Klimt's masterpiece 'The Kiss'.[515]

Among the array of Gustav Klimt-like gold symbols are embedded a double doll-like image of Siouxsie, one awake and one asleep, rendered as though she is looking at herself in the centre of the composition, and a triangulation, reflecting the abundance of decorative three-sided polygons, of Steve Severin, John McGeoch and Budgie, all asleep.

The back cover is an image of a sleeping Siouxsie bathed in Hundertwasser-esque[516] swirling symbols, as though in a Jean Cocteau dream sequence. The liquidity of the image is anchored by a red, gold and turquoise mosaic embellishment.

Beginning Of The End

'John just went a little further over the edge than the rest of us. When it happened, it came very fast'.[517]

Steve Severin

The band had taken a touring break of three months between 31 July, when they headlined the Elephant Fayre[518] in Cornwall, UK, and 29 October, flying to Madrid to play two dates at the Rock Ola Club, a stretch of twenty-five European and UK dates in total, which would culminate in two homecoming shows at London's Hammersmith Odeon on 28 and 29 December 1982.

But that was all it was, a break from gigging. The band returned to Playground Studio on 17 August to mix 'Painted Bird', and subsequently remixing 'Melt!' and then 'Obsession', 'Obsession II' and 'Cascade'.

'Slowdive' was also pared down to a seven-inch version. With the album completed, including the rearranging and running order of the tracks, 'the band rewarded themselves by getting mindlessly drunk around 2:00am on 21 August.[519]

The one remaining recording was undertaken at Marcus Studios,[520] a new version of 'Cannibal Roses', done in one take, produced by the whole band jamming around the original version, previously recorded on 11 July. There were also the dance rehearsals and subsequent filming of 'Slowdive' on 7 October.

The travails of touring, combined with the intensity of making *A Kiss In The Dreamhouse* and overdose of interviews, had taken its toll on all of the band but no more so than McGeoch.

A coalescence of ambition, recovery and ensuring the three-month touring hiatus rendered the band match fit for the remainder of the 1982 tour. Budgie recalls, 'I remember McGeoch taking me aside early on and saying. "You gotta watch your drinking". I thought, "That's rich coming from you!" He was being sincere and concerned, but I never took it seriously. I don't suppose either of us thought we had a problem. I wish I had been mature enough to help him when we got to Spain'.[521]

It wasn't only alcohol which was untethering McGeoch from the rest of the band. While cocaine had become a fairly regular feature of the band's extracurricular activities, McGeoch was developing his own habit, as Budgie explains, 'We were no saints, there was a lot of amphetamine going around... that kept us going, and all those sessions going, all night, so I could drink more, or we could all put more marks on the bottle of Frascati in the fridge – it was all quite pathetic'.[522]

One telling sign of McGeoch's creeping addiction was when, Budgie explains, 'He'd be on the other side of the mixing desk, rather than on the side where the band were. He'd keep ducking down and then popping up again'.[523]

Regarding cocaine, Siouxsie also acknowledges the discernible change in McGeoch, while also acknowledging that the environment at the time was akin to being on the inside of a snow globe, 'It's a bit of a curse. I didn't see it at the time – obviously hindsight is a wonderful thing. He'd have been better off not to have been introduced to it, but I don't know how he could have avoided it, because it was everywhere. There are certain personalities that it just hooks into – it was his little "voodoo dolly", if you like'.[524]

Robert Smith spent quite a bit of time in the studio during the recording sessions for the 'Dreamhouse' album and it was clear that Severin was developing an ever-closer friendship with the Cure frontman, and Severin's relationship with McGeoch was dissipating; conceivably catalysed, at least in part, by Smith's presence, adding to the increasing perturbation felt by McGeoch.

There is also the perhaps contributory detail of John McGeoch's musical éclat, which, along with Budgie's extraordinary brio, while being a spur for Severin's own development as a musician, could also have created some tension. Severin tells a rather different story; one of onerously won liberation through hard work, determination and chutzpah, which, he recounts, 'fed into the new material and working process'.[525]

If the band were immersed in the recording of 'Dreamhouse', not entirely unaware of the unfurling drama, slogging through, but 'heads down, in the studio, and pretty much working through it all, even though the hours were ridiculous',[526] with a job to be done.

Peter Hook, formerly bass player in Joy Division[527] and then New Order,[528]visiting Playground Studios to see Siouxsie, recollects, 'I sat down and, to be honest, I'd never got on with Robert (Smith), because the rivalry with Joy Division was too immense, but John was lovely and you could tell he wasn't too happy with the set up. I turned to Siouxsie and said, "You've got a fucking atmosphere here, haven't you, love?" She said, "Fucking tell me about it!" So I just said, "Well, I'm not hanging about, I'm off!"'[529]

One fermenting episode thought to have put the match to the powder barrel and 'sown the seeds for irrevocable damage',[530] was when the band, minus McGeoch, paid a visit to the local Greek taverna, down the road from Playground Studios. Budgie relates that, '…John hadn't come with us because he wanted to do a mix. When we came back, it wasn't awful, but it was just someone else's take on what we were doing. We'd never done that in the studio before. We only did that when we were all ready, when we all had our hands on the faders'.[531]

Budgie hypothesises that one of the reasons for John's nocturnal modification of the band's work was wanting to be more than the guitarist and more a part of the writing team. However, considering McGeoch's proliferating cocaine habit, Budgie also questions whether it was a case of "'Everybody's out and can I get stuck into the lines?'"[532]

Whatever the rationale, Budgie surmises that there was an

irrevocable fissure between McGeoch, Siouxsie and Severin. Financially, McGeoch had benefited from his work with Visage, whose first album had earned him, Billy 'Chainsaw' Houlston remarks, '…a shedload of money… Back then records sold a lot more and you could make a lot of money from royalties alone. So, because of his financial situation, he was able to introduce the Banshees to expensive red wine! I remember that vividly. He got a taste for the finer things in life… Money wasn't the motivation for John, I don't think. The Visage thing just happened, and nobody could have guessed how successful that would become'.[533]

The Rock Ola, Madrid

Neither Siouxsie, Severin or Budgie is a hundred percent sure, or can remember with any semblance of clarity, why Banshees' manager Dave Woods[534] booked two gigs at the Rock Ola in Madrid on the eve of Halloween, and the geography of the gigs is a little strange when looking at the tour schedule for the remainder of 1982.

The topography pales into relative insignificance with the spiralling events on 29 and 30 October 1982. Musical differences had already caused minor ripples between Siouxsie and McGeoch, one of which was the recording of 'Il Est Né Le Divin Enfant', a song which the guitarist didn't like, stating, "I really can't see this working, so if you don't mind, I'm not gonna take part".[535]

However, the beauty of the of the recording studio is that elements can be re-recorded, edited and deleted in pursuit of the polished article. Not the case with live performances, especially where one of the key musicians is in the throes of a drug and alcohol-fuelled calamity.

Essentially, John McGeoch was in a desperate state; one of the telltale signs was at the Rock Ola soundcheck, where McGeoch was struggling to remember guitar parts and this was both literally and metaphorically amplified during the first gig, Siouxsie recalls, 'He went downhill quite quickly. Bottom line is, I didn't really care what the band got up to as long as the band wasn't put out or compromised and the audience wasn't let down, i.e. a show didn't happen because of someone else'.[536]

Earlier on that day, Siouxsie recalls that the band had been to a park in Madrid and jumped into a cable car. 'John was slugging from a bottle of wine. His lips were black and he was raving. I was getting so pissed off with him that I was ready to throw him out of it'.[537]

Later on, it transpires that Dave Woods, in a bid to prevent McGeoch's falling apart, had put McGeoch in the shower to try and render him compos mentis for the gig. Budgie expounds, '...he was really shaky because he was having withdrawal from the booze the night before and he (Dave Woods) gave him a Valium or half a Valium'.[538]

It was common knowledge among band members that Woods' 'favourite nightcap was a Valium and a Campari and soda'.[539] However, the net result of the Valium, plus one or several glasses of wine from the wine box the guitarist kept next to his hotel bed, Severin recalls, 'so he could have a drink first thing in the morning when he woke up',[540] and the bottle he had taken to the park, was that McGeoch was well and truly soused come showtime.

Siouxsie recollects, 'During the first show we were playing 'Spellbound'. He didn't even realise. He just carried on playing something completely different to the rest of us. Luckily it was only a fairly small club in Madrid, so it wasn't to much of a disaster, but it was a bit odd'.[541]

McGeoch would later acknowledge, with no little remorse, the part benzodiazepine played in helping him 'ruin the gig'.[542]

A twelve-song set on the first night, depending on one's source, resulted in John McGeoch collapsing on stage, although some people refute this. It is a discernibly shorter set when compared to the second night; twelve songs without encores, as opposed to seventeen.

There is some debate about Dave Woods' involvement in sobering McGeoch up for the gig: Siouxsie's retrospective ire about giving him Valium and Budgie's feeling that Woods 'was trying to get his best out of John on the stage that night'.[543]

There is also speculation about Woods' business relationship with McGeoch, as Woods oversaw the band's finances and McGeoch 'was always pretty fierce about making sure he got the money owed to him, which Dave (Woods) obviously found threatening'.[544]

McGeoch's close friend the musician Russell Webb[545] was in Madrid at McGeoch's request, as someone he could turn to outside of the band during his dark night of the soul, but no amount of greasing the wheels that first evening could avert, as Budgie reflects, '...the first major fuck up. We were just bemused on stage because John could play in his sleep – his hands would do it if his brain wasn't really engaged... I listen back and sometimes I know when there's a bit of sloppy playing going on... He could be bang on when he's really slamming the chords, on say 'Christine', but again with this lack of rigidity that no one could get afterwards'.[546]

The second night in Madrid, although still not an easy listen, is an overall more competent gig, consisting of fourteen songs[547] for the main set and two encores. It may have been longer in duration but that first night had sown the seeds of what would become McGeoch's exit from the band. There was no band pow wow or mediation after the first night, just, Budgie remembers, '...an icy kind of silence, an embarrassed kind of silence. An inability to just say, "Hey, shall we all sit over there a minute and have a little talk about what happened last night?" We never did that. We just flew back home'.[548]

Siouxsie reflects on events some forty plus years later, 'That one gig was the last straw that broke the camel's back. It was a gradual build-up and I think we weren't able to be adult about it, we weren't really adults yet. We thought we were, (despite) our naivety about the situation and maybe his too, of not being able to ask for help'.[549]

Siouxsie also views McGeoch's malaise as cumulative and not just a case of bottoming out during one or two gigs. Siouxsie, Severin and Budgie had set such great store on McGeoch's brilliance, with Siouxsie saying he was given '...chance after chance. Then with the last gig of him playing a different song to everyone else on the stage, it was like, "WHAT"! It was almost like he'd lost his mind for a while and there was a thing of trying to look after him for a while and he'd hide bottles of stuff outside on the windowsill'.[550]

There would have been the inevitable jumpiness about bailing on a tour, as happened in Aberdeen three years earlier with the absconding of Kenny Morris and John McKay, not least from Dave Woods who'd allegedly stumped up his own money to finance the

1979 tour, which would have been a commercial disaster if Robert Smith hadn't stepped in, and who would have been, to put it mildly, unwilling to write off the not inconsiderable revenue generated from the remaining twenty-five gigs in 1982.

Siouxsie, Severin and Budgie were also resolute that they would not be derailed, Siouxsie commenting, '…it sounds really callous but it wasn't. It was like we were thinking, "What the fuck are you doing, John?" It's just so sad, really sad, that he got sucked into this. What a waste, what a real waste of his talent'.[551]

McGeoch reflects on his departure from Siouxsie and The Banshees, 'It was a bit of a misunderstanding… I think Siouxsie thought I was disenfranchised from the Banshees. Much later she said to me, "I thought you didn't want to be a Banshee anymore". I did. I just felt overburdened and I wasn't dealing with it very well'.

Budgie reflects that, in hindsight, the best course of action would have been for John McGeoch, and the rest of the band, to step away and take a break, but felt the band '…never learned the lesson. We continued and we saw another guitarist fail, and another guitarist, and individually we were all falling apart at times, but we never stopped. We never gave ourselves space to take some rest'.[552]

The band flew back to the UK after the second Madrid gig and McGeoch's wife Janet sought professional psychiatric counselling in London, the result of which was a stint at the Priory,[553] during which time the Banshees sacked him,[554] the Madrid gig being the main impetus.

Before McGeoch's ousting, with a two-month tour starting on 13 November, a further fifty-one planned gigs were planned for the new year, which would include Japan, Europe and the UK and the inevitable promotional duties for *A Kiss In The Dreamhouse*, due for release on 5 November.

There was also an appearance booked for *The Old Grey Whistle Test* on 8 November. Out of concern for the band's health, just as much as McGeoch's, Severin and Dave Woods visited McGeoch at the Priory on 2 November.

Neither were quite prepared for what they encountered, with Severin recalling, 'We were told John was only available in the evenings, so Dave and I arrived at the Priory around 8:00pm. only to be told that he was down the local pub! He had left a weird, scribbled note with a map so off we went. There was John surrounded by his new fast friends, sporting a still-fresh tattoo and with his head shaved on the sides'.[555]

Severin, wondering if McGeoch's striking new hairstyle was in fact him being prepared for a lobotomy, coupled with the affectionate hugs and kisses he received from McGeoch, recalls Dave Woods doing most of the talking, as he was '…too stunned by it all'.[556]

Severin and Woods' visit elucidated one steadfast certainty, 'that John was never going to be ready for the *Whistle Test* or the tour and that we needed a back-up plan'.[557]

Siouxsie, reflecting on the resolution to fire McGeoch from the band, deliberates, 'If he'd fought to stay in the band, maybe it would have been different, but he rolled over pretty easily, so I think part of him didn't want to continue'.[558]

With the end of any relationship, there is no easy goodbye, and this was especially the case with McGeoch as his tenure with the band marked their high point of inventiveness and creativity.

Siouxsie remarked, 'John was very upset about it at the time, but he was in hospital and he was receiving treatment. A combination of drugs, alcohol, and I think he suffered with a little bit of depression… There were other issues, but I'm pissed off it was handled that way. At the time we thought we were doing the right thing and protecting the band's integrity'.[559]

Budgie reflects on the lack of esprit de corps within the band as far as McGeoch was concerned, commenting, 'If something would fill me with grief and guilt, it would be that. It would be why couldn't we together or individually take him to one side? I wasn't aware of anything being wrong musically, really, until that (Madrid) gig, and not equipped to say anything about it either… I was developing my own set of addictions or whatever they were, which certainly messed me up. Is it that with John, once the ball started rolling, it went much faster for him?'[560]

In hindsight, Budgie acknowledges that every member of the band had their vices on the road, analysing his own alcohol problem as, 'I knew very early that I couldn't take a drink before I'd got the gig out of the way. Then I'd probably drink all night and have the rest of the day to recover... I wasn't seeing the band the day after the night before... It was the loneliest place, on the road'.[561]

Budgie certainly wasn't inured to McGeoch's Hadean descent, but his own proclivities made him unable to offer useful advice, remarking, 'Yeah, I noticed it, but you didn't notice. You don't notice because, who am I to point the finger?'[562]

Although John McGeoch's tenure in Siouxsie and The Banshees was, for all parties concerned, sadly attenuated, while the guitarist may have been down, he most certainly wasn't out.

In 1983, taking a break from making music, McGeoch produced Swedish 'punk-funk' band Zzzang Tumb's self-titled debut album,[563]a satisfying, melodious and poppy, hybridisation of Talking Heads, Can, Chic[564] and Visage, with discernible elements of Magazine, peppered with some Siouxsie and The Banshees.

In the same year, McGeoch formed The Armoury Show with ex-Skids singer Richard Jobson, bass guitarist Russell Webb[565] and drummer John Doyle.[566]

McGeoch's time in the band saw the release of the 1985 album *Waiting For The Floods*,[567] which puts McGeoch's guitar-playing artistry and dexterity very much in the foreground; what one would call a 'return to form'.

His guitar attacks, swoops and swirls, creating giddy sonic landscapes on a slice of quintessential 1980s New Wave.[568]

McGeoch joined Public Image Ltd. in 1986 and recorded three albums with the band, *Happy*,[569]released in 1987, *9*,[570] released in 1989, and *That What Is Not*,[571] released in 1992.

With more 'attack' called for with the band's more rock-oriented sensibilities, McGeoch again adopts the mantle with flair and adroitness, especially on *That What Is Not*, which would be the last full album McGeoch would play on, as well as the last tour with a band he would undertake.

His majestic playing can also be heard on the Sugarcubes' 'Gold' on the band's third and final album *Stick Around For Joy*,[572] released within a hair's breadth of PIL's *That What Is Not*.

There were a couple of short-lived projects McGeoch undertook with singer and songwriter Glenn Gregory[573] and John Keeble[574] of Spandau Ballet, but no recorded material came from these collaborations.

With the advent of what had been a prolific and financially rewarding sideline as a session musician running aground, McGeoch subsequently retrained as a nurse in the mid-1990s, managing to moderate his alcohol intake considerably, and, by the end of 2003, had stopped drinking entirely. However, years of substance abuse didn't mitigate McGeoch's epilepsy, a condition that he had been diagnosed with in the late 1990s.

His seizures became increasingly acute and, as described by his partner Sophie in *The Light Pours Out Of Me* by Rory Sullivan-Burke, '…while he was asleep, he suffered a seizure which effectively switched off his brain and stopped his breathing'.[575]

Sullivan-Burke elaborates, 'Sophie raised the alarm upon waking, but it was too late. John Alexander McGeoch died on 5 March 2004 as a result of SUDEP (sudden unexpected death in epilepsy). He was 48'.[576]

John McGeoch's swan song with Siouxsie and The Banshees elicited some favourable reviews, not least from the NME's Richard Cook[577], stating that it was rare for '…a group to make their fourth LP and still be provocative',[578]calling *A Kiss In The Dreamhouse* '…a feat of imagination scarcely ever recorded. It's breathtaking'.[579]

Of McGeoch's playing, Cook remarks, 'In John McGeoch's guitars a shattered beauty settles on the tattooed skin of the songs'.[580] *A Kiss In The Dreamhouse* peaked at 11 in the UK Album Chart and spent 11 weeks in the Top 100.

The album was and remains a colossus of sonic dissection. What had previously been a band in its own stream was now well and truly a 'Cascade', with *A Kiss In The Dreamhouse* overflowing with phantasmagorical soundscapes.

However, '…as none of the protagonists could talk openly to each other about what they were going through, the terror, desire, depression and anger was poured into the stunningly beautiful music that emerged from a small room in Camden Town'.[581] It would also prove yet another test of mettle for a band within spitting distance of total wreckage.

Budgie recalls, 'We were caught up in the insanity of that moment …We were losing the studio. We were losing a member. We were losing our minds. You try to manufacture those things, where you're trying to live on the edge, take away the safety-net, risk everything, and you're hoping that, out of the risk-taking, comes something magic. And that's what 'Dreamhouse' is. But you can't continue that way'.[582]

Regarding the Banshees' popularity, Siouxsie's face continued to be a regular feature on the cover of a plethora of music, fashion and culture-oriented weekly and monthly papers and magazines including *The Face*, *ZigZag*, *Melody Maker*, *NME*, *Record Mirror*, *Sounds* and *Fool's Mate*. Several of the images reflect Siouxsie's penchant for traditional Japanese accoutrements.

The Show Goes On

With the band at the second impasse of their career, bereft of a guitarist and with a burgeoning number of commitments on the horizon, the most imperative of which was to fulfil their touring commitments, step forward Robert Smith, lead singer and guitarist for The Cure, saving the day as he had in 1979 when Siouxsie and The Banshees were barely halfway through the 'Join Hands' tour.

With scant rehearsal time before the remainder of the 1982 gigs, the first of which was at the Birmingham Odeon[583] on 13 November, Smith nonetheless didn't need much persuading. *Pornography*,[584] described as The Cure's 'darkest hour',[585] with the nihilistic opening lyric on the first track 'One Hundred Years' 'It doesn't matter if we all die',[586] is the band's fourth studio album and one, Lol Tolhurst writes, 'Robert (Smith) said, 'I wanted it to be the ultimate "fuck off" record'. I think on that front we succeeded'.[587]

Beset by prolific drug use, in-fighting and Smith's increasingly desolate lyrics, the convergent events led to the departure of bass guitarist Simon Gallup[588] while the band were on tour.[589]

This took place after an altercation over a bar bill between Gallup and Smith in Strasbourg on 27 May 1982, which resulted in Smith taking a flight back to the UK, only to be castigated by his father, who would not let Smith over the family threshold in Crawley.

So Smith had to fly back and re-join the tour, with remaining Swiss, Belgian and French dates to fulfil. Lol Tolhurst, in his autobiography *Cured: The Tale of Two Imaginary Boys*[590] recounts the final gig of the 'Pornography' tour: 'On this occasion we changed it around a little and swapped instruments. I played bass, Simon (Gallup) played guitar and Robert played the drums. Our roadie, Gary Biddles, came on stage and started singing about Robert and me being wankers and only Simon was any good… Robert threw the drumsticks at him, and eventually we all stopped and left the stage'.[591]

This denouement presaged a nineteen-month hiatus for The Cure from November 1982 to June 1984. Lol Tolhurst recollects the strain which touring alone had put on the band, 'By the time we rolled onto Strasbourg on 27 May 1982, we had already played around thirty-three very intense gigs promoting *Pornography*.

We were both tired and mentally drained'.[592] Reflecting further on the 'Pornography' tour, Tolhurst expounds, 'It's not hard to see why the tour turned out that way. We had been cooped up together for an awful long time on the road and in the studio the previous three years. We had played 377 gigs, approximately one every three days for over a thousand days… we were just plain exhausted'.[593]

Exhaustion, disarray and dissolution weren't the only abiding memories of the 'Pornography' tour. The band's 'look, previously alluded to in the context of the *Pornography* album, had also changed, especially Robert Smith's.

Lol Tolhurst remarks, '…nobody could have predicted the bright red lipstick that now adorned Robert's face and eyes! The sheer shock of his appearance was tremendous to anybody that encountered him in the backstage area before the gig. It looked like his eyes were bleeding and someone had taken a knife to his face'.[594]

Smith's first 1982 performance with Siouxsie and The Banshees was on *The Old Grey Whistle Test* on 12 November 1982, playing two songs from *A Kiss In The Dreamhouse*: 'Melt!' and 'Painted Bird'.

Smith recalls that becoming a Banshee would allow him '…to play serious music, big chords and, crucially, I was no longer the focal point: I was just the guitarist'.[595]

The two songs were played live in front of an appreciative studio audience. This was the third live outing for 'Melt!', having been showcased at the Elephant Fayre on 31 July. 'Painted Bird' had become a regular feature of the Banshees 1982 setlist since its initial outing on 20 February 1982 at Vinyl Feest[596] in Amsterdam.

For 'Melt!', Smith plays a Squier Paranormal Jazzmaster XII twelve-string, which hits the spot completely. Excepting the white of the guitar body and the strap, Smith is ostensibly incognito, head to toe in black, melding into the background, studied and focused. A pitch-perfect Siouxsie is adorned with the glamorous garb seen in the video for 'Slowdive', and a besuited Severin wears his paisley high neck Nehru jacket with style, strumming his Music Man Stingray bass.

Budgie, replete with bleached blond hair, keeps a steady aerobic shuffle for 'Melt!'. Barely pausing for breath, excepting Smith swapping his twelve-string for a black Vox Teardrop, Budgie's drumsticks signal the introduction to 'Painted Bird'.

The emotive, melancholic timbre of the song is made all the more histrionic with the spectre of John McGeoch, whose panache and transcendent artistry aided and abetted the beautiful Siren call of the song.

However, this doesn't divert away from Smith's playing, which serves the song with unflinching immersion. Smith was just the elixir the band needed at this point; and the antidote for Smith's own precariousness had he continued with The Cure.

Of The Cure's own trajectory, there are parallels with Siouxsie and The Banshees regarding being fellow emigres of the pop world. There is, of course, the 'Goth'[597] tag, which alludes to the downbeat, often dramatic and tension-fuelled emotive nature of the music, charged with the hallucinatory nature of the lyrics and the Gothic influences of writers such as Edgar Allen Poe, Oscar Wilde[598] and Daphne du Maurier,[599] although musically and lyrically, for both bands this is only part of the equation, if such a thing exists, which made both bands what they were, or in the instance of The Cure, continue to be.

If one were looking for further parallels or 'outsider' tropes, there was also the commonality between Siouxsie, Severin and Smith of growing up in the suburban London hinterlands of Horley,[600] Bromley and Chislehurst respectively. However, Siouxsie was originally from Southwark, Severin from Archway and Smith, Blackpool.[601]

Smith, two years younger than Siouxsie and four years younger than Severin, had achieved critical plaudits for The Cure albums *Three Imaginary Boys*, *Seventeen Seconds*, *Faith* and *Pornography*.

The Cure's success with single releases started to gain traction in the early 1980s, after the first five releases, 'Killing An Arab', '10:15 Saturday Night', 'Boys Don't Cry', 'Jumping Someone Else's Train' and 'I'm A Cult Hero' (released under the pseudonym Cult Hero) failed to chart in the UK.

It was with the advent of 'A Forest', released on 28 March 1980, that the band would hit their singles stride. As for Siouxsie and The Banshees, Smith had, for the most part, the musical chops, the right look and, perhaps most importantly, was mustard keen to step into the Banshees fray.[602]

Steve Severin takes a pragmatic view of this time in the band's history, commenting, 'John McGeoch was a full partner in the band by this time, so, even though somewhere in his addled brain he'd thought he'd be rejoining us again as soon as he'd got his head together, I'm glad we got Robert in so quickly. He would have lost quarter of the money if we had to cancel the tour'.[603]

Severin also acknowledged that Smith would never be a full-time indissoluble Banshee, but there was categorically no chance that McGeoch would ever re-join the band again. In the 2003 Mark Paytress' biography, Severin also remarks, with no little judiciousness, how he '...found it hard at the time to have a lot of sympathy for John, because he seemed to have a lot more stability in his life than the rest of us. He was married, had made a wedge of money from Visage, and he was the only one of us who actually owned a house'.[604]

Billy 'Chainsaw' Houlston recalls John McGeoch appearing at the 13 November Birmingham Odeon gig, the first night of the UK and European tour with Robert Smith ensconced, recounting, 'I remember John showing up... and not being the full shilling. He came up to the merchandising stand and said, "Wanna see my new tattoos, lads?"'

Chainsaw acknowledges that the acquisition of tattoos was nothing unusual but, '...it was the way he said it that seemed to be a sign of his state of mind'.[605]

Chainsaw also acknowledges the fallout of the situation, commenting, 'It's always difficult to get rid of someone but that's the way it had to be'.

The Birmingham show, consisting of fifteen songs in total, are all *Kaleidoscope*, *Juju* and *A Kiss In The Dreamhouse* in orientation, with the inclusion of 'Red Over White', The Creatures' 'But Not Them' and singles 'Fireworks' and 'Israel'.

The transcendentally beautiful arpeggio run of the latter is perhaps rather sensibly re-structured by Smith throughout the tour, falling into the category of both serving the song and being, frankly, a little bit tuneless.

While this might seem unfair on Smith, it does highlight what an extraordinary guitarist McGeoch was, and both studio and live versions of 'Israel' during his incumbency are, simply, majestic.

Although not quite what Tommy Bolin[606] was to Ritchie Blackmore in Deep Purple, regarding falling short of the mark regarding litheness, it is certainly in that ballpark. However, this is not to detract from Smith's sheer doggedness and determination to master songs that were simply not his own.

Squeezing in a live studio performance on the BBC2 *Oxford Road Show*[607] on 3 December 1982 between dates at the Hammersmith Palais on 29 November and 6 December at Bochum[608] in Germany, Siouxsie and The Banshees play two songs, 'Melt!' and 'Overground', originally on 'The Scream', with the orchestral accompaniment of The Venomettes,[609] comprising Anne Stephenson and Virginia Hewes, with the addition of Audrey Riley.[610]

A Kiss In The Dreamhouse clearly whetted Siouxsie and The Banshees' appetite for the inclusion of orchestral elements, a plethora of which they would incorporate into all subsequent studio albums until they disbanded in 1995.

The Creatures

'We wanted to go somewhere as far away from Camden as possible'.[611]

Siouxsie Sioux

With commitments for the 1982 tour fulfilled, perhaps not before time, the band took some time off. 1982 was both the best of times creatively and the worst of times, as they narrowly missed being set adrift for the second time during their career.

This should be qualified: Robert Smith and Steve Severin hired a studio in late December 1982 and began writing and recording material for The Glove early in 1983, the first song of which, 'Punish Me With Kisses',[612] would become their second single release.

Siouxsie and Budgie headed out to Hawaii to record what would become The Creatures' album *Feast*,[613] accompanied by producer Mike Hedges.

Asked in an interview about the purpose of *Feast*, Siouxsie responds more broadly to the Siouxsie and Budgie musical affair thus, 'The purpose of the Creatures is being able to do something a lot more relaxed – not laid-back relaxed, but without having a monster around what you're doing. It allows different atmospheres, and there's none of the tension you have with the Banshees because that's so... big'.[614]

Both Siouxsie and Budgie's literal direction of travel dictating where they were going to record the album was a bit of a pin the tail on the donkey affair, Budgie remembers, 'We sat in the office with a map and pointed a finger at a country at random. We picked Mexico, then started ringing round trying to find out what the studios were like, but no one spoke English'.[615]

Siouxsie and Budgie then set their sights on Hawaii, which had just been through a tropical tempest. Budgie further recounts, '... so everyone was sitting there by candlelight listening to this weird request for studio time by a British band they had never heard of'.[616]

There was also some difficulty in understanding the austere, Spinal Tap-esque request for 'Just drums... And maybe a bit of percussion if you've got it'.[617]

Going to Hawaii was also the perfect opportunity for Siouxsie and Budgie to spend time together and, Siouxsie opines, '...not have to hide from anyone'.[618]

Budgie also recalls the excitement of passing through several time zones, which meant celebrating the New Year several times over, '... It was nine o'clock in Vancouver and midnight in London so it was 'Happy New Year!'.

Three hours later on the flight from Vancouver to Honolulu the Canadians went crazy, then we arrived in Honolulu at half past ten the same night so one and a half hours later they went crazy again and we were having our third New Year's Eve celebration!'[619]

One can only surmise that being seven thousand miles away on a beautiful tropical archipelago without the pressurised cocktail of delerium, including one large measure of incessant touring, a sizeable volume of seeking a replacement band member at short notice to complete a tour, and a not inconsiderable amount of recording and mixing an album, was a healing remedy for both Siouxsie and Budgie.

It would also allow them both to really spread their wings creatively, unattenuated and uninterrupted. The resulting album, *Feast*[620] is a milestone for both Siouxsie and Budgie and, frankly, remarkable.

Musically, the album is a feat of ingenuity, not least because of its two constituent parts: vocals and drums which, rather than being subsidiary without the addition of guitars, are made all the more bountiful, bringing into focus Siouxsie and Budgie's significance as artists of substance, not only within the context of Siouxsie and The Banshees but also in their own right.

The symbiosis of drum and vocal, bringing in a plethora of Polynesian influences that imbue the album, reflects a triumphant liberation; a consummation of desires, both musical and amatory.

One of the many remarkable features of the project is Siouxsie and Budgie picking up of The Creatures baton twenty-one months after the recording of the 'Wild Things' EP in May 1981.

Feast also comprises completely new material and represents an orgy of ingenuity, a euphoric revivification. The album was essentially written and recorded from scratch, Siouxsie recollects, 'There was nothing planned before we went... Ideas for lyrics, but nothing pinned down. All that happened when we were soaking things up out there'.[621]

Siouxsie and Budgie proceeded, magpie-like, to assimilate as much of their surroundings possible, including the language. Siouxsie explains, 'I used to be fixed to the telly watching Hawaiian Sesame Street... It's brilliant. It's a great language, really easy. They've only got about eight letters in the alphabet. These little monsters teach the American kids who live there to speak Hawaiian...'[622]

The duo also included a Hawaiian choir, credited on three songs on the album: 'Morning Dawning', 'Inoa 'Ole' and 'A Strutting Rooster'. Siouxsie remarked, '...We found out they lived in the next village and invited them along'.[623]

When Siouxsie and Budgie arrived in Hawaii, equipment-wise, they had nothing more than a tambourine and drumsticks for their odyssey. Retrospectively, the spontaneous nature of the project was unconventional (in 1980s pop cultural terms), with Siouxsie recollecting, 'There's only one studio there... and it's what people might call a demo studio.

Everything is custom-made for what is like a house and it's in the middle of the Hawaiian jungle. There's no soundproofing. If you're making a cup of tea out the back you've got to be quiet if someone's doing a vocal at the same time, otherwise it comes through'.[624]

It was also clearly something of an antidote to the Playground Studios *A Kiss In The Dreamhouse* experience, Siouxsie opining, 'You applied yourself somehow, just get on with it without people dropping in going, 'hey, let's have a party'. In fact we did organise a party in the studio for one of the tracks, 'Flesh''.[625]

Warming to the theme of the song, Siouxsie goes on to say, 'We taped a party while we went off to a hot-tub in the jungle. There was this jacuzzi in the middle of all the plants. It was really jungley. The party nearly ended up in the tub'.[626]

Budgie adds, 'We made this really lethal punch and put all these tropical fruit juices in it, and gave it to people as they came in, then left them to it with mikes hidden in the studio'.[627]

Did *Feast* take the temperature of the time it was made? To put it bluntly, it didn't. Why? Perhaps it was a combination of head-scratching incredulity and dismissiveness (at least in the UK), and well as possibly being too ahead of the curve.

The Creatures weren't Siouxsie and The Banshees, and therefore how did they fit in with 'the big pop family'?[628]

Also, the project only confirmed the wariness Siouxsie and The Banshees had of the music press; the band, especially Siouxsie and Severin, being somewhat a conduit for the perceived 'friend or foe' disposition of the interviewer or nature of question.

Regarding the evolution of the Siouxsie and The Banshees' philosophy, Siouxsie states, 'Our attitudes haven't changed. We still don't really care'.[629]

As for the band's contemporaries and the current musical terrain, Siouxsie declares, '…we miss the unfamiliarity that we had when we first started. People were interested but didn't know exactly what to expect. That's why we've been working abroad a lot, not just as The Creatures but with the Banshees too – Japan, Scandinavia, one-offs in Italy. We like them wondering what we're going to be like. We don't like the idea of a gig circuit'.[630]

Rhythmically and experimentally, there are parallels with *The Dreaming*[631] album released by Kate Bush,[632] which employs an array of instruments such uilleann pipes,[633] mandolins, didgeridoos,[634] polyrhythmic percussion, transposed time signatures and textures, vocal loops and samples.

Regarding The Creatures' own exclusive sonic laboratory, Siouxsie remembers, 'That's the way we worked, using things lying around that fitted in. I didn't want to use a drumkit on every track… coconuts! There's no synthetic noise on there. Everything's being hit, blown or sucked'.[635]

Using the maxim you can't take the Ballard out of the Banshee, the *Feast* track 'Miss The Girl'[636] took its lead from the 1973 novel *Crash*.[637] The video for 'Miss The Girl' is directed by Tim Pope[638] who latterly became synonymous with The Cure, directing thirty-seven of their videos between 1982 and 1995.

It would be incorrect to suggest that *Feast* was met with a lukewarm critical and commercial reception. *Melody Maker* heralded it as 'an album of filtered brilliance, fertile, sensual and erotic; an album that, in its desperate naivety, attempts to articulate that moment when the monsoon ends, when the smell and the heat conspire in a perfumed mist and life sprouts instantly, green and luxurious'.[639]

Similar praise was heaped by the *NME*, offering, 'The Creatures have assembled a multifarious sonic boom that is as various and kaleidoscopic as can be imagined. The humours of Sioux's frosty larynx are nakedly outlined against skins of sometimes fabulous quality. The drum sound on 'Ice House' must be one of the greatest on record'.[640]

The photography for the striking album cover, denoting Siouxsie and Budgie's immersion in the making of *Feast*, was undertaken by Gil Gilbert,[641] with designer Rob O'Connor at the helm for his last Siouxsie and The Banshees-related assignment.

Siouxsie is emblazoned with a majestic Hawaiian cadmium red, yellow and orange feathered cloak and beaded headdress, and Budgie wears a spiked necklace; both are fully assimilated into their Aloha State idyll. They stand together united, inscrutable.

A Boy Called Robert

'We probably should have just done the tour with him, but Robert insisted that he wanted to document his time with us. Back in 1979, it had just been one tour then it was gone, but this time he wanted to at least do an album with us. It seemed like a good idea at the time'.[642]

Steve Severin

In an *NME* interview with Paul Du Noyer[643] in 1983, when asked about Robert Smith's status as a full time Banshee, Siouxsie mused, 'In future, there's gonna be a status in the group that no one's ever permanent. He's permanent as he can be'.[644]

Well, at least for the twenty-two live dates in 1983, Smith would be on board the Banshees' bus for appearances in Japan, New Zealand, Australia, Denmark, Sweden, Holland, Switzerland, Italy, Israel and the UK.

Siouxsie, increasingly protective of her voice and the potential havoc wreaked by air-conditioned hotels, decided the only course of action at the beginning of the 1983 sojourn, while staying in a

Japanese hotel with, Siouxsie recalls, 'suicide locks on the windows',[645] was to pick up a telephone and throw it through the glass. Imbibing the fresh air, Siouxsie recounts, 'I thought, "That's better!" Robert Smith was a real copycat, and when he heard what I'd done, he had to do it too'.[646]

In her first autobiography, *Bedsit Disco Queen: How I Grew Up And Tried To Be A Pop Star*[647] Tracey Thorn[648] discusses the touring experience in relation to hotels, in particular the perception and the reality, 'The days seem on the surface to be luxurious and lazy, but in the middle of it all you can feel powerless, useless and without choice. If the room you're in is too hot or cold, for instance, you can't do anything about it, like finding the heating control and turning it up or down – you have to ask someone to fix it, you have to complain. Immediately, you're a diva'.[649]

It wasn't only the removal of humidity in hotel rooms that was a problem. Siouxsie seemed to be allocated rooms in various hotels during the 1983 tour which came with their own unwelcome aural accompaniment; Severin explains, 'At one point, every hotel we checked into seemed to put Siouxsie in a room next to some building works. It was as if there was a secret network of hoteliers ringing each other up and arranging to give her the room with the most noise outside it'.[650]

There was also Robert Smith's torpidity, which, putting it mildly, wasn't conducive to a rigorous and rote-oriented tour schedule, much to the other band members' chagrin. Siouxsie explains, 'We were in Italy once and we couldn't wake him up. That was a pretty regular problem because he was incapable of getting up on time for anything.[651] He'd unplug his phone and barricade himself in … prepared to sleep for a week if necessary. Something had to be done, so I climbed out of my window and into his'.[652]

Realising that nothing but a swingeing course of action was required to rouse Smith, Siouxsie recalls, 'I could see his big boots on the floor… so I picked them up and started hitting him with them, screaming, "Get up, you bastard!"'[653]

Robert Smith's dormouse proclivities aside, it was clear that he and Steve Severin were forming a very close bond, which would manifest itself in The Glove project, seemingly aided by Smith's penchant for LSD at the time.

He recollects, 'Acid made me feel very connected to Severin. We had a fantastic time making The Glove album… We were living in a *Yellow Submarine* cartoon world. We'd walk around London, and when you're taking acid with someone you really like, it's really funny. It was a very upbeat time… it got rid of all the bad stuff that happened when I was making (The Cure's) *Pornography*'.[654]

Smith, while also espousing the drug's liberating and ameliorative benefits, counters, 'It's great, but when it takes over, you can find yourself encountering mental problems. There are people from that era… that were close to The Cure, who went seriously mental. They never really recovered'.[655]

Smith also bought into Severin's hybridised Goth-esque, Beatnik-esque style including '…shades, crucifixes and beads. And he nicked loads of clothes off me, too'.[656]

It was around this time when The Batcave Club[657] was in full swing. The Batcave, based in Dean Street, Soho, is credited with resurrecting the 1980s' Goth movement and, even though both Siouxsie and Severin balked at the term 'Goth', it was, nonetheless, a vital part of the early 1980s' music scene frequented by Siouxsie Sioux[658], Steve Severin, Nick Cave,[659] Lydia Lunch,[660] Nik Fiend,[661] Foetus[662] and Robert Smith, '…paying homage to all things goth and hosting a range of arthouse films, cabaret extravaganzas and live music nights.

Cobwebs lined the ceilings, black bin-liners decorated the walls and to enter, you had to walk through a (real) coffin with the bottom taken out; its interior could only be described as spooky'.[663] It also '…provided sonic sanctuary for punk refugees who had held onto their subversive sensibilities and thus couldn't face the prospect of dancing to Kid Creole and The Coconuts or Spandau Ballet'.[664]

The Batcave's house band were Specimen[665] and there were many other groups, including Alien Sex Fiend[666] playing the club night regularly. Co-founder Jon Klein[667] recalls, 'The Banshees and The Birthday Party also used to turn up at The Batcave, which Specimen started at The Gargoyle Club in Soho. It wasn't really a goth club, more of an arts space with us as the host band and a diverse crowd of people – from Test Department to (Sham 69's) Jimmy Pursey – who were into music'.[668]

The Glove

1983 was a more truncated year in Siouxsie and The Banshees' touring schedule, relatively speaking, with twelve dates in February, straddling both Northern and Southern Hemispheres, two festival appearances in July at Roskilde[669] in Denmark and Langholmen[670] in Stockholm, Sweden, two further September festival dates in Rotterdam[671] and Arbon in Switzerland,[672] with further September dates in Modena in Italy and in Tel Aviv, and two dates at the Royal Albert Hall in London on 30 September and 1 October.[673]

With more time at their disposal than was the norm for the Banshees, as well as an opportunity to explore their individual creativity, Steve Severin and Robert Smith made headway with The Glove. Severin, embracing his innermost bohemian aesthete, was inspired by, he says, '60s psychedelia… as well as that kind of Britishness inspired by *The Avengers* and Dirk Bogarde in *Modesty Blaise*… we'd sit watching video nasties like Dario Argento's *Inferno & Tenebrae* and Abel Ferrara's *Driller Killer* and *Ms. 45 – Angel of Vengeance*. All those things permeated our dreams and we brought them to bear on record'.[674]

In keeping with the music's psychedelic influences, the band name The Glove comes directly from The Dreadful Flying Glove[675] in The Beatles film *Yellow Submarine*.[676]

The Glove also chose Britannia Row Studios,[677] Robert Smith recollecting, 'We chose Britannia Row out of irony. It was Pink Floyd's studio and the album was psychedelic…'[678]

It was important for both Severin and Smith to make an album of substance, Severin says, 'The idea that The Glove could get away with anything vanished very quickly because it became a real responsibility to get it to sound not indulgent'.[679]

In the same vein, Smith explains, 'We didn't want it to sound like a self-indulgent album made by two aging hippies… it's light in texture, up-sounding'.[680]

The *Blue Sunshine* album title is culled from the 1977 American horror film of the same name, written and directed by Jeff Lieberman.[681] The plot of the film pivots around a series of random murders in Los Angeles, in which the only common thread between the killers is an enigmatic haul of LSD, called 'Blue Sunshine' that they had all dropped ten years previously, as well as the loss of their hair, seemingly attributed to the 'Blue Sunshine' drug.

The aligning of stars, brought about in no small measure by The Cure's inactivity and Severin in search of an elixir vitae to Siouxsie and The Banshees, set The Glove on course for an initial nine days of recording in January 1983, caveated by Smith's contractual obligations to Fiction records, prohibiting him from recording vocals for any band other than The Cure.[682]

The Glove's narrative isn't entirely linear or clearcut, not least because nothing rarely is in the realms of Siouxsie and The Banshees. At the end of the Banshees' 1983 tour, Robert Smith was '...approached by Nicholas Dixon, a young choreographer with the Royal Ballet and asked to write the music for 'Les Enfants Terrible'.

Robert was intrigued but hesitant so, as a test, he suggested they try out a choreographed Cure song. A spot was offered on BBC2's *Riverside* and, with Lol (Tolhurst) on drums, Severin disguised under a hat on bass and the Venomettes on strings, Robert played 'Siamese Twins' live in the studio while two dancers danced. It was an interesting if not entirely successful experiment, and the ballet project was indefinitely shelved'.[683]

The performance provides a snapshot of what would become almost de rigueur regarding the coalescence of disparate art forms, not least instigated by dancer and choreographer Michael Clark,[684] among whose musical collaborators include The Fall, resulting in 'I Am Kurious Oranj'[685], initially intended as the soundtrack for the ballet 'I Am Curious, Orange'.[686]

Wayne McGregor[687] has also been important in this respect, choreographing music videos for Radiohead, Atoms For Peace[688] and The Chemical Brothers.[689]

Riverside[690] was broadcast on BBC2 in the UK from 1982 to 1983 and showcased a variety of musicians, bands, fashion designers, actors, artists and comedians. Consisting of interviews, sketches and live performances, guests included, among others, Alice Cooper, Steve Strange, Martin Rushent, Alan Adler,[691] Clare Grogan, Paul Weller, Martin Fry,[692] The Cure, The Smiths, New Order and Pauline Black.

Necessity being the mother of invention, Smith asked David "Kid" Jensen to read out a request for female vocalists to apply for an audition during his BBC Radio 1 weekday evening show. The subsequent interlude, while Severin and Smith waited for demo tapes, meant that they could set about writing enough material for a whole album; fifteen songs, in fact.

To effectuate the sound Severin and Smith wanted, they engaged the services of The Venomettes on strings and Brilliant's Andy Anderson[693] on drums. Anderson's playing, it transpired, would be juxtaposed with the patterns already committed to tape courtesy of a drum machine. A substantial number of songs were composed using keyboards and sequencers by Severin and, from there, rearranged on guitar by Smith.

A glut of tapes arrived, accompanied by letters and photographs, from potential singers. However, it was dancer Jeanette Landray, choreographer for the Banshees' 'Slowdive' video, who landed the gig, insisting that she was precisely what Severin and Smith were looking for.

Landray could sing at least as well as any of the voices heard on tape; it was also the case that Landray was on the inside track and would not be averse either to the mercurial nature of creativity or its (especially in the case of Severin and Smith) non-9 to 5 regimen.

With Landray on board, instrumental songs were rethought and reimagined and lyrics introduced during the latter part of the recording process; the antithesis of the way Siouxsie and The Banshees worked.

This was, Billy 'Chainsaw' Houlston observed, 'a whole new experience for Steve when compared to the way the Banshees work… Sioux and Budgie write their own individual parts because in doing so they'd create things that maybe Steve wouldn't think of… which is in effect what makes a Banshees song a group song…'[694]

In the instance of The Glove, Severin and Smith had to fashion those other segments between the two of them. Entire songs had been written in instrumental form, which would then necessitate the weaving in of lyrics; the converse methodology to the Banshees, which was more synergistic in nature.

Severin and Smith realised that their approach would mean no small measure of lateral chicanery to ensure that first the lyrics, and subsequently vocals, would meld with the musical arrangements. This approach would prove labour intensive.

The eventual make-up of the album was Landry providing vocals for six songs, two songs with Smith on vocals, (trying his level best to not sound like The Cure vocalist lest it contravened any contractual arrangement he had with Fiction) and two tracks remained instrumental. In common with *A Kiss In The Dreamhouse*, there are quirky sonic vignettes, some of which aren't dissimilar to scintillas of electronica on David Bowie's 'Art Decade', which are interpolated at various points on the album, one of which begins and ends on 'Looking Glass Girl' and is reprised on 'A Blues In Drag', sounding like a forerunner of the 'Super Mario Bros. theme'.[695] It is echoed in part on the introduction of 'Punish Me With Kisses'.

Excerpts from a 'tape recording that Steve (Severin) took from a Japanese TV programme during the Banshees '82 visit... of a Japanese chase during a kung fu movie...'[696] can be discerned on 'This Green City'.[697]

Another fragment from the same programme, this time more spoken dialogue in feel, can be discerned on 'Relax',[698] the final track on the album.

Other than the unanticipated protracted recording process, Severin and Smith took an apparently relaxed approach to working in the studio and making the album. Spontaneous binges were a regular feature during the *Blue Sunshine* sessions and encroached on the business of getting any actual work done.

Severin acknowledges that his creative partnership with Smith was interwoven with the duo's fondness for revelry, commenting, 'We were a bad influence on each other. It was difficult getting anything done with all the impromptu parties that took place in the studio. I know that Robert's wife regretted him doing the album because she hardly got to see him for months'.[699]

Blue Sunshine is an eclectic assortment of songs and luscious soundscapes. The New Order-esque, bass-guitar-driven 'Like An Animal' heralds Landray's operatic vocal, swooping over the apex of the song's multi-layered instrumentation. It is an upbeat wedge of feelgood, ebullient pop music.

'Looking Glass Girl', preluded and concluded by the tinny keyboard sound (no doubt culled from one of the many trashily satisfying videos Severin and Smith watched while making the album), sees The Venomettes in full flow; accompanying melodious acoustic and bass guitars with the addition of a metronomic, synthetic drumbeat.

Landray's vocal is, again, perfect for the song, channelling her inner chanteuse. 'Sex-Eye-Make-Up' is Soho seedy, with a 'Scary Monsters (and Super Creeps)' rancorous-sounding guitar solo adding to the song's squalid overtones.

'Mr Alphabet Says' could readily slip into any of The Cure's more whimsical repertoire, bearing all the hallmarks of 'The Love Cats',[700] which would be recorded and released as a single towards the tail end of 1983.

'A Blues In Drag' is a wistful David Bowie *Low* era interlude, including piano, strings, synthesiser and bass guitar. The sadomasochistic sounding 'Punish Me With Kisses', which became the second single release for the band, is another slice of lightweight pop, albeit slightly singed with Smith's dissonant guitar playing.

'This Green City' is another showcase for Smith's dexterity as a guitar player, with some superb proggy/poppy keyboard playing, the opening and ending of the song composed of the aforementioned Japanese kung fu film music.

In full flow, the song emanates a J.G. Ballard-esque intensity, energised by Smith's metallurgic guitar playing. 'Orgy' is a smorgasbord of different influences and sounds, including a mesmeric, melodramatic Middle Eastern timbre, sounding like a string loop. The sound of a synthesised recorder ensemble, as well as the booming bass guitar and drums, make for an intense experience.

'A Perfect Murder', Smith's only other vocal on the album, is another sumptuously overlayed melancholy song, aided and abetted in no small part by Smith's expressive lugubrious cantillation. The last song on *Blue Sunshine* is a six-minute three-second opus, full of suspense; an unwitting precursor of the portentous predilection discerned on Massive Attack's *Heligoland*[701] album.

In terms of commercial success, *Blue Sunshine* spent three weeks in the Top 100 UK Official Albums Chart, peaking at 35. The two singles, 'Like An Animal',[702] released on 12 August 1983, and 'Punish Me With Kisses',[703] released on 18 November 1983, didn't trouble the UK Singles Chart with any great fanfare, peaking at 52 and 97 respectively.

'Orgy' and 'Punish Me With Kisses' appeared in video form on BBC2s *Riverside*, and 'A Blues In Drag' makes an appearance on Siouxsie and The Banshees 'Play At Home' video. The photo-montage-oriented artwork[704] for both album and single releases reflects the musical and lyrical content, as well as both Severin and Smith's absorption in 1960s kaleidoscopic cultural elements.

Among the discernible cultural figures on the cover of *Blue Sunshine* are Jackie Kennedy Onassis,[705] Illya Kuryakin,[706] Patrick McGoohan,[707] Lady Penelope[708] and Jeff Tracy,[709] as well as posterised images of Severin and Smith, all set against a hypnotic psychedelic swirl.

Artwork for the two single releases is similarly playful and irreverent, with a clandestine, subliminal glimpse of Ukiyo-e[710] erotic drawing in the mix of other titillating minutia.

Blue Sunshine's three week run in the top 100 Albums Chart somewhat belies its musical accomplishment and sonic experimentation. The album is part of an investigative continuum of cutting up, splicing and looping that can be traced back at least as far as King Tubby[711] and Steve Reich,[712] and is particularly prevalent on The Beatles' mind-bending psychedelic sound collage 'Revolution 9'[713] from the album *The Beatles*, which samples, among a plethora of other musical and spoken tidbits, 'A Day In The Life',[714] George Martin[715] uttering "Geoff, put the red light on", Ralph Vaughan Williams,[716] Robert Schumann[717] and inverted violins and mellotron.[718]

Both The Creatures and The Glove projects demonstrate an

enthusiasm for embracing the world beyond the realms of Siouxsie and The Banshees; an opportunity to flex musical ideas with greater autonomy and a cathartic escape from the fraught intensity of the Banshees' non-stop cavalcade.

Regarding any conceivable duel between The Creatures and The Glove, Siouxsie remarks, 'Even though Severin denies it, I think The Glove album was a response to Budgie and I doing The Creatures record'.[719]

Severin takes the contrary view. Siouxsie and The Banshees had the mettle to pursue musical avenues separately from the band, taking a 360-degree panorama of everyone's endeavours, commenting, '... We were all having a break from the band and Robert and I had always talked about writing together... we could do separate projects without affecting what we did with the Banshees – and it paid off. Throughout 1983 we were hardly ever out of the charts. If it wasn't the Banshees, it was The Creatures or The Glove, Robert with The Cure or our contribution on a Marc Almond record'.[720]

Siouxsie isn't so exultant about The Glove, however, remarking, '...Despite the fact that they (Severin and Smith) had spent so much time and money and effort on it, and released it at the most opportune time, The Glove album and single did nothing. It didn't really happen'.[721]

The Creatures recorded the Herbie Mann[722] and Carl Sigman[723] standard 'Right Now'[724] as a standalone single, released 8 July 1983 while Siouxsie and The Banshees were in the midst of their 1983 tour.

Rather than adopting the distinctive bossa nova[725] piano and vibraphone sound used on the Mel Torme[726] version, The Creatures' interpretation is more big-band in orientation, replete with a brass section, including saxophone, trombone, trumpet and timpani.[727]

An aggregate of happenstance and circumstance led to the song's recording, while Siouxsie and The Banshees were on hold while The Glove project was being completed.

'Right Now' was also one of Siouxsie's childhood infatuations, remembering it being played at the family home by her brother and sister. 'Right Now' was also the highest UK Singles Chart position

Siouxsie had occupied since 'Hong Kong Garden' was released in 1978, peaking at number 14.

The Tim Pope-directed video for the song reflects its ostentatious musical production, Siouxsie channelling several different characters including Cleopatra[728] on a chaise longue, as well as a variant of the sun goddess Amaterasu,[729] and, of course, Siouxsie herself mostly dressed in black.

Budgie hams it up as white-tail-coated, baton-wielding band leader and timpani and tom-tom thumper, alternating with sequences of the percussionist in varying states of undress. Siouxsie and Budgie, faces painted gold, are intertwined with golden rope which adorns suspended mirror balls.

The video's cunning lies in its choreography, direction and set design. The backcloth is a graphically depicted besuited big band, conducted by Budgie. Dynamic and dizzying camera work reflects the frenzied cadence of the song. The video is glamorous, irreverent, striking and sensuous.

Tim Pope's inventiveness and Siouxsie and Budgie's sense of the burlesque make for a perfect cinematic union; in stark contrast with the *Top Of The Pops* performance which errs on the perfunctory and reflects the limitations of the format rather than the performers.

It is also the first *Top Of The Pops* appearance by Siouxsie and Budgie as a two-piece, without the presence of Steve Severin or a guitarist, so the experience could also have been slightly counterintuitive for the singer and drummer.

There is a new hairstyle for Siouxsie, cascading over her forehead and tied up at the back, wearing a silver and black trouser suit, miming into a vintage microphone. Budgie has adopted his own, more casual dress code, with a white shirt caught in at the waist by a black cummerbund, and black leggings. To give the appearance a little more visual chutzpah, there are several fleeting camera shots of dancers wearing zoot suits, trilbies and shades – sort of Dick Tracy[730] meets Miami Vice.[731]

The B-side of 'Right Now' showcases 'Weathercade', two minutes and forty-six seconds of blissful, polyrhythmic percussion, harmonica and voice, with the additional textural layer of xylophone and tubular bells.

'Weathercade' makes an appearance in video form on 'Play At Home', with Siouxsie a visual hybrid of Sally Bowles, Gene Kelly[732] in 'Singin' In The Rain'[733] and Droog. The white-room minimalism catalyses the harmonious black attire of Siouxsie and Budgie, coalescing in their harmonica playing, centred around a weathervane prop, with the sporadic camera punctuation of Siouxsie playing the tubular bells and Budgie on drums.

The Alex McDowell/Da Gama artwork for the 'Right Now' gatefold sleeve reflects the monochromatic ink-painted big-band backcloth for the video, with the addition of two luminous, delineated green, orange and violet figures, conceivably representing Siouxsie and Budgie as saxophonist and band leader.

There is a trickle of cadmium yellow on the front cover and a monochromatic, painterly, stormy-weather front on the back of the sleeve, juxtaposed with a streak of yellow lightening and what appears to be a suspended green, violet and orange horse swing, above a truncated photographic image of Spaghetti Junction.[734]

The inner gatefold is a riotous montage of black and white Siouxsie and Budgie photographic cameos, song lyrics and big band, with the focal point the polychromatic protagonists kissing on the horse swing.

'Dear Prudence'

Perhaps it isn't entirely unsurprising that Siouxsie and The Banshees should continue their dalliance with The Beatles; in fact, it never went away in the interceding years between introducing 'Helter Skelter' to the band's setlist on 17 May 1977 at The Oaks Hotel, in Manchester[735] and the recording of 'Dear Prudence'[736] in Stockholm at Europafilm[737] studio, which was later completed at Angel Studios[738] in London in July 1983.

Siouxsie has always acknowledged her love of *The Beatles* album, and Robert Smith and Steve Severin saturated The Glove's musical aesthetic with psychedelic 'Beatle-esque' allusions.

Mike Hedges was engaged again as co-producer, now proving something of a constant, indomitable presence in the mercurial world of the Banshees, having produced The Cure, The Creatures and Siouxsie and The Banshees. The decision to record 'Dear Prudence' was not immediately clearcut, nor entirely consensual.

Robert Smith was no great enthusiast of *The Beatles* album, unlike the rest of his bandmates, and, during the recording process, Siouxsie had misgivings about how the song was sounding, feeling it was antithetical to the version she had in her head, which was a far more distorted transposition of the original.

Siouxsie recounts, 'I could see ('Dear Prudence')... was turning out to be really commercial, so much so that I suggested putting it on the B-side instead'.[739]

Rather than deeming the potential mass appeal of the single an advantage, Siouxsie speculates that... 'it all seemed a bit nice and I was concerned that it might actually be very successful. It didn't seem subversive enough and was far too damn catchy'.[740]

Worried about how a commercially successful single could potentially depreciate the Banshees' 'craft or sullen art',[741] Siouxsie was more inclined towards the ethereal and otherworldly experimentation of their own composition, 'Tattoo'.

Budgie's suggestion of 'Glass Onion' was usurped in favour of 'Dear Prudence', which, Budgie recalls, '...was a good choice because we all felt The Beatles' version sounded unfinished, more like a sketch'.[742]

One can readily discern what Budgie means by the almost epigrammatic nature of The Beatles' original and how it would readily lend itself to a more embroidered rendition, which Siouxsie and The Banshees, despite Siouxsie's inclination towards antithetical alacrity, showcases a rich, cohesive and reinvigorated Banshees with Robert Smith's melodious guitar playing attuned to Severin's euphonious bass playing.

Budgie's two-second snare drum introduction sets the song on its way as 'Dear Prudence' is bathed in sumptuous, swirling sonic overlays. One of the most remarkable aspects of the song is Siouxsie's mellifluous vocal, an indication that this was both song and album she knew inside out, having developed an obsession with it in her teens.

It's conceivable that any misgivings about covering 'Dear

Prudence' are more adoringly reverential towards the original and not wanting to make a complete hash with a cover version.

Whatever surmise one might draw from Siouxsie's rhetoric, the Siouxsie and The Banshees' version encompasses an ardour all of its own. 'Dear Prudence', Robert Smith's inaugural recorded Banshees' outing, turned out to be something of a family affair, with his sister Janet Smith on harpsichord.

It was more than feasible that both The Creatures and The Glove projects proved the sonic palate cleanser needed for Siouxsie and The Banshees to continue as a viable and germane band well into the 1980s.

The video for 'Dear Prudence' employs the surreal filmic fairy dust of Tim Pope, who had worked with The Creatures and was the go-to video director and collaborator for The Cure, involved with no less than thirty-seven videos for the band between 1982 and 1987.[743]

Shot in Venice, en route to the Banshees' gigs in Israel, the video employs a myriad of different colour filter overlays and polarisation techniques which, coupled with footage of Venetian alleyways, canals and bridges, sees the band intertwined in a carousing, chaotic and exuberant dance, as well as individual shots of band members, some more naturally cinematically and choreographically disposed than others.

All Banshees count the song in: Budgie, Smith, Severin and Siouxsie, hands over eyes, mouthing 'One, Two, Three, Four', echoing Budgie's snare drum, as their hands lift to let the sunshine in. One by one, the band walk through a beautifully sun-drenched arcade, firstly Siouxsie, then Steve Severin, Budgie and, finally, Robert Smith, head to toe in black, including shades and dyed black hair, conceivably denoting the chronology of band members joining the Banshees.

Siouxsie, dressed in black and red lace and silk, adopting the role of a cross between Vampire Elder and matriarchal disciplinarian, curtails her Banshees' fervour to escape the *callette*'s murkiness, arms outstretched, protecting their pale, ghostly, heavily made-up faces from the sun's rays. Cut to Siouxsie staring wistfully and longingly out over the Venetian Lagoon,[744] nestled among Venetian *bricole*.[745]

Pope includes sporadic Venetian scenes of gondolas and the

shimmering, dappled flicker of water, conjecturally filmed while aboard a speeding vaporetto.[746]

A cross between slapstick, physical theatre and the absurdist, surreal elements of Salvador Dali and Luis Bunuel's[747] 'Un Chien Andalou',[748]Pope's video is deliciously irreverent.

Of particular note is Robert Smith's, inadvertent or otherwise, complete lack of choreography, latterly a mischievous trademark of The Cure videos, adding to the pandemonium. There is a particularly notable scene in the video, which sees Steve Severin walking down some stone steps, having been confronted by the local carabinieri, of which Siouxsie explains, 'You weren't supposed to film in Venice without getting permission and paying money, which of course we ignored. If you get caught, you either get stopped or you have to pay...'[749]

Of the band's tight time schedule, coupled with the prospect of imminent incarceration, Siouxsie says, '...trying to get in as much as possible we were there until very late, all day. By then the wine was flowing a bit, for some more than others, and everyone was running around by the end of the evening. It goes from day shots to night shots...'

The Keystone Cop[750] aura of the episode wasn't curtailed with Severin's buttonholing, as Siouxsie explains, 'The evening ended with Budgie trying to climb a wall and falling off and damaging his foot and being in agony. He then decided to drink a bottle of brandy to take away the pain. He was carted off in a Venice ambulance – which is a wheelbarrow. I always remember him with this silk-like top and pants, and he had his make-up on and he was totally legless in this wheelbarrow with his balls hanging out'.[751]

Siouxsie remembers Budgie taking on the visual mantle of '...a sleazy Coco The Clown'.[752]

Siouxsie recalls, 'I think he (Budgie) woke up in an amputees' hospital... they put him on a drip and gave him some painkillers and a bandage for his foot... it was so funny. He was wheelbarrowed and then taken on a boat, because the transport is all by canal there. Sadly I think the cameras had packed up by then. It should have been the finale'.

Budgie's recollection of his mishap is vividly macabre, akin to one of one of Francisco Goya's 'Black Paintings',[753] commenting on both his agonising situation and his attire, 'I woke up in hospital surrounded by surgical amputees with dark hairy skin and big grins all talking a different language. I knew I was''t in heaven because I was confused and scared and hurt like hell. Dave Woods picked me up and I hopped back out into the Venetian sun, still dressed head to toe in crumpled gold Tibetan silk, with smudged make-up and matted bleached hair'.[754]

Released 23 September 1983, with the B-side 'Tattoo' on the seven-inch vinyl and 'There's A Planet In My Kitchen' on the twelve-inch, the band's misgivings about recording 'Dear Prudence' contradicts its huge chart success, peaking at number three in the UK Official Singles Chart, surpassing Siouxsie and The Banshees' biggest chart hit to date, 'Hong Kong Garden', which reached peaked at number seven in 1978.

With this commercial triumph came the band's 13th 'performance' on *Top Of The Pops* on 29 September 1983, if one were to count the panoply of mimed appearances, videos and studio audiences dancing to Siouxsie and The Banshees' songs.

The first of three *Top Of The Pops* airings for 'Dear Prudence' sees the band emanating nonchalance; an agglomeration of Velvet Underground cool, confidence and a pinch of rebellion, which, rather refreshingly, had left its indelible imprint on the band's genealogy since 20 September 1976.[755]

Siouxsie fronts the band like a gothic hybrid of Judith in the Gustav Klimt painting 'Judith and the Head of Holofernes'[756] and pagan goddess of magic Hecate,[757] dressed from head to toe in black, with an elaborate black beaded fringe necklace, surrounded by Robert Smith, Steve Severin and Budgie, each absorbed in their apportioned role.

Severin and Smith adopt enigmatic sunshades, and Smith barely attempts to mime any semblance of chord sequence, angling his fingers over rather than under the fretboard; a metaphorical two-fingered gesture at banality of miming.

As is the case with any Siouxsie and The Banshees' *Top Of The*

Pops performance, there is the key element of pageantry; a spectacle to be taken in and regurgitated, like a sublime apparition or visitation, gawped at through the fissures of a budget wooden configuration, reflecting the 1980s design 'trend' of appropriating the geometrically oriented work of De Stijl[758] artist Piet Mondrian, yet looking as though it was a presentiment for the fixtures and fittings of Linton Travel Tavern.[759]

If one had to select a singular object that sums up the ersatz nature of the Banshees' mise-en-scène, it is the comatose mirrorball looming above the band. To quote Talking Heads, 'This ain't no party, this ain't no disco'.[760] No matter, Siouxsie and The Banshees look marvellous.

Reflecting the accomplishment of the single, and its seven weeks in the Top Forty Singles Chart, Siouxsie and The Banshees appear on *Top Of The Pops* for a second time, if one discounts the video airing for 'Dear Prudence' on 13 October 1983. The occasion this time is a Christmas special; a 1983 retrospective to celebrate all the acts with high charting hit singles that year, including the Banshees, The Police, The Cure, Phil Collins,[761] Spandau Ballet[762] and Rod Stewart.[763]

This time, stuck in the middle of the same *Top Of The Pops* travel tavern decor, this time with the addition of what appear to be tinsel stalagmites, the band are even more contradictorily stylishly avant-garde, symbiotically attired in black.

Siouxsie adopts her stalwart amour propre in a wide-neck leather dress, and Steve Severin and Robert Smith, looking as though they have dashed from an Allan Ginsberg[764] Beat poetry reading, are doyens of inscrutability; Severin's spirited performance contrasting with Smith's machine-like affectation. Budgie, secreted so much out of camera shot as to be virtually imperceptible, implements pretend drumming with his usual indomitable brio.

Siouxsie, pondering the unexpected chart success of the single, recounts, 'It was a surprise, but it didn't really sink in until we'd finished the touring and we were back home for the winter. Then we thought, 'Blimey! We got to number three!' Dear Prudence got played a lot on the radio, and of course we did the Christmas/New Year *Top Of The Pops*'.[765]

The first live airing of 'Dear Prudence' was at the Kolnoa Dan Club in Tel Aviv on 10 September 1983.

Without wishing to underplay the commercial success of their highest-charting single, there lurks the B-side masterpiece 'Tattoo'; three minutes and twenty-nine seconds of ghostly and mysterious experimentation that is the band's most unorthodox, yet perhaps most "Siouxsie and The Banshees at its source" song to date, evincing their preternatural eccentricities.

Siouxsie's sense of the macabre, her innate understanding of sonic phenomena, conjoined with Severin's remarkable musicality and ability to write multi-sensorial songs, collude to produce a piece of music that has antecedents in *Kaleidoscope* and *A Kiss In The Dreamhouse*, but is an entire universe away from anything the band have committed to vinyl before.

In many ways, the song belongs to Severin, playing a repeat harmonics[766] motif, with all the melody of a Tibetan singing bowl or temple bell,[767] as Budgie's drums, underpinned by an ominous snare-drum shuffle, are worked like a relentless industrial metal-stamping machine.

'Tattoo' is ushered in by the sound of what sounds like a rocket firework, joined swiftly by timpani mallets hitting piano strings, then bass, drums, and Siouxsie's low vocal, reciting a beguiling and alluring narrative with echoes of the LSD-infused 'Cocoon' on *A Kiss In The Dreamhouse*.

'Tattoo' appears to be an altogether darker, more visually ill-boding affair, the gist of which centres around a possession that renders the protagonist indelibly scarred or tattooed on the inside, sitting in the middle of the floor, all alone.

For 'Tattoo', it was Mike Hedges who encouraged the band to use the mixing desk as an instrument in its own right, creating an aural succubus and, conceivably, unwittingly contributing to the invention of Trip Hop[768] in the process.

'There's A Planet In My Kitchen' on the B-side of the 'Dear Prudence' twelve-inch single, plays out as its own 'kitchen sink' drama, complete with a key turning in a creaking door, running water, what sounds like a pan lid finding its centre of gravity, a tweeting bird, a bumble bee, a duck's quack, conceivably a croaking frog, someone whistling, the siren denoting that a fairground dodgem ride is about to elapse, a Teddy Bear growler,[769] a mechanical chirrup and the Apollo Eleven[770] countdown, as well as the blasting-off sequence; no doubt an oblique allusion to the 'planet' of the song.

The 'jam' like nature of 'There's A Planet In My Kitchen' allows the band to indulge in an array of sonic whimsy. The lyric suggests that the kitchen of the song has metamorphosed into a fantastical organism, part Walt Disney's 'Sorcerer's Apprentice'[771] from *Fantasia* and part Pink Floyd's 'Alan's Psychedelic Breakfast'.[772]

The song conveys a disorientation comparable with an altered state, as well as, perhaps, the utter bewilderment of confronting your own home after living out of a suitcase for weeks and months on end.

With De Gama at the design helm for the single, the band opts for the photographic image 'Shiroi hana' or 'White Flower' by Japanese photographer Sakae Tamura.[773]

The image is a portrait of a young girl holding a white daisy, as though about to give it up to someone else. There is an unsullied purity about the image, which takes on the narrative features of Pictorialism[774] whereby late nineteenth and early twentieth century photography was concerned with the aesthetics of an image and the emotional response it could evoke in the viewer.

This gave a painterly quality to many of the photographs made by Pictorialists, many of which are slightly blurred, often utilising brushstrokes of photographic developer to manipulate the image.

The photograph also represents the evolution of photography, bringing image making into a realm beyond the perimeters of mechanisation and simply 'recording' what was seen.

The striking photographic image on the front cover is encased by a light green border, which proliferates the entirety of the seven-inch gatefold sleeve, decorated with a more lucent green fleur-de-lis[775] and the blue outline of clouds, which continue throughout the design, punctuated by the inner gatefold image of the four band members set within the delineation of castle turrets, white fleur-de-lis and exquisitely drawn white fish.

The gatefold also includes a blue and silver alchemical[776] sun, seemingly glowering with an expression disdain and incredulity. Other versions of the single, both seven and twelve inch, are non-gatefold and are 'flamingo' pink and 'fuchsia' respectively.

Chapter Six
Everything All Of The Time

Despite the potential fallout and repercussions of losing a virtuoso guitarist and the perpetual merry-go-round of touring, interviews and not insignificant side projects, Siouxsie and The Banshees are at their peak.

The success of 'Dear Prudence' marked, after approximately seven years of indomitable persistence, bloody-mindedness, uninterrupted gigging and uncompromising determination, what the band had always wanted, to make their mark.

Billy Chainsaw ventures, 'It was great growing up with the band and getting to the point where 'Dear Prudence' went Top 3. That was when we all agreed, "Now it's all really happening"'.[777]

Chainsaw also muses on the Banshees' modus operandi and their determination to escape the suburbs in search of a more attractive alternative, 'They were the original punks who'd come from nowhere, but they all wanted to be on *Top Of The Pops*. The Banshees wanted to be famous from day one'.[778]

'Play At Home'

'…we were working for some people who were making a documentary series for Channel 4. The format for these hour-long Play At Home shows was that you'd broadcast half an hour of live music and then do what you liked with the other half… All of the other bands did earnest things. Level 42 did some kind of music workshop, Angelic Upstarts covered a Jarrow workers' march, which was really dull and worthy, and Big Country included footage of themselves packing their van. There was no way we were going to do anything like that, so we decided to make our own little movie'.[779]

Siouxsie Sioux

The aforementioned Channel 4 film *Play At Home* affords all four Siouxsie and The Banshees members creative latitude to showcase music by the band, as well as subsidiary projects The Creatures and The Glove. The initial "Wonderland' slant" of the programme has its origins in The Glove's *Blue Sunshine* album recording when Robert Smith had something of a lightbulb moment, uttering, 'the Banshees shouldn't be doing tours, they should be doing something really ambitious like *The Wizard Of Oz* on stage'.[780]

With the commissioning of the programme, after some collective indecision regarding the programme's thematic direction of travel, they went with Steve Severin's design based on the storyline on *Alice's Adventures In Wonderland*, dovetailing perfectly with Wonderland Records.

What could have been readily kiboshed by the band as a frivolous notion was embraced enthusiastically. 'Play At Home' would also form a not insignificant part of the multi-format *Nocturne*[781] live double album and DVD renewal after its 1984 release.

The film starts amid an office of Wonderland HQ, where there is an animated telephone exchange between Dave Woods and 'John' on the other end of the line about the acquisition of tickets for the Banshees' two sold-out shows at the Royal Albert Hall.

Woods states categorically and vehemently that he can't even stretch to two tickets and that there was '...literally no room',[782] at which point Don Grain[783] interjects, echoing Woods' 'no room' sentiment twice as the Banshees enter, one by one, and, when assembled, offer the riposte, 'There's plenty of room'.[784] Woods, holding the telephone receiver, looks at his watch, makes his excuses, uttering '...I've got to go. I'm late. I'm late'.[785]

The opening scene segues into the chaotically preposterous context of 'The Mad Tea Party',[786] appropriated from the Lewis Carroll 1865 novel, hosted by The Hatter,[787] Jos Grain, with Dave Woods as the perpetually time-troubled White Rabbit.

The cast, a somewhat 'Banshees' family' affair of sorts, includes Don Ash as Tweedle Dee and Billy Chainsaw Tweedle Dum, Annie

Hogan[788] as the Dormouse, Tim Collins[789] playing the Mad March Hare, Mike Hedges the Queen Of Hearts, and all members of Siouxsie and The Banshees playing Alice, huddled together, identical in pink puff sleeve dresses, white pinafores and blond wigs.

Various props laid out for tea include an array of discordant paraphernalia including a typewriter, dead flowers, watering can, telephone, desk lamp and, the centrepiece, a substantial grey and white cake in the form of the Royal Albert Hall. A series of disparate video backdrops play behind the 'Mad Tea Party', including a running horse in a field, a looming cat head and office buildings.

There are two immutable ingredients to the Banshees 'Play At Home' project, one being the 'Mad Tea Party' tableau and the other Siouxsie and The Banshees' 'The Circle', which, for the programme, is the backward string section from the song as a looped aural keynote throughout all the 'Mad Tea Party' sequences, latterly becoming one of the musical interludes, with Siouxsie dressed as whip-yielding ringmistress, replete with yellow slim coat, black peaked cap, calf-length leather boots and leather trousers.

She and the other band members – Severin in a black Kentucky bowtie and waistcoat and Smith, half-dressed in a baggy white shirt and Rosary beads[790] – are juxtaposed with video footage of a grimy, dystopian-looking yet visually effective London underpass, and fleeting shots of the London Underground, Piccadilly Circus neon and views of the London skyline from one of the Capital's bridges. With reference to the placing of 'The Circle', sequentially, it was felt that it should be a Banshees' performance that bookended the programme, for the sake of cohesion; it was, after all, a Siouxsie and The Banshees project.

There are also Banshees' Royal Albert Hall live performances of 'Eve Black/Eve White', 'Voodoo Dolly' and 'Helter Skelter'. Musical diversions are integrated with The Creatures' hitherto vignetted 'Weathercade' and The Glove's 'A Blues In Drag' from the *Blue Sunshine* album, which sees Robert Smith playing a Fender Rhodes electric piano and Steve Severin plucking and bowing a cello, set against the blue and yellow spiral backcloth seen on the 'Like An Animal' single artwork.

The Hatter introduces The Glove as 'Rupert The Riddles', giving a knowing glance as he gestures to suggest that some form of alcoholic revelry might be involved. The moody, melancholically reflective song synergises with evocatively visual close-ups of both band members, yellow chrysanthemums and ornate wine glasses.

Both band members mirror one another in black sunglasses, black polo neck sweaters and white formal jackets. There were also philosophical reasons why an instrumental song from The Glove's *Blue Sunshine* was chosen, as using a track with Robert Smith singing would have conceivably given more attention to him.

The decision to exclude Jeanette Landray was born out of practical necessity, as the inclusion of any third party would not have allowed the musical intervals to be kept within the Banshees' nucleus of the four band members.

Amid the 'Mad Tea Party' pandemonium and musical intervals, all four band members narrate an original self-penned story. Robert Smith spins the first, apparently rather hastily cobbled together, yarn.

'Nothing's so perfect' is set within the confines of a subterranean interrogation room. During the course of the interview, three menacing, suited figures swap several different clown masks, exchange glances, take notes and stir and drink tea, the sound of which has been put through a distortion effect to render its amplification slightly nauseating.

Smith, dressed in a blue and white striped shirt, wearing Rosary beads,[791] sitting at a table surrounded by dead flowers, an overflowing ashtray, a piece of blank paper and a full cup of tea, is the central figure actually undertaking the cross-examination while the clowns remain mute.

Smith's narrative appears to join together a series of surreal, jumbled non-sequiturs that reference an invisible ensemble cast. The entire, seemingly distressing, episode is aggravated by close-ups of Smith's face as he periodically holds his head in his hands. Throughout Smith's exposition, there is a miscellany of dissonant sounds that wouldn't be out of place in any of the possession scenes witnessed in the film *The Exorcist*.

Budgie's story 'The famous Prince Albert', is based on the Stanley

Holloway[792] soliloquy-like reading of 'The Lion And Albert'.[793] Budgie pieced together disjointed memories of t' monologue which include nascent recollections of Holloway's narration on a 78rpm record, with synapses firing intermittently as he tried to recount the piece '...with his mates down the local pub',[794] as well as recording the monologue on cassette tape.

In a moment of serendipity, '...when he sat down to write what he could remember of the words (as providence would have it), a half hour Stanley Holloway special came on the radio'. Budgie recorded the radio programme, reproduced the original words, '...then changed them to tie in with the inclusion of one of the animals he and Siouxsie (as The Creatures) adopted at London Zoo... Gregory Peccary,[795] in the place of the lion'.

The inevitably close comedic proximity to 'The Lion And Albert' meant seeking permission from Stanley Holloway's estate, which was duly granted. Budgie's characterful and expressive delivery of the monologue, the filming of which is set among Kensington Gardens and London Zoo, is clearly a heartfelt, almost eulogistic glimpse into his childhood, as, when piecing together his recollections of 'The Lion And Albert', Budgie had unearthed a cassette tape of the monologue, part of which included the voice of his mother who died when Budgie was twelve years of age.

'Night Adventurer returns home' is Siouxsie's anecdote, the initial impetus of which was a sort of 'Yellow Brick Road' inversion,[796] with its roots firmly embedded within the realms of Siouxsie's lived experience pertaining, initially, to interminable questions about the last time she went home, prompting the singer to venture back to the suburbs, somewhere she was only too eager to escape as a teenager, with apparently disastrous results. Apparently, the crux of the account alludes to a time when 'Siouxsie felt as though she was part of a living nightmare, just like the character in her story'.[797]

The opening visual of 'Night Adventurer returns home' juxtaposes Siouxsie's face, shot using chiaroscuro, and not entirely dissimilar to the opening sequence of Queen's video for 'Bohemian Rhapsody',[798] is one which sees the narrator's journey from the metropolis, a place that oozed excitement and promise but, ultimately, the transience of which left her feeling that she needed something more solid and steadfast, to the flattened and more predictable environs of the suburbs.

Most of the initial narrative is shot so only Siouxsie's illuminated mouth, appearing amidst an inky blackness with as much visual plangency as one of the oral fissures in a Francis Bacon painting, so the viewer fixates, mesmerised, on the story being expressed by this disembodied mystic. We hear the clatter of the train, and Siouxsie's face appears lit intermittently with a stroboscopic effect.

Once off the train, the darkness of the local woods need to be negotiated. This first part of the story is plunged into the realms of apprehension, as the trees appear to come to life in pursuit of the narrator.

Having negotiated the thicket-grown adversary, the storyteller arrives safely to the intimate surroundings of her home, only quickly to discover that what she thought would bring great solace turns out to be torment. In bed later that night, tossing and turning, our storyteller catches sight of what she thinks is either a real or imagined spectre at the bottom of her bed.

Now completely disturbed and alarmed, she creeps down the stairs, only to find her mother, on her hands and knees, squabbling and grappling with her sister over something raw and bloody, as their eyes pin the protagonist to the spot.

Siouxsie's story is a mixture of the real, imagined and the reoccurring, whether interpretively rendered through an unconscious dream-state or fully cognisant, as personified in the lyrics of 'The Circle' and Siouxsie's own personal childhood trauma.

The finale, perhaps unwittingly, also has a hint of the 'something sinister lurks behind the picket fence and net curtains…' trashy horror movies such as *Motel Hell* Siouxsie so savoured.

The story ends with Siouxsie's cautionary and sagely uttering to 'Look to where you have arrived, not where you have come from'.[799]

Siouxsie's tale of familial dysfunction reflects the maladjusted incoherence of the 'Play At Home' 'Mad Tea Party' convocation as it reaches its nadir of degeneration.

Steve Severin's anecdote centres around a long-held fixation with assassins, especially the all-consuming obsession of someone who is planning to shoot a famous figure.

Severin's synopsis was to render the story so it could have been set at any point in history by introducing an age-old assassin protagonist.

Utilising a Teleprinter[800] for the story, Severin reads the unfolding script as ink hits the paper, creating the duality of a cogent unfolding of events with the confused melange of a series of successful and failed assassinations, including John F Kennedy,[801] Pope John Paul II[802] and President Ronald Reagan.[803]

Severin's assassin assembles his sniper rifle with the utmost forensic precision, channelling Edward Fox[804] in *Day Of The Jackal.* [805]

Budgie and John McGeoch,
Swansea, 1980.

Sheffield, 1980.

© Peter Anderson

Tropicana Motel, West Hollywood,
November, 1980.

© David Arnoff

© David Arnoff

1981.

© Simon Fowler

John McGeoch and Siouxsie, North America 'Juju' tour, New York, 1981.

John McGeoch, North America 'Juju' tour, New York, 1981.

North America
'Juju' tour,
New York,
1981.

© Ray Stevenson

Siouxsie and John
McGeoch, North America
'Juju' tour, New York,
1981.

© Ray Stevenson

Siouxsie and John McGeoch,
North America 'Juju' tour,
Hot Klub, Dallas, Texas,
1981.

© Ray Stevenson

North America 'Juju' tour,
Ole Man River's,
Avondale, Louisiana,
1981.

© Ray Stevenson

Robert Smith playing an Ovation
Electric Guitar, Royal Albert Hall,
London, 1983.

Photograph taken from a contact sheet,
courtesy of Tony Mottram

Siouxsie playing her
Vox Teardrop guitar,
Royal Albert Hall, London,
1983.

Photograph taken from a contact sheet,
courtesy of Tony Mottram

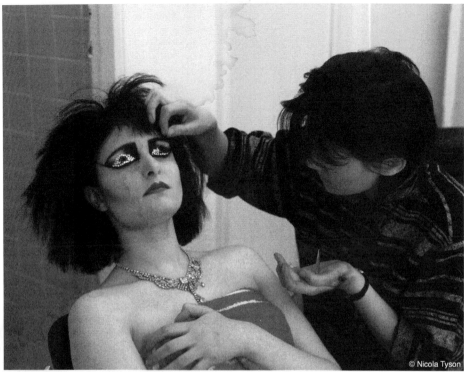

Tiny jewel adornments being applied to Siouxsie's eyelids for the 'Dazzle' video shoot, 1984.

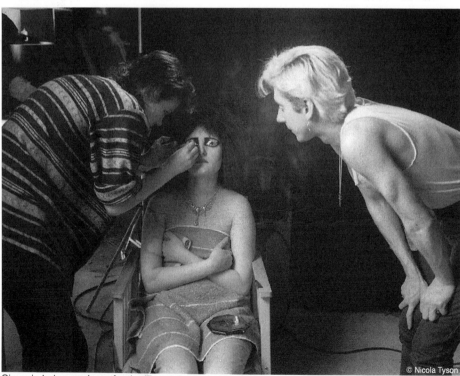

Siouxsie being made up for the 'Dazzle' video while Budgie looks on, 1984.

Steve Severin, 'Dazzle' shoot, 1984.

© Nicola Tyson

'Dazzle' video shoot, 1984.

© Nicola Tyson

'Dazzle' shoot, 1984.

© Nicola Tyson

Budgie, 'Dazzle' shoot, 1984.

© Nicola Tyson

© Nicola Tyson

'Dazzle' shoot, 1984.

© Nicola Tyson

Face to face with her waxwork head, 1984.

© Nicola Tyson

Hamming it up with her waxwork hand, 1984.

Siouxsie with a box of eyes, 1984.

© Nicola Tyson

John Valentine Carruthers.

© Nicola Tyson

San Sebastian, 1985.

© Peter Anderson

Siouxsie and Severin, Shoreditch, 1986.

© Peter Anderson

Shoreditch, 1987.

© Peter Anderson

Severin,
Siouxsie and
Budgie,
Shoreditch,
1987.

© Peter Anderson

Budgie and
Martin McCarrick.

© Jon Klein

Jon Klein wearing raw silk,
Tampa, Florida, 1987.

Siouxsie, Martin McCarrick and Budgie, 1987.

Siouxsie's backstage
motor home, 1987.

© Jon Klein

The Greek Theatre,
Berkeley, California, 1987.

© Jon Klein

Chapter Seven
Nocturne

'A short gentle piece of music, often one written to be played on the piano'.[806]

'I didn't think Nocturne was as bad as everyone thought at the time. I didn't so much go for the video but the live album would have made a good single LP. I don't think The Banshees knew what they were doing at the time and I don't think I had any clear idea of what they wanted me to do'.[807]

Robert Smith

Marking the two momentous dates at the Royal Albert Hall in London on 30 September and 1 October 1983, *Nocturne*, a sixteen-track, double live album, is perhaps the embodiment of the Banshees' mercurial nature, continuing to make their own rules and not caring a damn what anyone else might say or think regarding playing a 19th-century Victorian venue which might seem to embody all things dusty and conventional, suggestive of a bygone, antiquated, entrenched conservatism.

On the contrary, the Royal Albert Hall was probably the most symbolically 'Punk' gig the Banshees had played to date, reinforcing their hard-won autonomy and unstoppable and unassailable drive to be at the very top of their game.

The album is a timely testimony to the band's several incarnations, covering material from *The Scream*, *Kaleidoscope*, *Juju* and *A Kiss In The Dreamhouse*.

'Dear Prudence' would latterly make an appearance on 1984's *Hyæna*[808] and there is an absence of any song from *Join Hands*, except, perhaps vicariously, 'Pulled To Bits', the sulkier B-side of 'Playground Twist'.

'Israel'

Following a powerful orchestral scintilla of Igor Stravinsky's 'The Rite Of Spring',[809] the crowd erupts when the band hits the stage, and the first bars of 'Israel' make for a spine-tingling opening. The assembled crowd couldn't wish for more. This is a song befitting the magnificent splendour of the Royal Albert Hall and it is an absolute masterstroke to begin the set with it. The band sounds incredible. Robert Smith does opt for a non-arpeggio-oriented guitar break but the song is undiminished, replete with Siouxsie's swooping vocal and wrist bells, with Budgie and Severin rhythmically joined at the hip.

'Dear Prudence'

Introduced beautifully with Robert Smith's psychedelic-sounding whammy bar, Severin plays a steady bass, and Smith's melodious playing is an absolute treat, all underscored by Budgie's Ringo-esque drumming. Siouxsie sings with a gorgeous nonchalance and terrific, tremulous range, intoning clear adoration for a song from her beloved Beatles album.

'Paradise Place'

Belted out and a distinctly juxtaposed change of tempo from 'Dear Prudence', Siouxsie takes up Vox Teardrop guitar duties with aplomb as Smith matches the sonic brilliance of McGeoch's urgent, visceral playing. This is an absolutely barnstorming rendition of 'Paradise Place', creating the evocation of its botched-cosmetic-surgery subject matter origins perfectly. Severin's sweltering bass guitar and Budgie's drumming make the song a euphoric and magnificent standout on the album.

'Melt!'

Without pausing for breath, 'Melt!' swelters and envelops the auditorium imperiously, with Siouxsie's vocal articulation at its most expressive. Smith's ability to alternate guitar parts to serve the melodrama of the song represents his adroitness and accomplishment as a player.

The song is delivered by Siouxsie with all the emotive electrification of a Shakespearian tragedy crossed with the familial misanthropic chicanery of Mario Puzo's 'The Godfather'.[810]

'Cascade'
The quickening heartbeat of the song emits a frenzied and almost fatalistic urgency. Again, Smith demonstrates his agility as a player, undertaking the myriad facets of the song with depth of understanding, as the power duo of Severin and Budgie create a rumble so powerful that it sends reverberations through every captivated audience member. Siouxsie's vocal is, yet again, extraordinarily eloquent, dextrous and on point.

'Pulled To Bits'
Slowing the pace, 'Pulled To Bits' is played with austere menacing power, with Smith's acoustic guitar cutting through the song with pure melancholia, underpinned by Severin's poignant and beautiful bass playing. Budgie's percussion ebbs and flows with the song's changing tempo as Siouxsie delivers another heart-wrenching vocal performance.

'Night Shift'
Casting its vampiric spell as the sinister night-crawling of the song takes full effect, Smith's guitar playing captures the spikily barbed mood of the song perfectly, as the footstep and heartbeat of Budgie's drumming creates a seemingly perpetual pattern of woe, aided and abetted by the dour, plodding, menacing narrative of Severin's bass. Siouxsie's vocal is complicit in expressing the deeds of a notorious psychopath. The song ends with a wailing wall of eardrum-piercing feedback.

'Sin In My Heart'
'Sin In My Heart' continues in a similar vein, descending into a rabbit hole of gorgeous desperation, as Siouxsie takes up the Vox Teardrop guitar. Introduced by Severin's atmospheric bass playing, the song builds up a head of steam as it gallops as if trying to keep up with itself.

Budgie's extraordinary, fast-paced, intense drumming provides an imperative backbeat for the astonishing essence of the song, which is both testament to and showcase for the tightness of the band, substantiating thousands of hours of playing.

'Slowdive'

Shifting gear, although 'Slowdive' has none of the string orchestration of the studio version it is no less effective, perhaps even more so, as Robert Smith plays with a slide at the higher end of the guitar neck's octave range, making sound redolent of a pedal string guitar.

The song is a rhythmical tour de force for Budgie and Severin, as Siouxsie has impish fun with the vocal. A superb example of the Banshees' gift for deftly crafting and exploiting the space between the notes.

'Painted Bird'

Picking up the pace, 'Painted Bird' reprises the Banshees' existential angst as the band play at lightning speed; Robert Smith proving his brilliance and expressiveness as a guitar player, matching the McGeoch template with agility and playing to perfection, as do the other band members. The tremulous, seductive nature of the song has all the theatrics synonymous with the studio cut.

'Happy House'

Introduced by Siouxsie's dry-witted comment about how quickly Robert Smith's guitar goes out of tune, the band launch into 'Happy House', which fits the band like a glove.

It is another illustration of the contemporaneousness of Siouxsie and The Banshees playing at the very top of their game. If there is any proving that the band are indestructible, this live version of 'Happy House' does just that. It rumbles along defiantly; a middle finger up to anyone who had at, any point, written the band off. The phoenix not only rises but transcends.

'Switch'

Harking back to 1978's *The Scream*, 'Switch' is a sonic aggregate of everything mistrustful about authority or doctrine, whether scientific, political or religious in orientation. Again, this is a note-perfect version of a song which yells angst, especially in Siouxsie's remarkable vocal delivery.

As with all the songs on the double album, there is nothing but inextinguishable conviction conveyed by the band. The wistful nature of the song is captured beautifully, as it waves goodbye and good riddance to the wearying tedium of suburbia.

The melancholia is exacerbated through Robert Smith's barbed, yet melodious guitar attack and the resonating phased and flanged echoing of Severin bass, articulated with emotive thrum. Budgie's backbeat is a hybrid of straight up four-to-the-floor and nuanced jazz inflections. Siouxsie's vocal whooshes throughout the lofty venue. Masterful.

'Spellbound'

The first of four encores, the Banshees return to the stage and, like a melodious cudgel, launch into 'Spellbound'. Retrospectively, it seems almost like an act of contempt or abandonment that, as a single, the song peaked at number 22 in the UK Official Singles Chart.

However, this is moot now as, cannily, the band bring out the big guns and, with complete disregard for anything except putting on the best show on Earth, play out of their skins. Siouxsie and The Banshees at their absolute blinding best.

This live version moves at such a blisteringly feverish and skittish pace, it is all the four band members can do to keep up with it. But keep up they do, well and truly wigging out in this pure act of dramaturgy.

'Helter Skelter'

The second song the band plays from *The Scream*, the introduction to 'Helter Skelter' heralds the beginning of the apocalypse through Robert Smith's strident, wailing wall of feedback, underpinned by the lugubrious singular *durm and strang* of Steve Severin's bass guitar.

At fifty-two seconds, Siouxsie is accompanied by the stabbing thwack of Budgie's snare drum, Smith's guitar and Severin's bass, as the song gathers impetus to explode.

Nothing has been lost since Siouxsie and The Banshees first played 'Helter Skelter' live at The Oaks Hotel, Manchester, as their opening number on 17 May 1977. It has all the attack, attitude, freshness, aggression and intimacy one might associate with any number of spit-and-sawdust venues where the band learned their chops and cut their musical teeth.

If there was any doubt that Robert Smith was the right choice as the band's guitarist, here is complete vindication for The Cure figurehead.

'Eve White/Eve Black'

The only time the song was played live in 1983, this B-side to the 1980 single 'Christine', is a delicious rarity to be savoured. Two minutes and forty-six seconds of unbridled feedback and rhythmical tumult, enveloped by Siouxsie's agonised vocal, capturing the subject of the song, Christine Sizemore,[811] diagnosed with Dissociative Identity Disorder in the 1950s, as depicted in the book *The Three Faces Of Eve*.[812]

The song captures the warring factions of the mind, a slow burn when, at one minute and ten seconds, the mania takes complete control as Siouxsie channels the initial meek soliloquy, transmogrifying into multiple bellicose agonising cries. Extraordinary.

'Voodoo Dolly'

Leading in from 'Eve White/Eve Black', 'Voodoo Dolly' is the evening's 'Sister Ray' meets *The Exorcist*. Beginning with the metallic shards of Robert Smith's guitar feedback and Steve Severin's perilous bass playing, both Banshees lure Siouxsie and Budgie into the throes of the song and slap bang into the heart of darkness as the ritual begins, nonchalantly, gradually.

At one minute and twenty-four seconds, Smith transposes feedback for menacing chords, rejoined by Budgie at one minute and fifty seconds. Everyone is in; the ceremony begins. There is peril as the voodoo of the song starts to play out. Smith leads the charge, every chord and note resounding and indeterminate fracas.

At around four minutes and ten seconds, 'Voodoo Dolly' enters sonic hyperspace as Smith's guitar playing enters a whole other sublime realm like the scuttling of a million metallic spiders.

The whole band manages the balancing act between restraint and the fantastical, with temperance prevailing around five minutes and fifty seconds, with Siouxsie's extemporised, didactically sounding lyric, a conceivable nod to 'The Lord's Prayer', winding the song down like the ebbing of a zoetrope.[813]

Symbolically, at eight minutes and three seconds, Siouxsie's microphone is switched off and the audience are left with forty-seven seconds of encircling feedback.

For the VHS[814] footage of the two nights, Siouxsie and The Banshees not only sound magnificent but look spectacular as well. Playing in front of a panoramic, moving cloudscape backcloth, Siouxsie, both literally and metaphorically, sparkles; barefoot, bejewelled and shamanistic, she wears a black and grey Art Nouveau dress with a myriad accessories, including choker necklace, white scarves tied around her legs and one dangling from her waist on one night, and a black Devore dress, shoulder necklace and matching wristbands with embossed circular designs, for the other night; all topped off by an explosion of black crimped hair.

She is formidably mettlesome, mesmerising and born to command an audience. Robert Smith, bedecked in rock 'n' roll black leather trousers, studded belt, elaborately patterned shirt one night and a thin blue striped shirt the next, is the epitome of volitional Banshee; the music will do the showboating, all he needs to do is play brilliantly and serve the songs.

Stalwart Severin, stage right, wears a light blue ruffled shirt with an abstract patterned jacket and pegged trousers, juxtaposed with light-coloured trousers and dark shirt for the other night's performance.

Budgie, wearing a striking bleached leonine mane, errs on dressing down, no doubt due to the physicality and practicality of his role; wearing a sleeveless tee shirt, equipped and safe in the knowledge that the spotlight will be on Siouxsie. His role is to keep the beat, no Edwardian attire necessary.

The multi-camera nature of the filming is ostensibly without frills but brings to the fore how one song segues into another, broken up with some slow motion and oscillated transitions of coloured patterned cloth.

We see the animated Banshee audience crowded around the front of the stage, the odd mohican in silhouette. There is dry ice, and the band and stage are beautifully lit, Siouxsie dances. But this snapshot, committed to film for posterity, is the band stripped bare to reveal nothing more and nothing less than indefatigable brilliance.

The *Nocturne* video sees the band performing twelve songs, in contrast to the album's sixteen. There is also a different running order for the songs: 1. 'Israel', 2. 'Cascade', 3. 'Melt!', 4. 'Pulled To Bits', 5. 'Night Shift', 6. 'Sin In My Heart', 7. 'Painted Bird', 8. 'Switch', 9. 'Eve White/Eve Black', 10. 'Voodoo Dolly', 11. 'Spellbound' and 12. 'Helter Skelter'.

Bonus features include 'Play At Home', *Old Grey Whistle Test* performances of 'Painted Bird' and 'Melt!' and the promo for 'Dear Prudence'.

The concept of a double album, and, in the instance of *Nocturne*, with the embellishment of the concert video, itself with abundant additional material, isn't completely unimaginable in the early 1980s, not least with the October 1983 release of David Bowie's *Ziggy Stardust The Motion Picture*,[815] as well as Talking Heads' *The Name Of This Band Is Talking Heads*, [816] which features live recordings by the original quartet from 1977 to 1979 and the expanded live lineup from 1980 to 1981.

This is rather small change compared to The Clash's *Sandinista*,[817] a triple album with thirty-six tracks, released in 1980. And, as the subject in question is Siouxsie and The Banshees during their most commanding manifestation, having released their most experimentally rich studio album to date, the format of the release is indubitably germane.

Reflecting the protean nature of the band, the Da Gama artwork for the double album expedites the Baudelairean aesthetic of *A Kiss In The Dreamhouse* template, becoming more Neo-Plasticist in the process, with playfully deconstructed mosaic-like geometric patterns centred around the configuration of a six-pointed star, evocative of the 'Israel'

Star Of David motif on the front gatefold, and also echoing the work of Dutch artist Piet Mondrian in paintings such as 'Evolution'[818] from 1911, which dangles on a representational thread, betwixt figuration and abstraction.

On the front cover of *Nocturne*, the only figurative is a still of Budgie from one of the Royal Albert Hall performances placed within the frame of the star motif. Elsewhere, there is an elaborate multi-coloured triangular marquetry, juxtaposed with areas of graphically manipulated explosive sgraffito, echoing the album's namesake 'Nocturne In Black And Gold'[819] by artist James Abbott McNeil Whistler.[820]

The band name as it appears on the front cover has also undergone a playful abstraction, utilising asterisk-like stars yet keeping its hybridised Secessionist and Art Nouveau chromosomes. The album title *Nocturne* employs Objectiv Mk 1 font.

The inner gatefold is no less magisterial, with photographs of all four band members, from left to right Budgie, Severin, Sioux and Smith, captured during the two performances. The back cover has a full band photograph and the full track listing. For additional colour, the two dust sleeves are florescent blue, denoted by SHAH 1 for the A and B-sides and fluorescent pink SHAH 2 for the C and D-sides.

Conceivably, due to there never being any Banshees' 'blueprint', nor any apparent concern about what musical furrow their musical contemporaries were ploughing. In an article written by Lynden Barber for *Melody Maker*,[821] where two albums are reviewed, The Birthday Party's *Mutiny!*[822] and *Nocturne*, Barber makes allusions to the need for music, if it is to have any resonance and relevance, to have an element of suffering and sacrifice, especially in the case of The Birthday Party, commenting, 'I doubt if anything will sound quite so distressed and distended and downright nasty as 'Mutiny In Heaven' and 'Swampland', anthems of disease that kick aside 'King Ink' and 'Sonny's Burning' as moments of greatness with the grace of a yob pushing over dustbins at midnight'.[823]

Barber fathoms the essential nature of art as spectacle; entertainment to make the listener sit bolt upright and take notice. It is therefore opportune, if perhaps a little expedient, that Siouxsie and

The Banshees should be perceived in the same vein.

Barber's exposition isn't entirely effusive, reflecting, 'Like all double albums it should have been a single platter'.[824] And although there is unreserved flattery for 'Sin In My Heart', Barber comments, 'Siouxsie's voice is so flat on the opening track, 'Israel', that it is impossible to listen to without flinching'.[825]

For a little equity, Barber comments on the band's elan and a '...dedication that is magnificent to behold. They care about every second that is passing by; they play their instruments like they are making love; inaccuracies drop casually, slight errors are committed, yet fade away into irrelevance as the collective spirit blossoms'.[826]

For a greater degree of discernible contextualisation, Barney Hoskyn's interview with Siouxsie and The Banshees provides an insight into the collective Banshees' psyche, as they enter into a phase of inverse fraternité with the music press on the back of *Nocturne*.

Hoskyns identifies that, at the time he wrote the article for the *NME*, a period of seven years would have elapsed between then and Punk coming to fruition. Did *Nocturne* represent a renaissance for the Banshees or was it an indicator of musical deadlock? Could the band carry on?

Siouxsie is slightly mournful about how music has shifted, reflecting, 'Everything has changed, there's no such thing as an underground. It's impossible to get that atmosphere of being at something special that no one is aware of. Everything is always a media thing before it even happens'.[827]

Warming to her elder statesman motif, Siouxsie continues, 'It must be really hard to be young now and hate your parents, because that's always been fed by the animosity between kids and grown-ups. It must be tough for young people to sift through the quagmire. There's so many groups trying to be noticed, and in the way that they're trying to be noticed they're all the same'.[828]

On that note of generalisation, Siouxsie discerns between the then and now, the then being the Wild West, and the now more of a magnetic, drone-like pull back to the pedestrian beige of predictability, 'Earlier, I think there were groups who came along who didn't have a musical identity. People saw them and thought, what was that? Whereas now people know what to expect from things they've heard about. They know how they'll dress, and they know the kind of people they'll meet there. Before it was always such a diverse audience, because it was always by chance that people turned up at things'.[829]

Hoskyns also suggests the Banshees' path, en route to success, is itself an act of subversion. It is as though the band are the last bastions of Punk in terms of attitude and thinking but they have a volatility that is perhaps too nuanced, subtle and intellectual to pigeonhole.

It is complete anathema for the band to simply 'play the hits' like a human jukebox, and they have fought too hard for anything resembling compromise. Siouxsie crystallises the impasse, 'I suppose the difficulty is coping with being lumped along with all the other pop groups. We're finding it a bit frustrating that it's not obvious why we're different from any number of people who are in the charts for a few months… When you're frustrated like that, you feel really aggressive, and it usually ends up with you cutting off your nose to spite your face. We could have done more interviews to explain things, and its particularly me who's said no, I don't want to do anything, I think it's been good, but the motive behind it has been that aggression'.[830]

Hoskyns elaborates, 'So they will not be this, and they will not be that. They will be Siouxsie & The Banshees… their music is beautiful – that it is styled and very stylish, that it refers to no "style", no subtext of behaviour or belief, that it is not factional… I love Siouxsie because she is not vain and she is not a sex goddess and she is not a drug fiend and she is not a liar'.[831]

Hoskyns also empathises with the fact that the band '…find themselves at an unenviable point on the exponential curve of fame. People like to suppose they know what Siouxsie & The Banshees are about: a few masks, a couple of images'.[832]

Alluding to a curtailed longevity that has ushered in the death knell of multitudes of bands, Hoskyns muses, '…it's difficult, it has to be said, to get any perspective on these groups, the ones that stay with us'.[833]

Turning to the subject of the Royal Albert Hall gigs, Siouxsie says, '…I don't think I'd ever considered us playing there. Earl's Court or Wembley, yes, and I still say we'll never play there. It's not just a question of scale, it's a question of how perverse it is as well... We've seen some of the footage we filmed and it's like this grand concert performance and all these diverse people arriving next to these huge portraits and busts and all the pomp and everything. There's nothing wrong with all that, if it's in the right place at the right time'.

When Hoskyns points out that Echo And The Bunnymen played at the Royal Albert Hall, Siouxsie retorts, 'Well, yeah, but we've never worn raincoats or had camouflage... we never tried to blend in with the audience! It's always been a show. At the beginning it was always frustrating that it wasn't bigger. Now it's frustrating to contain the simplicity. But it's good that there's that combat, still wanting something that isn't perfect'.

Siouxsie and The Banshees are keen to emphasise the synergy between the visual impact of the gig and the music: 'All the visual drama is only there to enhance the mood of a song, as opposed to bands who just use it as a sideshow. If you have an audience that large, you have to project, but it's the way you project that matters. But with us, it's always real smoke, never dry ice!'[834]

And what of the connotations of the live double album format? Siouxsie: 'Well, yes. I always said we'll never bring out a live album, and I was being a real old boot about it, but when we played it all back with the visuals, I really thought it worked. Comparing it with what everyone else was doing with their live stuff, it was a million times better. I also think a lot of the songs were better live, like 'Cascade' and 'Pulled To Bits', because they were just so much less controlled'.[835]

There might have been an undercurrent of ambivalence about the future of Siouxsie and The Banshees, but there remains one constant, the steadfast nucleus of Siouxsie and Severin.

Regardless of changes of personnel, whether band members or management, there are still philosophically existential conversations to be had, pondering the meaning of, well, life. Siouxsie takes a moment to reflect on the more gratifying aspects of our limited existence, pondering, 'The fear is just seeing and being aware that things that might be pleasing to you... can be your downfall. People included. All the good things, all the happiness can be very negative in that they numb you. That's where the danger is, when you're numbed to other people's pain and other people's pleasure. That applies to anyone but more so given the unreality of being a pop star'.[836]

Severin, meanwhile, discerns the melee of contradictions inherent in trying to convey complex ideas through the ostensibly binary mechanism of pop music, 'It's like anything, it takes a bit of concentration and concern to find those things within the lyric, which you can't really demand of a listener and shouldn't really expect… because it's such a supposedly trivial medium. So it's almost inevitable that you get tagged with doom 'n' gloom etcetera, simply because most people haven't got the inclination to open up and discuss some of the subjects. But I don't see why we should not try and do that. It's ridiculous to do anything else'.[837]

Ancillary ventures for The Glove and The Creatures are postulated, with the inevitable well-trodden and apparently mirth-inducing 'will they, won't they' Banshees' split guessing game. Severin remarks, 'With the special projects, it was like all these new avenues had opened up in the media and we could suddenly give them two new names. We could get away with things that we couldn't have done as Siouxsie & The Banshees, because so many people are scared off by the name. And we liked all the confusion of are the Banshees splitting up? That's always fun'.[838]

In Hoskyn's interview, with no little impishness, Siouxsie and Severin proclaim their love of The Shaggs,[839] palpably a more intense and dissonant variant of The Velvet Underground. Siouxsie critiques the band's second album with '…they've got a bit more proficient by the second record. These little sparks will get polluted. I mean 'Foot Foot', that's my favourite. I love to imagine them in a swamp somewhere, with Pa and Ma and all the aunts and uncles involved. There's a live song with all these babies screaming along. It's like the whole clan has been gathered'.[840]

The discussion refocuses to mull over the Banshees' prospects. Did the band think that they would still be together? Siouxsie replies, 'Of course not, but in a way that's what I like about pop music, that you can't be sure of what's going to happen. It's knowing that things can be turned upside down and people who look like they're in a very secure position suddenly find the bottom falls out on them. I enjoy that. It's annoying sometimes, but that kind of letdown or uplift within the pop market is a big part of what it's about'.

Riffing on the theme, Severin ponders the question and relates it to the vested interest of others, explaining, 'We used to have these people around us who were always telling us how to keep everything rolling and still be in the public eye...'[841]

At which point, Siouxsie interrupts sardonically, 'The rules and regulations of how to be a pop star...'[842] Stoically, Severin reflects, 'It's only really in retrospect that we think of things as successes or failures. At the time, what happened with 'Melt!' and 'Slowdive' didn't really bother us. We were too busy with (John) McGeoch'.[843]

There is a bitter sweetness to the *Nocturne* experience, Siouxsie meditating, 'That was our first live album, but we should have done one when John McGeoch was in the band. We'd built up such a good reputation as a live group and hadn't really exploited it ...'[844]

Tim Collins, the Banshees' road manager at the time of *Nocturne*, comments, 'A ridiculous amount of time and effort went into that record. One night we stayed up at Pete Townshend's Eel Pie Studios, fortified by endless bottles of wine, finally finishing the session at eight in the morning. We'd spent all that time inserting this fan's yell for 'Love In A Void', a song they'd not played in years, between every track on the album'.[845]

The support act for the Banshees over the two nights, Frank Tovey, AKA Fad Gadget,[846]was, if nothing else, illustration of the hybridised conglomeration of various musical genres, past, present and future. Inclined towards Synth-Pop,[847] with roots firmly embedded in the terrain of Kraftwerk[848] and Suicide,[849] Tovey's oeuvre also reflected the zeitgeist, with Depeche Mode, The Human League, Ultravox and Soft Cell all purveying their post-Joy Division canon.

Nocturne reached its apex Official Albums Chart position at 29. Excepting the *Once Upon A Time/The Singles* compilation, which peaked at number 21, *Nocturne* proved, by far, to be the Banshees' least commercially successful album to date.

Chapter Eight
Hyæna

To be, or not to be. A Banshee.

Hyæna: noun. Any of several large strong nocturnal carnivorous Old World mammals (family Hyaenidae) that usually feed as scavengers.[850]

'We probably should have just done the tour with him, but Robert (Smith) insisted that he wanted to document his time with us… this time he wanted to do an album with us… it seemed like a good idea at the time'.[851]

Steve Severin

'Hyæna was, I suppose, chaotic in its approach. And fragmented'.[852]

Siouxsie Sioux

'I kept going until the end of 1983, when it all caught up with me, and I had a kind of breakdown. I was physically exhausted. It was like the vengeance of God; I had all these boils… It was like my body was saying, "If you refuse to stop, I will stop you". I had everything you can imagine go wrong. My system simply couldn't cope'.[853]

Robert Smith

It would be deceptive to think that Robert Smith had dissolved all enterprises with The Cure, as this was not the case. In fact, perhaps rather fortuitously in relation to Smith's moonlighting with Siouxsie and The Banshees, the band played its shortest tour to date, at least in terms of actual gigs per year – twenty-two in total between 5 February and 1 October 1983, even though they accomplished a fair few air miles, playing in Australia, New Zealand and Japan. This gave Smith the latitude to re-establish his day job, all the while undertaking his parallel universe commission as a jobbing Banshee. This state of affairs had some provocative consequences.

'Swimming Horses'

The inaugural idea for 'Swimming Horses', released as a single on 16 March 1984, was prompted by a programme Siouxsie saw "…about a female version of Amnesty, called 'Les Sentinelle".[854]

Siouxsie explains, 'They rescue women who are trapped in certain religious climates in the Middle East, religions that view any kind of pre-marital sexual aspersion as punishable by death – either by the hand of the eldest brother in the family, or by public stoning. And there was this instance of a woman whose daughter had developed a tumour, and, of course, gossip abounded that she was pregnant. The doctor who removed the tumour allowed her to take it back to the village to prove that, no, it wasn't a baby – but they wouldn't believe her. The woman knew her daughter would have to be stoned to death so she poisoned her, out of kindness, to save her from a worse fate'.[855]

The unfolding narrative of the programme catalysed the lyric, Siouxsie remarks, 'Kinder than with poison... 'I also used the imagery of 'He gives birth to swimming horses', from the fact that male sea horses give birth to the children, so they're the only species that have a maternal feel for the young. It was, I suppose, an abstract way of linking it all together without being sensationalist. I remember just being really moved by that programme and wanting to get the sorrow out of me'.[856]

The musical impetus for 'Swimming Horses' came from some initial piano noodling from Siouxsie and Severin, with Siouxsie's tinkling the ivories of a toy piano creating a nicely whimsical ocular vignette, at Angel Studios.

Preceding the recording of 'Dear Prudence', during a late night in June 1983, both Siouxsie and Severin have the kernel of a song they think can be developed further. Enter Robert Smith to augment the composition; only he doesn't.

Smith starts playing a refrain on the piano that contradicts what

Siouxsie and Severin have come up with, and is met with a chorus of approval, with Budgie chipping in and establishing the initial drumbeat for the song. Fortuitously, all was captured on tape by Mike Hedges 'with the aid of his newly acquired toy, a 'dummy head microphone' (this is a fibre glass mannequin's head with built in microphones in its ears, which is supposed to simulate the sound(s) you (the listener) would hear – in fact it produces a binaural effect, something that Lou Reed has experimented with on his solo recordings in the past).[857]

Hedges installed the mic in the piano and a six-minute backing track comprising piano and drums was recorded. Several weeks elapsed before the band undertook any subsequent work on the song, at which point Siouxsie had penned the lyrics and recorded a vocal sketch.

With the addition of Robert Smith's guitar part and Steve Severin's bass contribution, and the six minutes of the original song edited to four minutes and four seconds, the 'Swimming Horses' jigsaw was completed by December 1983. Mike Hedges suggested that the more protracted version of the song be released as a single, an idea vetoed until all the tracks on what would become *Hyæna* had been recorded.

The paradiddle drumbeat, guitar harmonics and choppy piano refrain, which has a semblance of cod-reggae[858] inflexion about it, not a universe away from the keyboard playing on Led Zeppelin's 'D'yer Mak'er',[859] laced with upper register embellishments, are joined, seven second in, by Siouxsie's otherworldly, swooping vocal.

As the song progresses it becomes a rococo tapestry of instrumentation, including flanged electric guitar, acoustic guitar, tambourine and bass xylophone, all held steady by the stripped down, effective resonance of Severin's bass. The overall tonality of 'Swimming Horses' possesses a delicious melancholy that is the sound of a band reawakened and rejuvenated.

'Between thought and expression, Lies a lifetime'.[860]

Lou Reed

Recruiting the directorial services of Tim Pope again, on deciding that 'Swimming Horses' would be released as a single, filming commenced for an accompanying promotional video.

Pope was now a regular feature in the Banshees' filmic landscape, having made films to support The Creatures' 'Miss The Girl', 'Right Now' and the Banshees' 'Dear Prudence'. On the day preceding the shoot for the video, Tim Pope visited a special horse hospital therapy centre to film one of the 'patients' in the pool, where exercise in water was part of its rehabilitation programme.

Pope's well-meaning but rather too literal interpretation of the song title resulted in footage of the horse's body and legs as it, well, swam. This was not what the band had imagined; instead, it had envisaged that there would be scenes of the horse's head hovering about in the water.

Siouxsie's recollections of the filming and subsequent video are, '…a fiasco. The idea was we'd have these coloured screens moving in and out of focus behind us. It was meant to be abstract and blurry, but it came out looking flat and really cheap.'[861]

Regarding the swimming horse footage, Siouxsie says, '…we had to get footage of a real horse swimming underwater, so they filmed it in a pool where they take horses to exercise after they have been injured. When the cameraman came back, he said they hadn't realised that when a horse enters the water it spontaneously pisses. These were the only shots I liked'.[862]

The video is a patchwork of ideas somewhat haphazardly sewn together. Its central focus is Siouxsie, dressed in a white snood-like jumper, and adorned with elaborate jewellery, looking stellar. While Siouxsie dances, swoops and mimes the lyric, Robert Smith and Steve Severin, dressed in various permutations of white starched collarless garments, and Budgie, who has dropped the hospital auxiliary nurse/ Droog look in favour of his default sleeveless vest, stand either stock-still or sway slightly, alternating between masked and unmasked, as what appears to be a shimmering drape oscillates in the background.

Severin comments, 'The basic idea was to use three males as a screen onto which a swimming horse could be projected but it didn't work very well. As with everything at this time, it was done in too much of a rush'.[863]

The video isn't without aesthetic merit, especially in terms of the dappled, chiaroscuro-oriented blue lighting, evoking the reflection of water on Smith, Severin and Budgie. Siouxsie dances with a white plaster cast bust among an entanglement of straw-coloured string as the Banshees, this time more animated, weave in and out of camera shot.

Then, at two minutes and fifty-two seconds, Siouxsie, unwittingly channelling The Lady In The Radiator from *Eraserhead*, compounded with the luminous disposition of a children's television presenter, is seen in a straight-to-camera chromatic shot for nearly a whole minute.

All the peculiarity is juxtaposed with sketches of swimming horses. Siouxsie describes the dissatisfaction with the video, '…because everyone kept telling me that I should let myself be pampered for a bit, I got a make-up artist in… she gave me this bright orange face. The whole thing was a complete disaster and we never allowed it to be shown on TV'.[864]

Tim Pope did not disagree with the less than favourable critique of the video, commenting, 'It's a failure as a video. The only funny thing in it is Robert in his wide white shirt'.[865]

With 'Swimming Horses' breaking into the UK Top Thirty Singles Chart at number 28, the band appears on *Top Of The Pops*. Comparatively speaking, Tim Pope's promo, although the result is still a mimed performance, proves to be a far more cohesive affair. Siouxsie, of course, steals the show, dressed in an elaborate pointy-sleeved white dress, over which she wears an Art Deco style beaded top. Siouxsie's crimped, backcombed hair is echoed by the coiffure of Robert Smith, who is playing electric piano. Steve Severin, alternating between bass and keyboard, looks rakish in waistcoat and tie. Both he and Budgie complement the black-haired Siouxsie and Smith with dazzling peroxide headdresses.

The B-side for 'Swimming Horses' includes 'Let Go' on the seven-inch version, with the additional track 'The Humming Wires' on the twelve-inch. 'Let Go', apparently inspired by Stanley Kubrick's 1968 epic *2001: A Space Odyssey*,[866] possesses a nonchalance the listener can discern in 'Swimming Horses', due in part to the seductive, improvisational sounding piano and languorous percussion, with

Budgie's stealthy 'When The Levee Breaks'[867] type rhythm. Siouxsie's relaxed vocal completes the subterranean-sounding lullaby. Another B-side cut reflecting the Banshees' brilliance when they... let go.

'The Humming Wires' is a far more frenetic affair, with the curious yet effective conjoining of ambient keyboard loops with a skiffle-esque drumbeat, 'Interstellar Overdrive'[868] like guitar and Siouxsie's vocal evoking the aural equivalent of a John Wyndham novel.

Relocating from Angel Studios, Both B-side songs were recorded at The Garden Studio,[869] in Shoreditch, London, which had been built by musician John Foxx[870] and studio designer Andy Munro.

Both Robert Smith and Steve Severin had used The Garden for The Glove and were familiar with the setup, enabling them to work with brio. Robert Smith, for his part adds tints and hues to the Banshees' musical palette, facilitating the band's melodramatic and cinematic aesthetic, and creating another layer of depth to their diorama, not least due to his tendency to emotive histrionics.

Regardless of Severin's subsequent ambivalence about Smith's tenure in Siouxsie and The Banshees, Smith provides the much-needed impetus to sustain the band's development.

The Da Gama artwork for the single sleeve marks another step in the band's visual evolution, with a rich and expressive painting, awash with Ken Kiff[871] and Oskar Kokoschka,[872] of a monochromatic male seahorse giving birth to one of its lurid pink offspring.

The Siouxsie and The Banshees logo is rendered as though being viewed underwater and the scene, which wraps around the back cover, is offset by a series of figurative automatic doodles in green against a yellow background. The exuberance of the cover rather negates the not entirely satisfactory nature of the Tim Pope promo video.

'Swimming Horses' crested just inside the Top Thirty, prompting Billy Chainsaw to remark, '...considering the success of its predecessor 'Dear Prudence', I had expected it to enter the charts at a reasonably high position and then climb to one deserving of its originality and quality... having entered the chart in the upper thirties, it climbed few places and not even an appearance on *Top Of The Pops* could prevent it from sinking out of sight in the weeks that followed...'[873]

'Swimming Horses' debuted live on 22 March 1984 at the Espace De Foire in Lille, France.

Meanwhile, Robert Smith had not actually ceased activity with The Cure, with several stand-alone single releases post *Pornography*, 'Let's Go To Bed',[874] 'The Walk',[875] and 'The Love Cats', the latter of which saw The Cure double in number as a four piece,[876] after initially comprising Smith and Lol Tolhurst (this time on keyboards) with Andy Anderson on percussion and Phil Thornalley[877] on double bass.

Smith's wish to dismantle The Cure after the woes of *Pornography* was to prove an act of shrewd reinvention, both artistically and commercially. Very much at the helm of The Cure, by stealthily building the band from the ground upwards again and keeping the band on the radar, Robert Smith, much to the relief of Fiction Records founder Chris Parry, would lead The Cure into its most successful commercial period, not least through the Tim Pope-directed videos for a then new MTV[878] generation.

Lol Tolhurst recollects, 'Although MTV started out in a little place in Hell's Kitchen in New York City, it was growing rapidly and there weren't enough videos of bands to fill the programming slots. I believe in the early days there were only six to eight new videos released each week, so that's pretty much what got played. As soon as we found out, some heavy rotation on MTV, together with our rigorous touring, would start to accelerate the rise of the band'.[879]

Regarding what would become a long and fruitful relationship with Tim Pope, Tolhurst recalls, 'We had a great rapport with Tim. The first video we did with him was 'Let's Go To Bed', which was really quite an exercise in absurdist thought. Parry, Robert and myself had spent quite a long night trying to devise ideas for 'Let's Go To Bed'. We threw all the strange abstract ideas we thought of that night at Tim, and, remarkably, he was able to make sense of it enough to make the first excellent video of The Cure'.[880]

Between June 1983 and April 1984, The Cure prove to be on a commercially successful roll, with 'The Walk' reaching number 12 in the UK Singles Chart, 'The Love Cats' peaking at seven and 'The Caterpillar',[881] released ten days after 'Swimming Horses, peaking at number 14, proving more profitable than the Banshees' single and persisting in the Top Forty for six weeks, in comparison to the Banshees' three-week occupation.

After the fissure caused by the *Pornography* album and tour, Robert Smith was now putting The Cure not only back on track, but future-proofing the band through the trilateral axis of memorable pop songs, MTV-friendly promotional videos and a wave of hit singles. However, there was still the not insignificant detail of Smith's other band.

'Dazzle'

The second and final single to be released from *Hyæna* sees the Banshees in bullish mode. Employing the Chandos Players, the twenty-seven-strong string section from the London Symphony Orchestra,[882] about which Martin McCarrick[883] provides some context: 'I'd been recording a Peel session with Marc Almond and it was all going horribly wrong. Marc was screaming, everyone else was screaming, and then there was this shout from down the corridor. It was Sioux and Budgie. She looked about seven feet tall and with the most piercing blue eyes – a terrifying vision in real life, like a big strutting cockatoo. Shortly afterwards, she sent a tape over to me, Anne (Stephenson) and Gini (Hewes). It was her playing a piano part which she wanted arranged for a big string section. That turned out to be the introduction to 'Dazzle''.[884]

Siouxsie's lyric for the song, embedded within the orchestration, is less than berceuse in nature, Siouxsie commenting, 'The sentiment behind it is of lying in the gutter but still looking up at the stars. I'd seen *Marathon Man*, and I was really intrigued by the guy swallowing diamonds to keep them, and then realising it was like swallowing glass – that they would pass through his system and tear him apart. So that's the line – "Swallowing diamonds, cutting throats"'.[885]

Siouxsie also transposed visual symbolism from the first time she visited Israel, commenting '"The sea of fluid mercury" in the lyric, is the Dead Sea'.[886]

Her recollections of visiting the iconic Salt Lake when Siouxsie and The Banshees played three gigs in Tel Aviv in 1983 are not exactly imbued with the romanticism one might infer, reflecting, 'We did this crazy thing and hired a car to go to the Red Sea – Robert had to be the chauffeur, he was the only one that could drive. But, when we got there, it was like *The Hills Have Eyes* – all barbed wire and tanks and flags with skull and crossbones on them!

In Tel Aviv, most of the audience were on acid – which was available after the show, so we took it too! We ended up on a beach, having a party until sunrise, and of course, we ended up swimming. The sea was very clear but there were all these little fish flying about. It wasn't the drugs, honest!'[887]

As with 'Swimming Horses', the initial impetus for recording the song went back to June 1983, with Siouxsie playing the toy piano with an almost waltz-like lilt. The baton was picked up and committed to a fully-fledged studio recording in March 1984.

The opening lilt of 'Dazzle' is fifty-six seconds of engorged ebbing and flowing string orchestration, not entirely dissimilar to 'Sailing By',[888] forever synonymous with the BBC Radio 4 Shipping Forecast theme by composer Ronald Binge.[889]

Enter Siouxsie's on point vocal, a dreamscape of intoxicating harmonisation with the string section as she opens with 'The stars that shine and the stars that shrink', alluding to the Oscar Wilde quotation from *Lady Windermere's Fan*, "We are all in the gutter, but some of us are looking at the stars".[890]

Then, the jolt heralded by the snap and clatter of Budgie's drumming and the rich, overlayed strings, trademark flanged bass guitar, tambourine and Robert Smith's guitar playing melodious overtones as the song is underpinned by a subterranean rumble. At four minutes and nineteen seconds, the orchestral motif is reprised, along with Siouxsie's opening lyric.

'Dazzle' creates the paradoxical aural sensation of being, at five minutes and thirty-one seconds, one of the longer cuts on *Hyæna* yet strangely abbreviated, in many ways the architecture that defines the album. The twelve-inch single reflects the zeitgeist of club-friendly dance remixes, with various instrumentation and vocals chopped up and spliced, all to Budgie's pulsating backbeat. Severin's bass guitar creates a particularly swampy sound, in delicious contrast to the jabbing interjections of orchestral strings.

In stark contrast to the shambolic video for 'Swimming Horses' and more dynamically MTV friendly, with the video clocking in at three minutes and thirty-seven seconds, nearly a whole two minutes shy of the single version, Tim Pope directs a fast-paced promo which looks to be far more on the Banshees' usual 'cut to the chase' terms.

Beginning with the slow motion of luminous cascading water, akin to an aqueous art installation, the film segues into Siouxsie's redoubtably penetrative Eye of Horus[891] gaze, which has regained much of its poise and conviction after her appearing slightly embarrassed in the video for 'Swimming Horses', as she alternates between a crystal-beaded and bejewelled demigoddess, dressed in black, with her other self in a shimmering white spaghetti-strapped white dress.

Both magnificent outfits are completed with opera gloves. The shots of Siouxsie, one of which sees her eyelids encrusted in jewels to create another pair of eyes with the shape of a star replacing the irises, are interspersed with an array of fleeting shots of the band, minus Smith (fulfilling European tour duties with The Cure).

So it's almost an unwitting symbolism that Severin plays a six-string bass guitar acquired during the time the band recorded 'Slowdive', a gun's revolving bullet chamber, a tambourine, Severin's diamanté jacket, a solitary gemstone sinking into mercury, and long exposure light shots; all conspire to make a credible and compelling video that is shot and edited to maximise all things scintillatingly luxurious, even the crumpled cellophane strewn on the floor of the studio.

Photographer Nicola Tyson[892] recollects the video shoot and her perception of Siouxsie, '…I thought her image encompassed many things – doll, cat, *maitresse*, Amazon, comic-book character, each one an aspect of herself that had been heightened'.[893]

Of Siouxsie's particular and unique iconography, Tyson continues, '…the war paint, the enigmatic glamour, all felt like a perfectly natural extension of herself. She was a subversive character, a new category of woman. And she has such a strong face, and knew exactly how to use it by keeping it expressionless and iconic'.[894]

The myriad photographs Tyson took of Siouxsie, both in preparing for the video and the shoot itself, attests to the care and painstaking attention to detail invested in ensuring she looked flawless.

The B-side for 'Dazzle' is 'I Promise' for the seven-inch format, with the additional track 'Throw Them To The Lions' on the twelve-inch. 'I Promise', which sees Siouxsie embrace a discernible Eastern timbre to her vocal, includes the recording of a music box given to the band by a fan as its ten-second introduction, evocative of 'Mother/O Mein Papa' from the 1979 *Join Hands* album.

Proving yet again, that the Banshees' B-sides are frankly better than most band's A-side offerings', 'I Promise' takes the band into ever circumlocutory terrain.

Just as John Cale's electric viola provides atonal menace on The Velvet Underground's 'Venus In Furs',[895] and the constant of distorted keyboard playing on Suicide's 'Cheree', Robert Smith's organ playing provides an unnerving discord, alongside an array of other electronic keyboards, one of which evokes the sound of a glass harmonica,[896] and a shamisen,[897] while Siouxsie's vocal undulates and everything is underpinned by Budgie's Taiko-esque drumming.

'Throw Them To The Lions' is another, almost frivolous, Banshees' late-night studio session one liner; an opportunity to de-pressurise, have fun, let rip, throw everything at the song and experiment with an array of juxtaposed and opposing yet somehow simpatico instrumentation, including a wall of guitar feedback, named the 'videodrome guitar sound'[898] by guitar tech Murray Mitchell,[899] thrash metal drumming, jauntily upbeat bass guitar, which almost sounds like Severin is playing in a different band, such is its temporary incongruity, until Siouxsie's vocal kicks in and the ensemble reach a Damascene-like synergy.

The lyrics of the song are peppered with biblical allusions, in particular Moses, Jesus and the martyrs of early Christianity. Steve Severin recalls the song being '…written over Easter in response to one of those tiresome Charlton Heston biblical epics… Don't ask me why, but it felt appropriate to add: a) an imagined Wilson Pickett style bass line, b) a back keyboard figure and c) some T. Rex "hey's"… It's a collage thing! Murray Mitchell, our guitar roadie at the time, worked a really grotesque guitar howling sound for me, which was really fun to play'".[900]

At two minutes and forty-nine seconds, 'Throw Them To The Lions' stops dead in its tracks as the baroque strains of a harpsichord kick in, over which Siouxsie's 'Hey Hey Hey' commences on repeat. Joyous!

The Da Gama sleeve design for the single uses Brian Griffin[901] photographs for both front and back covers; two monochromatic images of Siouxsie, pared down to what have become two of her most memorable features: piercing eyes surrounded by dense warpaint triangulations, revealed by a ribbon of light, and a shock of black crimped, backcombed hair. Griffin's cover photograph is a double exposure, which creates more of an unnerving proposition when the original photograph is viewed, as it emphasises the off-kilter Picasso-esque Cubistic[902] effect.

Griffin's original is also a head and shoulders shot. It is entirely conceivable that, used in its initial form, such an image would have proved a little too avant garde and non-commercial for public consumption. The back image for the single is one of Siouxsie with her eyes closed, again revealed by an aperture of light. The only hint of colour on both back and front sleeves takes the form of a shower of delicately illustrated jewels rendered in blue.

The narrative behind the photoshoot and the rapport between artist and sitter remain as enigmatic as the photographs themselves, as 'Siouxsie Sioux never said a word to him (Griffin) throughout their entire session'.[903]

'Dazzle', the Banshees' fifteenth single, was released 25 May 1984 and reached three places shy of the Top Thirty Singles Chart, peaking at number 33. Its first live airing was on 22 March 1984 at the Espace Foire[904] in Lille, France.

'We Hunger'

A bass guitar sound dredged from the bowels of the underworld and polyrhythmic percussion that could signal the ensuing apocalypse, plus the wailing siren of Robert Smith's guitar and Siouxsie's cannibalistic vocal delivery all conspire to make this song a terrifying white-knuckle ride.

Three minutes and twenty-two seconds of what is tantamount to an exercise in creating sonic delirium. Another song that has its origins back in June 1983 at Angel Studios, 'We Hunger' was the first track recorded that Siouxsie had already penned the lyrics for, which allowed Budgie to use the words as a basis around which he could start working on a suitable drum sound.

Essentially, the song was built upwards from Siouxsie's words, and after establishing what was deemed to be the right drum beat for the song, Budgie was then accompanied by Siouxsie on vocals. Steve Severin and Robert Smith worked on their parts, dovetailing them into the song as they progressed.

'It took three or four different 'takes' involving just Siouxsie and Budgie before a backing track was recorded, to which Steve and Robert added their individual contributions and the song had remained virtually untouched since then'.[905]

Of the lyrics, Siouxsie reflects, 'I'd just bought a video machine, that was three years ago, and everybody I knew seemed to be, like, in a video nasty club. I mean, there was a lot of unreality, waking up to video images. A song like 'We Hunger' arose out of that environment. I wasn't really living with any subtlety then'.[906]

The content of Siouxsie's prose suggests an almost unsatisfiable appetite 'We Hunger' was debuted live on 2 September 1983 at the Pandora's Music Box[907] music festival at De Doelen in Rotterdam.

'Take Me Back'

'It was if my parents had projected their dreams onto film emulsion. I was in my mid-thirties and longing for the intimacy, security, and comfort I associated with home. But whose home? Which version of the family'?

Larry Sultan[908]

A song with its origins in Siouxsie's 'Play At Home' story, it can be seen as a companion piece, with Siouxsie relaying '…the story of girl who has grown tired of the city and leaves for the country to return 'home' to visit her mother and sister. When things in the country do not turn out as planned the girl reaches an epiphany that her real 'home' is back in the city and it is there that she longs to return'.[909]

The song possesses a melancholia reflecting the displaced and dispossessed sentiment of the song; being caught in the gap between the sleepy comfort of familiarity and the beckoning allure of excitement offered by city life, something Siouxsie understood all too well.

Essentially, 'Take Me Back' is delivered by Siouxsie as a Gospel song, complete with the most emotive of sweeping harmonies and replete with the enveloping warm glow of Robert Smith's keyboard playing, with Steve Severin's understated bass guitar adding punctuation marks to the song and Budgie's jazz-oriented shuffle, with the addition of the marimba.[910]

The inclusion of bar chimes for the bridge of the song at one minute and forty-one seconds give the song another layer of yearning. The bittersweet liberation of the song parallels the coming-of-age sentiment expressed in The Beatles' 'She's Leaving Home'.

'Belladonna'
'Here is Belladonna, the Lady of the Rocks'[911]

From 'The Waste Land' by T.S. Eliot

The first of the three tracks on *Hyæna* to have lyrics provided by Steve Severin, 'Belladonna' started life during the *A Kiss In The Dreamhouse* sessions, in particular Severin's acquisition of a six-string bass guitar around the time of 'Slowdive'.

Billy 'Chainsaw' Houlston comments, 'During recording he took it away from the studio and, in the self-imposed solitude, wrote all the chords to 'Belladonna'. Then, during a day when Budgie and McGeoch weren't in the studio, Steve began playing the 'Belladonna' tune on a six-string bass, to which Siouxsie sang the lyrics to 'Cocoon'.

It was recorded, but on hearing the 'playback' they both decided that the music wasn't suitable for the lyrics, so it was shelved. Then one evening in the Angel (during the *Hyæna* sessions), Steve showed Robert all the 'Belladonna' chord changes and Robert went into the studio and started playing it. Budgie joined in and Steve wrote a bassline for it, on the spot'.[912]

The seductive, rich imagery of the lyrics are akin to a siren song of beguiling charm, with the 'Atropa Belladonna', part of the Deadly Nightshade family, including toxins atropine,[913] scopolamine[914]and hyoscyamine,[915]which precipitate hallucinations and delirium.

It is also conceivable that Severin would have been familiar with the cult Japanese animated film *Belladonna Of Sadness*,[916] based on the book *Satanism and Witchcraft*[917] by Jules Michelet,[918]which explores witchcraft from a historical and sociological perspective, seeing it as an act of insurrection against the serfdom of feudalism and the Catholic Church.

Certainly, a considerable proportion of Severin's lyrics insinuate something more than deleterious verdure, an example of which is the viscerally clandestine 'In a halo of sharks and a skeleton mask'.[919]

Expert in the art of juxtaposition, the underlying theme of the song is repudiated by its upbeat inflection, recalling *The Wicker Man* 'Maypole Song'[920] and 'The Rattlin' Bog',[921] with its theme of fertility rites and, in the film, pagan ritual, masking Sergeant Neil Howie's visit to Summerisle to investigate the case of a missing child.

The introduction of the song has the ensemble of oboe, played by the classically trained musician Robin Canter, melodious bass guitar, snap and shuffle of Budgie's percussion and Robert Smith's guitar refrain. It is only at one minute and forty-nine seconds that there is a distinctive change, which induces uncertainty in the listener until equilibrium is established and the song sails away into the realms of what is essentially pure instrumentation, except for some enchantress-like overlayed chorally oriented vocals provided by Siouxsie.

'Bring Me The Head Of The Preacher Man'

Opening with all the ostentation and melodrama of a spaghetti western,[922] 'Bring Me The Head Of The Preacher Man' began life as a jamming session while the band were on tour in Japan and Australia.

It was subsequently reinvigorated and was the last track recorded for *Hyæna* in November 1983 at Powerplant Studios, with bass and guitar added and the final mix completed at Roundhouse Studios, also in November, and made complete in March 1984.

The band's original soundcheck extemporising was demoed at Angel Studios in the first instance; back then, synonymous with other embryonic incarnations of *Hyæna* songs, it was eight minutes in duration, and with no discernible lyrics, which proved to be the status quo for quite a while.

However, Steve Severin was convinced that the song had potential. Billy 'Chainsaw' Houlston recalls the track re-emerging at Powerplant, '…but instead of recording a long version and later editing it down to a more compact length, they continually rehearsed it in the studio until they had eventually reduced it to what they thought would end up being the song and then recording it'.[923]

Contrarily, Houlston continues, '…It was one of the only tracks recorded (originally) with all four of them in the studio at the same time, but of that version they only kept the drum track; the bass and guitar were added later (at the Roundhouse), which was one of the last times Robert joined the group in the studio, because of his commitments recording The Cure album *The Top*'.[924]

The song's initial slow burn is reminiscent of the final scene of *For A Few Dollars More*[925], with the distant sound of a harpsichord evoking the 'Carillon's Theme'[926] music-box chimes emitting from El Indio's[927] pocket watch when he shoots the gun out of Mortimer's[928] hand.

When the chimes end, it signals the start of a duel, with Mortimer's gun still lying on the ground. With the chimes about to come to an end, Manco[929] suddenly appears with an identical pocket watch that plays the same tune as Indio's.

To even the odds, Manco points a Henry rifle at El Indio and gives his gun belt and pistol to Mortimer, who then outdraws and guns down Indio.

Lyrically, 'Bring Me The Head Of The Preacher Man' also shares commonality with its semi-analogous namesake 'Bring Me The Head Of Alfred Garcia',[930] which adopts similar adumbrations to Leone's 'Dollars' trilogy regarding revenge and bounty hunting, with its cinematic allusions to vultures picking bones until they are stripped of flesh, moonshine and El Dorado.[931]

Mariachi-style guitar playing and the sound of castanets conspire to create this fast-moving pictorial odyssey, which is predicated on Steve Severin's bumpy bass guitar riff and the echo of Budgie's mellifluous drumming.

Proving once again that the band are masters of illumination and penumbra, at two minutes and forty seconds, the song slows in pace, akin to a lingering camera shot, takes a breath before it speeds up again.

A screeching Middle-Eastern sounding oboe adds an extra deranged piquancy as Siouxsie enacts Severin's lyrics, turning them into an ethereal vocal. Perhaps there is even a nod to Robbie Krieger's[932] opening notes on The Doors' 'People Are Strange'[933] as Robert Smith closes the song. 'Bring Me The Head Of The Preacher Man' was debuted live on the same night as 'Swimming Horses', at the Espace De Foire, Lille, France on 22 March 1984.

'Running Town'

Another Banshees' song with Angel Studios provenance in June 1983, 'Running Town' was almost shelved due to Severin's chagrin about the initial axis of jamming between bass and drums, with Budgie playing a military-style marching drumbeat.

Mike Hedges saw potential in Severin's bass line and set about some suggested modifications, as Billy 'Chainsaw' Houlston reflects, 'For ages it was referred to as 'Dead and Barryed', because of a recording they did of it with a James Bond-type intro (hence the reference to John Barry... he being the composer of the Bond theme... in the title) but this was changed'.[934]

A backing track ensued, with Robert Smith following Severin's bass line on the piano, all the while elucidating what the piano and guitar parts would be. After Siouxsie's lyrics were added, a myriad rehearsals ensued to modify and refine what would be the song proper. Siouxsie's prose alludes to her loathing of the Australian city of Sydney, although, Siouxsie suggests, her words are caustic rather than an expression of outright abhorrence,

'...Everyone is in a hurry and walks around grinding their teeth. Instead of making an 'I hate Australia' statement I tried to make it more general so that it can be applied by anyone to their hometown in the same way that when reading a book you can often apply it to your own situation. It's important to be allowed to use your imagination. In that respect it's a pity that reading books is not a more popular pastime'.[935]

Siouxsie is as acutely aware of her own 'Martian'-like incongruity in a world professedly packed to capacity with beige conservatism.

With an expedient, tight drumbeat, demonstrating both Budgie's versatility and restrained percussive economy, an almost ragtime-esque piano, Severin's pugnacious bass, Robert Smith's vivid multi-tracked guitar playing, attacking like a swarm of killer bees, and Siouxsie's acerbic alliteration, the song takes full flight, swaying between the realms of the knockabout and the ambush, as a dog barks in the background.

Dead on two minutes and twenty-four seconds, the cavalcade disperses and the Banshees demonstrate their quietude with Budgie's echoing 'Bela Lugosi's Dead'[936] -like tapping on the snare drum rim and Siouxsie's sweltering, reverb-saturated vocal as the song shifts gear towards the frenzied denouement. 'Running Town' was first played live at the Royal Albert Hall on 30 September 1983.[937]

'Pointing Bone'

The shamanistic introduction, a slow, languorous build of the song with the lofty, echoing clatter of Budgie's snare (syn) drum and whiff of Robert Smith's wha-wha guitar, Severin's phased bass, under which lies the discernible sturm and drang of a Leslie speaker and Siouxsie's delirious 'Pointing Bone' incantation prefaces another array of interwoven textures, with an emotively poetic lyric penned by Steve Severin, brimming with imagery and metaphor.

As 'Pointing Bone' picks up the pace, and Robert Smith goes full Jimi-Hendrix, Budgie furnishes the song with the pneumatic drumbeat. At two minutes and twenty-two seconds, the light and dark motif of several songs on *Hyæna* kicks in and the song veritably stalls, only to rush on, reaching maximum celerity during the final ten seconds, as the embers of Siouxsie's vocal linger and Budgie's paradiddle is encroached on by Severin's concise bass, as Robert Smith goes into an apogee of wha-wha furore.

Steve Severin's lyric is an opulent array of adjective and metaphor, with the pervasive spectacle of ritual sacrifice and ancient mythology, as all the forces of nature gather to conspire with humankind in grisly benefaction.

A fevered chimera of flayed animal skin, flambeaus, wizards, jackals, a weeping moon and perspiring sun complete this epic, bloodthirsty odyssey. Severin's allusions are endemically Aboriginal in source, commenting, '...the pointing of the bone... was believed to cause death.

People who had been 'pointed' often died, not as a result of the magic itself, but because of their belief that they would die i.e., death through superstition or imagination'.[938] The specific term for what Severin describes is Kurdaitcha[939] or Kurdaitcha man, a kind of shaman among the Arrernte[940] people, an Aboriginal group in Central Australia in the ritual of bone-pointing.[941] 'Pointing Bone' was first played live on 26 March 1984 at the Palais d'Hiver, Lyon, France.

'Blow The House Down'
'Then I'll huff and I'll puff and I'll blow your house down'.[942]

From *The Three Little Pigs*

Never loth to pull out all the stops for a tumultuous finale, clocking in at seven minutes, 'Blow The House Down' is the Banshees' one-second-shy-of-seven-minute, sonic annihilation in widescreen.

Siouxsie's lyrical prologue lets the listener know in no uncertain terms the score that needs to be settled, that this is the consummate shock wave and no amount of caterpillar-like weaving, crawling or seeking subterranean refuge can allow them to avoid the ensuing tempest.

Perhaps fanciful in hypothesis, the lyrics suggest allusions to a plethora of authoritarian doctrine, of which Siouxsie had never been diffident in expressing an opinion. Dervishes, pillars of salt, crumbling castles and wicker men all provoke an angry outburst.

And, as the song progresses, the habitat, whether secular or non-secular, will also be set ablaze in one absolute inferno. One line in the song' 'Bishops Falling From The Windows', 'takes its inspiration from the Luis Bunuel film *L'Age d'Or*.[943] A sequel of sorts to *Un Chien Andalou*, *L'Âge d'Or* (The Golden Age) is the tale of two lovers who, despite their failure to marry, find themselves in the predicament of being jolted together and apart.

Awash with surrealistic symbolism and themes of libertarianism, and a storyline that begins with several minutes' examination of the lives of scorpions, the film shifts to four bishops in full ceremonial apparel on a craggy outcrop, latterly reprised as skeletons as a large gathering of local dignitaries pay their respects, only to be interrupted by the lovers, amorously vocal, writhing around in the mud. A bedraggled vagabond makes his way back to his hovel to join his other undernourished and forlorn brethren. A hubristic matriarch is slapped; a father shoots his son.

Thematically, *L'Age d'Or* follows similar themes to *Un Chien Andalou*, including tangled relationships, society's suppression of sexuality, the inevitability of physical violence and attacks on the clergy.

When the film premiered in 1930, it was met with a mixture of humour, befuddlement and politeness. However, it subsequently caused scandal and was censored when it was screened at Studio 28[944] in Montmartre, where ink was thrown at the screen, patrons were attacked and the display of work by Surrealist artists Man Ray, Salvador Dali and Joan Miro[945] was defaced by right-wing extremists.

The outrage shown during the event spread as far as the Italian embassy, 'which notified the French Foreign Minister of its dissatisfaction with the film's presentation. Religious leaders, the media and politicians fervently protested against *L'Âge d'Or*.[946]

Subsequently, 'Showing the film was banned in December 1930 by the Paris Prefect of Police. Despite being defended by the Surrealists, notably by the famous author André Breton, it would remain censored for fifty-one years, until 1981, when its original negative was restored by the Pompidou Centre'.[947]

The urgency of the song, after Siouxsie's initial siren call, to the accompaniment of howling wind, hybridises the myriad Middle Eastern and Far Eastern influences discerned throughout the album.

It uses screeching Chandos Players' strings, Robin Canter's

caterwauling oboe, Robert Smith's lightning-fast guitar and sitar playing, and the ominous cavernous accent of Steve Severin's bass, all on the verge of rupture if not cemented by Budgie's Kodo-esque percussion, punctuated with clangorous cymbals and snare drum.

Billy 'Chainsaw' Houlston remembers the jamboree of instruments in 'Blow The House Down', the result of foraging in Angel Studios in June 1983, 'Their spree unearthed an Hawaiian steel guitar, a Chinese fiddle, an assortment of peculiar percussive pieces and the most prized find, an ancient sitar with all its strings missing. They bought replacement strings, returned to the studio and restrung it'.[948]

Houlston elaborates 'Budgie began playing along on drums, both of them (Budgie and Smith) repeating the same thing for about ten minutes and it was all recorded. Then two or three weeks later, Robert translated the recorded sitar piece for piano, by which time Siouxsie had written some lyrics and she, Robert and Budgie recorded a backing track (with Siouxsie doing a guide vocal) which ran too long, so it was edited until they were all satisfied with it'.[949]

If this were the last song the Banshees ever wrote and performed, they'd have exited with a bang, rather than a whimper. 'Blow The House Down' was played live for the first time at the Royal Albert Hall on 1 October 1983.

The Da Gama artwork for the album sees another change in stylistic direction, with the image a medley of folk-art-oriented iconography, with overtones of Cubism and a not dissimilar visual appearance to the interlocking primordial forms in Jackson Pollock's 1938–40 painting 'Naked Man With Knife'.[950]

Surrounding the writhing, pattern-laden multicoloured forms, all teeth and claws, is a Jean Dubuffet[951] -like repeat motif. The back cover of the album employs the same theme, albeit more discernibly human than mammal in nature. All song titles are written at the top. The inner sleeve has four single monochromatic shots of every band member through a patternistic out-of-focus gauze on one side and the song titles and lyrics on the other.

Both band name and *Hyæna* title, as with all written elements of the design, are rendered with an expressionistic, loose, painterly technique. Siouxsie comments, 'The artwork was put together by this strange Indian woman who was like a female shaman. She was supposed to be on a higher spiritual plane, though I thought she looked like a bag lady. When I met her for the first time, she looked at me strangely and started waving her fingers in the air... she was probably checking out my aura'.[952]

There is no shortage of interest in the band throughout 1984 from weekly and monthly periodicals, with Siouxsie the steadfast cover star for the most part. However, the front-of-house magnetism depended on to maximise profitability is beginning to look more like a Hollywood backlot façade, as column inches focus on the Banshees' well-trodden backstory, a Siouxsie pull-out poster, or finding out whether or not Robert Smith is the band's whipping boy, or what the band thought of the current state of pop music.

Contextually, there had been a breakthrough regarding the Channel 4 music television programme *The Tube*,[953] which enabled Siouxsie and The Banshees to play live and showcase three songs from *Hyæna* during the 10 February 1984 broadcast: 'Running Town', 'Bring Me The Head Of The Preacher Man' and 'Blow the House Down'.

Although an opportunity to 'warm up' before the band's thirty-nine-date UK, European and North American 'Hyæna' tour, which began on 22 March 1984, Steve Severin, never a shrinking violet when expressing an opinion, recounts, 'The format for *The Tube* is very different from *Top Of The Pops*, for a start virtually every band that goes on there uses backing tapes.

We were up there and I just thought it was hilarious. You had Kool & The Gang who are just a bunch of session musicians and it was going to sound okay whatever they did. You had the Thompson Twins who were basically just miming and you had us with a really bad sound. We were basically stitched up but I thought it looked pretty exciting. At least it showed us sweating a bit'.[954]

It is perhaps unsurprising that, for the most part, actual press coverage for *Hyæna* on its release was not all unmitigated praise.

Creem magazine [955] offered the following scrutiny, 'We Hunger''s stark African drums and anti-sexual heebie-jeebies are lightened considerably by Siouxsie's tongue-in-cheek reading, while Cure guitarist Robert Smith fans the flames with his call-and-response jangle. 'Swimming Horses' evokes, of all people, Miss Linda Ronstadt, in her pre-prom-dress Stone Poneys California psychedelic pop period, and the song's highly graphic, darkly comic version of sexual reproduction reminds me of Woody Allen playing the hapless, doomed sperm in his *Everything You Always Wanted To Know About Sex... But Were Afraid To Ask* – which would make a marvellous title for a Banshees concept album, by the way. There›s still more where those came from, too, including a lovely, loony, drug-crazed version of the Beatles› 'Dear Prudence' (which may be even better than the group's old cover of 'Helter Skelter'), and Siouxsie dishing it out to Grace Slick on the LSD raver, 'Bring Me The Head Of The Preacher Man'.[956]

The review ends with the trenchant, slightly weary observation that *Hyæna* was somehow the punchline to a joke that started seven years ago when the band played The 100 Club.

The *NME* ventures, "Dazzle' opens this wild rumpus so well you'll wish for it to go on all night, or at least as long as the twelve-inch version, which has Sioux queening it rather splendidly, marshalling massive blocks of orchestral noise and sending them to do battle with marvellous queenly irresponsibility'.[957]

However, this effusive rhetoric is rather meagre regarding the remaining nine songs, observing, '…Not even the giddy chain of exotic noise and naughty phrase, nor the intrusion of phantom organ and the guitars' spidery sideways scuttles, nor the rapidly expanding majesty of Sioux's voice, can disguise the frailty of *Hyæna's* paper video palace'.[958]

Hyæna spent one week in the Top Twenty UK Official Albums Chart and six weeks in the Top One Hundred.

The band themselves weren't completely enamoured of *Hyæna*, Steve Severin reflecting, 'I associate that time with things being a real struggle. The album was really difficult to make and it got more and more frustrating. We didn't have enough new ideas, and because 'Dear Prudence' had been such a hit, we were under all this pressure to follow it up. When it finally came out, it was a relief to see the back of it'.[959]

Severin's dissatisfaction alludes, for the most part, to the band's near collapse when Robert Smith's double life started to catch up with him, with the seeds of doubt sown in late 1983, Smith revealing to *International Musician and Recording World* magazine,[960] "'A lot of the time I'm still trying to play John McGeoch's guitar parts and failing… If I went on like this for another few months… um… I'd be the next one to have a breakdown. No, it's fine at the moment. It's a balancing act, and as long as I don't fall over, it'll be alright…'"[961]

Smith reflects on the Banshees' way of working in the studio compared to The Cure's, as well as underlying and impending tensions, especially in relation to the timeframe for both *Hyæna* and *The Top* albums. "'We'd started *Hyæna* about ten or eleven months before and, in that time, The Cure had done 'The Walk', 'The Love Cats', released 'Japanese Whispers', gone to America and recorded most of *The Top*. The Banshees seemed to be getting slower and slower and, although they often blamed me for not being there, I knew it wasn't all my fault'".[962]

Smith, increasingly feeling like a hired hand, would be in the studio recording a guitar part for a Banshees' song on his own, during the fleeting moments when he wasn't with The Cure, feeling increasingly adrift from the rest of the band, commenting on the *Hyæna* sessions, "'It dragged on and on… recorded in spare moments. At the beginning, everyone had three or four ideas for songs, but they were exhausted pretty quickly so I found myself doing guitar parts for a song where I didn't know the title or the lyrics and Sioux didn't like it anyway, saying that it wouldn't go with the words she couldn't give me because they weren't finished yet!'"[963]

One of the reasons why Smith wanted to complete *Hyæna* was not wanting to lose his friendship with Steve Severin; other than that, Smith had become disillusioned with *Hyæna*, venturing, '…I thought the album would be a hybrid of *The Scream* and *A Kiss In The Dreamhouse*, I wanted it to be really hard but, obviously, the others didn't see it the same way. I didn't mind – I'd lost interest in it really; it had become a really grinding process and was beginning to wear me down. The funny thing is, I was only in the Banshees to get away from all that – I thought it was going to be really vibrant'.[964]

There was also the fact of Smith leading the charge for The Cure and what he perceived as the Banshees' dismissal of this progressively significant part of his musical career. The 'Hyæna' tour began, and, no sooner had Smith played seven European dates with the Banshees, in France and Italy, he was out on the road with The Cure, embarking on a seventy-date world tour.

The interceding time between the last Banshees date on 31 March 1984 and picking up The Cure baton on 6 April 1984 led Smith to within a hair's breadth of a complete physiological and psychological meltdown, tantamount to what he had virtually, albeit semi-laconically, prophesied back in 1983. Smith takes up the story, when on 26 May 1984,[965] less than two weeks before the Banshees would re-embark on the 'Hyæna' tour on 8 June, he called Steve Severin from Hamburg to break the news, 'I couldn't sleep. I was so bad that each night in the hotel, I'd be sitting there in bed, really wild-eyed and shaking and sweating and I thought 'it's finished – I mustn't seriously damage my health just for the sake of not letting the Banshees down'.[966]

Having called multiple times, only to find Severin unavailable, Smith left a long and rambling answerphone message, the essence of which was that Smith would honour the thirteen UK dates with the Banshees, at a push, but he could not commit to the American leg of their tour.

On hearing the message, Severin phoned Smith the next morning. Severin's initial reaction was incredulity. However, he could tell that Smith was in a bad way and, Smith says, '…he was really concerned. He asked me to come back to England to see them (the Banshees) and I agreed. So The Cure cancelled two gigs and I flew over – but I was really cursing them because it was the worst flight I'd ever had; the plane got hit by lightning, all the lights went out and I was thinking 'The bastards! It's all their fault! I'm gonna plummet from the sky!'. That was the last straw'.[967]

However, it wasn't the Banshees that Smith ran to immediately. It was his doctor, who, on seeing Smith's crumbling physical and mental state, Smith recalls, '…insisted I check into a health farm immediately or he wouldn't be answerable for the consequences'.[968]

Smith railed against the advice, but it did prove, in perhaps no uncertain terms where his loyalties and priorities lay – with The Cure. Smith's mind made up, his doctor wrote him a doctor's note which was then sent to the Banshees, explaining that Smith needed a period of rest and quiet.

Smith recalls Siouxsie's incandescence, "'How come you can do The Cure tour but not the Banshees tour?' but I think Severin understood and anyway, by then my mind was made up. After all, I'd given them two weeks' notice, which was longer than any guitarist had given them before!"'[969]

Siouxsie takes up the story, recollecting, 'I wasn't sad to see him go but his timing was atrocious. We'd (Siouxsie and Budgie) got back from Bali on my birthday having struggled to finish *Hyæna*, and Budgie was greeted by all these angry "Hope you fucking enjoyed yourselves!" messages from Severin on his answerphone. It was ten days before our biggest show, which was the Brixton Academy and opened a thirteen-date British tour'.[970]

Siouxsie, retrospectively, makes the following less-than-laudatory observations regarding Smith's departure, seeing his departure a more underhand ruse, 'I never trusted Robert. I always thought he had another agenda, that he was using the situation. Look at the facts. In October, 'Dear Prudence' made it to No. 3, thanks in part to The Creatures keeping the band's profile high. The Cure's first hit, 'The Love Cats', came out just as 'Dear Prudence' was peaking. When he left, it felt a bit like "Thanks for the ride, I'm off". All that bollocks about a sick note. That wounded sparrow act doesn't wash with me'.[971]

Siouxsie is also a little bemused about Severin's verbal attack on her and Budgie and that he did not have any inkling of Smith's intentions, remarking Severin '...was with Smith all the time. Why didn't he see it was happening?'[972]

In a live MTV interview during the band's two-gig stint in New York on 13 and 14 July, when the question is asked about why Smith departed from the band, Siouxsie's less-is-more riposte was, 'He was a guitarist'.[973]

John Valentine Carruthers

Born in Wortley, in the West Riding of Yorkshire, Carruthers' had been the guitarist in Clock DVA, after the release of the band's second album *Thirst*,[974] initially recording the *Passions Still Aflame*[975] EP, which was released 26 May 1982.

Although the Banshees' predicament necessitated celerity in finding another guitarist so they could fulfil their touring commitments, Carruthers proved to be a good fit. A versatile player, his work also evokes the urgency and bite of John McGeoch's playing, especially on Clock DVA songs 'Beautiful Losers',[976] 'Resistance'[977] and 'The Secret Life Of The Big Black Suit'[978] from the *Advantage* album.[979]

Among Carruthers' guitars was also the Yamaha SG1000, favoured by McGeoch. Clock DVA also, to some extent, reflected the 1980s zeitgeist of bands adopting a range of traditional instrumentation, melded with synthesizers, electronic innovation and tape loops, in the mould of Cabaret Voltaire. This was unsurprising as Clock DVA founder member Adi Newton[980] had previously worked with members of Cabaret Voltaire in a collective called The Studs,[981] as well as musicians Martyn Ware[982] and Ian Craig Marsh[983] in The Future.[984]

The guitarist's tenure in Clock DVA came to a halt when he walked out of a gig the band were playing at Le Bains Douches in Paris[985] on 18 October 1983 '…where an altercation occurred which resulted in …Carruthers allegedly stamping on Adi's favourite trumpet…'[986]

Carruthers, through a recommendation from Polydor, as Clock DVA were Banshees' label mates and were familiar with his work, got the gig. A ticking clock and another absent guitarist meant the Banshees, by now pretty much Houdini-like[987] in escaping potential tour disaster, were auditioning another guitarist. Budgie recalls, 'When we were auditioning guitarists in a rehearsal room in Camden, my head was still infused with Bali. I was still looking for coconuts and wearing sandals in the rainy North London streets. I was unfazed by the fact Robert wasn't there. We'd been there before'.[988]

Siouxsie takes a similarly pragmatic view of the band's predicament, reflecting, '…he was the best of the bunch we had to choose from …he was very blokey and it was the first time we'd had anyone like that in the band'.[989]

Although, if Carruthers were to join the Banshees gang, at least for the remainder of the 1984 tour, Siouxsie would need to take the guitarist to task about his casual 'sweatpants with stains'[990] attire, commenting, 'Even the roadies dressed better than that'.[991]

More pressingly, Carruthers would need to learn the Banshees' back catalogue in preparation for the two Brixton Academy gigs. It transpired that he couldn't have been a better or more timely fit. A snapshot of the Banshees playing 'Israel' on the *Angel Casas* show,[992] live at Barcelona's Studio 54, is indicative of Carruthers' studied aptitude, pulling off the short delay guitar part, tactically reinterpreted live by Robert Smith, with virtuosity supported by the Yamaha SG.

Similarly, from the same broadcast, 'Cascade' is played with adroitness and, most importantly, the band sounds great. Among the nineteen songs spanning *The Scream, Kaleidoscope, Juju, A Kiss In The Dreamhouse* and *Hyæna*, a new song is debuted at Studio 54, 'Cannons', whetting the audience's appetite for a rejuvenated Siouxsie and The Banshees.

The impetus for the song, Siouxsie recalls, was watching '…a documentary about this period of freak weather in the twenties, when it was either incredibly hot or ridiculously cold. T.S. Eliot had written a poem about it… the locals would fire a cannon into this oppressive sky each night in the hope of bursting a rain cloud'.[993]

The writing of new material suggested that Robert Smith's departure may have meant the band was momentarily down, but it was, come hell or high water, certainly far from out.

The King's Head

Perhaps no story of any band is incomplete without at least an allusion to some extracurricular activities. In the Banshees' case, The King's Head,[994] located at 49 Chiswell Street, between London's Barbican and Moorgate, provided what became the Banshees' unofficial HQ for a some substance-oriented diversions.

Conveniently placed a stone's throw away from manager Dave Wood's office on nearby Aldersgate Street, it was a place where the Banshees, and their coterie of close friends, could seek sanctuary from the public gaze and the scrutiny of the tabloid press, without the worry of appearing '…as this fucked up band… it would have been damaging to their image.

Severin occasionally popped up in the gossip columns, with this running joke about him being a Gary Numan lookalike, but that was about it'.[995]

The landlord at the time, Rick, became a huge Siouxsie and The Banshees' fan, to such an extent that the pub jukebox was brimming with Banshees' vinyl. Lock-ins were a common occurrence, with the notional idea of popping in for a quick drink, even with the best intentions, anathema.

As Severin recalls, 'We'd nip in for a swift half after sorting out some artwork or something, and the next thing we knew it would be 5:00am. As soon as we'd had a few drinks, Rick would be straight off to get some rifles out of his cabinet and start skulking around the pub "looking for intruders" …it was a strange period in our lives'.

The King's Head sessions would also provide a welcome antidote to the slow process of writing the band's next album, 'Tinderbox'.[996]

The capstone of the partying, at least for Rick, happened not at The King's Head, but at Siouxsie's basement flat, when Siouxsie introduced Rick to LSD. Among both Siouxsie and Rick's hallucinogenic haze was the knock on the door by a priest living upstairs, complaining about the bedlam below. Siouxsie's response, telling the priest, apparently accompanied by Sisters, to 'piss off',[997] proved the catalyst for her exasperated neighbours to knock again, this time with the threat of calling the police.

Siouxsie's 'by all means, be my guest' demeanour proved at odds with Rick's, as, Siouxsie recounts, 'He had vast amounts of drugs on him and, because the police were on their way, decided we had to take them all – coke, acid, dope, everything. By the time they arrived, I'd turned the music down, and they went away. But, because of all the drugs we'd taken, things got a bit weird'.[998]

In essence, the upshot of the strangeness Siouxsie refers to was Rick's paranoia that '…someone was trying to break in… insisting we should all get knives'.[999]

After Siouxsie's party, Rick's drug-induced escapade and the realisation that nocturnal shenanigans at The King's Head had led to a little more than was bargained for, especially regarding Rick's subsequent erratic behaviour, imagining himself part vigilante and part Banshees' 'personal security',[1000] the Banshees sought to put some distance between them and The King's Head proprietor.

The Thorn EP

If not exactly an act of ground-breaking maturation, what might be construed as 'wheeling out' material from the band's back catalogue was perhaps cathartic for the Banshees, or even a test of their songs' enduring substance as they revisited several McKay/Morris and McGeoch era compositions: 'Overground', 'Voices', 'Placebo Effect'[1001] and 'Red Over White', carefully chosen, orchestrally refashioned and reimagined with greater preponderance.

The songs were always cinematically psychodramatic in sonority. However, this time they are more grandiosely panoramic. Recorded '...in the middle of Bavaria'[1002] in Germany, the band thought it would be a good way to initiate Carruthers into the Banshees' fold.

It also gave Siouxsie an opportunity to use a string section again, commenting, 'I've always loved the discordant tension that you often get with violins and orchestras'.[1003]

Siouxsie also thought the reconceptualised songs would place greater emphasis on the band's synergy, rather than the scrutiny of Carruthers' guitar playing. The Chandos Players were re-engaged to provide orchestration, with Martin McCarrick and Bill McGee[1004] arranging and Gini Hewes and Anne Stephenson both scoring and playing.

'Overground'

Possessing all the angst and tension of the original 1978 *The Scream* recording, it is something of a thumbnail sketch in comparison to the vast, painterly canvas served up on *The Thorn* EP version.

The initial repose of the song's beginning: politely plucked strings, classical guitar and bass, and Siouxsie's initial vocal, discernibly several octaves lower than the original, at one minute and sixteen seconds, explodes, united by Budgie's drumming, into a fully blown symphonious saga. Two minutes and twenty-two seconds debuts the intuitive dexterity of Carruthers' guitar playing, as it alternates between pianissimo and fortissimo, acoustic and electric.

'Voices'

Originally the B-side of the band's first single 'Hong Kong Garden' and awash with all of the tension worthy of a Bernard Hermann film score, compounded by Siouxsie sounding like a demonically possessed child giving their first public singing recital, *The Thorn* EP recording of 'Voices' loses nothing of the original, with the first fifty seconds of complete pandemonium slowing to a halt as the flanged, metallic timbre of Carruthers' guitar kicks in.

With the strident disharmony of strings creating a sense of foreboding malaise, coupled with the echoing bang and clatter of Budgie's drumming, and Siouxsie's reverse reverb vocal as the 'Voices' motif chimes in, the listener is trapped in a chimaeric no man's land; definitely not a place for the faint hearted.

'Placebo Effect'

Join Hands, the Banshees' second studio album, released in 1979, wasn't shown a great deal of love by the band, not least because it marks the time when, on the very day of its release, John McKay and Kenny Morris ran away.

Songs from the album make sporadic live appearances in the band's live set during the 1980s, including 'Icon', 'Regal Zone', one outing for 'Mother/Oh Mein Papa' and 'Placebo Effect'.

If not quite recreating John McKay's stannic-sounding guitar on the original 'Join Hands' version using an MXR Flanger pedal, the EP incarnation, abundant again with orchestral strings, sees Siouxsie's initial chanteuse vocal, infused with her bilious lyrical attack on various strains of doctrinal snake-oil salesmen, prologue this blistering song, with Budgie channelling the metaphorical ghost of Kenny Morris.

'Red Over White'

Originally the B-side of the single release 'Israel', 'Red Over White' lends itself perfectly to this multilayered string arrangement.

Clocking in at nearly two minutes longer than the initial version, this newly painted 'Red Over White' incarnation ups the ante in terms of drama, with Carruthers' chorus/delay effect evocative of Geordie Walker's[1005] playing with Killing Joke.[1006]

The new version comes with supplementary menace, due in no small part to the under stream of strings, which add a furtive, lingering presence. As in 'The Juniper Tree', Siouxsie's assonant rumble conveys rivulets of haemoglobin dripping, not from a cut finger, but from sleigh bells into the snow.

The Da Gama design is a striking close-up of a rose, infused with red, white and pink hues, becoming enveloped by a brier-like motif, which covers the back of the EP, with the blue and pink barbs covering most of the back cover, through which what resembles a crumpled gold pelisse appears. The Banshees' logo has gone through another transformation, with an abundance of Arabesque flourishes, like the unfurling of a fern.

In common with the Banshees' 1979 'Mittageisen' release, *The Thorn* EP peaked at number 47 in the UK Official Singles Chart: if nothing else, a barometer of the band's ebb and flow of commercial fortune.

However, the Banshees' show per se endured, although there were times when the wheels, literally, detach from the bus. Siouxsie explains of the UK leg of the 1984 tour, 'We had a lovely driver called Tuna, who we'd met in Scandinavia… And one time he saved our lives. We were driving along a motorway when the axle of our van broke… if the road hadn't been empty we would definitely have hit something. I was behind Tuna and could see the muscles in his arms and neck bulging as he wrestled with the steering wheel…'[1007]

A further anecdote, which could probably only come straight from the pages of the Banshees' vivid playbook, is, after forestalling a near-death experience, the band found themselves within a stone's throw of Brookland's motor-racing circuit and aerodrome[1008] near Weybridge in Surrey, where they were given a tour of a breaker's yard by one of the workers there and almost gleefully told about the number of fatalities caused through car accidents.[1009]

Siouxsie elaborates, '…he'd point out various cars, saying things like, "Three died in that one". He seemed to be getting an unnatural amount of job satisfaction. In fact, all the people who worked there seemed disappointed that no one had been injured in our crash'.[1010]

The months after the band's final tour date at the Pavilion Baltard[1011] in Nogent Sur Marne in France on 28 November 1984 sees the Banshees, if not exactly on the brink of absolute implosion, then very near it. A pretty exhaustive inventory of everything colluding to capsize the band into the realms of oblivion? Step this way…

'That whole time was a period of growing up', recalled Siouxsie. 'But it was a torture test. It was as if we could only become stronger by going through some sort of pain or by mentally surviving extreme circumstances'.[1012]

In no particular order, there is the fracas with Marc Almond's manager Stevo,[1013] resulting in Tim Collins head-butting him after an animated discussion about a plexiglass grand piano, when Almond was the Banshees' special guest for one of the Hammersmith Odeon gigs – although this is somewhat speculative as Almond was gigging in Newcastle and Scotland on 24, 25 and 26 October when the Banshees played the same three dates in London.

However, the actual head-butting of Stevo can't be entirely discredited, having '…been stabbed and repeatedly headbutted; he (Stevo) terrorised record labels, even threatening to shoot Seymour Stein of Sire Records in the kneecaps; he was banned from the Sony building after trying to strangle someone from the legal department; and he instructed an office intern to plant a fake bomb under a music executive's car'.[1014]

The Banshees decided on a whim to try out Bob Ezrin[1015] as a producer, instigated by Geffen. He asked the band whom they wanted to produce their next album, as he had produced Lou Reed's *Berlin* album,[1016] as well as working with Alice Cooper.

The bottom line is that the Banshees needed a producer that they could trust to do their bidding while they fulfilled their touring commitments; that fifth member of the band whom they could leave in the control room to get everything just so.

It is unsurprising that the Banshees had co-produced all their albums to date, retaining autonomy. It was an almost self-fulfilling prophecy as far as Ezrin's try-out was concerned; he wanted a little too much autonomy for the Banshees' liking and, after some pre-production, he was promptly shown the (revolving) door.

An indication of Siouxsie's dislike for Ezrin's modus operandi as a producer, as well as her less-than-favourable opinion about their dysfunctional encounter, is encapsulated in the blunt observation, '... we can't stand you, there is no way that you're even going to have an opinion'.[1017]

Producer and engineer Hugh Jones[1018] was then called in, a suggestion of John Valentine Carruthers, whom he had worked with on the Clock DVA *Advantage* album. Jones had also worked with Echo And The Bunnymen, Adam And The Ants,[1019] Simple Minds and The Damned.[1020]

Hugh introduced the band to a more structured way of working, involving, Budgie recalls, '...different keys, chord structures and tempos... chords would be scribbled up on a blackboard'.[1021]

Demos of new material were worked on during 13 and 14 April 1984 at Matrix Studios, London,[1022] and, on 15 April, 12 days of pre-production took place at The NOMIS Complex[1023] with Jones at the production helm.

Severin, meanwhile, with a touch of Phil Spector-like posturing, was instructing Carruthers in the polished sound the band wanted for the subsequent album, which would involve listening to the guitar playing on records by Burt Bacharach[1024] and the Walker Brothers.[1025]

This didactic instruction, the first time the Banshees had implemented such a method, was predicated on the legacy and weightiness of being 'the Banshees' guitarist' and mitigated any potential existential crisis about whether the band wanted Carruthers to sound more like John McKay, John McGeoch or Robert Smith. In essence, Carruthers would be told what to play and add his own tweaks and inflections on top of what was already there.

On paper, one would expect the Banshees' choice of recording studio for the album, Hansa Tonstudio[1026] in Berlin, located near Potsdamer Platz,[1027] was going to be the catalyst for some really inspired sessions for the band; it was to prove the opposite.

Carruthers' live rehearsals with the band had been effervescent, but, as soon as the band entered Hansa, the disposition of his playing changed, and the crackling 'tinder' he was providing during the practice sessions became extinguished as soon as the 'Recording In Progress' light went on, prompting Budgie to recollect, 'When we were playing the material live in a room it was great but, unfortunately, when we got to Berlin (4 May) we didn't record them like that'.[1028]

One of the reasons for the drying of the liquidity in Carruthers' playing (although this isn't something the listener would necessarily discern) is the weight of expectation inherent in a space where two of the most iconic and revered albums of all time were recorded, David Bowie's *Low* and *Heroes*, as well as Iggy Pop's *The Idiot*.[1029]

Regarding anticipation, Steve Severin had perhaps placed in Carruthers' mind an altogether more glittering affair regarding Hansa, only to have his preconceptions dashed by a space, which he recalls, perhaps unfairly as resembling a 'scout hut'.[1030]

It might be the case that Severin is referring to a different studio from the neoclassical Meistersaal studio, a former chamber music concert hall built in 1910 with a polished floor and elaborately coffered ceiling, overlooking the Berlin Wall[1031] towards Soviet-occupied East Berlin, which became Studio Two in 1975.

What Severin encountered as dreary, proved different for David Bowie in 1977, the '...desolate wasteland setting sparked a creative resurgence in Bowie, who had moved to Germany to cope with a cocaine addiction and a collapsing marriage. 'It was literally like being reborn, he admitted later'.[1032]

It wasn't only the setting that was proving a little problematic, as equipment was glitchy. Fortunately, Hugh Jones had the technical wherewithal to fix studio equipment when it malfunctioned.

Away from Hansa, Budgie and Siouxsie had a spat in Berlin that resulted in Budgie's inebriation and Siouxie kicking in a glass door, the upshot of which saw Budgie blacked out and collapsed in a gutter and Siouxsie's foot resembling something from the gore-spattered trashy horror movies she loved.

The episode also dredged up the scarring that hadn't healed from Siouxsie's assault as a child, evoking flashbacks and prompting Siouxsie to confront her mother when the band return to the UK from

Berlin, about why there hadn't been more vociferous condemnation of her attacker.

Siouxsie was unable to elicit any response from her mother. Memories and the mental trauma of the episode were exacerbated by Siouxsie's physical wound, reminding her of being hospitalised as a teenager with ulcerative colitis.

Conversely, although unsurprisingly in the Banshees' hall of mirrors universe, Siouxsie was invited to sit among other high-profile women, luminaries from the world of sport and commerce, for Woman Of The Year at the Savoy Hotel, '…in the presence of the Dutchess of Kent'.[1033]

In what can only be described as inverted normalisation, Siouxsie is measured up for a waxwork to go on display at the Virgin Megastore in London's Oxford Street.[1034] One can only imagine the glee Siouxsie experienced among the dismembered wax limbs, wigs and boxes of glass eyes.

Before the Banshees recorded *Tinderbox*, initially in May and subsequently September 1985, the band played their first 1985 gig, a benefit in aid of Pete Townshend's Anti-Heroin Campaign,[1035] on 10 April 1985 at St James's Church, Piccadilly,[1036] road testing several songs they had been working on for the new album.

Alongside the previously heard 'Cannons', the band debuted 'The Sweetest Chill', '92°', 'Party's Fall', and 'This Unrest'.

The gig is also of significance as it was the only time the band performed 'Mother/Oh Mein Papa' from the 1979 *Join Hands* album. It was also at the same gig that the band brought in Adam Peters from The Flowerpot Men[1037] to play cello and keyboards, so were able to play material that had hitherto never been given a live excursion.

Chapter Nine
Tinderbox

A tinderbox is a metal box which contains tinder, ordinarily small pieces of something dry that will burn readily, for instance, dried wood or grass, and is used for lighting fires. Its origins can be traced back to prehistoric Europe where flint and iron pyrites, commonly known as fool's gold, were struck against one another sequentially to create a spark for lighting fires. Colloquially, it refers to a highly inflammable object or a potentially explosive situation or place.

'It's called Tinderbox *because everything seemed to happen either around situations or the effect of weather...'*[1038]

Siouxsie Sioux

'The world has no end, and what is good among one people is an abomination with others'.[1039]

Chinua Achebe

'Cities In Dust'
Before completion of the Banshees' seventh studio album, 'Cities In Dust' is released as a single. Although Steve Severin, having recorded a home demo instrumental version, envisaged it as a solid B-side,[1040] on hearing the results, Siouxsie deemed it too much an earworm for the band's usual esoteric flipside forays.

Siouxsie reflected on the song's beginnings, 'We were aware of trying to create a sense of place as well as atmosphere and sentiment... While touring in Italy last year we were en route to Taranto, and on the way there we found out it was possible to visit Pompeii, so of course we did. That trip did leave a very strong impression, the culmination of which was seeing the petrified bodies on display in the glass caskets. There was no specific, conscious effort to write a song about it, but one night in the studio the band was just playing around doing demos and the music was suddenly in the making and I immediately wrote 'Cities in Dust' for it'.[1041]

Of the powerful impression left on her of how Pompeii had retained its atmosphere and mystique despite the tourism, Siouxsie commented, '...American accents and German sausages...',[1042] imagining what it must have been like when the Mount Vesuvius[1043] erupted, destroying the cities of Pompeii, Herculaneum, Oplontis and Stabiae, among several other settlements. Siouxsie's lyrics are an imagined conversation with one of the petrified bodies in a glass vitrine she witnessed in Pompeii, ostensibly explaining to the Pompeian what happened to their homes, culminating in a richly observed song about a city bustling with activity suddenly being engulfed by an eruption of molten rock and shattered pumice; the liquified magma entering the Pompeians' open mouths, as well as enveloping and encasing them. Lare's Shrine, referred to in Siouxsie's lyric, otherwise known as the Sanctuary Of The Public Lares, was a formidable building, completely open on the Forum,[1044] furnished with a central altar '...where sacrifices could be offered for the emperor as well as for citizens of Lari. There are two large exedras on the two sides of the central apse and several niches intended to house the statues of the imperial family. Only a few fragments of the rich marble covering are preserved, which was destroyed shortly after the eruption 79 AD'.[1045]

Beginning with the sound of a Jew's harp, percussion, running water, and the scuttling sound created by John Valentine Carruthers' echoing the song's beginning lyrical refrain – Pompeiian calm before the smelted cataclysm – with the crystalline sound of synthesized glass bells, this is a new, reinvigorated and poppier-sounding Siouxsie and The Banshees, embracing a harder-edged, Mondrian-esque primary colour palette with the addition of black and white.

Although it would be reductive to observe that the song has a distinctive 1980s sound, there are certain production values and sonic techniques in the foreground that are indicative of a particular identity, especially where there is a certain 'brightness' of sound, especially with the Yamaha DX7,[1046] which could emulate the sound of lavish strings, marimbas and electric pianos.

There was also the inescapable 'gated reverb', which was conceivably one of the most defining 1980s' effects, with 'gated drums' being used on virtually every track from the decade. One of the most distinctive features of 'Cities In Dust', and conceivably a throwback to when the Banshees worked with Nigel Gray, is the luxuriance of the song, without being overcooked, with spaces between the notes so the music can exhale.

Steve Severin's bass playing has become increasingly melodious, Siouxsie's voice is imbued with her trademark operatically inclined acrobatics but is far more relaxed and intuitive sounding. Carruthers' playing fits like a glove, playing a miscellany of ascending scales and sleek Echoplex[1047] stabs.

'Cities In Dust' was initially recorded between 29 July 1985 and 1 August 1985 at Hansa Studios, with the final mix undertaken at Air Studios between 10 and 11 September 1985. 'Cities In Dust' came late to the feast for *Tinderbox*, but the experience of Pompeii had proved so profound that the band felt magnetically drawn to write a song about their visit.

It was also the time when the band realised that Hugh Jones was not the ideal choice to work on the album; Jones's mix of 'Cities In Dust' was to prove less than satisfying for the band who heard the results when they returned to the UK from the eleven-day Italian, Belgium and French leg of their 1985 tour, when they found Jones wrestling with the material that had been laid down at Hansa Studios.

Jones was let go and, at Polydor's suggestion, mixing engineer Steve Churchyard,[1048] proving a much better fit for the sound the Banshees envisaged, stepped in to make the necessary modifications, saving the day.

Churchyard was also responsible for the 'Cities In Dust (Extended Eruption Mix)',[1049] an eight-minute-fifteen-second extravaganza, driven by a mesmerising drumbeat, and allowing for an array of electronic splicing and experimentation, the Banshees of the dance floor, for which he received a credit alongside engineer Julian Standen.[1050]

The US Geffen release also included a 'Cities In Dust' remix by Canadian producer Bob Rock,[1051] which proved to be an epiphanic breakthrough for the Banshees in the USA, reaching number 17 in the US Dance chart. The song was debuted live at the Preston Guildhall[1052] in Lancashire on 5 October 1985.

'Cities In Dust' was released in both seven-inch and twelve-inch single formats, with 'An Execution' appearing on the B-side of the seven-inch, and the addition of 'The Quarterdrawing Of The Dog' on the twelve-inch offering.

There is also a limited edition of the seven-inch single that comes with a fold-out poster, including a full-colour image of the band, as well as six Pompeii-related images. 'An Execution' begins with gladiatorial menace, like the evil twin of Led Zeppelin's 'Kashmir', the listener picturing a Roman amphitheatre during a bloodthirsty melee.

The song is based on the life of Elizabeth Báthory,[1053] allegedly the inspiration for Bram Stoker's novel *Dracula*[1054] due to the (now generally acknowledged as apocryphal) stories of Bathory bathing in the blood of her virgin victims as an elixir of eternal youth.

Báthory, a Hungarian noblewoman, was a purported serial murderer and, along with four of her servants, accused and convicted of torturing and killing several hundred girls and women between 1590 and 1610.

Siouxsie's slaughterous spoken-word lyric, entering the song after a passage of evocative chanting, reflects the dispassionate, calculating nonchalance of the song's psychopathic protagonist against the backdrop of John Valentine Carruthers' wailing wall of feedback, as a melancholic, repetitive minor note refrain is played on the electric piano against a backdrop of a synthesized Jew's Harp and metronomic percussion. 'An Execution' was recorded at Matrix Studios on 31 May 1985.

'The Quarterdrawing Of The Dog', continuing the Pompeiian theme, is a reference to the petrified guard dog, preserved with the collar around its neck that made any attempt to flee the ensuing fallout from the eruption futile.

Tethered to a post in the house of Marcus Vesonius Primus,

a senator and general of the Roman Empire, when the eruption occurred and volcanic ash began to engulf the atrium, the dog was unable to climb higher and was subsequently buried alive.

The contorted dog, its teeth bared, is seemingly hung, drawn and quartered, hence the song title, which derives from 14th-century punishment for high treason during the English rule of King Edward III,[1055] whereby the victim was either drawn by a horse to a gallows, hanged, and then cut into four pieces and scattered, or was hanged, disembowelled while still alive, otherwise known as 'drawn', then beheaded and dismembered.

The ambient introduction to the song heralds a plethora of rich instrumentation from Carruthers' alternate picking technique to the melodic top line of Severin's bass, a sprightly keyboard chime and Budgie's snare to tom-tom tub thumping. At three minutes and fifteen seconds, Carruthers' guitar adopts the tone of a muted scream.

The B-side Banshees at their playful best, in disaccord with the pathetic spectacle of the blighted dog of the song's title. 'The Quarterdrawing Of The Dog was recorded 30 August 1985 at Matrix Studios, with final mix taking place at Eel Pie Studios on 3 September 1985.

With Tim Pope again assuming video promo duties, Siouxsie and The Banshees opt for what can be a fairly literal interpretation of 'Cities In Dust', a juxtaposition of imagery including Siouxsie lying horizontally in a dress with cutouts, assuming the configuration of a petrified body. Steve Severin, Budgie and John Valentine Carruthers, filmed in monochrome, are dressed in white, excepting Severin's knee-length leather boots.

All appear encrusted in ghostly white make up to simulate the ash-covered Pompeiians as they run, contort and endeavour to escape the imagined liquefied avalanche. The accelerated long-distance shots of Severin render the bass guitarist startled and mouse-like, a cross between mime artist Lindsay Kemp[1056] and one of the apparitions conjured up from the fertile imaginations of Luis Bunuel and Salvador Dali.

Budgie appears fully immersed in adopting the guise of a Pompeiian being consumed by volcanic magma, his bare-chested writhing, twisting and turning elevating his portrayal into the realms of performance art, with his cast shadow at one point resembling the Pompeiian dog.

The border of a curtain, the backdrop used for a dancing skeleton puppet, utilises a decorative Meander motif.[1057] A Romanesque pediment with pillars is seen being swallowed up by the molten lava that flows as a visual constant throughout the video. The filming was undertaken at Fulham Studios on 27 September 1985.

The art direction for the 'Cities In Dust' single was undertaken by Banshees' inner-circle stalwart and Banshees' fan club lantern bearer Billy 'Chainsaw' Houlston, another surefire sign that the Banshees had entered a phase of what one might describe as streamlined consolidation, tantamount to slaying the serpentine machinations of *A Kiss In The Dreamhouse* and *Hyæna*, both of which represented the conceivable end of the band due to the untimely departures of John McGeoch and Robert Smith.

Chainsaw's design heralds an incisive and direct approach, adopting the Euclidean axiom 'to draw a straight line from any point to any point',[1058] perhaps fitting given the provenance of Euclid, from Ancient Greece, and the subject of 'Cities In Dust'.

The standalone image is a tinted photograph of the petrified guard dog, but flipped, as if in the throes of a convulsion, effecting a reanimation of the calcified animal and changing the context of the work, while also resembling one of the mutated figures in Francis Bacon's 1944 triptych painting 'Three Studies For Figures At The Base Of A Crucifixion',[1059] another serendipitous symbiosis as the three canvasses are based on the Ancient Greek 'Eumenides', or 'Furies', of Aeschylus's 'Oresteia',[1060] and depict three tortured, writhing anthropomorphic aberrations set against a rough-hewn cadmium orange background.

The dog is flanked by pale orange and black meanders, with both Siouxsie and The Banshees logo and 'Cities In Dust' in Latin Roman alphabetical font. The reverse cover for the seven-inch single has the 'Cities In Dust' lyrics with the meander border motif, while the fold-out poster edition has a magisterial and moody shot of the band, all dressed in black, seen through a mesh of pink and violet translucent wires, with two drawings of the guard dog in the bottom left and top right corners.

The reverse side of the poster has both petrified guard dog and an image of Pompeii's Cave Canem (Beware Of The Dog) mosaic on the floor of the entrance to the House of the Tragic Poet.[1061]

Two of the other images are the cymbal and timpani players from the 'Trio of musicians playing an aulos, cymbala, and tympanum'[1062] mosaic in Pompeii. Other images include vignettes of the fresco paintings 'Portrait of a young girl' (conceivably the poetess Sappho)[1063] and 'The Three Graces'.[1064]

The background colour for all 'Cities In Dust' imagery is an approximation of the iron oxide 'Pompeiian red' so common in the ancient city, although it is thought that large areas of the vivid red frescoes in Pompeii actually began life as yellow and were subsequently turned red by the gases emitted from Vesuvius as it erupted.

The label for the twelve-inch 'Extended Eruption' edition of 'Cities In Dust', is a print taken from an Etruscan plate,[1065] which depicts an erotic scene that some retail outlets refused to keep in stock.

'Cities In Dust' spent seven weeks in the Top One Hundred Singles Chart and peaked at number 21, the Banshees' highest UK chart placing since 1983's 'Dear Prudence'.

Siouxsie and The Banshees made a cameo appearance in the 1986 Richard Tuggle[1066]-directed American neo noir crime film *Out Of Bounds*,[1067] playing 'Cities In Dust' in a Los Angeles nightclub among a crowd of rather gentrified looking punk wannabes and dismembered mannequins hanging from the club's ceiling.

Of the Banshees' part in the film, Siouxsie reflects, 'It was just us being ourselves in a club scene. There weren't really any stars in it, just a lot of young people, superbrats'.[1068]

The band's role isn't a million miles away from The Yardbirds'[1069] 'Stroll On' appearance in Michelangelo Antonioni's 1966 film *Blow Up*[1070] in terms of the naturalistic performance, as well as the crime genus of the two movies.

The film soundtrack also includes songs by The Cult,[1071] Stewart Copeland[1072] and Belinda Carlisle,[1073] among other bands and solo musicians.

Although not vetoed by the band, as was the case with 'Love In A Void', which, on seeing their portrayal in the 1978 film *Jubilee*,[1074] the Banshees had withdrawn the song from the soundtrack, they were not entirely convinced of the aesthetic merits of *Out Of Bounds*, prompting Steve Severin's assessment, '…seemed a bit smarter than your usual action thriller. Unfortunately, *Out Of Bounds* was rubbish'.[1075]

'Candyman'

"'Candyman' was trying to put across the unspeakability of child abuse, and, again, trying not to sensationalise it, just coming up with a very strong picture of a character that was sickly sweet and oozing repulsiveness. The amount of people who've been abused is incredible, and it's only lately that the subject's been brought out into the open. The whole thing's such a power trip, and you realise the victims must have been so in fear of saying anything – cos they've been told by the perpetrator that they'll go to hell or something'.[1076]

Siouxsie Sioux

'…Certain people have suggested that it's also about drugs and drug-pushers, but it isn't really. Or at least it could be – Sioux's lyrics are always ambiguous. Even in Berlin where we were recording, we heard about the shocking rise in child abuse. If there's one thing Sioux really hates it's children being used against their will. It's a prime concern of hers'.[1077]

John Valentine Carruthers

'That is not what I meant at all; That is not it, at all'.[1078]

T.S. Eliot

The first track on *Tinderbox* and the second single release from the album on 28 February 1986, 'Candyman' nails its colours to the mast as a breathtaking, exhilarating album-opening gambit.

From John Valentine Carruthers' opening notes onwards, this is a mellifluously bludgeoning Banshees. Severin has got the shiny guitar sound he wanted and, not that Siouxsie and The Banshees are ones to look back, ever, there is a new-found confidence reminiscent of when John McGeoch was in the band – all twists and turns, several songs in one, changing tempo and into the realms of soliloquy at

202

one minute and twenty-five seconds, as Siouxsie's cathartic lyric lays down the exactitude of revenge for the generic perpetrator of the song, including a 'nyah nyah na-nyah nyah' playground taunt.

This is no approbatory vignette about the gratification of sugar from *Willy Wonka And The Chocolate Factory*[1079] with Aubrey Woods[1080] espousing sunrises, rainbows and the world tasting good.

On this occasion, it is poison, misery, guilt and shame being purveyed. Seldom has a song sounded so deliciously effervescent yet cut with arsenic. Although the Banshees are not prone to repeating themselves, they confound expectation masterfully, making the listener sit up and take notice, of both music and the lyrics.

It is little wonder that the band spent so much time in interviews correcting what has been incorrectly put on record, or explaining what the lyrics are about, in order to avoid them being misconstrued.

'Candyman' demonstrates the band's mercurial heterogeneity in showcasing a harder, sharper sound. Gone are the smooth, hallucinatory and equatorial Jean Cocteau-esque proclivities of *Hyæna* into the realms of the absolute.

Severin's bass guitar playing punches its way through 'Candyman' with all the bravura assault of *The Scream's* 'Jigsaw Feeling'. Never has the grotesque sounded so gorgeous.

Chronologically, 'Candyman' was recorded from 6 May to 14 May at Hansa Studios, with overdubs added from 3 June to 30 June 1985 at The Garden Studios in London, and the final mixing on 4 December 1985 at Air Studios, London. 'Candyman's live debut was on 10 July 1985 at the Théâtre de Verdure, Nice, France.[1081] It was recorded for a BBC John Peel Session on 28 January 1986 at Maida Vale Studios, which subsequently aired on 3 February 1986.

The single release of 'Candyman' has 'Lullaby' as the B-side of the seven-inch and 'Lullaby' and 'Umbrella' on both twelve-inch and limited edition double-pack formats.

'Lullaby' has a beautiful dissonance about it, as well as all the loafing ease of T. Rex's 'Cosmic Dancer', the Severin-penned lyric and lilt of Siouxsie's voice oscillating, as nighttime encroaches and leads the listener down an alleyway of nocturnal revery.

The song takes inspiration from the life of King Ludwig II of

Bavaria, otherwise known as the 'Swan King'[1082] because of his ancestral use of the swan as a heraldic motif, as well as the 'Fairytale King' due to his commissioning of Neuschwanstein Castle[1083] in the Schwangau region of Bavaria in Germany, used as the model for Walt Disney's *Sleeping Beauty* fortress.

Neuschwanstein, ostentatiously decorated with Byzantine and mediaeval motifs, was, first and foremost, built for Ludwig's entertainment, a shrine to his musical deity Richard Wagner, with allusions to the composer's work in every corner of the two-hundred-room edifice.

Ludwig II suffered from insomnia, preferring long carriage rides in the middle of the night or roaming from room to room in one of his many castles, hence the night-veiled 'Lullaby' motif. Perhaps unsurprisingly, due to his family's history of mental illness, Ludwig latterly became increasingly paranoid, megalomaniacal and suicidal.

He died in mysterious circumstances: his body was recovered from Lake Starnberg, along with that of his physician Dr Gudden, on 13 June 1886. Luscious woodwind and string embellishments, befitting Ludwig's Wagnerian infatuation, are meted out electronically in contradistinction to the live orchestral arrangements on *Hyæna*, reflecting the Banshees' dismantling of multiple strata.

Clearly, the brief time the band spent in the Bavarian countryside before recording 'Lullaby' at Hansa Studios between 29 and 30 May 1985, wasn't all in vain. 'Lullaby' was played live for the first time at the Hollywood Palladium Los Angeles on 7 June 1986.

'Umbrella' is all delirious incantations and dark instrumental passages, Budgie's percussive introduction akin to the reverberating drumbeat played by Ian Paice, again harking back to the beginning of Deep Purple's 'Living Wreck'. John Valentine Carruthers channels Link Wray's distortion as heard on 'Rumble',[1084] with the addition of a Johnny Marr-esque jangle. Siouxsie's vocal lilt conjures the cocoon-like protection of the canopy under forbidding skies, with saline tears the only antidote to the phantasmagorical torrent.

The band, after taking a break from using their long-standing film director Clive Richardson, not employed since the making of the video for 'Slowdive' in 1982, eschew the services of Tim Pope, at least temporarily, so they can reprise the Banshees' more straightforward 'performance-oriented' promos.

The band also uses photographer Joe Lyons, whose band images adorn both *Kaleidoscope* and *Juju*, to undertake the set and lighting design for the promo shoot, which takes place on 11 and 12 February 1986.

Akin to the pared down, cut to the bone machinations of the song itself, the video for 'Candyman', except for some trichromatic filter video overlays and costume changes; Siouxsie's black and white ruched dresses and Severin and Carruthers' appearing either shirted or coated, plus the addition of a wind machine directed at Siouxsie, this is a fast-paced, dynamic video, the band set against the austerely effective white backdrop, punctuated by white, pillar-like vertical strips to facilitate camera angles of the band behind and in front of the segments, as well as projections of their shadows.

The cover for the 'Candyman' single, designed by Billy 'Chainsaw' Houlston, revisits a familiar Banshees' motif, as four red delineated dancers, not a huge visual leap from Henri Matisse's 'Le Danse'[1085] paintings, parade, hands joined, around a blue delineated phallus-like ball top cane.

'Candyman' is written in the chromatic circus font pioneered by George F Nesbitt,[1086] while the Siouxsie and The Banshees insignia is a variant of the Hammer House Of Horror ITC Tiffany font.[1087] The back of the single sleeve has a Matisse-like white dove on a blue background, within red and yellow circles. 'Candyman' peaked at number 34 on the UK Singles Chart.

'The Sweetest Chill'

The lament on the death of a loved one, either real or imagined, feasibly the mourning of a love lost, 'Sweetest Chill' is an example of what the Banshees do best: writing paeans that dissect the viscera of human behaviour, whether through the lens of literature, poetry, film or veiled autobiography.

This isn't any run of the mill shedding of a tear over the departed; instead, it explores a whole diapason of physical manifestations of grief. John Valentine Carruthers commented on the song's theme being '…a visitation from a lover's spirit who is already dead – someone who comes back from the grave and greets her as a lover'.[1088]

The title implies discord, another Banshees' reoccurring theme. However, within the realms of 'The Sweetest Chill', there is succour to be found in the presence of absence, whether through physical keepsake or experienced in sleep.[1089]

Siouxsie's lyrics allude to spectral iciness and the duality of feeling both lachrymose but also solace in knowing that the departed will always endure in the memory. As with Siouxsie's lyric, there is a beautiful yearning through the instrumentation, as though vocals, bass, guitar, keyboard and drums conspire in holistic veneration.

The first nine seconds of 'The Sweetest Chill', Siouxsie's siren call and several acoustic guitar notes and a couple of chords, are glacially rousing. 'The Sweetest Chill' is a felicitous reminder of John Valentine Carruthers being an opportune conduit for the band to deliver their musical vision; whether stentorian or gentle, weeping or carnivalesque, Carruthers' guitar playing is consummately germane.

'The Sweetest Chill' was recorded from 14 to 23 May 1985 at Hansa Studios, with overdubs taking place between 3 and 30 June 1985 at The Garden Studios. The song's final mix was executed on 21 December 1985 at Air Studios in London. It was played live for the first time at St James's Church Piccadilly on 10 April 1985.

'This Unrest'

Themes explored by the Banshees previously in 'Premature Burial' and 'Jigsaw Feeling', of being overwhelmed and displaced, whether mentally or physically, drowning in the morass of multisensory overload, giving rise to feelings of being eaten or buried alive, are floodlit in 'This Unrest'.

It calls to mind the insomnia experienced by King Ludwig II expressed on 'Lullaby'. With the accepted Banshees' norm of confounding expectation, the beginning of 'This Unrest' turns on a pin from a gentle twilight stroll with nonchalant snare drum rim clicks; the Banshees' stamp of using the spaces between the notes in full effect, into the realms of the nocturnal succubus, thronged with the protagonist brim-full of psychological debris. Siouxsie's lyric describes a cavalcade of unprocessed and unresolved thoughts spreading, entangled, malignant; pleading for the carcinoma to be expunged.

Severin's sinister bass, increasingly coming to the fore of Banshees' songs, accompanies Budgie's polyrhythmic workout, including his bandsaw-like high hat, and Carruthers' volatile guitar playing. 'This Unrest' is formed of several parts, the first one a catharsis, expressing how the malaise is manifesting itself; the second passage moves into the realms of momentary psychosis, before regaining composure, although this equilibrium is short-lived as another phase takes hold and John Valentine Carruthers' guitar commences with all the tension of Richard Wagner's 'Ride Of The Valkyries',[1090] combined with the sonorous, low-pitched reverberation of Duane Eddy.[1091]

Budgie's use of the high hat quickens, and the Banshees are joined by a synthesised choir of angels, the antithesis of Siouxsie's backward reverb-laden vocals as she tries to put the nefarious genie back in the bottle. Siouxsie's lyrical contribution, through the flume of a sublime vocal, reflects, as always, a studied eclecticism of material from Wes Craven's 'A Nightmare On Elm Street'[1092] to the poetry of T.S. Eliot, providing both resin and cantilever of the song.

'This Unrest' debuted at St James's Church Piccadilly on 10 April 1985. It is another cut from 'Tinderbox' which started its recording life at Hansa Studios between 16 and 25 May 1985, with subsequent overdubs taking place at The Garden Studios between 3 and 30 June 1985. The final mix was at Air Studios on 16 December 1985.

'Cannons'

In T.S. Eliot's *The Waste Land* there is an absence of rain, except in April, 'the cruellest month'[1093], and the poem '...is dominated by images of drought. There are landscapes of dust, red rock without water, cracked mouths, dry bones, beating sun and "dry sterile thunder without rain".[1094]

'Cannons', Siouxsie's inaugural lyrical refrain alluding to the ensuing meteorological cataclysm, is delivered with adventitious composure. Weather patterns have become anarchical, with hailstones pelting down during the summer months, while winter yields a sunbaked and burning landscape.

The 'Cannons' in question, although not actually in Eliot's poem, which explores a plethora of themes including the impotence of modern life, religion and The Fisher King,[1095] in the Banshees' song are employed to precipitate rainfall from the overcast, forlorn skies but to no consequence, the only result being to perturb the sleeping.

The theme of expediting rainfall isn't entirely fictional as 'cloud seeding' can be traced back 1891, when German-American engineer and inventor Louis Gathmann[1096] suggested firing liquid carbon dioxide into rain clouds to cause them to rain.

Subsequently, meteorologists Alfred Wegener,[1097] Tor Bergeron[1098] and Walter Findeisen[1099] theorised that supercooled water droplets present, while ice crystals are released into clouds, would induce rain. While researching aircraft icing, the process whereby water droplets in the atmosphere at high altitudes spread over the surface area of an aeroplane wing, Vincent Schaefer[1100] and Irving Langmuir[1101] confirmed the merits of the theory.

The song 'Cloudbusting' by Kate Bush also alludes to Austrian psychoanalyst Wilhelm Reich's[1102] proclamation that he could generate rain by shaping what he referred to as 'Orgone Energy'[1103] pervading the atmosphere.

The 'Cloudbuster' was contrived to be used in a not dissimilar way to a lightning rod, which he would position towards a particular area of sky and anchor it in a material that was presumed to soak up orgone, most likely a body of water, and elicit the orgone energy from the atmosphere, instigating the construction of clouds and rain. Reich conducted a myriad experiments with the 'Cloudbuster', naming the investigation 'Cosmic Orgone Engineering'.[1104]

The prettiness of the song, including Siouxsie's deadpan apologue, John Valentine Carruthers' dizzying twelve-string acoustic guitar playing, in tandem with the deluge of hail Siouxsie intones, and the inclusion of a probably unintentionally cheerful fire bell passage played fleetingly and adroitly by Budgie.

The 'dum da dum' vocal that provides the bridge of the song is akin to a shrug of the shoulders, at one minute and thirty-six seconds. Seldom has the apocalypse been presented with such detached sobriety.

'Cannons' was recorded at Hansa Studios on 26 May 1985, with resultant overdubs on 3 June to 30 June 1985 at The Garden Studios. The concluding mix took place on 14 December 1985 at Air Studios. 'Cannons' was also recorded for a BBC John Peel Session on 26 January 1986 at Maida Vale Studios and first aired on 3 February 1986.

'Party's Fall'

Desolately cautionary and distinctly antithetical to any Noël Coward-like aspirations of attending a 'Marvellous Party',[1105] although perhaps falling short of the Morrissey[1106]-penned lyric in The Smiths' 'How Soon Is Now',[1107] which alludes to standing alone at a club and leaving on one's own. The wretchedness and loneliness of which only a swift demise would ameliorate, 'Party's Fall' tells the story of making a career from attending one blow-out too many, and the miserable undertaking of adorning oneself with ostrich feathers to pander to the assembled company, all of one's friends that really aren't friends at all but just transient acquaintances.

Siouxsie comments on the shelf life of such a preoccupation, 'The parties spoil perhaps when you get too old to do it'.[1108] John Valentine Carruthers opines, 'This is about people who go to thousands of parties and talk to everyone and leave the party and find they haven't a friend in the world. In London there's a ...vacuous circus of meeting pop stars and film stars and then departing and feeling sorry for yourself'.[1109]

Tinderbox's leitmotif, reflected in the aerodynamics of the music, spotlights shedding the carapace of the past and is a rethink of where the band is at, as well as demonstrating acute understanding of Chaos Theory,[1110] with the looping inevitability of pandemonium manifest in every enclave of the universe or, in this instance, the life and times of Siouxsie and The Banshees.

'Party's Fall' is conceivably semi-autobiographical and a part of the band's life they find cumulatively enervating. However, the sparkling patina of the song braves it out, with vocal harmonies and inflections worthy of any yearning song by The Ronettes[1111] or Shangri-Las.

Although no doubt the Banshees would rail against this observation, 'Party's Fall' shares much of the sonic elegance and pop-oriented sensibilities of Blondie, in particular Debbie Harry's latitudinous, sugar-coated vocal delivery, lulling and blindsiding the listener with her cooing lyrics about desire, revenge and heartbreak.

One can see why 'Party's Fall' was mooted for single release. It's upbeat tempo, memorable guitar riff and, that Blondie reference again, Budgie given carte blanche to let rip on his crash cymbals with gleeful abandon, does sound coincidentally like Clem Burke channelling Ringo Starr[1112] on 'The Beatles' 'Tomorrow Never Knows'.

John Valentine Carruthers' pithy introduction to 'Party's Fall' is a beckoningly seductive sketch as the song changes tempo thirty seconds in, as Carruthers adopts a Johnny Marr-esque jangle that transmogrifies into choppily muted chords, subsequently reprising the initial effervescence to the augmentation of Siouxsie's tambourine.

The song's saga-like character is predicated on an exuberance of synergistic cadence. It is a band unequivocally locked in. Lest we think the subject of 'Party's Fall' has induced a Rubicon regarding exhausting their party privileges, Siouxsie's lyrical denouement provides a hint that a party of one or two in the privacy of one's home might be acceptable.

'Party's Fall' was recorded between 7 and 17 May 1985 at Hansa Studios, with ensuing overdubs on 3 to 30 June 1985 at The Garden Studios. The final mix took place on 12 December 1985 at Air Studios. 'Party's Fall' was debuted at St James's Church Piccadilly on 10 April 1985.

'92°'

"'There's a book by Ray Bradbury called The October Country, *and there's one story about these two old men who are travelling somewhere and they're trying to spread this message of the danger of 92° because they'd been witnesses to an event that happened in some other town where there'd been so many murders and madness and mayhem at this magical figure. Meanwhile, it was coming close and people were losing their tempers – 'don't tell me about 92°'. It was a great story and almost the sort of thing that to me is believable because it's so far-fetched'".*[1113]

Siouxsie Sioux

The '92°' spoken-word introduction comes directly from the 1953 American science fiction/ horror film *It Came From Outer Space*.[1114] Siouxsie elaborates on the literary kernel of the song, 'sparked off by a short story I read where crimes would escalate when the temperature reached 92 degrees. It's about the rising panic of the people who know what's going to happen as the temperature rises towards that number. I mentioned it to Steve, who'd seen some alien from outer space film, in which, right at the end, a sheriff says: "Yeah, just about at this temperature everybody goes crazy"'.[1115]

The plot of the film centres around the town of Sand Rock, Arizona, and the character of author and amateur astronomer John Putnam, played by actor Richard Carlson,[1116] who is stargazing when he sees through his telescope what appears to be a meteor shower but, it transpires, is a crash-landed alien spacecraft. Putnam investigates the crater caused by the wreckage, informing Sheriff Matt Warren[1117] of the cause of the pit, only to be ridiculed because the large disc-like object had been covered in debris from a landslide after Putman saw it.

After initial scepticism and derision, even from Putnam's fiancée, Ellen Fields,[1118] it transpires that Putnam's sighting of the spaceship was real. Its alien inhabitants are amorphous and jellyfish-like with an ability to take on the human forms of townsfolk they have abducted so they can move around incognito to collect much-needed supplies to repair their damaged craft. However, their imperfect replication arouses suspicion and leads to the killing of two of the aliens.

Subsequently, to aid the extraterrestrial visitors' departure, Putnam creates a protective barricade for them so they can return home. Of note, and slightly contradicting Sheriff Warren's assertion that 'more people are murdered at ninety-two degrees Fahrenheit than any other temperature'[1119] is echoed by the original impetus for '92°', the Ray Bradbury short story *Touched With Fire*, from Bradbury's 1955 collection *The October Country*.[1120]

The synopsis of *Touched With Fire* involves two main characters, Mr Foxe and Mr Shaw, both retired insurance salesman, who have taken up a new sleuthing hobby. During a heatwave, they discover that murders most commonly occur at 92°, at which point people become exceedingly aggravated. Both men follow a woman, Mrs Shrike, as they believe she will be the next person to be murdered because of her irritating and obstreperous behaviour.

Foxe and Shaw's aim is to make Shrife to a more serene and loving, to mitigate the chances of her murder. Foxe's deeds, however, take a sharp turn and appear to accelerate the process of Shrike's decline; when the temperature hits 92°, overwhelmed by Shrike's unremitting yelling, Foxe raises his cane to strike her.

Bradbury often employs the metaphor of fire to highlight the dark forces at play in the world. Shrike's voice is described as like 'pure blazing sunlight'[1121] and she swears at Foxe and Shaw with language 'like great searing torches'. Shrike is also described as a 'feverish dragon'[1122] who lives in a 'fire clouded room'[1123], uttering nothing but 'fire and smoke'.[1124]

The 1990 *Ray Bradbury Theatre*[1125] television series adaptation of the short story moves the temperature gauge up to 102°. However, the 1956 *Alfred Hitchcock Presents*[1126] adaptation, *Shopping For Death*[1127] is true to the original story regarding the temperature; Mr Shaw has become Elmer Shore and Mr Foxe, Clarence Fox.

The penultimate song in this collection of literal and metaphorical baroscopic forays, '92°' leads us again into Pompeiian terrain, evoking the corollary of the mercury hitting its Fahrenheit target.

Its ambient keyboard beginning, alongside the *It Came From Outer Space* monologue, as Budgie, in the guise of Hal Blaine[1128], with an iconic 'boom, ba-boom BOP' drumbeat used on The Ronettes' 'Be My Baby'[1129] and subsequently adopted by Blaine for Frank Sinatra's 'Strangers In The Night',[1130] leads us into the heart of the song, the snare drum arid and brittle.

The song's dilatory pace, as it swirls and swelters with all the steaminess of an impending geyser deluge, reflects Bradbury's thesis that any temperature under or over 92° makes any plausibility of doing anything angry or violent less likely. The article Sheriff Warren refers to claims that below 92° everyone remains unruffled, and over 92° they are too hot to move. In the world of the Banshees, '92°' is the imminent flashpoint; the forecast that something will inevitably kick-off; the consequences of Chaos Theory never far away.

Siouxsie's lyrics envelop the listener in a multi-sensory landscape, visualising the heat shimmer as the day barely nudges along. At one minute and fourteen seconds, the countdown to the metaphorically inevitable atomic blast commences.

With allusions to Hades and volcanic eruptions, Siouxsie's desolate prognostication is infused by the emotive, heartrending and expressive playing of Severin, Carruthers and Budgie. The mini opera is far from new territory for the Banshees, and '92°' is another realisation of a spectacular sweeping diorama. '92°' recording credentials are 8 to 23 May 1985 at Hansa Studios, with overdubs taking place at The Garden Studios from 3 to 30 June 1985, with the definitive mix taking place on 6 December 1985 at Air Studios. Its first live outing was at St James's Church Piccadilly on 10 April 1985.

'Land's End'

'Thus hath the candle singed the moth'[1131]

William Shakespeare

'Now they stand chin-deep in the sway of ocean,
Firm West, two stringy bodies face to face,
And come, together, in the water's motion,
The full caught pause of their embrace'.[1132]

Thom Gunn[1133] 'The Discovery Of The Pacific'

Scampering drum reverberations usher in the final cut on *Tinderbox*, which sees Siouxsie's lyrics in the realms of a hybridised *Casablanca*[1134] and *Romeo and Juliet*,[1135] suffused with Homeric[1136] elements. It is a tale of yearning and clandestine assignation, with all the hallmarks of a moonlight flit; imagery of water proliferates, whether driving rain or the swell of the sea.

Although the consequences of such a tryst has implied consequences for the star-crossed lovers, the jeopardy proves too alluring to rebuff. Paraphrased in other songs on *Tinderbox*, the prevailing trajectory is that of avoiding any given catastrophe; on this occasion it is dangerous liaison with the metaphorical moth attracted to a flame and the inexorable flotsam of current lives or lives to be.

John Valentine Carruthers' multi-faceted guitar playing, expressing the fervour of the song, in accordance with Severin's understated bass playing and Budgie's cumulatively locomotive playing. Siouxsie's nocturne articulates the inevitability of running out of road, or land in the instance of the song, as the infatuated couple reach the boundary of their desires but persevere in contemplating the infinite.

'Land's End' was recorded between the 22 and 24 May 1985 at Hansa Studios, with overdubs taking place between 3 and 30 June 1985 at The Garden Studios, with the completed mix on 17 December 1985 at Air Studios. Alongside 'Candyman' and 'Cannons', 'Land's End' was recorded for a BBC John Peel Session on 28 January 1986 at Maida Vale Studios and was subsequently aired on 3 February 1986. Live, 'Land's End debuted on 10 July 1985 at the Théâtre de Verdure, Nice, France.

Eagle-eyed music trivia fiends will notice a certain similarity between the cover of *Tinderbox*, that of Deep Purple's 1975 album *Stormbringer*,[1137] and Miles Davies' 1970 four-sided opus, *Bitches Brew*[1138], as all three albums adopted and modified versions of what has become an iconic photograph taken by Lucille Handberg of a tornado striking Jasper, Minnesota, on 8 July 1927.

At the time, the now defunct publication *The Illustrated London News*[1139] hailed it as 'the finest photograph of a tornado ever taken'.[1140]

Handberg took three photographs, one before the celebrated image and one after. The first photograph, which seems to have been taken just after Handberg set foot outside her house, shows the dust-encased tube of the tornado extending almost horizontally beyond some farm roofs and a windmill.

Deep Purple opted for transforming the original black and white photograph by presenting it as a mirrored image and turning it into a painterly, colour landscape with the addition of a winged Pegasus[1141] riding atop the tornado, reflecting, at least in part, the David Coverdale lyric alluding to the Stormbringer's imminent approach, and supposedly alluding to the mythological predilections in the Michael Moorcock[1142] 1965 *Stormbringer*[1143] novel.

Miles Davies' *Bitches Brew* appropriates Handberg's image in a more poetically multifaceted way, reflecting the rich layering of musical styles which took Davies into a more rock-oriented realm with the addition of the virtuoso guitarist and pioneer of Jazz Fusion[1144] John McLaughlin.[1145]

The artist responsible for the *Bitches Brew* album cover, a French Surrealist painter of German origin, Malti Klarwein,[1146] was renowned for his 'vivid and colourful style of painting, consisting of popular psychedelic imagery, and on themes of religion, race and sexuality'.[1147]

Klarwein developed an oeuvre which he named 'Mischtechnik', a method incorporating different tempera and oil paint techniques to create a luminescent effect. The cover features an array of figures and pictorial components, of which, again, transformed from monochrome to colour, Handberg's tornado is at the core, depicted as a force of nature as it radiates spectacularly from the head of one of the embracing figures standing on the edge of the ocean, amid the side profile of a perspiring head and an oriental poppy, disseminating ideas including 'a fusion of the dark and the light, the relationship between nature and humans, and certainly an amalgamation of cultures'.[1148]

In interview, Matti Klarwein commented, 'While it's easy to see how the cover might represent dichotomies, it is really more about tandems and shared experiences, coupled with the acknowledgement that individual perspectives can create an otherworldly experience'.[1149]

Billy 'Chainsaw' Houlston's design for *Tinderbox* is the tornedo witnessed as if one were inside a theatre or cinema, replete with the top half of rich velvet auditorium seats, watching the spectacle unfold. There is no Pegasus or additional figurative content as with the other Handberg-appropriated manifestations; instead, the image is effectively in a Mark Rothko[1150] maroon, excepting the fragmented magenta stripes that adorn the two tapering vertical panels that act as a perspectival device to lead the viewer into the central tempest.

The dark hanging detritus at the top creates the sensation that there is a blurring of the edges between the sanctuary of the viewer's intimate surroundings. The Siouxsie and The Banshees logo typography has had a considerable makeover post-*Hyaena*, with a more defined and hard-edged look, opting for Times New Roman[1151] capitalisation for both band name and album title, except for the decadently ostentatious ampersand.

The back cover of the album uses solarised stills of The Banshees from the video of 'Candyman'. The inner sleeve has portrait photographs of all four band members taken by Joe Lyons, looking sullenly baroque except for Siouxsie, who wears an elaborately plumed fascinator,[1152] off-the-shoulder ball gown and black evening gloves, channelling Audrey Hepburn[1153] in *My Fair Lady*.[1154]

The flip side of the inner sleeve contains the lyrics from all eight *Tinderbox* songs. Both inner and outer sleeves are unified by a maroon tint.

Tinderbox rose to its highest peak at number 13 in the UK Top Twenty Albums Chart, its best placing by far when looking at its chart positioning around the world; the nearest being Sweden, where *Tinderbox* placed at 32.

Even though the band had label representation across the Atlantic, *Tinderbox* reached its apex at number 88 in the US. Reviews for the album are as divergent as the Banshees' experience of interviews, the nadir of which was an article written by *NME* journalist David Quantick,[1155] in which zero punches are pulled regarding his assessment of the new album, deeming it 'perhaps the least interesting Siouxsie and The Banshees album yet; only its deranged predecessor, *Hyæna*, is worse and even that was fascinating for its wilfulness. This time round, the Banshees seem to have played it very safe, made a record that takes no risks and offers no surprises. *Tinderbox* offers up an aspect of the Banshees that one hoped not to see; competence without verve'.[1156]

The album review, or rather critique, appears in tandem with the transcription of a Quantick interview with Siouxsie and Severin, the opening gambit of which is Quantick letting his interviewees know that the only discernibly distinguishing feature of Tinderbox is that it sounds like Siouxsie and The Banshees, and that it has no sense of adventure about it.

Siouxsie's counter retort is, as well as a perceptible rolling of the eyes, 'That kind of accusation doesn't really penetrate because it's been said of every album since *The Scream*. As far as reviews go, it's always been, oh, another Banshees record. That criticism always sounds like the right thing to say from the other side'.[1157]

As is the well-trodden default trope reminiscent of too many Banshees interviews to mention, Quantick ostensibly comes back with 'Yes but, you used to be good until the mess of *Hyæna*' response, the thrust of his thesis being that the band is becoming risk averse.

This, in turn, elicits a response from Siouxsie which, with her usual unflinching candour, expresses the band's less than overjoyed countenance about the album, commenting, 'We were unhappy with *Hyæna* and the memory of how it was put together, and we need to put some distance behind the memory of doing it'.[1158]

Severin also alludes to the band adopting a pragmatically consolidated approach when making the album, commenting, 'It's just basically an album of really strong songs, and that's all we wanted to do. We just wanted to sit down with the new guitarist (John Carruthers) and write songs, as opposed to being the Banshees zooming off in one direction or another. It was all done to be one complete overall album'.[1159]

Quantick meets this statement incredulity, his counter-argument being that, as he perceives it, the album is 'A nice complete staid unadventurous album that's incredibly samey'.[1160]

The interview continues in the same interrogative vein, with Quantick's combustible ace card, in essence to draw Siouxsie and Severin's ire, proposing that *Tinderbox* is 'complete in its seamless texture, that the Banshees have approached making *Tinderbox* with that desire for rock consistency so beloved of U2 and Simple Minds'.[1161]

On the back of this comment, the Banshees' *The Scream* producer Steve Lillywhite is alluded to regarding the 'saminess'[1162] of production, as he sees it, evident on the albums of U2 and Simple Minds, a far more pejorative lens on what the Banshees feel is a striving for less unevenness and greater consistency.

Close one's eyes, and, even though Siouxsie and The Banshees are not ones for looking over their shoulders and raking over the coals of the past, the band's 'don't give a damn' attitude, which got them initially onto the stage of The 100 Club and over the threshold of Punk with such deftness and panache, still prevails; when David

Quantick suggests that 'today's Banshees are lacking a certain spark', Siouxsie smiles and utters, 'What a shame!'[1163]

For context, it's worth specifying that David Quantick is a Siouxsie and The Banshees acolyte, as the following comment attests, when ruminating on 'The Great Lost Album', 'One of my favourite albums is Siouxsie & The Banshees' *Join Hands*, the last album they made before half the band walked out and Sioux and Severin were forced to reinvent themselves as a pop group. I like to imagine how things would have gone if McKay and Morris had stayed'.[1164]

Siouxsie and The Banshees continue to garner music press column inches throughout 1985 and 1986, and Siouxsie, with the occasional Banshee in shot, adorns the cover of a myriad different publications, some dyed-in-the-wool established, focusing on the band's musical craft, some riding the wave of the 1980s' synergistically marketable music, fashion and culture zeitgeist, others pedalling the well-trodden tropes ranging from the Banshees being Punk survivors, black magic, good and evil, whether Siouxsie believes in astrology, will she have children, or making veiled and not so veiled allusions to the fact that, in her late twenties, she might be knocking on a bit, and asking what her spirit animal is.

Among the covers of *Record Mirror*, *Sounds*, *Blitz*, *Fool's Mate*, *Melody Maker* and *ZigZag* stalwarts, Budgie, Severin and Carruthers make the cover of *International Musician And Recording World*[1165] magazine and Budgie, alongside Duran Duran's Roger Taylor[1166], appears on the cover of *Rhythm* magazine.[1167]

There are also a fair few television interviews and performances, one of which is the band's appearance on the hundredth episode of *The Tube* on 4 April 1986, introduced by Nicholas Parsons,[1168] playing 'Candyman' and '92°', looking commandingly stunning, more so than the apparent live sound mix imposed on the two songs.

What is unremittingly apparent is the unerring seriousness with which the band continues to take making music, when interviews have the, albeit subliminal, latitude in allowing them to do so amidst the inanity of interviewer superfluity.

Perhaps one of the more thoughtfully music-oriented interviews is the CBS *Nightwatch*[1169] dialogue with Charlie Rose,[1170] during the band's thirty-two North American tour dates in 1986, the same year Rose interviewed Charles Manson[1171] at San Quentin State Prison.[1172]

One of the frequent topics of conversation is Siouxsie's literal breaking of a leg during the first of three nights at the Hammersmith Odeon on 24, 25 and 26 October 1985, Steve Severin recounting, 'Halfway through 'Christine', with Siouxsie leaping all over the stage as usual, I heard this thump. I turned round and she was on the floor holding her leg and screaming her head off'.[1173]

Severin, clearly still on red alert after all the years gigging and the de rigueur expectation that some faction in the audience might fancy a little bit of a skirmish, surmised Siouxsie had had something thrown at her. This was not the case, Severin recalls, 'It transpired that she'd caught her foot in some cabling, fallen over and her kneecap had popped out. I went off stage and she was in this little anteroom with our security man, who was an SAS marine. She was shouting, "Knock me out or whack it back in!"'[1174]

Siouxsie was bundled off to Charing Cross Hospital where her leg was put in a cast. Siouxsie, remembering the traumatic ghosts of maladies past, comments, 'My kneecap ended up round the other side of my leg. I looked down and couldn't believe what I was seeing. Total agony. I was kept waiting for hours. It was a Saturday night, and waiting in a bed next to me was this guy who'd been in a knife fight groaning and clutching his stomach. When I finally got seen to, the doctor literally did whack it back in, put it in a plaster cast and gave me loads of painkillers'.[1175]

Rather than curtail the Banshees' tour which, given Siouxsie's penchant for acrobatics, an integral part of her stage performance, would have been understandable, the remainder of the tour went ahead, with the modifications of Siouxsie perching on a stool during gigs and Severin's acquisition of a cane with a skull on top of it.

The resolution to carry on with the tour was made for several reasons, including economic pragmatism; the band were acutely aware of the financial fallout were they to cancel the twenty remaining dates, culminating in a concert at the Royal Albert Hall on 28 November 1985.

Siouxsie's stool bound performances, although yielding the

benefits of Siouxsie enjoying singing much more, adapting her voice to her imposed immobility, resulted in a trapped nerve in her back.

Siouxsie's previous assignation with a glass door and now her broken leg, plus the seemingly interminable travails of a conveyer belt of guitarists, were all taking their toll, culminating in Siouxsie's *The Picture Of Dorian Gray*[1176] moment, on viewing her leg after the cast was taken off on 29 November 1985, when she commented, 'I saw this shrivelled left leg, I was appalled. The physio stuck electrodes in my knee and I felt like Frankenstein's monster all over again'.[1177]

Tinderbox was released one day shy of the Banshees' 1986 tour, which commenced on 22 April 1986; forty-three dates that would begin in Belgium and end in Buenos Aires, the first English band to play in Argentina since the 1982 Falklands War[1178].

Steve Severin recounting, 'the show was the first time we'd been spat at in ten years. I've got this abiding image of the audience holding up Union Jacks and gobbing at us'.[1179]

Siouxsie recalls the make-up of the audience thus, '...the biggest shock was that there was a football pig element in the crowd... They were gobbing and throwing bubblegum an all that crap, and it was like – oh my God, all this way after all this time and it's like back in Hemel Hempstead eight or nine years ago! But that was just a few idiots, everyone else we saw – whether it was the huge menacing ones or the pretty ones – said they loved it'.[1180]

This was also the Banshees' longest stint in North America since 1981. Two dates into the 1986 tour, the band debuted 'Song From The Edge Of The World',[1181] at the Biskuithalle,[1182] Bonn, Germany, on 24 April 1986; demoed during the *Tinderbox* sessions but not released.

There was also an outing for the Bob Dylan[1183] and Rick Danko[1184] penned 'This Wheel's On Fire,'[1185] at the Palácio das Convenções do Anhembi,[1186] São Paulo, Brazil, on 1 December 1986.

After the thirty-two North American dates, including Washington, Chicago, Minneapolis, Dallas, New Orleans and bookending their stateside jaunt in New York City at Pier 84,[1187] the Banshees catch their breath before playing two festival gigs, Rockscene[1188] in France and WOMAD[1189] in Clevedon, England.

From a setlist averaging around seventeen or eighteen songs per show, five, six or seven, depending on how the band decides to mix things up, are from *Tinderbox*, including 'Cities In Dust', 'Candyman', 'Cannons', 'The Sweetest Chill', '92°', 'This Unrest' and 'Land's End'.

Although ordinarily averse to playing anything from *Join Hands*, 'Icon', featured eighteen times during the 1985 tour, after a four-year hiatus between 1981 and 1984, is given a one-off airing at the Hollywood Palladium, Los Angeles, on 7 June 1986.

The Banshees hadn't completely forsaken *Hyæna*, with 'Bring Me The Head Of The Preacher Man' featuring twenty-seven times during the 1986 tour. 'Dazzle' is also played but in a lesser capacity. Various live snapshots of the 1986 tour reveal the band in fine fettle. Songs from *Tinderbox* are played adroitly with conviction and pride. The Banshees are as tight as ever, striking the balance between 'The Hits', the chiaroscuro of *Kaleidoscope, Juju* and *A Kiss In The Dreamhouse* and deeper B-side cuts such as 'Red Over White', Pulled To Bits' and 'Eve White/Eve Black', demonstrating the depth and eclecticism of their repertoire and back catalogue.

The band continued to develop musically, as evidenced by these deft live performances, and John Valentine Carruthers proved an excellent live fit for the Banshees, his ability to serve the Banshees spectrum of McKay, McGeoch and Smith-era songs pretty much flawless. Siouxsie's vocal gymnastics were in full force, never giving anything less than one hundred percent for every show.

And there were still surprises to be had, as Siouxsie attests when reflecting on the South American leg of the 1986 tour, 'The shows in Brazil were amazing, and the audience went completely bonkers. It was so strange to see all these dark-skinned and tanned fans dressed in black. We had a day in Rio and did four shows in Sao Paulo, where we had our own crew of bodyguards called the Fonseca Gang, who resembled WWF wrestlers… the organisers were convinced we were going to get kidnapped'.[1190]

In terms of individual Banshees' members on tour, Severin and Carruthers made a point of fleeing to a nightclub after every Banshees show, Budgie decided to abstain from drinking alcohol for the duration of the 1986 tour and, following Siouxsie's dietary lead, became vegetarian, no mean feat when, during the band's South American jaunt, Severin comments, not only about the conspicuous meat consumption but also other appetites, 'I seem to remember the trip being a whirl of huge steaks, washed down with loads of drinks and uncut narcotics. I had a great time'.[1191]

Chapter Ten
Through The Looking Glass

What goes around comes around...

Before the Banshees embarked on their South American dates, they implemented a plan for an album of cover versions, with which they had been flirting for a while, with Pink Floyd's 'Arnold Lane', played during Banshees' rehearsals during the McGeoch era, under consideration, as well as Cream's 'White Room',[1192] which was thrown out as a song choice after the lyrics of the song were inspected more closely.

They set about raiding personal favourites from their individual record collections, the initial idea having been sparked by David Bowie's *Pin-Ups* album.[1193] The band had never been averse to recording cover versions, including single B-sides 'Supernatural Thing' and '20th Century Boy'.[1194]

The project marks the rekindling of the band's relationship with producer and engineer Mike Hedges. In the interceding time between *Hyæna* and *Through The Looking Glass*, Hedges had been working on albums with Marc Almond, Everything But The Girl[1195] and The Cure.

The Banshees had also got Martin McCarrick back on board, undertaking cello, keyboard and string arrangement duties, as well as Gini Hewes. There were also brass players Pete Thoms[1196] on trombone, Luke Tunney[1197] playing trumpet and Martin Dobson[1198] on saxophone. Julie Aliss[1199] played harp.

Indomitable and determined not to be derailed by any number or permutation of either literal or metaphorical flesh wounds, the *Through The Looking Glass* venture, the title derived from the Lewis

Carroll book of the same name,[1200] was intended to be a project that the whole band could get on board with to keep everyone's spirits buoyed, particularly after the protracted making of *Tinderbox*, which had proved a bittersweet experience for the band, both because of the amount of time invested and the ancillary physical and psychological woes for Siouxsie.

For John Valentine Carruthers, however, this strategy proved to be a step too far and his reluctance to participate a portent of things to come. On a purely pragmatic level, entertaining writing a whole album of new material was unbearable, even for the Banshees.

Entering Abbey Road Studios on 27 July 1986, the band started making inroads into the Bob Dylan and Rick Danko penned 'This Wheel's On Fire', a song that Siouxsie had always held a candle for, although this proved to be a perhaps less than auspicious start, and not really the springboard the Banshees felt they needed to propel them in the direction they desired.

Motown songs were also contenders in the preliminary mix but, Severin opines, 'The idea of Siouxsie singing something like 'You Can't Hurry Love" was horrible'.[1201]

'This Town Ain't Big Enough For Both Of Us'
The opening song on *Through The Looking Glass*, originally recorded by Sparks,[1202] and decided on by the band as the most obvious and best choice for an opener, keeps the spirit of the original, with an epic, thumping bass drumbeat replacing Ron Mael's keyboard.

Russell Mael's falsetto was always going to be the toughest of calls to try and replicate, so, rightly, Siouxsie opts for a lower range, delivering Russell Mael's cut-up style lyrics, which originally started life as a collection of movie cliches, hence the song's title, which was lifted from the 1932 film *The Western Code*.[1203]

She loses none of the expression of the original, which is driven forward by Budgie's fierce drumming; he is clearly having the time of his life. Severin's solid bass playing, not as pronounced as the Martin Gordon[1204] Rickenbacker 4001[1205] template, holds steady, and Carruthers' guitar playing, with the inclusion of a sitar, adds colour and texture.

The song's bridge, the apogee of the original, bangs and crashes with pure, unadulterated elation, as the band, no doubt egged on by Mike Hedges, throw everything at it, just shy of producer Muff Winwood's[1206] gunshots, implemented after the Maels raided the BBC sound effects library.

Sparks were beaten to the number one slot in the UK Singles Chart by The Rubettes' 'Sugar Baby Love'.[1207] The Banshees' version of 'This Town Ain't Big Enough For Both Of Us' was recorded between 26 August 1986 and September 1986 at Abbey Road Studios, with the final mix executed on 2 October 1986.

The Sparks original appears on their 1974 album *Kimono My House*.[1208] There is no live performance by the Banshees of 'This Town Ain't Big Enough For Both Of Us', but the band gave a mimed performance of the song on *Get Fresh*,[1209] a weekend children's television programme that was broadcast from a different location in the UK every week during the time it aired from 1986 to 1987, which, for the Banshees is the bandstand at Clydebank Shopping Centre in Scotland.

Siouxsie appears as a vision in red with a feather boa to shield her from the horizontal rain. Siouxsie and The Banshees also performed 'Song From The Edge Of The World'.[1210]

'Hall Of Mirrors'

'Hall Of Mirrors', from Kraftwerk's 1977 album *Trans-Europe Express* [1211] turns out to be an inspired, rather than oblique, choice of song, considering the Kraftwerk pure electronic original.

Ralf Hütter's[1212] inscrutable baritone strains, articulating an exposition about vanity and self-image, suit Siouxsie perfectly, and 'Hall Of Mirrors' is transformed into a dance song, complete with Severin's funk-laden bass guitar, Budgie's four-on-the-floor drumbeat, Carruthers' occasional moody Link Wray-esque guitar interjection, and the effective inclusion of Julie Aliss's melodic and poetic harp playing, as though it were actually included on the Kraftwerk original.

The 'looking glass' lyric of the original is a nifty bit of congruence with the title of the Banshees' album. 'Hall Of Mirrors' was recorded between 28 August 1986 and 8 September 1986 at Abbey Road

Studios, and the final mix took place on 29 September 1986. 'Hall Of Mirrors' was first played live by the band on 10 July 1987 at the Bizarre Festival in Berlin.[1213]

'Trust In Me'

Although initially considered a song that would be better suited for The Creatures, 'Trust in Me (The Python's Song)'[1214] originally appears in the Walt Disney film *The Jungle Book*.[1215]

The song was sung by Sterling Holloway playing the part of Kaa, the snake. Siouxsie saw the song as 'very erotic... A seductive snake – what more could you want'.[1216]

The original song begins with the alluring sound of the flute and finger cymbals, leading the listener into a romantic melody, which belies the scene of the Disney film in which endeavours to hypnotise Mowgli[1217] with a view to eating him.

In the Siouxsie and The Banshees version, there is clearly nothing but adoration for the original, with Siouxsie's adaptation erring more towards the chanteuse: Edith Piaf[1218] meets Eartha Kitt.[1219]

As with 'Hall Of Mirrors', the inclusion of a harp is inspired, hovering above Siouxsie's whispered assonance and Steve Severin's Vick Flick[1220]-like bass guitar playing, as Budgie's percussion mooches threateningly throughout the song.

'Trust In Me was recorded between 11 August 1986 and 4 September 1986 at Abbey Road Studios, with the final mix taking place on 7 October 1986. Live. 'Trust In Me' was also debuted at Berlin's Bizarre Festival on 10 July 1987.

'This Wheel's On Fire'

'Dylan's 'Wheels On Fire' was me giving my bow to Julie Driscoll who did this wonderful version of it and who I still admire a lot for having been this strong and proud cool woman at a time when there were all these cute little-doll-like pop girlies'.[1221]

Siouxsie Sioux

The Bob Dylan and The Band[1222] song was originally recorded in 1967, but not released until it appeared on *The Basement Tapes*,[1223] Bob

Dylan's sixteenth album and his second with The Band, with Bob Dylan on vocals.

The Band's version appeared on their debut album, *Music From Big Pink*,[1224] released in 1968, with Rick Danko on lead vocals.

The interpretation of Dylan's lyrics, with theses having pored over every minutiae of his oeuvre, vacillate, among other analyses, between a motorcycle accident Dylan had before writing the song, and any given trope involving god assuring redemption to the protagonist in return for them choosing a righteous path; the only fly in the ointment being the central character's favouring of the apocalypse.

There is also the story of Ixion, in Greek legend the son either of the god Ares or of Phlegyas, king of the Lapiths in Thessaly, who murdered his father-in-law and could find no one to purify him until Zeus took pity on him, admitting him as a guest to Olympus.

Instead of being grateful, Ixion tries to seduce Zeus's wife Hera. Zeus creates a cloud in the shape of Hera and tricks Ixion into coupling with it. This results in the birth of Centaurus, who fathered the Centaurs by the mares of Mount Pelion. Zeus, to punish him, bound him on a fiery wheel, which rolled unceasingly through the air or, according to the more common tradition, in the underworld.[1225]

There is also the wheel of fire as it appears in *King Lear*, 'Thou art a soul in bliss, but I am bound, Upon a wheel of fire, that mine own tears'.[1226]

The burning wheel also features in Ezekiel 10:6, 'Take fire from among the wheels, from among the cherubim'.[1227]

Literary provenance aside, it wasn't The Band's or Dylan's original version the Banshees, in particular Siouxsie, was interested in; it was the Julie Driscoll[1228] with Brian Auger and The Trinity[1229] version, released in 1968.

Siouxsie commented, 'I had the hots for Julie Driscoll! I can't remember when this originally came out, but I'd have been about 11, and I was besotted by her, by the way she looked, by her voice. It was very different to watching Lulu on *Top Of The Pops*, this woman with a shaven head and huge black eyes. I thought she was incredibly beautiful, very spiky and strong and tough – not at all cute and cuddly and feminine. And I loved the song. It conjured up all sorts of fantastic stories for me'.[1230]

Her infatuation with Driscoll and her interpretation of 'This Wheel's On Fire' were so inextricably intertwined for Siouxsie that, on realising that Driscoll was not the originator of the song, a disconsolate Siouxsie reflected, 'We nearly didn't do it when I found out it was a Bob Dylan song. I sulked for ages'.[1231]

Severin expressed similar, albeit less ornery, incredulity, on discovering the song's antecedent. The Banshees' variant is an up tempo, drums-and-bass-oriented take; the beat essentially rendering it a great song to dance to, particularly when one listens to the extended twelve-inch mix, with, again, the accompaniment of Julie Aliss' harp, as well as lush string arrangements, echoing Far Eastern sonority.

Severn's bass guitar chugs, while Carruthers' guitar echoes the Eastern-hemisphere flavour of the song. Before the release of *Through The Looking Glass*, 'This Wheel's On Fire' was the Banshees' first single from the album, distributed on 5 January 1987, with the B-side 'Shooting Sun' on the seven-inch version and 'Shooting Sun' and 'Sleepwalking (On The High Wire)' appearing on the twelve-inch format.

The A-side, 'This Wheel's On Fire (Incendiary Mix)', clocking in at seven minutes and twenty-seven seconds, appears with embellished orchestration, a chugging four-on-the-floor beat and an ending not far off The Beatles' 'A Day In The Life'.

With Clive Richardson taking the reins as video director, the Banshees, capitalising fully on their four-month pause between 1986 tour dates, embarked on the promo for 'This Wheel's On Fire', between 10 November and 13 November 1986, on location in Berkshire and Grip House Studios.[1232]

It was the most elaborate, cinematic, stylish and cohesive-looking video the band had shot to date, including Siouxsie hamming it up as part Snow Queen, part Cruella de Vil[1233] in *One Hundred And One Dalmations* wearing a faux Dalmatian fur coat, white Cossack hat and purple-and-black-striped catsuit, drenched in jewels, as she rides in a black horse-drawn[1234] funeral carriage, replete with black ostrich feathers, alternating between other black and violet floral catsuits, as various Banshee members endeavour to board the vehicle while it is in motion, driving along the water-sodden carriageway.

The video moves apace, due in no small part to Richardson's clever deployment of the spinning wagon wheels, filming the carriage as it barrels through water. There is Banshee action aplenty, as Richardson adopts a multi-layered approach to filming the band so there is never a single moment during the video when Siouxsie isn't pirouetting and dancing with ribbon bangles, or a sartorially brocaded Budgie, Severin or Carruthers aren't in the throes of acting, singing, spinning, colliding or playing their instruments, all dressed to the nines and looking a cross between fugitives from a successful bank heist and making their way to a Regency ball.

The band's *Top Of The Pops* performance, recorded on 22 January 1987, is correspondingly convincing, with Siouxsie's defiant straight-to-camera assuredness, dressed in a floral catsuit, black fur headband, bejewelled gilt bird skull brooch and conceivably the most embellished hip belt to ever grace the *Top Of The Pops* studio.

Budgie, Severin and Carruthers, attendant in monochrome, all cut a similar, if judiciously understated, dash. The Banshees also appeared on *TopPop*,[1235] the first regular television programme dedicated pop music in Holland, boasting an impressive roster of (albeit mimed) acts including David Bowie, Iggy Pop, Abba, Black Sabbath, Madonna and Bob Marley and The Wailers.[1236]

With Siouxsie attired in the black and purple catsuit worn in the 'This Wheel's On Fire' video, she and the other Banshee members performed on stage with a backdrop like a facsimile of a giant box of vegetables. Siouxsie was also fleetingly interviewed on the programme, with questions asked about breaking her leg, the secret to the band's longevity, the release of *Through The Looking Glass* and Siouxsie's on-the-record quote about not wishing to trade places with Madonna.

There was also an appearance to promote the single on the short-lived Belgian *Bingo!*[1237] pop programme on 9 March 1987, with the discernible absence of John Valentine Carruthers, the reasons for which will become apparent.

'Shooting Sun' was conceived on 10 January 1985, between the making of *Hyæna* and *Tinderbox*, although recording took place between 15 and 17 September 1986 at Firehouse Studios.

Beginning with a lulling introduction, the song contains a lyric that hints at reprisal, conjoined with Siouxsie's lyrics which parallel her Pompeii fixation, mentioning flames running in golden streams and breaking open years of stone. Although the band were in the throes of making an album of covers, there was still a rich seam of original material to be mined, and 'Shooting Sun' is testament to the ease with which the band could mesh a spectrum of musical ideas together with mellifluous results.

The final mix for 'Shooting Sun' took place on 26 October 1986. 'Shooting Sun' had two live airings, the first of which was on the BBC Radio 2 Janice Long Show, recorded on 11 January 1987 and transmitted on 2 February 1987. The other live performance was on 23 September 2004 at the House of Blues, West Hollywood, California, USA.[1238]

Initially intended for inclusion on *Tinderbox*,[1239] 'Sleepwalking (On The High Wire)' shares the same chronology as 'Shooting Sun'. Apparently influenced by the 1956 film *Trapeze*,[1240] the storyline of which involves Mike Ribble,[1241] a once renowned circus acrobat, now disabled due to a fall while performing, is emotionally split between two ambitious young trapeze artists, one a talented young American, Tino Orsini,[1242] and a less-gifted but beautiful Italian, Lola.[1243]

Ribble is the one of half a dozen trapeze performers who managed to successfully complete a triple somersault before his fall. Tino is resolute that he wants to be the seventh trapeze artist to complete Ribble's acrobatic feat, and Orsini's persistence and chutzpah wins Ribble over. However, Lola, an acrobat in the same circus, tries to disrupt Orsini's acrobatic schooling to ensure that the spotlight shines on her performance.

The vaguely lugubrious keyboard gives way to a splash of tambourine and some accented, reverb-soaked guitar playing, over the top of which there is a further high-pitched, dissonant wail, reminiscent of Robert Fripp's guitar playing on David Bowie's 'Beauty And The Beast'.[1244]

Bass and drums, Budgie keeping a simple four-on-the-floor rhythm, rumble through the song, with the punctuation of thunder-sounding synthesised notes, as well as a plethora of other sounds that conjure up images of a hallucinatory dank sub-terrestrial chamber. 'Sleepwalking (On The High Wire)' was recorded on 20 September 1986 at Firehouse Studios, and the final mix for the song took place on 26 October 1986. 'Sleepwalking (On The High Wire)' does not feature in the Banshees' repertoire of live songs.

The cover design for 'This Wheel's On Fire' opts for a hybridised motif, somewhere between a still from *The Jetsons*[1245] and a Soviet-era propaganda poster. Two metallic curved prongs create diagonal animation with a stylised hand with a pointing finger poking through a tractor tyre, as delicately illustrated, translucent black tulle opera gloves cascade throughout the image, which is rendered in modulations of greens, blues, oranges, pinks and reds.

The Siouxsie and The Banshees ampersand is again prominent in the top right-hand corner, and the band's name, as well as that of the single, a ribbon of red and white on front and back, is presented in a black and white dot-matrix design in two corners, while a simple white on black four-petal vector is repeated throughout. A monochromatic peacock feather embellishes the back cover.

'This Wheel's On Fire' was initially recorded and subsequently scrapped between 27 July 1986 and 12 August 1986 at Abbey Road Studios, then picked up again and recorded between 26 August 1986 and 4 September 1986, where the song also has its final mix.[1246]

Live, 'This Wheel's On Fire' was first performed at the Palácio das Convenções do Anhembi São Paulo, Brazil, on 28 November 1986. Released on 5 January 1987, in the UK Official Singles Chart it punctured the Top Twenty and peaked at number 14, becoming the Banshees' highest chart placing since 'Dear Prudence' and the band's third-best selling single since 'Hong Kong Garden'.

'Strange Fruit'

> *'Southern trees bear strange fruit*
> *Blood on the leaves and blood at the root*
> *Black bodies swinging in the southern breeze*
> *Strange fruit hanging from the poplar trees'*[1247]

Billie Holiday[1248]

Apparently, John Valentine Carruthers' initial idea, with Steve Severin's suggestion of adding a New Orleans-style funeral march in the middle of the song, 'Strange Fruit' is undoubtedly ubiquitous with the 1939 Billie Holiday version.

However, the origins of the lyrics begin with Abel Meeropol, who had written song lyrics for both Peggy Lee[1249] ('Apples, Peaches and Cherries') and Frank Sinatra ('The House I Live In').[1250]

But this poem, originally titled 'Bitter Fruit' on its publication in January 1937 after Meeropol saw the photograph of the 1930 lynching of Tom Shipp and Abe Smith[1251] in Marion, Indiana, was an altogether more desolate affair about the practice of lynching, a method of social control predicated on racial hatred, which predominantly took place in North American former Confederate states.

Mississippi, Florida, Arkansas and Louisiana claimed the highest statewide rates of lynching in the United States, and Mississippi, Georgia and Louisiana the highest number of lynchings across the USA.

The 'fruit' Meeropol refers to is the ravaged bodies hanging from the trees. This barbaric ritual, whereby 'Victims would be seized and subjected to every imaginable manner of physical torment, with the torture usually ending with being hung from a tree and set on fire.

More often than not, victims would be dismembered, and mob members would take pieces of their flesh and bone as souvenirs',[1252] was a method of social and racial decree, its main aim to terrorise black Americans into submission, rendering them an inferior racial caste.

Lynchings became widely practised in the USA's south from roughly 1877, the end of post-Civil War reconstruction, through to 1950.[1253]

'Strange Fruit' was originally sung by Meeropol's partner Laura Duncan[1254] as a protest song at Madison Square Garden in New York City in 1938. Billie Holiday's inaugural performance of 'Strange Fruit' was at a former speakeasy in New York City, called 'Cafe Society'.

It was Holiday's final number of the evening, and not what the audience was expecting, with, 'Blood on the leaves and blood at the root… Black bodies swinging in the Southern breeze'. Lynching? It's a song about lynching? The chatter from the tables dries up. Every eye in the room is on the singer, every ear on the song. After the last word – a long, abruptly severed cry of "crop" – the whole room snaps to black. When the house lights go up, she's gone'.[1255]

On the studio recording of 'Strange Fruit', the three-versed lyric begins at one minute and nine seconds, over a third of the song's length, making every word and phrase rupture with meaning; the burning flesh and sustenance for crows to eat and the southern sun to rot juxtaposed with decorous images of sweet-scented magnolia and the ironically phrased gallantry of the South, imbuing the song with barbed piquancy.

Siouxsie and The Banshees' 'Strange Fruit' cover begins with the sound of dust-infused wind, the strings ensemble and Siouxsie's emotive, characterful vocal, punctuated by the sound of a funeral bell before, at one minute and thirty-one seconds, the melancholically lugubrious strains of the New Orleans[1256] jazz ensemble begins, with the requisite strains of trumpet, saxophone and trombone, and the thump of a tonal bass drum leading the song into the depths of mourning.

The origins of the New Orleans Jazz Funeral are culturally complex and multi-faceted, including the colonisation of the region by the French, Spanish and British in turn, where military brass bands were sequestered to play at an array of official occasions and attended funerals throughout the 19th century.

New Orleans was also central to the domestic slave trade that was thriving in 1808. West African tribal traditions of rejoicing at death through music, drums and chants travelled with the slaves who found themselves forced into subjugation in the area. The premise of the ceremonial music was that it was meant to assist the dead to navigate the passage from Earth to Heaven; not a dissimilar premise to the Haitian Voodoo idea of celebrating after death in order to satiate the spirit gods.

The final verse of 'Strange Fruit', with its imagery of hanging bodies being plundered, feasted on and further beaten and destroyed, this time by the sun, wind and rain, enters the song at two minutes and forty seconds, accompanied by the orchestrated gloom of violin and cello, as 'Strange Fruit' deliquesces as it began, into the cinder-contaminated hot southern squall. 'Strange Fruit' was recorded between 20 August and 2 September 1986 at Abbey Road Studios, with the final mix taking place on 7 October 1986.[1257] The song was never included int band's live repertoire.

'You're Lost Little Girl'

Originally on The Doors' *Strange Days* album, Siouxsie and The Banshees pay homage to one of Siouxsie's favourite singers, Jim Morrison. Beginning with eight seconds of Doug Lubahn's downbeat bass guitar,[1258] Robbie Krieger's guitar jangle joins the fray, and the lilt of John Densmore's high hat and the idiosyncratic tones of Ray Manzarek's Vox Continental[1259] organ, an instrument also heard on The Animals' 'House Of The Rising Sun' and The Velvet Underground's 'Sister Ray'.

The lyrics are delivered by Morrison sotto voce, the result of producer Paul A. Rothchild's[1260] suggestion that the vocal wasn't forced and was delivered in a relaxed way, '…so that his voice would sound like that of Frank Sinatra',[1261] one of Morrison's singing heroes, the other being Elvis Presley.

It was also mooted by The Doors, not entirely seriously, '… whether no less a crooner than Frank Sinatra might deign to cover 'You're Lost Little Girl'… John Densmore thought it would have made a great serenade to his waifish wife, Mia Farrow'.[1262]

The title of the song is thought to have been inspired by William Blake's *The Little Girl Lost*, which first appeared in the second part of Blake's poetry collection *Songs of Innocence and of Experience*, first published in 1794.[1263]

The overall refrain of the song is uncomplicated, Siouxsie saying of Morrison, 'I like the empty songs best where it's just his voice and a single instrument. His voice was definitely the lead instrument in The Doors'.[1264]

The Banshees' arrangement of 'You're Lost Little Girl' finds the listener in the landscape of Ennio Morricone once again, with the inclusion of a western-style Tack piano[1265] and chimes, which could have come from 'Carillon's Theme' from *For A Few Dollars More*.

The 3/4 waltz time signature at the beginning of the song, underpinned by the bass guitar matching the pattern of the bass drum, and Siouxsie's Morrison-esque vocal, builds into a tambourine and tubular bells, matching the ebb and flow of the vocal-led carnival, with all the lush production values of The Four Tops' 'Reach Out I'll Be There',[1266] a nod to Siouxsie's love of the Motown sound.

Both 'You're Lost Little Girl' and 'Reach Out And I'll Be There', coincidentally, run at two minutes and fifty-eight seconds. The production, especially Budgie's drumming sound, also echoes the compressed reverberation used by Phil Spector, aforementioned with regard to Hal Blaine. However, it isn't just the percussive elements that are given the Spector/ Motown treatment; it's an aesthetic that pervades the entire song.

At one minute and forty-one seconds, something delightfully incongruous happens, as 'You're Lost Little Girl' spirals into fourteen seconds of disorienting mayhem, a dissonant cross between the circus-inspired 'Henry The Horse' waltz sequence in The Beatles' 'Being For The Benefit Of Mr. Kite!' from the 1967 album *Sgt. Pepper's Lonely Hearts Club Band*, driven by the distinctive sound of a calliope steam organ, the twelve seconds of Mick Ronson's wailing guitar on David Bowie's 'Time', a song which also deploys the aforesaid Tack piano, and the 'Pleasure Island'[1267] scene in the Walt Disney 1940 film *Pinocchio*.[1268]

The Banshees' psychedelic visitation deploys a carnivalesque 'oom pah pah' drumbeat and the caterwauling evocative of a conglomerated Laughing Sal[1269] and Banshee wail. 'You're Lost Little Girl' was recorded between 13 August 1986 and 5 September 1986 at Abbey Road Studios, where the final mix took place on 7 October 1986. There are no discernible live Siouxsie and The Banshees' renditions of the song.

'The Passenger'

Initial trepidation about doing a cover version of Iggy Pop's 'The Passenger'[1270] was trumped by the band wanting to try it out and see what ensued. Pop's original, co-written with guitarist Ricky

Gardiner[1271] and on the 1977 *Lust For Life* album, denotes a time in the singer's life when Pop was trying to get a derailed career back on track after the disbanding of The Stooges[1272] in 1974.

After a downward spiral of drug and alcohol abuse, he was admitted to the UCLA Neuropsychiatric Institute[1273] in 1975, where he underwent an array of treatments, including psychoanalysis, so he could undergo a complete detox. One of very few notable visitors during this period was David Bowie, who was resolute that Pop should join Bowie on his Isolar tour.[1274]

Bowie had previously worked with Pop on the Stooges' 1973 album *Raw Power*[1275] as co-producer. What transpired was two albums that essentially mark the resurrection of Pop's career and re-introduction into making music, beginning with 1977's *The Idiot*,[1276] produced solely by Bowie, and, in very quick succession, *Lust For Life*,[1277] with the triumvirate production of David Bowie, Iggy Pop and Colin Thurston.

These two albums dovetail with Bowie's own purple patch in making *Heroes* and *Low* at Hansa Studios in Berlin, where *Lust For Life* was also recorded.

At the time, Bowie was also in the throes of ridding himself of cocaine addiction and he and Iggy became flatmates for a spell. Pop, reflecting about this time in his career and Bowie's companionship and mentoring, comments, 'The friendship was basically that this guy salvaged me from certain professional and maybe personal annihilation – simple as that… A lot of people were curious about me, but only he was the one who had enough truly in common with me, who actually really liked what I did and could get on board with it, and who also had decent enough intentions to help me out. He did a good thing'.[1278]

Pop's 'The Passenger' alludes to the amount of time he spent travelling with David Bowie by car, driving throughout the day and night, while travelling across North America and Europe, as well as the influence of *The Lords*,[1279] a collection of poems written by Jim Morrison, reflecting on Morrison's thoughts on modern life, people, places and cinema.

Ricky Gardiner's guitar riff, was the result of the guitarist '…

walking around in the apple trees and it was apple blossom time... I had an old Les Paul Junior round my neck and I was just wandering about and enjoying this fantastic spring morning. I wasn't paying any attention at all to what I was playing but I heard these chords and I thought, 'Oh, I must remember that'.[1280]

The result is an intoxicating, infinitely memorable song, the musical arrangement of which is so perfectly composed as to facilitate Pop to almost scat over the top of it; the 'La la la la la la la la, la la's reminiscent of any mental distraction to relieve the monotony of a seemingly interminable car journey.

The Banshees' interpretation retains the spirit of Pop's original as it bounds along, John Valentine Carruthers' guitar playing a near-perfect enactment of the Gardiner primary source. Facilitated by Mike Hedges's trademark lavish production and the inclusion of the Banshees' adopted brass section, alongside tubular bells and that Midas Spector-dusted tambourine sound, the Banshees' 'The Passenger' cavorts with inexhaustible energy.

The second single from *Through The Looking Glass*, 'The Passenger' was released on 16 March 1987 and was available in both seven and twelve-inch formats. The B-side songs are 'She's Cuckoo' (seven inch) and 'She's Cuckoo' and 'Something Blue' (12 inch).[1281]

'The Passenger' twelve-inch is the 'Llllloco-Motion Mix' extended version, and indubitably a song that lends itself to a further three minutes and four seconds, replete with dub-style guitar and further brass and tubular bells frills.

Siouxsie and The Banshees performed 'The Passenger' on Channel 4's *The Tube*, where they were filmed in Portmeirion, the setting for the UK TV show *The Prisoner*. The performance, filmed in early January 1987, is delivered with gusto and conviction, juxtaposed with shots of Portmeirion beach and occasional footage from *The Prisoner* as Number Six, portrayed by Patrick McGoohan, is relentlessly pursued by Rover, the coercive floating white balloon whose role it was to keep control of fractious inhabitants of The Village,[1282] rendering them incapacitated or, if necessary, killing them.

Siouxsie and Budgie appear in near-matching black and white stripes – Siouxsie's horizontal, Budgie's vertical. The appearance of John Valentine Carruthers completes the quartet, although it is to prove his last official sighting with the band. There had been rumblings in the Banshee camp more or less throughout Carruthers' tenure, questioning both his motivation and commitment.

Severin commented, 'He was all front. I remember sitting in a hotel room with him telling me that Robert (Smith) had been a rubbish guitarist and that he could have played the stuff on *Hyæna* much better.

When he was called upon to prove it, though, he was remarkably uncreative. Trying to get a fresh sound out of him was like trying to get blood out of a stone'.[1283]

Siouxsie recalls, to the day, when, on 16 January 1987, Siouxsie, Severin and Budgie discussed Carruthers' departure from the band and how this was to be instigated. Severin recalls it was incumbent on him to do the deed, 'I had to go round to his flat and tell him, which I hated doing. I tried being as diplomatic as I could, and he looked up and said, "Well at least I got to go to Brazil". He obviously wasn't that gutted'.[1284]

Billy 'Chainsaw' Houlston, musing on Carruthers' departure, comments, 'There always seemed to be a whipping boy. (Robert) Smith may have been fronting The Cure, but when he was a Banshee he was "Fat Bob". Aside from learning the old stuff, he's got to come up with new ideas, too... I don't think John was allowed to spread his wings as much as much as he would have liked. Banshees guitarists were like the Spinal Tap drummer. They would always explode one way or another'.[1285]

Clive Richardson was called upon to direct the promo for the single, which took place between the 18 January and 20 January 1987 at Bell Studios. A dazzling vision in monochrome, with the stalwart trinity of Siouxsie, Severin and Budgie present, the Banshees and Clive Richardson made a video that pulls out every visual stop regarding its completeness.

Siouxsie's shock of raven hair is now a Liza Minnelli[1286]-as-Sally-Bowles bubikopf, restyled by Vidal Sassoon,[1287] as the singer appears in a giant suspended geometric leaded-glass pendant, with innumerable costume changes alternating between black backless dress, catsuits, waistcoats, 1920s' fringed flapper cap and a treasure trove of beaded necklaces, bangles and other accoutrements; she struts through every scene with exaltation.

Richardson and the Banshees have orchestrated a video whereby the monochromatic schema, a no-frills approach excepting the band's performance, gives both parties the latitude to be creative and inventive, including the cat's cradle of strings Severin plays across Siouxsie's backless dress and Budgie adopting the guise of Jackson Pollock and applying splashes of red and yellow paint on a clear perspex screen, alternating between timpani mallets and handprints.

Siouxsie appears through the underside of another transparent screen as she toys with a multitude of scattered cat's-eye marbles. At certain points, Severin tries not to corpse, as Siouxsie impishly tries to put him off his inscrutable stride. Elsewhere, Siouxsie, Severin and Budge dance the can-can, smile, laugh and generally goof off.

The seven and twelve-inch B-side of 'The Passenger', 'She's Cuckoo' (initially titled 'He's Cuckoo') names a litany of bird species, which Siouxsie clearly relishes singing in a domino effect of a birder's paradise.

The Budgie-penned lyrics were prompted initially by the 'cuckoo' sound of his boiling kettle, after which he rifled through his book of bird classifications[1288] to create an Edward Lear-esque feathered tapestry.

The 'Cuckoo' of the song also has the duality of either being the European parasite given to laying eggs in the nests of other birds or someone voraciously enamoured of someone else. The metronomic percussion is accompanied by a wooden agogo[1289] and various permutations of keyboards and xylophone, creating slow-moving ambience, the prelude almost elegiac.

'She's Cuckoo' was recorded between 6 January and 8 January 1987 at Abbey Road Studios.[1290] There is no live outing for the song. 'Something Blue' is imbued with all the percussive urgency heard on David Bowie's 'Weeping Wall'[1291] with its similar deployment of the xylophone as Siouxsie endeavours to catalogue a miscellany of blues, with their rich-sounding names, the blue in question literal and metaphorical as the song's denouement, after a Prussian, emerald and turquoise reverie plays on words, as, out of the blue, perhaps a long lost love is unexpectedly brought to mind, 'out of the blue'.

'Something Blue' was recorded between 6 January and 8 January 1987 at Abbey Road Studios.[1292] It is first played live on the BBC Radio 2 Janice Long Show, recorded on 11 January 1987 and transmitted on 2 February 1987.

The single's front cover design, originating from Crocodile Studios in London, is a cartographical Renaissance-inspired terrestrial and celestial affair with gold stars, not dissimilar to those that appear on Giotto's magnificent Cappella degli Scrovegni[1293] fresco in Padua, Italy.

The stars lie atop elements of the world globe, with colours centred around a pale green, yellow and orange cartographical palette, where one can discern the province of Mongolia[1294] next to China, as well as the Barents Sea,[1295] as a face with all the characteristics of an angel in Fra Angelico's 'Christ Glorified in the Court of Heaven', painted in 1423–24, looks on.

There is also an orange delineation of the nautilus shell[1296] as it appears in sacred geometry. The sense of movement is conflated by all the imagery being encircled, not only exemplifying the globetrotting theme but also adroitly echoing the shape of the disc within.

There are also discernibly grainy monochrome striations within the circular motif, again emulating the vinyl format. The Siouxsie and The Banshees ampersand remains dominant in the bottom left-hand corner of the image, and 'The Passenger' is rendered in a hybridised black font with both Gothic and cursive elements.

Both back and front designs have black and white halftone elements. The back cover of 'The Passenger' is a black and white photograph of a 1955 Chevrolet car Bel Air hood ornament, a three-dimensional chrome depiction of a bird airplane. There is also a chrome hood V in shot.[1297]

The cover for the 'Lllloco-motion Mix' twelve-inch expands a couple of the visual motifs such as the Fra Angelico face and a light blue 'The Passenger' design. The seven-inch single also comes with a limited-edition poster of Siouxsie.[1298] 'The Passenger' was recorded between 28 July and 15 August 1986 at Abbey Road Studios, where the final mix also took place on 26 September 1986.[1299] 'The Passenger' peaked at number 41 in the UK Singles Chart.

'Gun'

Both Siouxsie and Steve Severin found out they both had copies of John Cale's 1974 album *Fear*,[1300] so it is perhaps unsurprising that one of his songs should appear on *Through The Looking Glass*. Cale's original eight minute and four second version is a juxtaposition of an elegant deadpan vocal delivery belying the subject matter of the song, which concerns grisly murders and a subterranean world where the protagonist's very being has become the embodiment of a gun.

Cale, an expert narrator and storyteller, presents the objectified 'don't shoot the messenger' exposé, as if Bonnie And Clyde[1301] had teamed up with Freddie Kruger.[1302] There is also the gorgeous, mesmerising cacophony of Phil Manzanera's[1303] guitar playing, which twists and turns with all the wringing angst and tumult that can be heard on The Velvet Underground's 'I Heard Her Call My Name'.[1304]

The Siouxsie and The Banshees 'Gun' cover is an attenuated version of Cale's original, as well as being embellished by the Banshees' string and brass retinue, with percussive xylophone for added texture.

John Valentine Carruthers plays a hybrid of Rockabilly[1305] clean-sounding guitar melded with Robert Fripp-esque 'Scary Monsters (And Super Creeps)' low succubus growl. Jocelyn Pook and Ginny Hewes' viola and violin add a frisson of screeching *Psycho* strings.

Recording 'Gun' didn't pass without incident, with the hammer of the firearm well and truly pulled back and ready to strike the firing pin, as Siouxsie explained with regard to Carruthers' contribution to the song: 'On 'Gun', he added a really straight acoustic guitar bit which sounded like the theme tune to *Blue Peter* or something, so I had this idea of twisting the knobs on the mixing desk and really fucking up the sound to make it more exciting. John was outraged and came storming in accusing me of wrecking some great artistic piece of work'.[1306]

Siouxsie also reflected that Carruthers '…wasn't responsive to any kind of invention or creativity. We'd been spoiled by having McGeoch in the band because he was so capable of taking a vague idea and turning it into something. We had to work hard to get anything out of Carruthers. That's when a lot of the magic went from the band for me. It wasn't equal or spontaneous anymore'.[1307]

'Gun' was recorded between 28 July and 1 August 1986 at Abbey Road Studios, the final mix taking place on 1 October 1986. There are no apparent Siouxsie and The Banshees live performances of 'Gun'.

'Sea Breezes'

Originally on the eponymously titled Roxy Music debut album, the first half of the seven-minute-and-three-second song, ushered in with the gentle ebbing and flowing of the tide, is the austere-sounding trio of a Hohner Pianet,[1308] Andy Mackay's[1309] oboe and Bryan Ferry's quavering falsetto, latterly joined by Phil Manzanera's guitar.

The second half of 'Sea Breezes' moves the song from a carefree musing into the realms of a sharper, more brittle abstraction, as Manzanera's guitar wail travels between speakers, Paul Thompson's[1310] drums deliver an improvisational expressive slant, and Graham Simpson's[1311] bass guitar inclines towards the melody expressed in Ferry's voice, with the song sounding as though it is on the precipice of falling apart, further skewed by the experimental frizzle of Brian Eno's synthesizer. Around the six minute and fourteen second mark, the storm has calmed and the listener is soothed by lilting voice, oboe and pianet.

It seems appropriate that there should be the inclusion of a Roxy Music song on *Through The Looking Glass*, not least due to the fact that it was at a sold-out Roxy Music show at Wembley Arena on 18 October 1975, during the 'Sirens' tour, when Siouxsie Sioux and Steve Severin first met.

Severin comments, 'We tried 'Pyjamarama' and 'Street Life' for about two seconds, and we thought that it was too obvious to do. I think Sioux found it in the end, she really liked the melody'.[1312]

However, it would appear that 'Sea Breezes' was also an incongruous choice for the Banshees as it was not a favourite Roxy Music song of any of the band, plus, as Severin comments, they felt the song '…was just completely perfect'.[1313]

The Banshees' cover is similarly introspective, with a pared-back introduction, capturing the DNA of the original, with the addition of strings giving the song an additional emotive quality. As the Banshees' 'Sea Breezes' is an abbreviated take, around three minutes shorter than the Roxy Music original, the crescendo of the song barrels forwards around the one minute forty second mark, with John Valentine Carruthers' flanged guitar emulating the ripples of the sea. The song then pulls back, reverting to a softer timbre until it enters its final minute like a Vaughan Williams[1314] symphony, including crashing drums, guitars and evocative keyboards. 'Sea Breezes' was recorded between 11 August and 9 September 1986 at Abbey Road Studios, and the final mix for the song took place on 6 October 1986. 'Sea Breezes' was never played live by the Banshees.

'Little Johnny Jewel'

Perhaps it shouldn't be too much of a surprise that, rather than select a song from Television's opus *Marquee Moon*, Siouxsie and The Banshees favour Television's first single release, 'Little Johnny Jewel',[1315] a song that, when played live, could be improvised and extemporised for over fourteen minutes, as can be heard on *Live At The Old Waldorf*.[1316]

Originally recorded and released in 1975, the single version has 'Little Johnny Jewel Pt 1', running at three minutes and forty-seven seconds as an A-side and 'Little Johnny Jewel Pt 2' on the B-side, slightly longer at four minutes and eleven seconds.

Musically, one can see why the Banshees would be drawn to 'Little Johnny Jewel', a mini opera, with all the apparent improvisation and extemporisation of their beloved Can, with the twin guitars of Tom Verlaine[1317] and Richard Lloyd[1318] restrained and stripped down; a musical template that has been plundered by bands and guitarists too numerous to mention.

Billy Ficca's[1319] virtuoso drumming is the magnificent glue that holds the seeming autoschediasm together, along with the steady and unfussy bass playing of Fred Smith,[1320] whose opening rumbling notes are so powerful that the listener can almost feel the heat emitted from Smith's amplifier transistor.

Tom Verlaine educes a stifled, almost incidental vocal. A song the band, Severin comments, had been playing '...at soundchecks for years – basically because we've always liked it. But we also wanted an element of surprise on the record, we wanted to do songs which people wouldn't expect us to cover'.[1321]

The Banshees' version is a nonchalant ebb-and-flow take on the Television original, capturing its proto-punk disposition. Its initial languid pace, a melange of strings, guitars, drums and vocal, gives way to a quickening pace, one minute in, as lush, sweeping orchestration comes to the fore and Carruthers wrings a higher scale of notes from his guitar before resuming a lower range snarl.

Two minutes and fifty seconds sees the song move into the realms of melancholia, as we enter the final act, with Siouxsie's expert vocal narration heralding finger clicks, distant wailing guitar, muffled bass, drum rim clicks and eventual diffusion.

'Little Johnny Jewel' was recorded by the Banshees between 28 July and 1 August 1986 at Abbey Road Studios, with the final mix undertaken on 3 October 1986. It had one live airing, on the BBC Radio 2 Janice Long Show, recorded on 11 January 1987 and transmitted on 2 February 1987.

Of note, although not on the original pressing of the 1987 *Through The Looking Glass*, is the Banshees' blistering rendition of The Modern Lovers 'She Cracked'[1322], which has the almost perfect circularity of DNA with The Modern Lovers original cross-pollinated lineage with The Stooges' 'I Wanna Be Your Dog'[1323] and The Velvet Underground's 'What Goes On'[1324] and Talking Heads 'Once In A Lifetime'[1325] (produced by Bowie collaborator Brian Eno) regarding The Modern Lovers and Talking Heads keyboardist Jerry Harrison emulating John Cale's Vox Continental keyboard sound when it kicks in at three minutes and twenty six seconds. John Cale also produced The Modern Lovers' 'She Cracked' and The Stooges debut album.

In terms of chronology, after the release of 'This Wheel's On Fire' and before the distribution of 'The Passenger', the Strange Fruit label,[1326] established by John Peel and Clive Selwood, released a Siouxsie and The Banshees *The Peel Sessions* EP, featuring recordings made for John Peel's show, originally recorded at the BBC Studios in

Maida Vale on 29 November 1977 and broadcast on 5 December 1977. The four songs included are 'Love In A Void', 'Mirage', 'Mittageisen (Metal Postcard)' and 'Suburban Relapse'.

The front cover of the album includes a die-cut central square through which the inner sleeve can be viewed from both front and back, illustrated by Stephanie Atkins, under the art direction of Crocodile, is the dispersal of the eyes of all four band members superimposed over what appears to be monochromatic arid terrain, and through the die-cut aperture a hypnotic red, black, white and orange spiral collage is espied.

The back cover has four single head shots of every band member doused in white stage make up, evoking their Pompeiian foray, photographed by Ewan Fraser. The die-cut perforation reveals another, more hand-drawn spiral. The inner sleeve, once fully revealed, is, on one side, a rich palette of colours interspersed with further head shots of the band; the other side reveals a paler array of white and yellow tones, with the inclusion of all song titles. 'Through The Looking Glass' peaked at number 15 in the UK Official Albums Chart.

Chapter Eleven
Three Become Five

With John Valentine Carruthers out of the band, having fulfilled recording duties for *Tinderbox* and *Through The Looking Glass*, as well as undertaking 120 tour dates with the Banshees, Siouxsie, Budgie and Severin's situation as a three piece necessitated the search for another guitarist.

However, this wasn't before they recruited Martin McCarrick as a full time Banshee, having been impressed with his work on both The Glove's *Blue Sunshine* and *Through The Looking Glass*.

McCarrick recalls being wined and dined at Fuji, a Japanese restaurant on Brewer Street, Soho, where the band '... gave me more sake than I'd ever seen, but it was a slightly odd encounter. Severin discussed religion and Siouxsie talked about her brother'.[1327] McCarrick also recounts the disorientation Siouxsie's reconfigured hairstyle caused him, 'Siouxsie's big backcombed chignon had gone, and she was sporting a crop hairdo'.[1328]

As the evening progressed, McCarrick, wondering if someone was going to broach the subject of him joining the band, had his question answered when, he recalls, 'Eventually, there was a lull in the conversation and Severin leaned over and said, "Well, do you want to join?" I said, "Yes," and that was it. We carried on knocking back the sake and brandy'.[1329]

McCarrick's passage to becoming a Banshee was, initially, when he was given a copy of *Join Hands* for his 16th birthday, prompting the realisation that the Banshee musical aesthetic was about so much more than an attitude of, McCarrick proffers, '"Fuck off, I'm gonna do what I want cos I'm a punk"', the Sex Pistols' line'.[1330]

Subsequently, McCarrick met Anne Stephenson, through whose contacts McCarrick began undertaking session work. He eventually met Siouxsie and The Banshees through Marc Almond, which slightly irked Almond as McCarrick had been an important part of Almond's Willing Sinners[1331] backing band for quite some time.

With all their trials, tribulations and misfortunes, there was a question about whether the Banshees would continue. Billy 'Chainsaw' Houlston postulates, 'If Martin hadn't joined, I don't think the Banshees would have been able to sustain it for as long as they did... Martin had been classically trained and added a whole new dimension, especially in terms of songwriting. He just made everything bigger'.[1332]

There was also what Siouxsie, Budgie and Severin considered a brief period of enlightened reverie, when, unencumbered by the worry of what John Valentine Carruthers may or may not be adding to the band, not only were they rehearsing showing Carruthers the exit door, the Banshees started to go over new material – 'She's Cuckoo', 'Something Blue' and 'Peek-A-Boo'.

The Banshees also worked on another new song, 'The Killing Jar', Steve Severin having brought in the lyrics for the band to start working on some music. It was at this point, with the thought of yet another conveyer belt of wannabe guitarists insurmountably grim, that McCarrick was invited to work with the band on several occasions, each of which proved fruitful.

McCarrick also realised that there was more to Siouxsie and The Banshees than 'Spellbound', although it seemed to him that, even though the band had amassed an eclectic and adventurous back catalogue, with a cumulatively indifferent music press and a groundswell of what was tantamount to a backlash, at least in the UK, the band were not given the latitude or empathy to grow.

With Martin McCarrick in the Banshee fold, it was clear that the band needed to face the necessity of recruiting another guitarist. McCarrick recalls the majority of auditioning hopefuls tantamount to being a 'crock of shite'.[1333]

On this occasion, it turned out to be a two-horse race between Japan's Rob Dean,[1334] an accomplished player with a lot of session work under his belt, and aforementioned member of Specimen, Jon Klein.

The Cult's Ian Astbury describes Specimen's oeuvre as '…very dark, but they were as much German as they were The Addams Family. They were like a Death Bowie'.[1335]

The Specimen aesthetic, as the Batcave host band, was a melange of *The Rocky Horror Show*[1336] with aspects of *Blade Runner*,[1337] the New York Dolls and more than a touch of burlesque, dressed in fishnet stockings and liberal application of white foundation and eyeliner.

Musically, Specimen are a mixture of Glam stomp coupled with Klein's searing guitar sound, sharing the same addictive, glutinous texture as Killing Joke's Geordie Walker and a modicum of melodious Goth pop. Among the band's five single and EP releases between 1983 and 1986 are two singles that pierced the UK Top One Hundred Singles Chart, 'Returning (from a Journey)'[1338] and 'Beauty Of Poison'.[1339] The *Sharp Teeth* EP[1340] peaked at number 20 in the UK Indie Singles Chart.[1341]

For the Banshees, what marked Jon Klein out was that he had his own unique style, flamboyant but not dressing, as some did for the audition, as a carbon copy of Steve Severin. Klein's brief, when it was his turn to face his Banshee interviewers, came from Siouxsie, to play "an exploding horse going over a cliff".[1342]

The noise elicited from Klein's guitar, although his actual playing wasn't perhaps as accomplished and studied as some of the other players trying out, clearly did the trick. In tandem with McCarrick, Siouxsie and The Banshees had also left a lasting impression on Klein, having heard 'Metal Postcard' as a teenager on the John Peel Show, and also encountering the band live during the 'Juju' tour in 1981.

Klein, the third Banshees' Jo(h)n from an art school background, was given the nod by Severin, Budgie having opted for Rob Dean. Klein acknowledged that 'it was Severin's vote that counted'.[1343]

Klein was also at a pivotal point with his own career trajectory, although it looked as though Specimen were on the cusp of a breakthrough in America, having been signed to Sire Records[1344] in 1983, as well as a centre spread in *Rolling Stone*. However, despite the success of the Batcave, Klein reflects on Specimen's own throw of the dice, '…it looked like it was going big time but we managed to fuck it up. It was a good time to join the Banshees, just as they were having this shake up'.[1345]

With a semblance of balance and relative normality restored, courtesy of two new band members and a rekindled esprit de corps between Siouxsie and Severin, the new Banshees' chapter unfolded with the recording of a new single.

'Song From The Edge Of The World'[1346] had already been demoed during the writing and recording of *Tinderbox* in 1985, and had had its live debut during the WOMAD festival in 1986. Martin McCarrick remembers that recording the song was not an entirely joyous process, with a palpable tension within the band, 'Severin and Siouxsie were arguing. There was no creative spark, just this awful unrest. I thought, "Have I done the wrong thing by joining this band?"'[1347]

There was also the search for the right producer, this time opting for Mike Thorne, chosen for his work with the band Wire.[1348] However, the optimistic notion that Thorne could infuse the same distorted, choppy angularity into the Banshees' work as he had with *Pink Flag*,[1349] *Chairs Missing*[1350] and *154*[1351] proved to be folly. The band had underestimated, Severin recollects, Thorne's '…academic approach to everything, while at the same time thinking he was Brian Eno, which he wasn't'.[1352]

'Song From The Edge Of The World', due to its *Tinderbox* ancestry, shares the same Romeo and Juliet characteristics delineated in 'Land's End'.[1353] With lyrics written by Steve Severin, the song is a really touching love song with a myriad maritime and celestial imagery, including pearl diving, crashing waves and a shimmering, star-strewn night sky.

The song's rich opulence is underpinned by Martin McCarrick's harpsichord playing and Jon Klein's screeching guitar, approximating the atonal sound Klein really loved about John McGeoch's playing with the Banshees.

The Clive Richardson-directed promo video for the single, filmed in late June and early July 1987, sees the band with its two new members part of a rich tapestry of imagery, including Siouxsie swimming in a leopard print catsuit, clearly having recovered from the Tim Pope 'Swimming Horses' washout, numerous visual effects, including the deft deployment of several colours of marbling fluid, not dissimilar to the visual effects adopted by Pink Floyd during their early Syd Barrett-era gigs at London's UFO Club in the 1960s.[1354]

Richardson turns up the colour saturation to make Siouxsie's red-dyed ostrich feathers and feather boa particularly dazzling. Richardson's fast-paced, conglomerate technique adds to the kaleidoscopic spectacle. 'Song From The Edge Of The World' was recorded at Abbey Road Studios and Sigma Sound Studios, New York between 28 May and 3 June 1987.[1355] 'Song From The Edge Of The World' peaked at number 59 in the Official UK Singles Chart.

There are two B-side 'Song From The Edge Of The World' tracks, 'The Whole Price Of Blood' on the seven-inch and 'The Whole Price Of Blood' and 'Mechanical Eyes' on the twelve-inch format. 'Song From The Edge Of The World (Columbus Mix)' is the A-side twelve-inch version. There was also a limited-edition picture disc with an illustrated clam shell, prawns and fish on the A-side and an octopus with depictions of five tiny open mouths on the B-side, with the same marbling effect that appears in the video promo.

'The Whole Price Of Blood' is something of a companion piece to 'Swimming Horses', and was conceived during the *Hyæna* writing period, prompted by 'Les Sentinelles' Amnesty programme, where, Siouxsie comments, the Amnesty group '…rescue women who are trapped in certain religious climates in the Middle East, religions that view any kind of pre-marital sexual aspersion as punishable by death – either by the hand of the eldest brother, or by public stoning'.[1356]

The song is predominantly percussion driven, interspersed with an array of keyboard chimes and sitar, over which Siouxsie sings of evil and slaughter as the song reaches a vertiginous denouement. The song was recorded between 28 May and 3 June 1987 at Abbey Road Studios and Sigma Sound Studios, New York. The song was never performed live.

'Mechanical Eyes' is a J.G. Ballard-oriented dystopian song, with sensationalist National Enquirer[1357] type headline lyrics and austere, punchy Suicide-like instrumentation. 'Mechanical Eyes' was recorded between 28 May and 3 June 1987 at Abbey Road Studios and Sigma Sound Studios, New York. It was never performed live.

The artwork for 'Song From The Edge Of The World' adopts the same fantail fish seen on the cover of the Banshees' single 'Melt!' on the front cover, within a rectangular aperture with Siouxsie and The Banshees in italics, with the S of Siouxsie and B of Banshees in the configuration of a human figure intertwined with a serpent-like creature, simultaneously appearing like a scroll. All other writing is ornamental calligraphy, including song titles and the 'Design: Crocodile (London)/Banshees' inscription. The mirrored aperture on the back cover is a sweltering crimson abstract plane of colour.

On 10 July 1987, Siouxsie and The Banshees embarked on a sixteen-date tour, including two dates in Germany, one date in the UK and thirteen dates in North America. The first gig the Banshees play with Jon Klein and Marin McCarrick is at the Bizarre Festival in Berlin, with a nineteen-song setlist including songs from all eight studio albums.

'Playground Twist' is resurrected after a five-year hiatus, and the Banshees, with the addition of multi-instrumentalist McCarrick, now have the scope to develop their stagecraft more laterally and add texture to songs that that would otherwise have been too problematic to accomplish live.

The other two festivals the Banshees play are the Loreley festival[1358] in Germany and the 'Big Top' festival at Finsbury Park. Severin recalls, 'It was a brilliant bill: we were supported by Gaye Bykers On Acid, Psychic TV, Wire and The Fall'.[1359]

Siouxsie and The Banshees were also the support act for David Bowie at the Anaheim Stadium in California, during his 'Glass Spider'[1360] tour, despite Siouxsie's misgivings about the 1987 Bowie manifestation. Jon Klein remembers, 'She said, "He's crap now!"… It was the Glass Spider tour, though we preferred to call it the "Plastic Jiffy" tour because the set was terrible. It looked like a load of condoms hanging off one giant condom'.[1361]

The 1987 Siouxsie and The Banshees tour finished on 23 August 1987 with a gig at the 1235 Concert Hall in Miami.

The adventure continues…

Epilogue

A rollercoaster ride of twists, turns and loops which, if nothing else, illustrates the resolve of a band whose vision simply will not falter or be deterred by the departure of any given guitarist, or producer, all of whom contributed to the Banshees creative orbit, despite presages and subsequent miscalculations. It is solely because of the music that the band continues to ride the storm of hackneyed interviews, less than flattering reviews, fads, trends and indifference about their craft so they can pursue their sweeping panorama of imaginative possibilities, remaining unyieldingly in their own stream. The Banshees are now a very long way down the line from their initial 20 September 1976 100 Club appearance, but the unstoppable temerity remains the same.

Although perhaps not entirely satisfactory for Siouxsie and The Banshees completists, the albums discussed are the original recordings and not the subsequent reissues with various demos, remixes and remasters.

The door remains well and truly open for the Banshees' third and final act.

Acknowledgements

This book would not have come into existence without the unwavering support of Wymer Publishing impresario Jerry Bloom, whose encouragement and backing has given me no small amount of affirmation to keep writing.

I also extend huge thanks to the following wonderful people who have been incredibly helpful in terms of their generosity, insight, expertise, knowledge, encouragement and patience: Ray Stevenson, Rob O'Connor, John Robb, Peter Anderson, Simon Fowler, Tony Mottram, David Arnoff, Nicola Tyson, Tony Gleed, Jon Klein, Walthamstow Rock n Roll Book Club, Billy 'Chainsaw' Houlston, Cathi Unsworth, Rory Sullivan-Burke, Herman De Tollenaere, Yeah UhHuh, Painted Bird, Mark Paytress and the fantastic 'The Banshees And Other Creatures' website.

Most importantly of all, my thanks to Catharine, Hermione, Cicely and Jude for their constant and enduring love and support.

Footnotes

1 Siouxsie Sioux Latitude Festival BBC Sounds Stage 23 July 2023
2 French composer Camille Saint-Saëns 'Carnival Of The Animals', a musical suite comprising fourteen movements, 1922
3 Scottish fashion designer
4 Siouxsie and The Banshees, from the 1981 album *Juju*, released 19 June 1981, Polydor Records
5 songmeanings.com Source: Sounds 28 February 1981
6 Rory Sullivan-Burke *The Light Pours Out Of Me* Omnibus Press, published 2022
7 Siouxsie and The Banshees released Israel as a stand-alone single 28 November 1980 on Polydor Records
8 British rock and pop band formed in London in 1978. Years active 1978 to1985, 2002 to 2011 and 2012–2015
9 *Siouxsie and The Banshees The Authorised Biography* Mark Paytress, Sanctuary Publishing 2003
10 Rory Sullivan-Burke *The Light Pours Out Of Me* Omnibus Press, published 2022
11 *Siouxsie and The Banshees The Authorised Biography* Mark Paytress, Sanctuary Publishing 2003
12 *Siouxsie and The Banshees The Authorised Biography* Mark Paytress, Sanctuary Publishing 2003
13 *Siouxsie and The Banshees The Authorised Biography* Mark Paytress, Sanctuary Publishing 2003
14 *Siouxsie and The Banshees The Authorised Biography* Mark Paytress, Sanctuary Publishing 2003
15 Pink Floyd's ninth studio album, released 12 September 1975 EMI, London
16 untiedundone.com Rhythm magazine 'So you want to sound like', January 2005
17 Percussion Discussion podcast Episode 103, 26 November 2022
18 'Israel' lyric, Siouxsie and The Banshees
19 Rory Sullivan-Burke *The Light Pours Out Of Me*, Omnibus Press, published 2022
20 Interview with Mike Stavrou 31 October 2022
21 Originally known, when it was opened in 1929 as the Astoria Variety Cinema, and formally as the Carling Academy Brixton, the venue is currently known as the O2 Academy Brixton
22 Graphic Designer and founder of Stylorouge graphic design studio
23 Hans Christian Andersen *New Fairy Tales*. First Volume. Second Collection published 21 December 1844
24 Also known as 'The Almond Tree' is a German fairy tale published in Low German by the Brothers Grimm in the collection of *Grimm's Fairy Tales*, 1812
25 Jacob Grimm 1785 to 1863) and Wilhelm Grimm 1786 to 1859 were German academics who together collected and published folk stories, including 'Cinderella' 'Hansel and Gretel' and 'Snow White'
26 theguardian.com 'The Tale of the Juniper Tree' by the Brothers Grimm translated by Joyce Crick 29 September 2009
27 Percussion Discussion podcast Episode 103 26 November 2022
28 Released 30 January 1968 on Verve Records
29 Lead guitarist and keyboardist of Radiohead. Born 5 November 1971
30 BBC2 *Youth TV* television show 1978-1980 showcasing up and coming/ new bands
31 Audio effects delay pedal which creates a distinctive 'swooshing' sound
32 'Congo Conga' would become the B Side of the single 'Arabian Knights', alongside 'Supernatural Thing', originally recorded by Soul and R&B singer Ben E. King in 1974, released 24 July 1981
33 Sullivan-Burke
34 1980 documentary acknowledging female rock musicians, directed by Wolfgang Buld, running time approximately 45 minutes.
35 'Girls Bite Back'
36 'Girls Bite Back'
37 'Girls Bite Back'
38 'Girls Bite Back'
39 Annual Post-Punk and Gothic rock festival held at venues in Leeds, Stafford and Queensbury 1979-1980
40 Released 23 September 1977, produced by David Bowie and Tony Visconti RCA
41 Born 13 February 1950. English singer, songwriter, record producer and human rights activist. Original lead singer of rock band Genesis.
42 Released 30 May 1980, produced by Steve Lillywhite Charisma UK
43 American rock band founded in 1974 in New York City by vocalist Debbie Harry and guitarist Chris Stein.
44 Released September 1978 Produced by Mike Chapman Chrysalis
45 Released 3 August 1979 Produced by Brian Eno and Talking Heads Sire
46 Released 12 September 1980 Produced by Tony Visconti RCA
47 Paul Morley, New Musical Express, 20 September 1980
48 Paul Morley, New Musical Express, 20 September 1980
49 Paul Morley, New Musical Express, 20 September 1980
50 Excepting 'Voodoo Dolly' and 'Into The Light' which were showcased during the 1980 'Kaleidoscope' tour
51 Peel Sessions featured on John Peel's BBC Radio 1 show from 1967 until John Peel's death in 2004
52 Portland Place W1, London. First used by the BBC for broadcasting during the Second World War. The entire building was bought by the BBC in 1965 and sold in 1986.
53 Track three on The Creatures' *Wild Things* five track EP, released 25 September 1981
54 Band formed in 1981 by Siouxsie Sioux and Budgie
55 Song based on *The Premature Burial* short story by Edgar Allan Poe, published 1844
56 'The Tragedy of Hamlet, Prince of Denmark', often attenuated to 'Hamlet', is a tragedy written by William Shakespeare approximately between 1599 and 1601.
57 Sullivan-Burke
58 Oxford English Dictionary
59 thebansheesandothercreatures.co.uk
60 Paytress
61 Rory Sullivan-Burke interview, 31 July 2023
62 the bansheesandothercreatures.co.uk Source: Electron interview, 20 December 1982
63 thebansheesandothercreatures.co.uk Billy 'Chainsaw' Houlston, The File
64 Siouxsie and The Banshees' fourth studio album, produced by Nigel Gray and Siouxsie and The Banshees, released 19 June 1981, Polydor Records

65 B Side of the single 'Playground Twist', released 29 June 1979
66 In its original form, 'Goosey Goosey Gander' appears in Gammer Gurton's 'Garland'; otherwise known as 'The nursery Parnassus, a choice collection of pretty songs and verses, for the amusement of all little good children, who can neither read nor run' first published 1 January 1783
67 American psychological thriller based on the book 'The House of Dr. Edwardes' by Hilary Saint George Saunders and Francis Beeding. The film was released 31 October 1945
68 Swedish actor 29 August 1915 to 29 August 1982
69 American actor 5 April 1916 to 12 June 2003
70 Name for the residential psychiatric asylum in 'Spellbound'
71 Spanish Surrealist artist 11 May 1904 to 23 January 1989
72 faroutmagazine.co.uk 'FILM Rare footage of Alfred Hitchcock discussing his collaboration with Salvador Dali on 'Spellbound', 11 May 2020
73 'Christine' was released as the second single on 30 May 1980 from album 'Kaleidoscope' with 'Eve White/Eve Black' as the B Side
74 Nature reserve located in Buckinghamshire to the West of London
75   British film production company based in London, established in 1934 and renowned for making a series of Gothic horror and fantasy films made from the mid-1950s until the 1970s
76 The Oni mask is said to have derived from the Oni, or demons which appear in Japanese mythology
77 'Onibaba', also known as 'The Hole', is a 1964 Japanese factual drama and horror film written and directed by Kaneto Shindō
78 Japanese film director, screenwriter, film producer and writer 22 April 1912 to 29 May 2012
79 thebansheesandothercreatures.co.uk
80 thebansheesandothercreatures.co.uk Source: Trax Magazine 17 February 1981
81 Buddhist teaching founded by the former Tendai Japanese monk Shinran
82 Mark Kermode reviews 'Onibaba' BFI 15 May 2020
83 Comprehensive range of Japanese percussion instruments.
84 Contemporary Taiko drummer and film composer, born in New York 1963
85 Japanese actor 1 October 1924 to 22 December 1994
86 Japanese actor Born 18 April 1943
87 Sustainable rural Japanese villages nearby forest and mountains.
88 Japanese civil war civil war 1467 to 1477
89 Brought about by the Ōnin War in 1467 which collapsed the archaic system of Japan under the Ashikaga shogunate.
90 21 December 1928 to 2 May 1910
91 Michelangelo Merisi da Caravaggio, Italian painter 29 September 1571 to 18 July 1610
92 1973 American supernatural horror film, directed by Friedkin from a screenplay by William Peter Blatty
93 Entertainment 'The Exorcist director William Friedkin shares 13 must-see horror movies' by Mandi Bierly 29 October 2007
94 Paytress
95 'Follow The Sun' was played live twice by the band, the first time at the Paradiso Grote Zaal Amsterdam, Holland, 17 July 1981 and last time at the Gaumont Theatre, Ipswich, England
96 Indian one stringed instrument used in the traditional music of South Asia, also used in the modern-day music of Bangladesh, India and Pakistan
97 American writer of horror, science fiction, supernatural fiction, crime and suspense novels. Born 21 September 1947
98 1973 British folk horror film directed by Robin Hardy with Edward Woodward, Britt Ekland, Diane Cilento, Ingrid Pitt, and Christopher Lee
99 American film maker and writer and director of *Hereditary* 2018, *Midsommar* 2019, and *Beau Is Afraid* 2023. Born 15 July 1986
100 Folk horror film written and directed by Ari Aster starring Florence Pugh and Jack Reynor
101 Fairlight CMI (Computer Musical Instrument) is a digital synthesizer, sampler, and digital audio workstation introduced in 1979
102 Dutch painter and art theoretician 7 March 1872 to 1 February 1944
103 French Post-Impressionist painter 2 December 1859 to 29 March 1891
104 French Neo-Impressionist painter 11 November 1863 to 15 August 1935
105 Technique of painting with small, distinct dots, developed by Georges Seurat and Paul Signac in 1886
106 Also known as chromoluminarism, Pointillism is the style utilised in Neo-Impressionist painting defined by the separation of colours into discrete dots or patches that interact optically
107 American writer and visual artist 5 February 1914 to 2 August 1997
108 Early twentieth century European Avant-garde art movement established in 1916, lasting until the mid-1920s
109 Created in the 1960s by a group of British art school students in the 1960s, combining aspects of music hall, traditional jazz and psychedelia with surreal humour and avant-garde artwork. 1962–1970, 1972, 1988, 2002 onwards
110 Fourth studio album by Radiohead, produced by Nigel Goodrich, released 2 October 2000, Parlophone Records
111 https://www.musicvf.com
112 'Picasso: A Biography' Patrick O'Brien October 2010 Harper Collins
113 Genre of rock music that emerged from post-punk in the UK in the late 1970s. The first post-punk bands associated with the movement include Siouxsie and The Banshees, The Cure, Bauhaus and Joy Division
114 Paytress
115 Paytress
116 Paytress
117 American video streaming service owned by Netflix.Inc, established January 16, 2007
118 American science fiction horror drama TV series created by the Duffer Brothers, 15 July 2016 to present
119 Lars Hokanson, contemporary American illustrator 1942 to 2012
120 Relief print made from a motif cut in a block of wood, formerly widely used for book illustration
121 Modernist movement, initially in poetry and painting, with predominantly German origins at the beginning of the 20th century.
122 Emil Nolde, German-Danish painter and printmaker, 7 August 1867 to 13 April 1956
123 Woodcut made in 1917, collection of MoMA, New York
124 Creative consultancy founded in 1981 by Rob O'Connor
125 Rob O'Connor interview 8 August 2023
126 William Houlston aka Billy 'Chainsaw' Houlston ran the Siouxsie and The Banshees official fan club and was the band's personal assistant from 1979 to 1995. Quote taken from an evening with Billy 'Chainsaw' Houlston to coincide with his art exhibition 'It Is What It Is' at the Naked Gallery, Brighton, 26 August to 2 September 2023

127 Rob O'Connor interview 8 August 2023
128 The Museum of Mankind, situated in Burlington Gardens, London, was a branch of the British Museum, opened in 1970 and closed in 1997. In the official Mark Paytress biography, there is recollection of the Horniman museum as the source for the 'Juju' statue
129 Rob O'Connor interview 8 August 2023
130 Punk rock band formed in Sunderland, England, 1978 to 1983, 2007 to 2022
131 Rob O'Connor interview 8 August 2023
132 The Hammersmith Palais de Danse, latterly known as Hammersmith Palais, was a dance hall/ entertainment venue in Hammersmith, London, from 1919 until 2007
133 English guitarist who was a member of The Police 1977-1976; 2007-2008. Born 31 December 1942
134 Single from The Police album *Regatta De Blanc*, 'Walking On The Moon' was released 4 November 1979, A&M Records
135 English record producer, recording engineer and musician. Born 28 February 1971
136 Song by Radiohead, released 26 May 2003, from the band's sixth studio album *Hail To The Thief*
137 'Nigel Godrich: your questions answered on Radiohead, Macca and Marmite' Laura Snapes, The Guardian 25 February 2020
138 First published in 1899 in W.B. Yeats' third volume of poetry 'The Wind Among the Reeds'
139 Irish poet, dramatist, writer and politician 13 June 1865 to 28 January 1939
140 Paytress
141 Paytress
142 Paytress
143 Paytress
144 Paytress
145 Paytress
146 Paytress
147 Wayback Machine Internet Archive. Source: thecreatures.com
148 Music rehearsal studios in South West London
149 British music producer/engineer. Work includes The Cure, Siouxsie and the Banshees, and Manic Street Preachers. Born 1954
150 Camden recording studio, St Paul's Crescent, London
151 First release by The Creatures, issued 25 September 1981 Polydor Records
152 American author and illustrator of children's books. 10 June 1928 to 8 May 2012
153 Children's book, written and illustrated by American writer and illustrator Maurice Sendak, originally published by Harper & Row 13 November 1963
154 Scottish television presenter, filmmaker, director, writer and producer. Also known as the singer-songwriter of the band Skids. Born 6 October 1960
155 Paytress
156 The drumbeat isn't dissimilar to that on 'Chasing Shadows', Side one, track one, of Deep Purple's self-titled album, released 21 June 1969
157 Originally written by Wild Ones American songwriter Chip Taylor and made popular by UK band The Troggs who released 'Wild Thing' as a single 22 April 1966
158 Music photographer
159 Paytress. More likely the Special Olympics, which were inaugurated in Gateshead, Newcastle, 1981
160 Paytress
161 Paytress
162 Rob O'Connor interview thebansheesandothercreatures.co.uk 5 August 2004
163 First Studio Session Depeche Mode, 1 September 1980. Last Studio Session The Triffids 1 January 1989
164 thebansheesandothercreatures.co.uk Source *NME* 15 August 1981
165 American rock band formed in Los Angeles, 1965, with Jim Morrison, 8 December 1943 to 3 July 1971, Ray Manzarek, 12 February 1939 to 20 May 2013, Robby Krieger, born 8 January 1946 and John Densmore, born 1 December 1944. The Doors were active from 1965 to 1973
166 A collection of Middle Eastern folktales compiled in Arabic during the Islamic Golden Age
167 Originally a Persian name used as one of the most acclamatory titles of nobility, corresponding with 'King' or 'Grand Duke'
168 A high ranking official in some Muslim countries, especially in Turkey under Ottoman rule
169 thebansheesandothercreatures.co.uk Source: *Smash Hits* June 1986
170 thebansheesandothercreatures.co.uk Source: *Record Mirror* 11 November 1989
171 1960s American female band with Mary Weiss, Elizabeth "Betty" Weiss, Marguerite "Marge" Ganser, and Mary Ann Ganse. 1963 to 1968, 1977, 1989
172 Song written by George "Shadow" Morton, Jeff Barry, and Ellie Greenwich. Performed by the Shangri-Las It was a number one pop hit in 1964
173 Zills or zils (from Turkish zil 'cymbals'), small metallic finger cymbals used in belly dancing and comparable performances
174 Originally released 12 November 2002 (CD only), including recordings from 1978 to 1995. Subsequently re-released in 2004 to include double CD and DVD and again 1 October 2007
175 American epic historical drama film directed by Joseph L. Mankiewicz. Released 12 June 1963. Starring Elizabeth Taylor, Richard Burton and Rex Harrison
176 Rectangular vaulted hall, walled on three sides, with one end completely open
177 First appeared on the 'Once Upon A Time' video, released in 1981 to coincide with the compilation album of the same name
178 Second most populated city in France,
179 1980s audio processing technique brought to the fore in the late 1970s and early 1980s by producers Steve Lillywhite and Hugh Padgham
180 theguardian.com Alex Petridis 'Artists beginning with S' 21 November 2007
181 Petridis
182 First broadcast 7 December 1914
183 Also known as jaw harp, juice harp, or mouth harp. It is a lamellophone instrument, consisting of a pliable bamboo or metal tongue or reed attached to a mount
184 Bantu ethnic group native to Central Kenya
185 Central African Belgian colony from 1908 until its independence in 1960.
186 Cabell "Cab" Calloway III, American band leader and jazz singer, associated with the Cotton Club in Harlem. 25 December 1907 to 18 November 1994

187 Known professionally as Patrick Grant. American singer, born 5 January 1953
188 American singer-songwriter and pianist 9 July 1950 to 3 February 1999
189 United States Music industry standard record Chart for songs, published weekly by Billboard magazine
190 English drummer, best known for his work with Deep Purple and being the last remaining original member of the band. Born 29 June 1948
191 Fourth studio album by English rock band Deep Purple, released 5 June 1970
192 German artist that worked in painting, etching, lithography and woodcuts and sculpture 8 July 1867 to 22 April 1945
193 'Little Boy Lost' from William Blake's *Songs of Innocence and of Experience* first published 1789
194 thebansheesandothercreatures.co.uk Source: *Sounds* 7 March 1981
195 Written in 1874 by composer Camille Saint-Saëns 9 October 1835 to 16 December 1921
196 Final act of the ballet 'Gayane' 1942, where the dance troupe display their dexterity with sabres. Composed by Aram Khachaturian 6 June 1903 to 1 May 1978
197 Military march composed in 1897 by Julius Fucik 8 July 1872 to 25 September 1916
198 Composed by Gioachino Rossini 29 February 1792 to 13 November 1868. French language opera in four acts, premiered 3 August 1829 Salle Le Peletier, Paris
199 American song-writer and politician 4 March 1923 to 7 March 1949 'The Streets Of Cairo' is an established melody, published in various forms in the nineteenth century
200 Ordinarily translated as storm and stress. Proto-Romantic movement in German literature and music between the late 1760s and early 1780s
201 1978 American independent horror film directed and scored by John Carpenter and co-written with producer Debra Hill
202 Gaelic festival on 1 November denoting the end of the harvest season and beginning of winter
203 Christian festival celebrated in honour of all the saints of the church, both known and unknown
204 Percussion instrument consisting of a piece of stiff U- shaped wire connecting a wooden ball to a cavernous box of wood with metal 'teeth' inside
205 From 'Break On Through (To The Other Side)', track one of The Doors' debut album, released 4 January 1967. Lyrics written by The Doors' singer-songwriter and lead singer Jim Morrison
206 irr.org Fighting Sus! then and now Joseph Maggs 19 April 2019
207 Stop and search law that allowed a police officer to stop, search and potentially arrest people on suspicion of them contravening section 4 of the Vagrancy Act 1824
208 English novelist, short story writer, satirist and essayist 15 November 1930 to 19 April 2009
209 Public Switched Telephone Network
210 A structure for watching television where the viewer pays for particular programmes watched
211 thebansheesandothercreatures.co.uk
212 Genre of film that shows, or lays claim to show, scenes of actual homicide
213 1976 'splatter' film directed by Michael Findlay and Horacio Fredriksson. Released January 16, 1976
214 1983 Canadian science fiction horror film written and directed by David Cronenberg starring Deborah Harry, Sonja Smith and James Woods starring James Woods. Released 4 February 1984
215 imdb.com David Cronenberg Biography
216 Canadian film director, screenwriter, and actor. Born 15 March 1943
217 Video camera designed to record or stream to a computer or computer network. Primary uses include video telephony, live streaming, social media and security.
218 thebansheesandothercreatures.co.uk
219 English documentary filmmaker born 26 May 1955
220 An approach to the overseeing of information that perceives human attention as a scarce commodity. Its application is in economic theory to solve information management problems
221 time.com 'A Conversation with Filmmaker Adam Curtis on Power, Technology and How Ideas Get Into People's Heads' Billy Perrigo 23 February 2021
222 English musician and drummer of Led Zeppelin. 31 May 1948 to 25 September 1980
223 A harmonious vision of pastoralism and nature derived from the Greek province of the same name
224 Multi-use building in Portsmouth, built in 1890
225 Rory Sullivan-Burke interview 31 July 2023
226 Peter William Sutcliffe, serial killer born 2 June 1946, died 13 November 2020
227 An allusion to 'Jack The Ripper', undetermined serial killer active in and around the Whitechapel district of East London in 1888
228 Nickname given to John Samuel Humble 8 January 1956 to 30 July 2019. British man who pretended to be the Yorkshire Ripper in a counterfeit audio recording and several letters during 1978-1979
229 Also known as a machinist's hammer. Type of peening hammer used in metalworking
230 thebansheesandothercreatures.co.uk Source: Billy 'Chainsaw' Houlston, The File
231 Ballet by Russian composer Sergei Prokofiev 15 April 1891 to 15 March 1953. Based on William Shakespeare's 'Romeo and Juliet'. First composed in 1935
232 Song by Led Zeppelin. Included on their sixth studio album *Physical Graffiti* released 24 February 1975, Swan Song Records
233 Secular music and sacred music, both non-religious were the two main categories of Western music during the Middle Ages and Renaissance periods
234 Classification of vices within Christian doctrine: pride, greed, wrath, envy, lust, gluttony and sloth
235 Usually associated with a deity possessing the features of an animal
236 1963 British science fiction horror film produced by George Pitcher and Philip Yordan. Directed by Steve Sekely and Freddie Francis. Based on the John Wyndham 1951 novel 'The Day Of The Triffids', published by Michael Joseph
237 Electronic inductive string feedback circuit device used for playing string instruments, usually the electric guitar
238 Play first staged in October 1962. Written by American playwright Edward Albee 12 March 1928 to 16 September 2016. Subsequently adapted for the Mike Nichols 1966 film of the same name
239 From the iconic speech by actor Robert de Niro as Travis Bickle in the Martin Scorsese directed *Taxi Driver*, released 9 February 1976
240 thebansheesandothercreatures.co.uk Source: 'Enter The Dragon' *Sounds* interview with John Gill 20 June 1981
241 Erstwhile member of the band Rikki and the Last Days of Earth and music journalist
242 thebansheesandothercreatures.co.uk Source: 'Incest…and other obsessions' *Sounds* interview with Valac Van der Veene 28 February 1981

243 thebansheesandothercreatures.co.uk Source: Trax 'Through A Glass Darkly' interview with Johnny Black 17 February 1981
244 American pioneering and influential musical comprising vocalist Alan Vega and instrumentalist Martin Rev, sporadically active between 1970 and 2016.
245 American rock band formed in 1976 and working until 2009. Their lineup rotated frequently, with the husband and wife duo of singer Lux Interior and guitarist Poison Ivy the only constant members
246 thebansheesandothercreatures.co.uk Source: 'Enter The Dragon' Sounds interview with John Gill 20 June 1981
247 thebansheesandothercreatures.co.uk Source: 'Incest…and other obsessions' Sounds interview with Valac Van der Veene 28 February 1981
248 thebansheesandothercreatures.co.uk *ZigZag* magazine interview with Tom Vague May 1981
249 thebansheesandothercreatures.co.uk Source: 'Incest…and other obsessions' *Sounds* interview with Valac Van der Veene 28 February 1981
250 thebansheesandothercreatures.co.uk Source: 'The Magic Of Trance. The fetish speaks - part one. Mark Cooper goes ghost walking in the enchanted, perverted world of Siouxsie and the Banshees', *Record Mirror* 1981
251 thebansheesandothercreatures.co.uk Source: 'The Magic Of Trance. The fetish speaks - part one. Mark Cooper goes ghost walking in the enchanted, perverted world of Siouxsie and the Banshees', *Record Mirror* 1981
252 thebansheesadothercreatures.co.uk Source: 'The Magic Of Trance. The fetish speaks - part one. Mark Cooper goes ghost walking in the enchanted, perverted world of Siouxsie and the Banshees', *Record Mirror* 1981
253 This alludes to *NME* journalist Lynn Hanna's article 'Into The Valley Of The Voodoo Doll', Lynn Hanna joins The Banshees Farewell Tour. Source thebansheesandothercreatures.co.uk
254 thebansheesandothercreatures.co.uk Source: 'Incest…and other obsessions' *Sounds* interview with Valac Van der Veene, 28 February 1981
255 1977 David Lynch written, directed, produced and edited American surrealist body horror film
256 The name given by the Shuar people for a shrunken head
257 Museum of archaeological and anthropological artefacts, founded in 1884 by Augustus Pitt Rivers
258 Also known as Jivaro, Shuar are the earliest ethnic group to inhabit the Equadorean and Peruvian Amazonia
259 The 'river of wailing' in the underworld in Greek mythology
260 Song written by Scottish musicians Gerry Rafferty and Joe Egan. Performed by their band Stealers Wheel, released 27 April 1973. 'Stuck In The Middle With You' was used for the notorious ear cutting scene in the 1992 American crime film *Reservoir Dogs*, released January 21 1992, written and directed by Quentin Tarantino.
261 dictionary.cambridge.org
262 thebansheesandothercreatures.co.uk Source: *Sounds* 20 June 1981
263 American director, producer and writer of television and film. 12 August 1927 to 27 March 2006
264 1975 American made for television trilogy of short horror films
265 American screenwriter and author specialising primarily in fantasy, horror, and science fiction. 20 February 1926 to 23 June 2013
266 American actor, singer and screenwriter 1 July 1939 to 8 August 2013
267 Native American Pueblo peoples indigenous to the Zuni River valley
268 Eunice Kathleen Waymon, known professionally as Nina Simone. American singer, songwriter, pianist, and civil rights activist 21 February 1933 to 21 April 2003
269 Chanteuse that appears as a vision singing 'In Heaven' in the 1977 David Lynch film *Eraserhead*
270 Siouxsie and The Banshees headlined the Queen's Hall, Leeds two-day festival on Saturday 13 September
271 Three-day music festival 16, 17 and 18 June 1967, held at the Monterey County Fairgrounds in Monterey, California. It was the Jimi Hendrix Experience's first major live appearance
272 Fifth track from The Velvet Underground's second album, *White Light/White Heat*, released 30 January 1968
273 Track six on 1997s *OK Computer*, released as a single 25 August 1997
274 Guitarist, songwriter and member of Radiohead. O'Brien releases solo material under the name EOB. Born 15 April 1968
275 faroutmagazine.co.uk 'Listen to Siouxsie and The Banshees provocative debut at the 100 club, 1976' Jack Whately 24 September 2022
276 thebansheesandothercreatures.co.uk Source: 'Incest…and other obsessions' *Sounds* interview with Valac Van der Veene, 28 February 1981
277 Paytress
278 Paytress
279 Paytress
280 Paytress
281 Paytress
282 Paytress
283 Paytress
284 Paytress
285 American rock band, formed in Union City, New Jersey. The band name was shortened to Dr Hook in 1975. Years active 1968 to 1985, 1988 to 2015, 2019 to present
286 Paytress
287 Seminal venue which opened in October 1977. Open for five years, closing in the summer of 1982, it hosted acts such as Prince, Siouxsie and The Banshees, Percy Sledge, Todd Rundgren, Allen Toussaint, The Sheiks, Dr. John, Iggy Pop and The Cramps
288 Paytress
289 Paytress
290 Paytress
291 Paytress
292 Paytress
293 Paytress
294 Paytress
295 Popular disco located at 128 West 45th Street, New York City. Open from 1958 to 1965, although a subsequent incarnation was opened in 1980
296 Paytress
297 Non-album single debut, followed up by 'A Day's Wait', released in May 1981, also produced by Steve Severin which halted outside the UK Top 100 singles
298 John Winston Ono Lennon 9 October 1940 to 8 December 1980, English singer, songwriter, musician and peace activist. Founder, co-songwriter, rhythm guitarist and co-lead vocalist of The Beatles

299 Claire Patricia Grogan born 17 March 1962), known as Clare Grogan or C. P. Grogan, Scottish actress and singer
300 Altered Images debut album predominantly produced by Steven Severin and recorded at Rockfield Studios, excepting one track, 'Happy Birthday', produced by Martin Rushent and recorded at Genetic Sound. The single became the band›s biggest hit, peaking at number two on the UK Singles Chart, October 1981
301 Paytress
302 American singer, poet, writer, actress and self-empowerment speaker. Lunch's career began during the 1970s New York City 'No Wave' scene as the singer and guitarist of Teenage Jesus and the Jerks
303 Lydia Lunch's second album, released in June 1982 by record label Ruby
304 Paytress
305 Paytress
306 Also known as the 'Third Arab–Israeli War', it was fought between Israel and a coalition of Arab states including Egypt, Syria, and Jordan from 5 to 10 June 1967
307 Paytress
308 Paytress
309 Paytress
310 Scottish musician, singer-songwriter and record producer born 10 October 1953
311 Paytress
312 Ancient Greek king who had amassed immense wealth
313 New Zealand record producer and former musician. Former manager and producer for The Cure. Founder of Fiction Records. Born 7 January 1949
314 The Cure single released 2 November 1979
315 Disco-funk band formed in London, 1975
316 Scottish folk musician and founding member of the band Pentangle. 3 November 1943 to 5 October 2011
317 English composer and impresario of musical theatre. Born 22 March 1948
318 English lyricist and author. Born 10 November 1944
319 Northern Irish blues rock, hard rock, heavy metal and jazz fusion guitarist. 4 April 1952 to 6 February 2011
320 Interview with Ray Stevenson 18 September 2022
321 thebansheesandothercreatures.org.uk The File Phase Two Issue One 'Fireworks Unleashed At Last', Billy 'Chainsaw' Houlston
322 Paytress
323 Paytress
324 Single released on 21 May 1982. Polydor Records. Peaked at number 22 in the UK Singles Chart
325 The Nigel Gray produced version of 'Fireworks' appears on the 2006 remastered *Juju* CD
326 Second studio album by The Cure, released 18 April 1980 by Fiction Records
327 Paytress
328 Paytress
329 Recorded at Surrey Sound Studios 19 to 24 September 1981
330 English singer-songwriter most active during the 1980s and 1990s. Born 26 September 1959
331 Most likely the same quartet utilised on 'Obsession' featuring two cellists (Alison Briggs and Caroline Lavelle) and two violinists (Anne Stephenson and Virginia Hewes). The latter two musicians also feature on 'Slowdive'
332 Fourth studio album by Echo & the Bunnymen. Released 4 May 1984 on Korova Records
333 Debut album by The The, released 21 October 1983
334 Second studio album The The, released on 17 November 1986 by Some Bizzare and Epic
335 thebansheesandothercreatures.co.uk Source: Record Mirror 18 December 1982
336 thebansheesandothercreatures.co.uk Source: Record Hunter December 1992
337 Paytress
338 American musical fantasy film directed by Victor Fleming and produced by Metro-Goldwyn-Mayer. Released 10 August 1939
339 Paytress
340 American pianist, singer and songwriter. 29 September 1935 to 28 October 2022. Also known as 'The Killer' because of his reputation as the first wild man of rock.
341 Rob O'Connor interview 8 August 2023
342 thebansheesandothercreatures.co.uk
343 thebansheesandothercreatures.org.uk
344 Puzzle video game created in 1985 by Alexey Pajitnov, a Russian software engineer.
345 Paytress
346 Published initially as *Greenslaves*, *The Green Brain*, published in 1966, is a science fiction novel by American writer Frank Herbert
347 Franklin Patrick Herbert 8 October 1920 to 11 February 1986
348 Paytress
349 Song by Led Zeppelin and the opening track from the album *Houses of the Holy* released 28 March 1973, Atlantic Records
350 Paytress
351 Founded in 1978 by Alex McDowell and Glen Matlock, Rocking Russian was a graphic design studio where Neville Brody also began his career
352 Rob O'Connor interview 8 August 2023
353 1981 compilation album featuring Siouxsie and The Banshees UK single releases to date. Released 4 December 1981
354 Second singles compilation released by Siouxsie and the Banshees on 5 October 1992, following the same format as *Once Upon a Time/The Singles*
355 Rob O'Connor interview 8 August 2023
356 Rob O'Connor interview 8 August 2023
357 1897 to 1914. Formed by a group of Austrian painters, graphic artists, sculptors and architects, including Gustav Klimt Josef Hoffman, Koloman Moser and Otto Wagner
358 International style of art, applied art and architecture, especially the decorative arts. Active 1883 to 1914
359 Scottish architect, designer and artist 7 June 1868 to 10 December 1928
360 1946 French film directed by French poet and filmmaker Jean Cocteau
361 1950 French film directed by Jean Cocteau
362 1941 American film directed, produced and starring Orson Welles.
363 Niccolò di Bernardo dei Machiavelli[a] 3 May 1469 to 21 June 1527, Renaissance Italian diplomat, author, philosopher and historian

364 Fifth studio album by Siouxsie and the Banshees Released 5 November 1982
365 uncut.co.uk Siouxsie And The Banshees: 'We were losing our minds' written by Gary Mulholland 24 October 2014
366 Electrically amplified clavichord invented by Ernst Zacharias and made by Hohner of Trossingen, West Germany, from 1964 to 1982
367 Modernist district in Stockholm, Sweden. During the summer months, there are different events on 'the field' open space such as a circus, music and sport events
368 Paytress
369 Paytress
370 Paytress
371 Rory Sullivan-Burke interview 31 July 2023
372 Sullivan-Burke
373 Interview with Ray Stevenson, 12 November 2023
374 1971 American psychological thriller film directed by, and starring, Clint Eastwood
375 uncut.co.uk 'Siouxsie And The Banshees: "We were losing our minds"' 24 October 2014
376 Paytress
377 *The Beatles*, also referred to as the *White Album*, is the ninth studio album (and only double album) The Beatles, released on 22 November 1968
378 Paytress
379 American television series, comprising thirteen episodes in total, created by Stephen J. Cannell and Roy Huggins, also known for *The Rockford Files* 1974 to 1980
380 Paytress
381 Deep Purple *Made In Japan*, 1972.
382 English guitarist, songwriter and a founding member of Deep Purple in 1968. Born 14 April 1945
383 Recording studios (latterly called Maximum Sound) located on the Old Kent Road, London, England, owned consecutively by Vic Keary, Manfred Mann, Pete Hammond, then Pete Waterman. Active 1969 to late 1980s
384 Signature music of the James Bond films, featured in all Eon Productions James Bond film since *Dr. No*. Released in 1962 and composed in E minor by Monty Norman, with arrangements for film provided by John Barry et al
385 Western style of architecture, dance, music, painting, sculpture, poetry and other art forms that thrived from the early- to mid-seventeenth century
386 Cooking technique in which the remnants of one animal are stuffed into another animal. The method is purported to have originated during the Middle Ages
387 Lysergic acid diethylamide, more commonly known as LSD (from German Lysergsäure-diethylamid), and known idiomatically as acid, is a psychedelic drug
388 Paytress
389 Paytress
390 Paytress
391 1981 to 1984 weekday BBC Radio 1 evening show from 8pm to 10pm. The show was later extended to run from 7pm to 10 pm
392 uncut.co.uk Siouxsie And The Banshees 'We were losing our minds' written by Gary Mulholland 24 October 2014
393 Modern percussion instrument, consisting of a small flexible metal sheet suspended in a wire frame ending in a handle. Proliferate in classic cartoons
394 Variety of end-blown flute that includes the recorder, flageolet and tin whistle.
395 Clipped backbeat and muted chord that marks the off-beats or upbeats. Exemplified in the playing of Django Reindhardt, Nile Rodgers and Freddie Green
396 American record producer, guitarist, composer and co-founder of the band Chic. Born 19 September 1952
397 1972 episode of *Night Gallery* directed by British born American director John Badham, born 25 August 1939. The other two episodes shown at the same time were 'The Funeral' and 'The Tune In Dan's Cafe'. 'Green Fingers' was based on a story of the same name by author R.C.Cook
398 American playwright, screenwriter, television producer, narrator and on-screen host, celebrated for his live television dramas of the 1950s and anthology television series *The Twilight Zone*. 25 December 1924 to 28 June 1975
399 American horror anthology television series aired on NBC from 16 December 1970 to 27 May 1973
400 American television, film and stage actor 4 November 1918 to 6 July 1994
401 British actress known for her work in theatre, film and television, perhaps best known for her role as the title character in *Bride Of Frankenstein* 1935. 28 October 1902 to 26 December 1986
402 1980 American comedy horror film directed by Kevin Connor
403 Siouxsie and The Banshees' debut album, Polydor Records. Released 13 November 1978
404 Siouxsie and The Banshees' second album, Polydor Records. Released 7 September 1979
405 Tape looping method popularised by guitarist Robert Fripp which can be traced back to his initial collaborations with Brian Eno in 1972
406 thebansheesandothercreatures.co.uk Source: Sounds 10 May 1982
407 thebansheesandothercreatures.co.uk The File Phase Two Issue Two
408 thebansheesandothercreatures.co.uk The File Phase Two Issue Two
409 thebansheesandothercreatures.co.uk The File Phase Two Issue Two
410 thebansheesandothercreatures.co.uk The File Phase Two Issue Two. On the 12" version of 'Slowdive', there is a purely instrumental version where all of the sound effects can be heard in full
411 thebansheesandothercreatures.co.uk The File Phase Two Issue Two
412 uncut.co.uk Siouxsie And The Banshees: 'We were losing our minds' written by Gary Mulholland 24 October 2014
413 thebansheesandothercreatures.co.uk
414 'Princess Julia: the first lady of London's fashion scene' Lauren Cochrane, The Guardian, 23 May 2014
415 Princess Julia, real name Julia Fodor, born on 8 April 1960. English DJ and music writer.
416 The Blitz Kids were a group who regularly attended the Tuesday club-night at Blitz in Covent Garden, London1979 to 1980, also credited with launching the 'New Romantic' movement
417 English singer, songwriter, singer and DJ, best known for fronting the band Culture Club
418 British pop musician and DJ at Blitz. Former drummer of the Rich Kids and Visage. Born 19 September 1957
419 Common Mexican interjection, used as exclamation, cry or shout
420 American company started in Cincinnati in 1853 by German immigrant Franz Rudolph Wurlitzer. The company firstly imported stringed, brass and woodwind instruments from Germany which were subsequently re-sold in the United States

421 Electric organ invented by Laurens Hammond and John M. Hanert, first manufactured in 1935.

422 Online conversation with Rory Sullivan-Burke 31 October 2023

423 uncut.co.uk Siouxsie And The Banshees: 'We were losing our minds' written by Gary Mulholland 24 October 2014

424 uncut.co.uk Siouxsie And The Banshees: 'We were losing our minds' written by Gary Mulholland 24 October 2014

425 First recorded in 1842 by nursery rhyme and fairy-tale collector James Orchard Halliwell-Phillipps 21 June 1820 to 3 January 1889. The song was translated in different languages including French, German and Italian.

426 Italian narrative poem by Dante Alighieri, May 1265 to 14 September 1321, the poem was started in 1308 and completed circa 1321

427 John Ciardi, American poet, translator, and etymologist 24 June 1916 to 30 March 1986 *The Divine Comedy* published by W. W. Norton & Company,1 April 1977

428 Mostly subterranean transport system, otherwise known as 'The Tube' serving Greater London and some parts of adjacent English home counties including Buckinghamshire, Essex and Hertfordshire

429 American-British musician and founding member and the lead vocalist, guitarist, and primary songwriter of the rock band the Pretenders. Born 7 September 1951

430 English singer and lead vocalist of the band The Selecter, actress and author. Born 23 October 1953

431 American singer, songwriter, actress and lead vocalist of the band Blondie. Born 1 July 1945

432 Australian-born British musician, singer, songwriter and writer. Albertine is best known as the guitarist of The Slits, 1977 until 1982. Born 1 December 1958

433 English musician, singer-songwriter, and lead vocalist for the punk rock band X-Ray Spex. 3 July 1957 to 25 April 2011

434 Putland took a series of photographs of the group at the Royal Garden Hotel

435 English music photographer 27 May 1947 to 18 November 2019

436 The Act sought to clarify the law in Britain. It was introduced by Member of Parliament David Steel and subject to impassioned debate, allowing for legal abortion on numerous grounds, with the added protection of free provision through the National Health Service. The Act was passed on 27 October 1967, coming into effect on 27 April 1968

437 'Siouxsie And The Bitter Pill' Rosalind Russell *Record Mirror* 23 February 1980

438 One-off series of sixty minute shows where bands, including Siouxsie and The Banshees, Echo and the Bunnymen, XTC, Angelic Upstarts and The Specials, were given complete autonomy over the programme's content with no input from the production company or Channel 4

439 British free-to-air public broadcast television channel owned and operated by the state-owned Channel 4 Television Corporation

440 Nickname for the largest bell off five in the Elizabeth Tower, Palace of Westminster, London

441 Dave Morrison 'Twice Upon a time Siouxsie and the banshees' review, *Select* magazine November 1992

442 thebansheesandothercreatures.co.uk Source Banshees & Other Creatures Interview 2000

443 Expression that means the brief loss or weakening of consciousness and, in modern vernacular, refers specifically to the sensation of post orgasm akin, metaphorically, to death

444 uncut.co.uk Siouxsie And The Banshees: 'We were losing our minds' written by Gary Mulholland 24 October 2014

445 Long necked acoustic instrument popular in Greece

446 Hstorical drama film directed and produced by Italian filmmaker Luchino Visconti. *Death In Venice* was adapted by Visconti and Nicola Badalucco from the 1912 novella of the same name by German author Thomas Mann

447 Played by Swedish actor and musician Björn Johan Andrésen, born 26 January 1955

448 Part three of Mahler's Symphony No. 5, composed in 1901 and 1902

449 French organist, composer and publisher, 12 January 1815 to 13 February 1888

450 Roman Catholic church located in the town of Saint-Dié-des-Vosges in Lorraine, France and built on the site of two religious buildings built between 664 and 679

451 thebansheesandothercreatures.co.uk Melt! B Sides Billy 'Chainsaw' Houlston

452 Siouxsie and The Banshees four-disc box set of B-sides and additional material, released 29 November 2004

453 Spanish concert venue located at 5 Padre Xifré Street, Madrid 1979 to 1985

454 First broadcast on 7 January 1982 with its last programme aired June 1988

455 Friends and gang members in *A Clockwork Orange*, first published in 1962 by novelist Anthony Burges and latterly made into a film, directed by Stanley Kubrick, released in 1971

456 German experimental Krautrock band formed in Cologne. Years active 1968 to1979, 1986 to1988 and 1991 to 1999

457 Third studio album by Can, released 19 November 1972, United Artists

458 Instrument originating from the Shona inhabitants of Zimbabwe, consisting of a wooden board fitted with a resonator with attached staggered metal prongs

459 Japanese printmaker and painter and Ukiyo-e artist of the Edo period, active as a painter and printmaker 31 October 1760 to 10 May 1849

460 A graphic description of World War Two as seen through the eyes of a six-year-old boy, wandering through small villages strewn around a non-specific country in both Central and Eastern Europe

461 Polish-American novelist 14 June 1933 to 3 May 1991

462 thebansheesandothercreatures.co.uk Source *New Musical Express* 'Don't cry Kyoto. It's only Siouxsie And The Banshees taking Mount Fuji by strategy on their first Japanese tour' Paul De Noyer, published 17 April 1982

463 Spanish (Basque) artist 25 October 1881 to 8 April 1973

464 Large scale monochromatic painting, executed in 1937, depicting the carnage of the bombing of Guernica during the Spanish Civil War, on 26 April 1937

465 Norwegian Expressionistic artist 12 December 1863 to 23 January 1944

466 Oil, tempera, chalk pastel and oil pastel on cardboard, 1893

467 American drama television series created by Mark Frost and David Lynch. First aired on the ABC television network on 8 April 1990, and originally ran for two seasons until being cancelled in 1991. The show returned in 2017 for a third season on the Showtime channel

468 Debut album by American musician Patti Smith, released by Arista Records 10 November 1975

469 Eighth Pink Floyd studio album released 1 March 1973

470 theguardian.com 'Invention, grace and bloodlust ballet': post-punk guitarist John McGeoch written by Daniel Dylan Wray, 4 May 2022

471 Single released 13 November 1963 on Garrett Records, containing the repetitive lyric 'the bird is the word'. The Ramones cover appears on *Rocket To Russia*, released 4 November 1977, Sire Records

472 The Cramps version of 'Surfin' Bird' was recorded as a single and released in 1978 on Vengeance Records. It also appears on the *Gravest Hits* EP released July 1979

Footnotes

473 *Alice's Adventures In Wonderland* Lewis Carroll first published in November 1865, Macmillan Publishers
474 Charles Lutwidge Dodgson, 27 January 1832 to 14 January 1898, better known by the name Lewis Carroll was an English author, poet, photographer and mathematician
475 thebansheesandothercreatures.co.uk Source: *Melody Maker* 14 May 1983
476 uncut.co.uk Siouxsie And The Banshees: 'We were losing our minds' written by Gary Mulholland 24 October 2014
477 uncut.co.uk Siouxsie And The Banshees: 'We were losing our minds' written by Gary Mulholland 24 October 2014
478 Paytress
479 Paytress
480 Paytress
481 Paytress
482 thebansheesandothercreatures.co.uk The File, Phase Two, Issue Two
483 thebansheesandothercreatures.co.uk The File, Phase Two, Issue Two
484 American composer Angelo Badalamenti 22 March 1937 to 11 December 2022, wrote and composed the score for Twin Peaks. 'Dance Of The Dream Man' appears on *Soundtrack from Twin Peaks* (also known as *Music from Twin Peaks*) released 11 September 11 1990, on Warner Bros. Records
485 Paytress
486 Paytress
487 'Cocoon' lyrics written by Siouxsie Sioux
488 *Alice's Adventures In Wonderland*, Chapter One 'Down The Rabbit Hole'
489 uncut.co.uk Siouxsie And The Banshees: 'We were losing our minds' written by Gary Mulholland 24 October 2014
490 uncut.co.uk Siouxsie And The Banshees: 'We were losing our minds' written by Gary Mulholland 24 October 2014
491 Art Deco, Grade Two listed concert venue. Opened in 1938
492 thebansheesandothercreatures.co.uk Source: Melody Maker 17 October 1992
493 thebansheesandothercreatures.co.uk Source: Record Hunter December 1992
494 Paytress
495 uncut.co.uk Siouxsie And The Banshees: 'We were losing our minds' written by Gary Mulholland 24 October 2014
496 thebansheesandothercreatures.co.uk Source: *Electron* interview 20 December 1982
497 Audio processing technique that combines strong reverb and a noise gate that curtails the tail of the reverb. Pioneered by producers Steve Lillywhite and Hugh Padgham
498 uncut.co.uk Siouxsie And The Banshees: 'We were losing our minds' written by Gary Mulholland 24 October 2014
499 uncut.co.uk Siouxsie And The Banshees: 'We were losing our minds' written by Gary Mulholland 24 October 2014
500 thebansheesandothercreatures.org.uk The File Phase Two Issue Two *A Kiss In The Dreamhouse* Billy 'Chainsaw' Houlston
501 thebansheesandothercreatures.co.uk Source: *Record Mirror* October 1982
502 thebansheesandothercreatures.co.uk Source: *Smash Hits* October 1982
503 Fictional English heavy metal band created by the American musicians and comedians of the ABC television network's *The T.V. Show*, Michael McKean, Harry Shearer and Christopher Guest
504 Men's suit consisting of high-waisted, wide-legged, tight-cuffed, pegged trousers, and a long coat with wide lapels and wide padded shoulders, popularised in the 1940s, initially among African Americans and subsequently Filipino, Mexican, Italian and Japanese Americans
505 Dance troupe who appeared on the weekly British music series *Top of the Pops* between 1981 and 1983, choreographed by Flick Colby
506 The only studio album by The Glove, released 9 September 1983 by Wonderland Records/Polydor
507 thebansheesandothercreatures.co.uk
508 Paytress
509 Siouxsie and The Banshees four-disc box set of B-sides and additional material, released 29 November 2004
510 Roxy Music debut single released 4 August 1972 on E.G. Records
511 English artist known for viscerally autobiographical work. Born 3 July 1963
512 Irish-born British figurative painter 28 October 1909 to 28 April 1992
513 French artist renowned for his use of colour 31 December 1869 to 3 November 1954
514 An example of Symbolism, the canvas measures 77 x 83 cm, and resides in Galerie Würthle, Vienna
515 1907-1908, housed in the Österreichische Galerie Belvedere, Vienna, Austria
516 Austrian artist and architect who also worked in the field of environmental protection.15 December 1928 to 19 February 2000
517 29 July 29th to 1 August 1st 1982 Port Eliot, Cornwall. Billed as Siouxsie and The Banshees first 1982 date
518 29 July 29th to 1 August 1st 1982 Port Eliot, Cornwall. Billed as Siouxsie and The Banshees first 1982 date
519 thebansheesandothercreatures.co.uk The File Phase Two Issue Two 'A Kiss In The Dreamhouse' Billy 'Chainsaw' Houlston
520 Recording studio 17-21 Wyfold Road, London London, SW6 6SE
521 Paytress
522 Rory Sullivan-Burke *The Light Pours Out Of Me* Omnibus Press, published 2022
523 Sullivan-Burke
524 Sullivan-Burke
525 Sullivan-Burke
526 Sullivan-Burke
527 English rock band formed in Salford, consisting of vocalist, guitarist and lyricist Ian Curtis, guitarist/keyboardist Bernard Sumner, bassist Peter Hook and drummer Stephen Morris. Active 1976 to 1980
528 English rock band formed in 1980 by vocalist and guitarist Bernard Sumner, bassist Peter Hook and drummer Stephen Morris, latterly joined by Gillian Gilbert
529 Sullivan-Burke
530 Sullivan-Burke
531 Sullivan-Burke
532 Sullivan-Burke
533 Sullivan-Burke
534 Siouxsie and The Banshees tour manager then latterly manager 1981 to 1987 after the firing of Nils Stevenson
535 Paytress
536 Sullivan-Burke
537 Paytress

538 Sullivan-Burke
539 Paytress
540 Paytress
541 Paytress
542 Paytress
543 Sullivan-Burke
544 Paytress
545 Bass guitarist and member of Slik, PVC2, Zones, The Skids, The Armoury Show and Public Image Ltd.
546 Sullivan-Burke
547 It was also the first time 'Thumb' from The Creatures' 'Wild Things' EP had been played live. It was to feature intermittently during the 1982 tour with its last outing for the band on 29 December, the final date of the 1982 tour
548 Sullivan-Burke
549 Sullivan-Burke
550 Sullivan-Burke
551 Sullivan-Burke
552 Sullivan-Burke
553 Private mental health hospital in South West London. Little known back in the early 1980s and not known as the celebrity retreat it is today
554 There is some speculation whether McGeoch's sacking was by formal letter, although it could have been face to face or by telephone. Siouxsie maintains that McGeoch had been told of his dismissal by the band prior to receiving a letter
555 Sullivan-Burke
556 Sullivan-Burke
557 Sullivan-Burke
558 Sullivan-Burke
559 Sullivan-Burke
560 Sullivan-Burke
561 Sullivan-Burke
562 Sullivan-Burke
563 Active 1982 to 1983
564 Now known as Nile Rodgers & Chic. American disco-oriented band formed in 1972 by guitarist Nile Rodgers and bassist Bernard Edwards. Active 1972 to1983, 1990 to 1992 and 1996 to present
565 Born 1958 in Glasgow. Scottish new wave bass guitarist who played with Slik, the Skids, The Armoury Show and Public Image Ltd. among other bands
566 English drummer born 6 May 1959 and member Magazine and The Armoury Show.
567 One and only studio album released by The Armoury Show, September 1985, EMI America
568 Post- Punk Music genre from the late 1970s through to the 1980s.
569 Sixth PIL studio album, released 14 September 1987, Virgin Records
570 Seventh PIL studio album, released 30 May 1989 (UK), Virgin Records
571 Eighth PIL studio album, released 24 February 1982 (UK), Virgin Records
572 Third and final album by the Sugarcubes, released 18 February 1992. Elektra/ One Little Indian Records
573 British singer, songwriter and multi-instrumentalist. Born 16 May 1958
574 English pop and rock drummer, born 6 July 1959, best known for his work with Spandau Ballet
575 Sullivan-Burke
576 Sullivan-Burke
577 Richard David Cook, 7 February 1957 to 25 August 2007. British jazz writer, magazine editor and former record company executive
578 rocksbackpages.com 'Siouxsie and the Banshees: A Kiss in The Dreamhouse (Polydor)'
Richard Cook, *New Musical Express*, 6 November 1982
579 rocksbackpages.com 'Siouxsie and the Banshees: A Kiss in The Dreamhouse (Polydor)'
Richard Cook, *New Musical Express*, 6 November 1982
580 rocksbackpages.com 'Siouxsie and the Banshees: A Kiss in The Dreamhouse (Polydor)'
Richard Cook, *New Musical Express*, 6 November 1982
581 uncut.co.uk Siouxsie And The Banshees: 'We were losing our minds' written by Gary Mulholland 24 October 2014
582 uncut.co.uk Siouxsie And The Banshees: 'We were losing our minds' written by Gary Mulholland 24 October 2014
583 Cinema and former concert venue in Birmingham, England. Opened 4 September 1937
584 Released 4 May 1982 by Fiction Records
585 faroutmagazine.co.uk The Cure *Pornography*, Aimee Ferrier 3 May 2023
586 Track one, Side one of *Pornography*
587 Lol Tolhurst 'Cured. The Tale Of Two Imaginary Boys', Quercus Books, first published 22 Sept 2016
588 English musician and bassist with The Cure. Born 1 June 1960
589 Initially the 'Fourteen Explicit Moments' tour which subsequently became the 'Pornography' tour
590 Lol Tolhurst 'Cured. The Tale Of Two Imaginary Boys', Quercus Books, first published 22 Sept 2016
591 faroutmagazine.co.uk 'The bar bill that almost split up The Cure' Joe Taysom 18 April 2021
592 Lol Tolhurst 'Cured. The Tale Of Two Imaginary Boys', Quercus Books, first published 22 Sept 2016
593 Lol Tolhurst 'Cured. The Tale Of Two Imaginary Boys', Quercus Books, first published 22 Sept 2016
594 Lol Tolhurst 'Cured. The Tale Of Two Imaginary Boys', Quercus Books, first published 22 Sept 2016
595 Paytress
596 in 1982 Vinyl Feest was at the Theater de Meervaart Amsterdam, Netherlands
597 Style of rock music emerging from Post-Punk in the UK in the late 1970s. The first Post-Punk bands to err on the side of 'dark' music with gothic overtones include Siouxsie and the Banshees, Joy Division, Bauhaus, and the Cure, among others
598 Irish poet and playwright 16 October 1854 to 30 November 1900
599 English novelist, playwright and biographer 13 May 1907 to 19 April 1989
600 Town in the borough of Reigate and Banstead, Surrey, England
601 Seaside resort and town in Lancashire, England
602 Both Siouxsie and The Banshees and The Cure also shared a long and fruitful relationship with producer Mike Hedges

603 Paytress
604 Paytress
605 Paytress
606 American guitarist who played with Zephyr 1969 to 1971, The James Gang 1973 to 1974 and Deep Purple 1975 to 1976. 1 August 1951 to 4 December 1976
607 Music show that aired on BBC2, 16 January 1981 to 29 March 1985
608 Concert venue in Zeche, Bochum, a City in North Rhine-Westphalia
609 Formed of musicians Anne Stephenson and Virginia Hewes. The Venomettes would also make appearances on work by Marc And The Mambas and The Cure
610 English cellist and string arranger, based in the UK
611 rocksbackpages.com 'The Creatures: Love At First Bite' Kris Needs, Flexipop!, May 1983
612 Released 18 November 1983 on Wonderland (Polydor) Records, co-produced by Steve Severin, Robert Smith and Mike Hedges
613 Debut studio album by British duo The Creatures, composed of Siouxsie Sioux and Budgie. Recorded in January 1983, released in May 1983, at Sea-West Studios, Oahu, Hawaii. Co-produced by Siouxsie Sioux, Budge and Mike Hedges
614 rocksbackpages.com 'All Creatures Great and Small' Richard Cook, *New Musical Express*, 14 May 1983
615 Paytress
616 Paytress
617 Paytress
618 Paytress
619 rocksbackpages.com 'The Creatures: Love At First Bite,' Kris Needs, Flexipop!, May 1983
620 Debut studio album by The Creatures. It reached No.17 in the UK Albums Chart
621 rocksbackpages.com 'The Creatures: Love At First Bite', Kris Needs, Flexipop!, May 1983
622 rocksbackpages.com 'The Creatures: Love At First Bite', Kris Needs, Flexipop!, May 1983
623 rocksbackpages.com 'The Creatures: Love At First Bite', Kris Needs, Flexipop!, May 1983
624 rocksbackpages.com 'All Creatures Great and Small,' Richard Cook, New Musical Express, 14 May 1983
625 rocksbackpages.com 'The Creatures: Love At First Bite' Kris Needs, Flexipop!, May 1983
626 rocksbackpages.com 'The Creatures: Love At First Bite' Kris Needs, Flexipop!, May 1983
627 rocksbackpages.com 'The Creatures: Love At First Bite' Kris Needs, Flexipop!, May 1983
628 rocksbackpages.com 'All Creatures Great and Small', Richard Cook, *New Musical Express*, 14 May 1983
629 rocksbackpages.com 'All Creatures Great and Small', Richard Cook, *New Musical Express*, 14 May 1983
630 rocksbackpages.com 'All Creatures Great and Small', Richard Cook, *New Musical Express*, 14 May 1983
631 Fourth studio album by English singer and songwriter Kate Bush, released 13 September 1982, EMI Records.
632 Catherine Bush CBE, English singer, songwriter, dancer and record producer. Born 30 July 1958
633 National bagpipe of Ireland
634 Wind instrument, played with vibrating lips to produce a continuous sound while using circular breathing. Developed by the Aboriginal Peoples around a thousand years ago
635 rocksbackpages.com 'The Creatures: Love At First Bite' Kris Needs, Flexipop!, May 1983
636 'Miss The Girl' was released as a single from 'Feast on 15 April 1983. It peaked at number 21 in the UK Singles Chart. It was the first record released on Wonderland Records (Dreamhouse publishing), a subsidiary of Polydor UK and Geffen US, exclusively for the release of music by Siouxsie and The Banshees, The Creatures and The Glove
637 Novel based around a group of car-crash fetishists who become sexually excited by staging and participating in car accidents, inspired by celebrity car crashes
638 Film director mostly known for making music videos, directing feature films, and for a fleeting pop career. Born 12 February 1956
639 'Dancing on Glass', written by Steve Sutherland, *Melody Maker* 14 May 1983
640 rocksbackpages.com 'All Creatures Great and Small', Richard Cook, *New Musical Express*, 14 May 1983
641 Photographer, cinematographer, and filmmaker
642 Paytress
643 English rock journalist and author. Born 21 May 1954
644 thebansheesandothercreatures.co.uk *NME*, Paul Du Noyer 1983
645 Paytress
646 Paytress
647 British singer and songwriter, best known as a member of Everything but the Girl, active from 1982 to 1999, and 2022-
648 'Bedsit Disco Queen: How I Grew Up And Tried To Be A Pop Star' by Tracey Thorne first published 2013, Virago Press
649 'Bedsit Disco Queen: How I Grew Up And Tried To Be A Pop Star' by Tracey Thorne
650 Paytress
651 Paytress
652 Paytress
653 Paytress
654 Paytress
655 Paytress
656 Paytress
657 The Batcave was a weekly club-night at 69 Dean Street, Soho, Central London, 1982 to 1985. It is considered to be where Southern English goth subculture started
658 In Mark Paytress' *Siouxsie & The Banshees The Authorised Biography*, Siouxsie only recalls going to The Batcave infrequently, commenting that she thought it was 'all a bit after the fact ...'
659 Australian musician, writer and actor. Born 22 September 1957
660 American singer, writer, poet and actress. Born 2 June 1959
661 Co-member of Alien Sex Fiend 1982-
662 James George Thirlwell, otherwise known JG Thirlwell, Clint Ruin, Frank Want and Foetus, among other pseudonyms. Australian musician, composer, and record producer known for his use of a plethora of different musical styles. Born 29 January 1960
663 faroutmagazine.co.uk 'The Batcave Club, London: A venue that kickstarted the 1980s goth movement' Kelly Rankin 7 October 2020
664 the quietus.com 'In The Batcave With Mr & Mrs Fiend: Alien Sex Fiend On Goth & Marriage' Nix Lowrey 8 September 2010
665 British band founded in the 1980s, incorporating an eclecticism of different styles including Glam, Punk, Post-Punk and Goth. Active 1981-1985, 2006-

666 English Gothic rock band, formed in London,1982. The band consists of Nik Fiend and Mrs Fiend.
667 English guitarist and producer. Co-founder of The Batcave (with Ollie Wisdom). Member of Siouxsie and the Banshees from 1987 until 1994
668 Paytress
669 Dyrskuepladsen Roskilde, Region Zealand, Denmark
670 Island in Stockholm's inner city
671 De Doelen concert venue, Rotterdam, Holland
672 Sittertobel, St. Gallen, Switzerland
673 Material for both live dates would be used for the double live album *Nocturne*, released on 25 November 1983 on Polydor. There would also be a video release of the live performances
674 Paytress
675 The most formidable of the Blue Meanies, the main adversaries in *Yellow Submarine*
676 1968 animated musical conceptual film inspired by the music of the Beatles
677 Recording studio created by Pink Floyd and located in Islington, London N1 from 1975–1995. And then onwards Fulham, London SW6, England 1995 to 2015. Pink Floyd recorded their album *Animals*, released on 21 January 1977 and parts of *The Wall*, released 30 November 1979 there.
678 *The Cure. Ten Imaginary Years* by Babarian, Steve Sutherland and Robert Smith Zomba Books. First edition published 1 Dec 1987
679 *The Cure. Ten Imaginary Year*s Source: *Melody Maker* by Babarian, Steve Sutherland and Robert Smith Zomba Books. First edition published 1 Dec 1987
680 'The Cure. Ten Imaginary Years' Source: International Musician by Babarian, Steve Sutherland and Robert Smith Zomba Books. First edition published 1 Dec 1987
681 American film director and screenwriter born 16 October 1947) known for his cult horror and thriller films *Squirm* 1976, *Blue Sunshine* 1977 and *Just Before Dawn* 1981
682 Smith sings on two *Blue Sunshine* songs: 'Mr. Alphabet Says' and 'Perfect Murder'
683 *The Cure. Ten Imaginary Years* by Babarian, Steve Sutherland and Robert Smith Zomba Books. First edition published 1 Dec 1987
684 Scottish dancer and choreographer. Born 29 May 1962. Other collaborations include Wire, Laibach, Jarvis Cocker and Scritti Politti
685 Eleventh studio album by English band The Fall, released on 24 October 1988 through Beggars Banquet
686 Loosely based upon the life and intellect of William of Orange
687 British choreographer and director. Born 12 March 1970
688 Band comprising Thom Yorke, Flea, Joey Waronker and Nigel Godrich. Active 2009 to 2013 and 2018
689 English electronic music duo comprising Ed Simons and Tom Rowlands. Formed in Manchester,1989
690 Weekly arts magazine programme shown on BBC 2 in 1982 and 1983 with a focus on music, art, style and fashion
691 Australian ballet dancer and ballet teacher. 4 September 1937 to 15 July 2019
692 English singer, composer, songwriter, musician and record producer. Born 9 March 1958
693 British drummer, best known for work with The Cure and Steve Hillage. 30 January 1951 to 26 February 2019
694 thebansheesandothercreatures.co.uk 'Nocturne The File 'The Glove'
695 Officially known as the 'Ground Theme' or 'Overworld Theme' used in the initial stage of the 1985 Nintendo video game 'Super Mario Bros'.
696 thebansheesandothercreatures.co.uk 'Nocturne' The File 'The Glove'
697 Track seven on 'Blue Sunshine'
698 Track ten (instrumental) on 'Blue Sunshine'
699 Paytress
700 Released as a stand-alone single by The Cure on 21 October 1983, Fiction Records
701 Fifth studio album by Massive Attack, released on 8 February 2010, Virgin Records. 'Man Next Door' on Massive Attack's also uses a sample from The Cure's '10:15 Saturday Night'
702 B Side 'Like an Animal' and 'Mouth to Mouth'
703 B Side 'The Tightrope'
704 Artwork by Da Gama
705 American socialite, writer, photographer, and book editor. First lady of the USA from 1961 to 1963, as the wife of President John F. Kennedy. 20 January 1961 to 22 November 1963
706 Fictional character from the 1960s TV spy series The Man from U.N.C.L.E. played by actor David McCallum. 19 September 1933 to 25 September 2023
707 American-born Irish actor, director, screenwriter, and film, television and theatre producer 19 March 1928 to 13 January 2009. McGoohan appears as 'Number Six', the role he played in the television series *The Prisoner*, also created by McGoohan, which aired 29 September 1967 to1 February 1968.
708 Lady Penelope Creighton-Ward is a fictional character in the British 1960s Gerry and Sylvia Anderson Supermarionation television series *Thunderbirds*, first aired in 1965
709 Fictional character from Gerry and Sylvia Anderson's Supermarionation television show *Thunderbirds*, first aired in 1965
710 Genre of Japanese art prominent from the 17th to 19th centuries
711 Jamaican sound engineer, instrumental in the development of dub in the 1960s and 1970s. 28 January 1941 to 6 February 1989
712 American composer known for his contribution to the development of minimal music in the mid to late 1960s. Born 3 October 1936
713 Side four, track six sound collage from The Beatles' 1968 self-titled or *White Album*, released 22 November 1968 Apple Music
714 Side two, track six from The Beatles' *Sgt. Pepper's Lonely Hearts Club Band*, released 26 May 1967 Parlophone (UK) Capitol (US)
715 English record producer, composer, arranger, conductor, and musician. 3 January 1926 to 8 March 2016
716 Ralph Vaughan Williams, English composer 12 October 1872 to 26 August 1958
717 German composer, pianist, and music critic. 8 June 1810 to 29 July 1856
718 Electro-mechanical musical instrument cultivated in Birmingham, England,1963
719 Paytress
720 The album referred to by Severin is 'Torment And Toreros', released by Marc And The Mambas in 1983. The song 'Torment' was written by Steve Severin and Robert Smith
721 Paytress
722 Herbert Jay Solomon was an American jazz flute player known by his stage name Herbie Mann. 16 April 1930 to 1 July 1 2003
723 American songwriter 24 September 1909 to 26 September 2000

724 Upbeat 1962 jazz song with music by Herbie Mann and lyrics by Carl Sigman. Released as a single by The Creatures 8 July 1983

725 Relaxed style of samba initiated and developed in the late 1950s and early 1960s in Rio de Janeiro, Brazil

726 Melvin Howard Tormé 13 September 1925 to 5 June 1999) was an American musician, composer singer, arranger, drummer, actor, and author

727 Timpani or kettledrums are percussion instruments in the form of a drum with a large, hemispherical surface area

728 Queen of the Ptolemaic Kingdom of Egypt from 51 to 30 BC, and its last ruler. 0/69 BC – 10 August 30 BC

729 Goddess of the sun according to Japanese mythology

730 American comic strip featuring Dick Tracy (originally Plainclothes Tracy) debuted on Sunday, October 4, 1931

731 American crime drama television series created by Anthony Yerkovich and produced by Michael Mann for the NBC channel 1984 to 1989

732 American dancer, singer, actor, director and choreographer, 23 August 1912 to 2 February 1996

733 1952 American romantic musical comedy, directed and choreographed by Gene Kelly and Stanley Donen

734 Otherwise known as The Gravelly Hill Interchange. Sprawling road junction in Birmingham, England

735 Former Manchester pub and gig venue on Barlow Moor Road, Chorlton-Cum-Hardy, Manchester which closed in the 1990s

736 Originally recorded by The Beatles for *The Beatles* album, released 22 November 1968 about Prudence Farrow, daughter of film director John Farrow and actress Maureen O'Sullivan and younger sister of actress Mia Farrow. 'Dear Prudence' references Farrow's studying of Transcendental Meditation in Rishikesh with the Beatles in early 1968. The Siouxsie and The Banshees version was recorded July 1983 in Stockholm, Sweden and Islington, London and released 23 September 1983 by Siouxsie and The Banshees, with the B Side 'Tattoo' and additional 'There's A Planet In My Kitchen' on the twelve-inch version

737 Swedish film company established in 1929 by Schamyl Bauman and Gustaf Scheutz, located at Kungsgatan in central Stockholm. The film studio was located in Mariehäll, Bromma, northwest of Stockholm city

738 British recording studio based 311-312 Upper Street, Angel, Islington, active 5 December 1978 to December 2019

739 Paytress

740 Paytress

741 'In My Craft or Sullen Art' is a poem written by Welsh poet Dylan Thomas 1914 to 1953) First published 1946 in the volume of poetry 'Deaths and Entrances'

742 Paytress

743 The first Cure collaboration was 'Let's Go To Bed' in 1982 and the last was 'Wrong Number' in 1987

744 The Venetian Lagoon is an encircled bay of the Adriatic Sea, in northern Italy, in which Venice is situated

745 Wooden posts planted in the Venetian Lagoon to indicate the channels to boats

746 Venetian water taxi

747 Luis Buñuel Portolés was an influential Spanish filmmaker who worked in France, Mexico and Spain. 22 February 1900 to 29 July 1983

748 English translation 'An Andalusian Dog' is a 1929 French silent film produced, directed and edited by Luis Buñuel, who also co-wrote the screenplay with Salvador Dalí

749 loudersound.com 'The story behind the song: Dear Prudence by Siouxsie And The Banshees' written by Carol Clerk, 23 February 2022

750 Fictional, intentionally humorously incompetent policemen characterised in silent film 'slapstick' comedies produced by Mack Sennett for his Keystone Film Company between 1912 and 1917

751 loudersound.com 'The story behind the song: Dear Prudence by Siouxsie And The Banshees' written by Carol Clerk, 23 February 2022

752 Paytress

753 Group of fourteen paintings by artist Francisco Goya, made during the later years of his life, surmised to be between 1819 and 1823. Portraying intense, haunting themes, the works reflect both his paranoia of insanity and his bleak outlook on mankind

754 Paytress

755 The two day 100 Club Punk Special where Siouxsie and The Banshees played their first gig

756 Oil painting by Gustav Klimt, executed in 1901 depicting the biblical figure Judith holding the head of Holofernes after beheading him

757 Ancient Greek mythological Goddess, often shown holding a pair of torches, a key, or snakes, or accompanied by dog

758 Also known as Neoplasticism, De Stijl was a Dutch art movement founded in 1917 in Leiden, Holland

759 Fictionalised roadside hotel in the comedy series *I'm Alan Partridge* broadcast on BBC2 3 November 1997 to16 December 2002

760 Lyrics from the Talking Heads song 'Life During Wartime', released as the first single in September 1979 from the band's 1979 album 'Fear of Music', Sire Records

761 English drummer, singer songwriter, record producer and actor. Born 30 January 1951

762 English pop band formed in Islington, London, 1979. Years active 1979 to 1990 and 2009 to 2019

763 British pop and rock singer and songwriter. Born 10 January 1945

764 American poet and writer 3 June 1926 to 5 April 1997. Instrumental in forming the core of the Beat Generation along with William S.Burroughs and Jack Kerouac.

765 loudersound.com 'The story behind the song: Dear Prudence by Siouxsie And The Banshees' written by Carol Clerk, 23 February 2022

766 Harmonics come from the vibration of an open guitar string

767 North Indian and Nepalese type of bell that vibrates and produces a rich, deep tone when played

768 Musical genre which originated in Bristol, England the late 1980s. Described as a psychedelic fusion of hip hop and electronica with slow tempos and an atmospheric sound, its pioneers are Massive Attack, Portishead and Tricky

769 Mechanical device inside a toy bear which recreates the bear's 'growl', invented by Paul Steiff in 1908

770 American spaceflight that first landed humans on the Moon. Neil Armstrong and Buzz Aldrin landed the Apollo Lunar Module Eagle on 20 July 1969

771 From the American 1940 Walt Disney produced animated musical anthology film *Fantasia*, released 13 November 1940

772 Fifth and final three-part instrumental track from the Pink Floyd album *Atom Heart Mother*, credited to the whole band. Released 2 October 1970 in the UK, Harvest Records

773 Japanese photographer 17 September 1906 to 22 July 1987

774 International style and aesthetic movement which was at the vanguard of photography during the later nineteenth and early twentieth centuries

775 Common heraldic motif in the shape of a French flower

776 Relating to the science of alchemy, the medieval practice concerned with the transmutation of matter

777 Paytress

778 Paytress

779 Paytress

780 thebansheesandothercreatures.co.uk 'Play At Home'

781 Siouxsie and The Banshees live double album and video by released on 25 November 1983, Polydor Records.

782 Play at Home dialogue from the forty-five-minute show broadcast on Channel 4, RPM Productions. Aired September 1984

783 Grain became Iggy Pop's road manager in 1986

784 Play at Home dialogue from the 45-minute show broadcast on Channel 4, RPM Productions. Aired September 1984

785 Play at Home dialogue from the 45-minute show broadcast on Channel 4, RPM Productions. Aired September 1984

786 *Alice's Adventures In Wonderland*, Chapter Seven

787 fictional character first appearing in Lewis Caroll's 1865 *Alice's Adventures in Wonderland*, and subsequently in the 1871 sequel *Through the Looking-Glass*

788 British DJ, musician, record producer and composer, born in 1961

789 Beginning as sound engineer, stage crew supplier and promoter's rep, Tim stage managed Soft Cell, production managed UB40 and tour managed artists from Kajagoogoo to Captain Beefheart before moving into artist management in the late 1980s. Collins took over tour managing duties for Siouxsie and The Banshees in the late 1980s, subsequently becoming their longest serving manager (eight years in total). Collins was influential in regenerating the band's career in America, including the 1991 Lollapalooza American tour and securing the band the 'Face To Face' main song on the 1992 Tim Burton 'Batman Returns' film soundtrack

790 Predominantly used in the Catholic Church as a physical string of knots or beads used to count the components of a prayer

791 Predominantly used in the Catholic Church as a physical string of knots or beads used to count the components of a prayer

792 English actor, monologist, singer and comedian 1 October 1890 to 30 January 1982

793 Originally written by George Marriott Edgar, British poet, scriptwriter and comedian 5 October 1880 to 5 May 1951, recorded by Stanley Holloway in 1932

794 thebansheesandothercreatures.co.uk 'Play At Home', aired September 1984

795 Peccaries are pig-like ungulates found throughout Central and South America, Trinidad in the Caribbean, and in the North American southwest. Siouxsie and Budgie also adopted an armadillo called Amy

796 Scene in the 'Wizard Of Oz' American musical fantasy film produced by Metro-Goldwyn-Mayer. Released 10 August 1939

797 thebansheesandothercreatures.co.uk 'Play At Home', aired September 1984

798 The video for the song was shot in four hours on 10 November 1975 at Elstree Studios. 'Bohemian Rhapsody' was released as a single on 31 October 1975, EMI Records

799 Play at Home dialogue from the forty-five-minute show broadcast on Channel 4, RPM Productions. Aired September 1984

800 Electromechanical device used to send and receive typed messages through multiple communications channels, came into telegraphic use in 1887

801 John Fitzgerald Kennedy was the thirty fifth president of the United States Of America from 1961 until his assassination in 1963. 20 January 1961 to 22 November 1963

802 . Head of the Catholic Church and sovereign of the Vatican City State from 1978 until 2005. 16 October 1978 to 2 April 2005

803 American actor and politician; fortieth President of the United States Of America from 1981 to 1989. 6 February 1911 to 5 June 2004

804 English actor born 13 April 1937

805 1973 political thriller film directed by Fred Zinnemann, starring Edward Fox and Michael Lonsdale, based on the 1971 novel of the same name by author Frederick Forsyth

806 collinsdictionary.com

807 *The Cure. Ten Imaginary Years* by Babarian, Steve Sutherland and Robert Smith Zomba Books. First edition published 1 Dec 1987

808 Sixth studio album released by Siouxsie and The Banshees, released 8 June 1984. The only studio album to feature Robert Smith. Polydor Records. Geffen US

809 Both ballet and orchestral concert work by Russian composer Igor Stravinsky premiered 29 May 1913

810 Crime novel by American author Mario Puzo. Published originally in 1969 by G. P. Putnam's Sons, the novel involves the story of a fictional Mafia family residing in New York City and Long Island, headed by Vito Corleone, the Godfather of the story. Published 10 March 1969

811 In the 1950s, Sizemore, 4 April 1927 to 24 July 2016, was diagnosed with multiple personality disorder, latterly known as dissociative identity disorder

812 Book written by psychiatrists Corbett H. Thigpen and Hervey M. Cleckley about the life of Christine Costner Sizemore, subsequently turned into an American film noir, released in 1957

813 Pre-film animation device that produces the illusion of motion, the zoetrope is a cylindrical variant of the phénakisticope, an instrument mooted after the stroboscopic discs were introduced in 1833

814 The VHS (Video Home System) is a standard for consumer-level analogue video recording on tape cassettes, invented in 1976 by the Victor Company of Japan (JVC)

815 Double live album by David Bowie, recorded on 3 July 1973 and released in October 1983 in conjunction with the film of the same name. RCA Records

816 Double live album by the American new wave band Talking Heads, released 24 March 1982 by Sire Records

817 Fourth studio album by The Clash, released on the CBS Epic label 12 December 1980

818 Painted in 1911, after the artist had visited Paris. The work represents a mid-point in Mondrian's passage from realistic landscapes to far-reaching abstraction

819 1875 oil on canvas painting by James McNeill Whistler, Detroit Institute of Arts, America

820 American painter and printmaker, 10 July 1834 to 17 July 1903, active during the American Gilded Age. Whistler was based primarily in the United Kingdom

821 'The Birthday Party: Mutiny! (Mute 29); Siouxsie & the Banshees: Nocturne (Polydor Shah 1)'

822 Released in 1983 as two EPs, 'The Bad Seed' and 'Mutiny!' on 4AD and Mute Records

823 'The Birthday Party: Mutiny! (Mute 29); Siouxsie & the Banshees: Nocturne (Polydor Shah 1)', written by Lynden Barber for *Melody Maker*, 26 November 1983

824 'The Birthday Party: Mutiny! (Mute 29); Siouxsie & the Banshees: Nocturne (Polydor Shah 1)', written by Lynden Barber for *Melody Maker*, 26 November 1983

825 'The Birthday Party: Mutiny! (Mute 29); Siouxsie & the Banshees: Nocturne (Polydor Shah 1)', written by Lynden Barber for *Melody Maker*, 26 November 1983

826 'The Birthday Party: Mutiny! (Mute 29); Siouxsie & the Banshees: Nocturne (Polydor Shah 1)', written by Lynden Barber for *Melody Maker*, 26 November 1983

Footnotes

827 *Don't Look Black* Barney Hoskyns, *NME* 24 December 1983
828 *Don't Look Black* Barney Hoskyns, *NME* 24 December 1983
829 *Don't Look Black* Barney Hoskyns, *NME* 24 December 1983
830 *Don't Look Black* Barney Hoskyns, *NME* 24 December 1983
831 *Don't Look Black* Barney Hoskyns, *NME* 24 December 1983
832 *Don't Look Black* Barney Hoskyns, *NME* 24 December 1983
833 *Don't Look Black* Barney Hoskyns, *NME* 24 December 1983
834 *Don't Look Black* Barney Hoskyns, *NME* 24 December 1983
835 *Don't Look Black* Barney Hoskyns, *NME* 24 December 1983
836 *Don't Look Black* Barney Hoskyns, *NME* 24 December 1983
837 *Don't Look Black* Barney Hoskyns, *NME* 24 December 1983
838 *Don't Look Black* Barney Hoskyns, *NME* 24 December 1983
839 American rock band, formed in Fremont, New Hampshire, in 1965, comprising Dorothy "Dot" Wiggin on vocals and lead guitar, Betty Wiggin, also vocals and rhythm guitar, Helen Wiggin on drums and, latterly, Rachel Wiggin on bass guitar
840 *Don't Look Black* Barney Hoskyns, *NME* 24 December 1983
841 *Don't Look Black* Barney Hoskyns, *NME* 24 December 1983
842 *Don't Look Black* Barney Hoskyns, *NME* 24 December 1983
843 *Don't Look Black* Barney Hoskyns, *NME* 24 December 1983
844 Paytress
845 Paytress
846 Francis John Tovey 8 September 1956 to 3 April 2002), otherwise known as Fad Gadget, was a British avant-garde electronic vocalist and musician
847 Music genre that initially became prominent in the late 1970s and features the synthesizer as the principle musical instrument
848 German electronic band formed in Düsseldorf in 1970 by Florian Schneider and Ralf Hütter
849 American musical duo composed of vocalist Alan Vega and instrumentalist Martin Rev, periodically active between 1970 and 2016
850 miriam-webster.com
851 Paytress
852 rocksbackpages.com Source 'Siouxsie & The Banshees' Martin Aston, Rock's Backpages audio, 1986
853 Paytress
854 thebansheesandothercreatures.co.uk Source: *Melody Maker* 17 October 1992
855 thebansheesandothercreatures.co.uk Source: *Melody Maker* 17 October 1992
856 thebansheesandothercreatures.co.uk Source: *Melody Maker* 17 October 1992
857 thebansheesandothercreatures.co.uk The File- Phase Three Issue Two 'Hyaena'- 'Swimming Horses' The Record
858 A term used to describe reggae performed by non-Caribbean people, often in a defamatory manner because of perceived inauthenticity
859 Song by Led Zeppelin, from the 1973 album *Houses of the Holy*. The title is a play on the word Jamaica when uttered in an English accent
860 Lyric from the Velvet Underground song 'Some Kinda Love', from the band's third studio album, released March 1969, MGM Records
861 Paytress
862 Paytress
863 *The Cure. Ten Imaginary Years* by Babarian, Steve Sutherland and Robert Smith Zomba Books. First edition published 1 Dec 1987
864 Paytress
865 *The Cure. Ten Imaginary Years* by Babarian, Steve Sutherland and Robert Smith Zomba Books. First edition published 1 Dec 1987
866 1968 monumental science fiction film directed and produced by Stanley Kubrick. Released 2 April 1968
867 First recorded by Memphis Minnie and Kansas Joe McCoy in 1929 and re-worked by Led Zeppelin as the last song on the band's 1971 Untitled album, otherwise known as *Led Zeppelin IV*
868 English science fiction writer 10 July 1903 to 11 March 1969
869 Pink Floyd Instrumental composition, written in 1966 and appears on the band's 1967 debut album, *The Piper at the Gates of Dawn*, EMI Records
870 Foxx, born 26 September 1948 was the original lead singer of Ultravox and a musician, artist, photographer, graphic designer, writer, teacher and lecturer
871 English figurative artist 29 May 1935 to 15 February 2001
872 Austrian artist, poet, teacher and playwright 1 March 1886 to 22 February 1980
873 thebansheesandothercreatures.co.uk The File- Phase Three Issue Two 'Hyaena'- 'Swimming Horses' The Record
874 Released as a stand-alone single by The Cure in November 1982. Fiction Records
875 Released as a stand-alone single by The Cure in June 1983. Fiction Records
876 Strictly speaking a three piece, with Thornalley drafted in specifically for 'The Love Cats', his only studio recording with The Cure
877 English songwriter, musician, and producer. Born 5 January 1960
878 American cable television channel officially launched on 1 August 1981
879 Lol Tolhurst *Cured. The Tale Of Two Imaginary Boys*, Quercus Books, first published 22 Sept 2016
880 Lol Tolhurst *Cured. The Tale Of Two Imaginary Boys*, Quercus Books, first published 22 Sept 2016
881 Released on 26 March 1984 as the sole single from The Cure's fifth studio album *The Top*. Fiction Records
882 Founded in 1904, it is the oldest of London's symphony orchestras
883 English cellist, guitarist, keyboard player and composer born 29 July 1962. McCarrick is also a teacher and visiting lecturer in music. McCarrick also worked on The Glove 'Blue Sunshine' album
884 Paytress
885 thebansheesandothercreatures.co.uk Source: *Melody Maker* 17 October 1992
886 thebansheesandothercreatures.co.uk Source: *Melody Maker* 17 October 1992
887 *Season of the Witch: The Book of Goth* Cathi Unsworth first published in the UK in 2023 by Nine Eight Books
888 short piece of light music composed by Ronald Binge in 1963
889 British composer and arranger of light music 15 July 1910 to 6 September 1979
890 *Lady Windermere's Fan, A Play About a Good Woman* is a comedy in four acts by Oscar Wilde. It was first performed on 20 February 1892, at the St James's Theatre in London
891 Concept and symbol in ancient Egyptian religion that represents protection, well-being and healing

892 British artist based in New York, born in 1960

893 Paytress

894 Paytress

895 Velvet Underground song, written by Lou Reed. Originally released on the band's 1967 debut album 'The Velvet Underground & Nico' Verve Records

896 The glass harmonica, also known as the glass armonica, glass harmonium, bowl organ or hydrocrystalophone, was invented in 1761 by Benjamin Franklin

897 Three-stringed traditional Japanese musical instrument, originating from the Chinese instrument sanxian, which can be traced back to the thirteenth century

898 thebansheesandothercreatures.co.uk 'Hyaena'-The File Phase Three Issue Two 'Dazzle' The Record Billy 'Chainsaw' Houlston

899 Siouxsie and The Banshees guitar tech. Mitchell worked as a tech for a number of both American and UK bands

900 dailymotion.com The "hey's" in question come from the T.Rex song 'Solid Gold Easy Action', released as a single on 1 December 1972 EMI Records

901 British photographer whose portraits of 1980s pop musicians led to him being named 'photographer of the decade' by The Guardian in 1989. 13 April 1948 to 27 January 2024

902 Cubism was an early-20th-century avant-garde art movement that saw a revolution in European painting, drawing and sculpture, inspiring related movements in music, literature, and architecture. In Art, its main proponents were Pablo Picasso, Georges Braque, Juan Gris, Jean Metzinger and Robert Delauney, among others

903 newyorker.com 'The Stories Behind Brian Griffin's Portraits of Seventies and Eighties Rock Stars' Hua Hsu 24 October 2017

904 Concert venue in Lille, Hauts-de-France, France

905 thebansheesandothercreatures.co.uk 'Hyaena'- The File Phase Three Issue Three And Four The Origins Billy 'Chainsaw' Houlston

906 thebansheesandothercreatures.co.uk Source: NME 28 September 1985

907 Apparently Inspired by the UK's 'Futurama' festivals, 'Pandora's Music Box '83' was a two-day, indoor alternative music festival taking place on 2 and 3 September 1983

908 From the exhibition 'Don't Forget to Call Your Mother' at the Metropolitan Museum of Art, New York, USA. Larry Sultan was an American photographer from the San Fernando Valley in California, USA. 13 July 13, 1946 to 13 December 2009

909 thebansheesandothercreatures.co.uk 'Hyaena' Trivia

910 Musical instrument in the percussion family consisting of wooden bars that are hit with mallets.

911 'The Waste Land', a poem written by T.S. Eliot, 26 September 1888 to 4 January 1965, was first published 16 October 1922

912 thebansheesandothercreatures.co.uk 'Hyaena'- The File Phase Three Issue Three And Four The Origins Billy 'Chainsaw' Houlston

913 Medication used to treat certain types of nerve agent and pesticide poisonings

914 Synthetically or naturally produced tropane alkaloid and anticholinergic drug, utilised as a medication to manage motion sickness

915 Used to provide symptom relief of spasms caused by lower abdominal and bladder disorders

916 Part three of the 'Animerama' trilogy, *Belladonna Of Sadness* is a 1973 Japanese adult animated art film produced by the animation studio Mushi Production

917 Originally published in Paris as 'La Sorcière' in 1862

918 French historian and writer best known for his multi-volume work 'Histoire de France'. 21 August 1798 to 9 February 1874

919 From 'Belladonna'. Lyrics written by Steve Severin

920 From the 1973 British folk horror film directed by Robin Hardy with Edward Woodward, Britt Ekland, Diane Cilento, Ingrid Pitt, and Christopher Lee

921 Irish folk song included in the Roud Folk Song Index

922 Sub-category of Western films produced in Europe, emerging in the mid-1960s on the wave of Sergio Leone's filmmaking technique

923 thebansheesandothercreatures.co.uk 'Hyaena'- The File Phase Three Issue Three And Four The Origins Billy 'Chainsaw' Houlston

924 thebansheesandothercreatures.co.uk 'Hyaena'- The File Phase Three Issue Three And Four The Origins Billy 'Chainsaw' Houlston

925 1965 Sergio Leone directed Spaghetti Western film, the second film of Leone's 'Dollars Trilogy'

926 'Carillon' was written by Italian composer, conductor, trumpeter and pianist Ennio Morricone, 10 November 1928 to 6 July 2020 for the 1965 *For A Few Dollars More* soundtrack

927 Bank robber played by Italian actor and activist Gian Maria Volonté 9 April 1933 to 6 December 1994

928 Bounty hunter played by American actor Lee Van Cleef 9 January 1925 to 16 December 1989

929 Bounty hunter played by American actor and director Clint Eastwood, born 31 May 1930

930 1974 Mexican-American neo-Western film directed by Sam Peckinpah 21 February to 28 December 1984

931 Dating back to the sixteenth century, El Dorado is commonly associated with the legend of a gold city, kingdom, or empire said to be placed somewhere in the Americas

932 Guitarist and founder member of The Doors born 8 January 1945

933 Appears on The Doors' second studio album, *Strange Days*, released 25 September 1967, put out as a single on 4 September 1967, Elektra Records

934 thebansheesandothercreatures.co.uk 'Hyaena'- The File Phase Three Issue Three And Four The Origins, Billy 'Chainsaw' Houlston

935 thebansheesandothercreatures.co.uk 'Hyaena'- The File Phase Three Issue Three And Four The Origins, Billy 'Chainsaw' Houlston

936 Debut Bauhaus single, released on 6 August 1979 on Small Wonder Records

937 Author's note: 'Running Town', 'We Hunger' and 'Blow The House Down' were played during the Banshees' two night stint at the Royal Albert Hall on 30 September and 1 October 1983 but didn't make the vinyl cut

938 thebansheesandothercreatures.co.uk 'Hyaena' The Album

939 Also spelt gadaidja, cadiche, kadaitcha, karadji or kaditcha. In Arrernte orthography it is spelt kwertatye, is a type of shaman and traditional executioner amongst the Arrernte people, an Aboriginal group in Central Australia. The practice of Kurdaitcha had stopped in southern Australia by the twentieth century but it is believed to have continued in northern Australia

940 Also referred to as the Aranda, Arunta or Arrarnta. Aboriginal Australian peoples who live in the Arrernte lands, at Mparntwe, Alice Springs and surrounding enclaves of the Central Australia region of the Northern Territory

941 wellcomecollection.org

942 Fable dating back to the 1840s, but the story is presumed to be much older, with the earliest known version situated in Dartmoor with three pixies and a fox before appearing with the three pigs and a wolf in 'English Fairy Tales', published in 1890 by Joseph Jacobs 29 August 1854 to 30 January 1916. Jacobs credited James Halliwell-Phillipps 21 June 1820 to 3 January 1889, as the source

943 thebansheesandothercreatures.co.uk 'Hyaena' The Album

944 Opened in 1928 with *Napoleon*, directed by Abel Gance. Located in Montmartre, Paris, France

945 Spanish painter, sculptor and ceramist. 20 April 1893 to 25 December 1983

Footnotes

946 festival-cannes.com 'The scandal of L'Âge d'or (The Golden Age)' Andréa Mendes, published on 21 May 2019
947 festival-cannes.com 'The scandal of L'Âge d'or (The Golden Age)' Andréa Mendes, published on 21 May 2019
948 thebansheesandothercreatures.co.uk 'Hyaena'- The File Phase Three Issue Three And Four The Origins, Billy 'Chainsaw' Houlston
949 thebansheesandothercreatures.co.uk 'Hyaena'- The File Phase Three Issue Three And Four The Origins, Billy 'Chainsaw' Houlston
950 Oil on canvas painting in Tate Modern, London, England by American artist Jackson Pollock 28 January 1912 to 11 August 1956
951 French painter and sculptor of the Ecole de Paris (School of Paris). 31 July 1901 to 12 May 1985
952 Paytress
953 UK music television programme, broadcast on Channel 4 which ran for five series, from 5 November 1982 to 24 April 1987
954 thebansheesandothercreatures.co.uk 'Hyaena' Interviews/ Articles ZigZag magazine 'From Here To Eternity' Paul O' Reilly interview with Steve Severin June 1984
955 American rock music magazine and entertainment company, founded in Detroit. The magazine was in print form from 1969 to 1989
956 rocksbackpages.com 'Siouxsie and the Banshees: Hyaena' written by Roy Trakin, Creem Magazine, November 1984
957 rocksbackpages.com 'Siouxsie & The Banshees: Hyaena (Wonderland/Polydor)' written by Biba Kopf for the New Musical Express on 4 August 1984
958 rocksbackpages.com 'Siouxsie & The Banshees: Hyaena (Wonderland/Polydor)' written by Biba Kopf for the New Musical Express on 4 August 1984
959 Paytress
960 International Musician and Recording World was a magazine published from 1975 to 1991. Launched initially in the UK, with editions created for the United States, Europe, Australia, and Japan
961 The Cure. Ten Imaginary Years by Babarian, Steve Sutherland and Robert Smith Zomba Books. First edition published 1 Dec 1987
962 The Cure. Ten Imaginary Years by Babarian, Steve Sutherland and Robert Smith Zomba Books. First edition published 1 Dec 1987
963 The Cure. Ten Imaginary Years by Babarian, Steve Sutherland and Robert Smith Zomba Books. First edition published 1 Dec 1987
964 The Cure. Ten Imaginary Years by Babarian, Steve Sutherland and Robert Smith Zomba Books. First edition published 1 Dec 1987
965 Steve Severin maintains that Smith was calling from Milan in the Mark Paytress Authorised Biography, which would have been on 21 May 1984, coinciding with a gig at Teatro Tenda
966 The Cure. Ten Imaginary Years by Babarian, Steve Sutherland and Robert Smith Zomba Books. First edition published 1 Dec 1987
967 The Cure. Ten Imaginary Years by Babarian, Steve Sutherland and Robert Smith Zomba Books. First edition published 1 Dec 1987
968 The Cure. Ten Imaginary Years by Babarian, Steve Sutherland and Robert Smith Zomba Books. First edition published 1 Dec 1987
969 The Cure. Ten Imaginary Years by Babarian, Steve Sutherland and Robert Smith Zomba Books. First edition published 1 Dec 1987
970 Paytress
971 Paytress
972 Paytress
973 YouTube.com Siouxsie and the Banshees - 1984 MTV Interview (unedited)
974 Second Clock DVA album, released 24 January 1981 on Fetish Records
975 Released on 26 May 1982 on Polydor Records
976 Track two, Side one on the third Clock DVA studio album Advantage released 1983 on Polydor Records
977 Track three, Side one on the third Clock DVA studio album Advantage released 1983 on Polydor Records
978 Track one, Side two on the third Clock DVA studio album Advantage released 1983 on Polydor Records
979 Third Clock DVA studio album Advantage released 1983 on Polydor Records
980 Founder member of Clock DVA 1980 to present
981 Early 1970s multimedia collective
982 English musician, arranger, composer, record producer and music programmer. Ware was also a founding member of both the Human League and Heaven 17
983 English musician, composer and founding member of the Human League. Craig Marsh subsequently went on to form the British Electronic Foundation and latterly Heaven 17
984 Adi Newton, Martyn Ware and Ian Craig Marsh formed The Future wrote music and put together demos in a disused Sheffield cutlery workshop. The band were never signed and didn't put out any music commercially at the time
985 Former Parisian nightclub, originally founded in 1885
986 encyclopaediaelectronica.com 'Moments of Terror (A Tale of Clock DVA 1977-1983)' written by Steven B. O'Connor in January 1984
987 Erik Weisz 24 March 24 to 31 October 1926), known as Harry Houdini was a Hungarian-American escape artist and illusionist
988 Paytress. Siouxsie and Budgie had been holidaying in Bali when they returned, on Siouxsie's birthday, to be confronted by news of Robert Smith's departure from the Banshees
989 Paytress
990 Paytress
991 Paytress
992 Àngel Casas 17 April 1946 to 1 October 2022 was a Spanish journalist and writer. The Angel Casas talk show was broadcast from 1984 to 1988
993 Paytress
994 Re-named The Jugged Hare in 2012
995 Billy 'Chainsaw' Houlston. Source: Siouxsie and The Banshees The Authorised Biography Mark Paytress Sanctuary Publishing 2003
996 Siouxsie and The Banshees' seventh studio album released on 21 April 1986 by Wonderland and Polydor Records in the UK and Geffen Records in the US
997 Paytress
998 Paytress
999 Paytress
1000 Paytress
1001 'Overground', 'Voices', 'Placebo Effect' are discussed in Siouxsie And The Banshees The Early Years Laurence Hedges. Wymer Publishing 2023
1002 Steve Severin. Source: Siouxsie and The Banshees The Authorised Biography Mark Paytress Sanctuary Publishing 2003
1003 Paytress
1004 Classical musician, not to be confused with trumpeter Bill McGee, Grand Master Flash, The Sugar Hill Gang et.al
1005 English rock musician, songwriter and producer. Best known as the guitarist of post-punk group Killing Joke. 18 December 1958 to 26 November 2023

1006 English rock band formed by Jaz Coleman, born 26 February 1960, Paul Ferguson, born 31 March 1958, Geordie Walker, 18 December 1958 to 26 November 2023 and Youth (Martin Glover), born 27 December 1960
1007 Paytress
1008 Motor racing circuit and aerodrome built near Weybridge in Surrey, England, UK. Opened in 1907, it was the world's first purpose-built 'banked' motor racing circuit
1009 The inferred link between the breaker's yard and Brookland's car crashes could be a little coincidental and/ or fanciful as the racetrack was decommissioned in August 1939
1010 Paytress
1011 Concert hall located in Nogent-sur-Marne, France.
1012 Paytress
1013 Known as Stevo, Stephen John Pearce, born 26 December 1962 is a British record producer and music industry executive, although best known as the owner of indie label Some Bizzare Records
1014 theguardian.com Stevo of Some Bizzare Records: 'The delay in any kind of recognition is outrageous' written by Daniel Dylan Wray 23 February 2023
1015 Canadian music producer and keyboardist born 25 March 1949 known for his work with, among others, Lou Reed, Aerosmith, Alice Cooper Kiss, Deep Purple and Pink Floyd
1016 Reed's third solo studio album, released 5 October 1973, RCA Victor label
1017 rocksbackpages.com Source 'Siouxsie & The Banshees' Martin Aston, Rock's Backpages audio, 1986
1018 British record producer, associated with numerous Post-Punk and New Wave albums
1019 English rock band that formed in London, 1977. Disbanded in 1982
1020 English Punk Rock band formed IN 1976 comprising currently Dave Vanian, Rat Scabies, Captain Sensible and Paul Gray
1021 Paytress
1022 Studio complex in Parsons Green, West London.
1023 Rehearsal studio situated on Sinclair Road, Hammersmith, West London, founded and opened by producer Simon Napier-Bell, NOMIS bought by the Sanctuary Music Group in the mid-80s, it later reverted to its original name before being turned into offices and becoming vacant in 2008
1024 American composer, songwriter, pianist and record producer May 12 1928 to 8 February 2023
1025 American pop group formed in Los Angeles in 1964 by John Walker (John Maus) 12 November to 7 May 2011, Scott Walker (Noel Scott Engel) 9 January 1943 to 22 March 2019 and with Gary Walker (Gary Leeds) born 9 March 1942
1026 Recording studio located in the Kreuzberg district of Berlin, Germany
1027 Public square and traffic intersection in the city centre of Berlin
1028 Paytress
1029 Second solo studio album by Iggy Pop, released on September 9 1977 RCA Records
1030 Paytress
1031 Guarded concrete barrier that encircled West Berlin of the Federal Republic of Germany, West Germany, separating it from East Berlin and the German Democratic Republic from 1961 to 1989
1032 undiscovermusic.com 'Recording Studios: A History Of The Most Legendary Studios In Music' written by Martin Chilton, published 10 August 2023
1033 Paytress
1034 Siouxsie's waxwork went on display at the Virgin Megastore, London, alongside waxworks of Mick Jagger, David Bowie, John Lennon and Jimi Hendrix
1035 Pete Townshend, English musician, is the co-founder, principal songwriter, guitarist and second lead vocalist for The Who. The 10 April gig was the first one organised by the Anti-Heroin campaign, part of the 1980s anti-drug education movements in the UK
1036 Also known as St James's Church, Westminster, and St James-in-the-Fields. Anglican church on Piccadilly, London, England. Designed and built by Sir Christopher Wren and dedicated on 13 July 1684
1037 1980s British electronic music band. Steve Severin produced the 1984 *Jo's So Mean* EP
1038 undiscovermusic.com 'Tinderbox: How Siouxsie & The Banshees' Career Reignited In The Mid-1980s' written by Tim Peacock, published 21 April 2024
1039 From *Things Fall Apart*, the debut novel by Nigerian author Chinua Achebe 16 November 1930 to 21 March 2013, published by William Heinemann Ltd.
1040 'Cities In Dust' was envisaged as the B Side for the proposed single release of 'Party's Fall', Source: thebansheesandothercreatures. co.uk
1041 washingtonpost.com 'All's Wail With Siouxsie The Banshees' Icy Diva of Punk, Still Probing the 'Hidden Side', written by Richard Harrington 11 May 1986
1042 rocksbackpages.com Source 'Siouxsie & The Banshees' Martin Aston, Rock's Backpages audio, 1986
1043 Located on the Gulf of Naples in Campania, Italy, east of Naples and a short distance from the coastline
1044 The Pompeii Forum was the centre of politics, trade, culture and religion in ancient Rome
1045 https://pompeiisites.org/en/archaeological-site/sanctuary-of-the-public-lares/
1046 Yamaha synthesizer manufactured from 1983 to 1989. It was the first successful digital synthesizer and one of the most economically profitable in history
1047 Tape delay effect, first made in 1959. Designed by Mike Battle. Latterly digitised and produced by Dunlop Manufacturing
1048 English record producer, audio engineer and mixer with credits including Siouxsie and The Banshees, The Stranglers, Joni Mitchell and The Pretenders.
1049 'Cities In Dust' twelve-inch format
1050 Former House Engineer at Matrix Studios
1051 Born 19 April 1954. Record producer, musician and sound engineer
1052 Performance venue in Preston, Lancashire, England. Opened in 1973
1053 thebansheesandothercreatures.co.uk *Tinderbox* Trivia
1054 'Dracula' was first published on 26 May 1897 by Archibald Constable and Company
1055 King of England 1327–1377. There were similar rituals carried out during the reign of King Henry III 1216–1272
1056 British mime artist, choreographer, artist, actor and teacher. 3 May 1938 to 24 August 2018
1057 Decorative border created from an unbroken line and formed into a repeat motif
1058 Euclid was a Greek mathematician active as a geometer and logician, active 300 BC. Euclid developed a series of hypotheses, in which all theorems are derived from a small number of simple axioms
1059 1944 triptych painting in the Tate collection

Footnotes

1060 Trilogy of Greek tragedies written by Aeschylus in the 5th century BCE, appertaining to the murder of Agamemnon by Clytemnestra, the murder of Clytemnestra by Orestes and Orestes subsequent trial, the end of the curse on the House of Atreus and the appeasing of the Furies, also known as the Erinyes or Eumenides

1061 Roman house in Pompeii, dating to the 2nd century BC, famous for its intricate mosaics and frescoes depicting scenes from Greek mythology

1062 Music of ancient Rome was a central part of Roman culture and songs were an integral part of virtually every social occasion

1063 Archaic Greek poet from either Eresos or Mytilene, on the island of Lesbos, Greece

1064 Painted after the Hellenistic sculpture, now resides in the Naples Archaeological Museum, southern Italy

1065 In the collection of the National Archaeological Museum in Tarquinia, central Italy

1066 American film director and writer, born 8 August 1948, known foremost as the writer of 'Escape from Alcatraz', released in 1979 and the writer and director of 'Tightrope', released in 1984, both starring Clint Eastwood

1067 Starring the actor Anthony Michael Hall, playing the part of Daryl Cage who gets unwittingly embroiled in the LA drug scene and becomes the prime suspect after his brother is murdered

1068 thebansheesandothercreatures.co.uk 'Tinderbox' Interviews/Articles

1069 English rock band, formed in London in 1963. The band kickstarted the careers of Eric Clapton (1963–1965), Jeff Beck (1965–1966) and Jimmy Page (1966–1968)

1070 Film drama and thriller directed by Michelangelo Antonioni 29 September 1912 to 30 July 2007, starring David Hemmings, Vanessa Redgrave and Sarah Miles

1071 English rock band formed in Bradford in 1983. Initially called Southern Death Cult, the band renamed themselves The Cult in January 1984

1072 American musician and composer, born 16 July 1952 best known for his work as the drummer of The Police from 1977 to 1986, and 2007 to 2008

1073 American singer and songwriter born 17 August 1958

1074 1978 Derek Jarman directed British cult film

1075 Paytress

1076 thebansheesandothercreatures.co.uk 'Tinderbox' Trivia. Source: Melody Maker 17 October 1992

1077 thebansheesandothercreatures.co.uk 'Tinderbox' Trivia. Source: Melody Maker 17 October 1992

1078 From the poem 'The love song of J Alfred Prufrock', first published in 1915 by American-born British poet T. S. Eliot 1888 to 1965

1079 1971 American musical film directed by Mel Stuart from a screenplay by Roald Dahl, based on his 1964 novel *Charlie and the Chocolate Factory*

1080 English actor best remembered for playing the candy store owner Bill in Willy Wonka & the Chocolate Factory. The 'Candyman' song was originally written by Leslie Bricusse and Anthony Newley

1081 Open air concert venue opened in 1946

1082 The swan was the historic heraldic animal of the knights of Schwangau. Ludwig's father, the King of Bavaria from 1848 to 1864, saw himself as their successor and adopted their coat of arms

1083 Completed in 1886, Schloss Neuschwanstein is a historicist palace on a rugged hill in the foothills of the Bavarian Alps in the south of Germany, in close proximity to the Austrian border

1084 Instrumental song by American group Link Wray & His Wray Men. Released in USA on 31 March 1958, Cadence Records

1085 1910 Painting made by French artist Henri Matisse, 31 December 1869 to 3 November 1954

1086 American printer and typographer 13 January 13 1809 to 7 1869

1087 Serif typeface designed by Ed Benguiat in 1974.

1088 thebansheesandothercreatures.co.uk 'Tinderbox' Trivia. Source: Melody Maker 1986

1089 Ancient Greek god synonymous with sleep and dreams

1090 'Ride of the Valkyries' is in reference to the beginning of act 3 of 'Die Walküre', the second of the four music sagas constituting Richard Wagner's 'Der Ring des Nibelungen'

1091 American rock and roll guitarist born 26 April 1938. Eddy is best known for the song 'Peter Gunn' released in January 1959 on RCA Victor Records

1092 The first of a franchise consisting of nine films, a television series, novels, comic books, and various other media, started in 1984, *A Nightmare On Elm Street* is a horror slasher film directed by Wes Craven 2 August 1939 to 30 August 2015

1093 From T.S. Eliot's 'The Waste Land'

1094 theguardian.com 'TS Eliot's The Waste Land issues weather warning for our times' Written by David Hambling, published 16 April 2022

1095 Figure in Arthurian legend, alluding to the last in a long line of British kings tasked with protecting the Holy Grail. In literature, the story dates back to the twelfth century, explored by Chrétien de Troyes' in 'Perceval, the Story of the Grail' written between 1182 and 1190

1096 Inventor of the Gathmann gun. 11 August 11 1843 to 3 June 1917

1097 German geologist, climatologist, geophysicist, meteorologist, and polar researcher. 1 November 1890 to November 1930

1098 Swedish Meteorologist known for the 'Bergeron Process', believed to be the primary process by which rain precipitation is formed. 15 August 1891 to 13 June 1977

1099 Dutch Meteorologist 23 July 1909 to 9. May 1945

1100 American chemist and meteorologist who advanced cloud seeding. 4 July 1906 to 25 July 1993

1101 American engineer, physicist, and chemist. Langmuir was awarded the Nobel Prize in Chemistry in 1932 for his work in surface chemistry. 31 January 1881 to 16 August 1957

1102 Austrian doctor of medicine and psychoanalyst. 24 March 1897 to 3 November 1957

1103 Variantly described as a hypothetical universal life force or esoteric energy

1104 The (what is widely believed to be) pseudoscience developed by William Reich Reich whereby he claimed he could produce rain by manipulating what he called 'orgone energy' present in the atmosphere

1105 Written by Noël Coward 1938 and included in his Broadway revue 'Set to Music', where it was performed by Beatrice Lillie 29 May 1894 to 20 January 1989, in January 1939.

1106 Singer and songwriter Steven Patrick Morrissey, born 22 May 1959

1107 Song by English band The Smiths, written by singer Morrissey and guitarist Johnny Marr, born 31 October 1963

1108 thebansheesandothercreatures.co.uk Source: *NME* 28 September 1985

1109 thebansheesandothercreatures.co.uk Source: *Melody Maker* 1986

1110 Interdisciplinary field of scientific study and branch of mathematics, focusing on underlying patterns and stoical laws of systems that are highly sensitive to primary conditions

1111 American all-girl group from Washington Heights, Manhattan, New York City. Active 1957–1967, 1973–1974
1112 English musician, songwriter and actor and, foremost, the drummer for the Beatles. Born 7 July 1940
1113 rocksbackpages.com Source: 'A Match, a Flame, a Banshee Howls' written by Toby Goldstein for *Creem* magazine, October 1986
1114 The first film produced using the 3D process from Universal-International. The script is based on Ray Bradbury's 'The Meteor' a 110-page story treatment for the movie
1115 thebansheesandothercreatures.co.uk 'Tinderbox' Trivia. Source: *NME* 28 September 1985
1116 American actor, television and film director and screenwriter 29 April 1912 to 25 November 1977
1117 Played by American actor Charles Drake 2 October 1917 to 10 September 1994
1118 Played by American actor Barbara Rush 4 January 1927 to 31 March 2024
1119 Quotation from *It Came From Outer Space*, release date June 5 1953
1120 1955 collection of nineteen macabre short stories by American writer Ray Bradbury. First published on 16 November 1955 by Ballentine Books
1121 Quotation from *Touched With Fire*, from Ray Bradbury's 1955 collection 'The October Country'
1122 Quotation from *Touched With Fire*, from Ray Bradbury's 1955 collection 'The October Country'
1123 Quotation from *Touched With Fire*, from Ray Bradbury's 1955 collection 'The October Country'
1124 Quotation from '*Touched With Fire*, from Ray Bradbury's 1955 collection 'The October Country'
1125 Anthology series that ran for three seasons on First Choice Superchannel in Canada and HBO in the United States from 1985 to 1986, and subsequently on USA Network, where it aired for four additional seasons from 1988 to 1992
1126 American television anthology series created, hosted and produced by Alfred Hitchcock, airing on the CBS and NBC channels, alternately, between 1955 and 1965
1127 *Alfred Hitchcock Presents* Season One, directed by Robert Stevens, 2 December 1920 to 7 August 1989 and first aired 29 January 1956
1128 American drummer and session musician 5 February 1929 to 11 March 2019. Blaine was considered one of the most recorded studio drummers in the music industry, with 35,000 sessions undertaken
1129 Phil Spector produced single on Philles Records, released August 1963
1130 Song composed by Bert Kaempfert 16 October 1923 to 21 June 1980, with lyrics by Charles Singleton 17 September 1913 to 12 December 1985 and Eddie Snyder 22 February 1919 to 10 March 2011. Made famous by Frank Sinatra, American singer and actor, 12 December 1915 to 14 May 1998
1131 William Shakespeare *The Merchant of Venice* Act 2, Scene 9, Line 85, believed to have been written between 1596 and 1598
1132 Thom Gunn *Selected Poems* published by Faber and Faber 2017
1133 English poet 29 August 1929 to 25 April 2004
1134 American film directed by Michael Curtiz, released in 1942 starring Humphrey Bogart 25 December 1899 to 14 January 1957, Ingrid Bergman 29 August 1915 to 29 August 1982 and
Paul Henreid 10 January 1908 to 29 March 1992
1135 William Shakespeare tragedy, written early in his career about the feted romance between two Italian youths from feuding families, believed to have been written 1591 and 1595
1136 8th Century Greek poet credited as the author of epic poems 'The Iliad' and 'The Odyssey'
1137 Ninth studio album by English rock band Deep Purple, released 8 November 1974 on Purple Records
1138 Studio album by Miles Davis released 30 March 1970 Columbia Records
1139 Founded by Herbert Ingram and first published on Saturday 14 May 1842. *The London Illustrated News* was the first ever illustrated weekly news magazine which ran from 1842 to 2003 in various formats including weekly, monthly, quarterly and twice yearly
1140 Article published in *The London Illustrated News* on 18 August 1928
1141 Winged horse in Greek mythology, mostly depicted as a white stallion
1142 English-American fantasy and science fiction writer. Born 18 December 1939
1143 A magic sword featured in numerous fantasy stories by author Michael Moorcock. Stormbringer's first appearance was in Moorcock's 1961 novella *The Dreaming City*
1144 Music genre which developed from the late 1960s synergising elements of jazz harmony and improvisation with funk, rock music and rhythm and blues
1145 Born 4 January 1942 and also known as Mahavishnu, McLaughlin is an English guitarist, composer and bandleader
1146 French painter of German ancestry, 9 April 1932 to 7 March 2002, known for his works used on the covers of music albums, including Santana's *Abraxas*, released 23 September 1970, also on Columbia Records
1147 faroutmagazine.co.uk 'The Cover Uncovered: The story behind Miles Davis' album cover for Bitches Brew' by Malti Klarwein' written by Atreyi Banerji, published 27 January 2021
1148 faroutmagazine.co.uk 'The Cover Uncovered: The story behind Miles Davis' album cover for Bitches Brew' by Malti Klarwein' written by Atreyi Banerji, published 27 January 2021
1149 faroutmagazine.co.uk 'The Cover Uncovered: The story behind Miles Davis' album cover for Bitches Brew' by Malti Klarwein' written by Atreyi Banerji, published 27 January 2021
1150 Born Markus Yakovlevich Rothkowitz until changing his name in 1940, Mark Rothko was an American abstract expressionist painter. September 25 1903 to February 25, 1970
1151 Serif typeface commissioned by *The Times* newspaper in 1931
1152 Millinery dating back to the eighteenth century. In nineteenth century USA, the term 'fascinator' was first applied to headwear
1153 4 May 1929 to 20 January 1993
1154 1964 American musical comedy film, adapted from the 1956 Alan Jay Lerner 31 August 1918 to 14 June 1986 and Frederick Loewe 10 June 1901 to 14 February 1988, stage musical based on George Bernard Shaw's 1913 stage play 'Pygmalion'.
1155 English novelist, comedy writer and critic, who has also worked as a journalist, including the NME, and screenwriter. Born 14 May 1961
1156 rocksbackpages.com 'Siouxsie and The Banshees: How Many LPs Is It Now? "Fifteen, Love"'. Written by David Quantick, New Musical Express, 19 April 1986
1157 rocksbackpages.com 'Siouxsie and The Banshees: How Many LPs Is It Now? "Fifteen, Love"'. Written by David Quantick, New Musical Express, 19 April 1986
1158 rocksbackpages.com 'Siouxsie and The Banshees: How Many LPs Is It Now? "Fifteen, Love"'. Written by David Quantick, New Musical Express, 19 April 1986
1159 rocksbackpages.com 'Siouxsie and The Banshees: How Many LPs Is It Now? "Fifteen, Love"'. Written by David Quantick, New Musical Express, 19 April 1986
1160 rocksbackpages.com 'Siouxsie and The Banshees: How Many LPs Is It Now? "Fifteen, Love"'. Written by David Quantick, New

Musical Express, 19 April 1986

1161 rocksbackpages.com 'Siouxsie and The Banshees: How Many LPs Is It Now? "Fifteen, Love"'. Written by David Quantick, New Musical Express, 19 April 1986

1162 rocksbackpages.com 'Siouxsie and The Banshees: How Many LPs Is It Now? "Fifteen, Love"'. Written by David Quantick, New Musical Express, 19 April 1986

1163 rocksbackpages.com 'Siouxsie and The Banshees: How Many LPs Is It Now? "Fifteen, Love"'. Written by David Quantick, New Musical Express, 19 April 1986

1164 recordcollectormag.com 'The Great Lost Album' written by David Quantick 10 June 2019

1165 Magazine published from 1975 to 1991

1166 English drummer, best known for Taylor's work with Duran Duran

1167 English drumming and percussion magazine 1985 to 2021

1168 English actor, radio and television presenter 10 October 1983 to 28 January 2020

1169 American news program broadcast by New York City based CBS 1982-1992, subsequently renamed CBS Overnight News

1170 American journalist and talk show host. Born 5 January 1942

1171 American criminal, musician and cult leader who fronted the Manson Family, a late 1960s cult based in California. Some members of the cult committed a series of at least nine murders at four locations in July and August 1969

1172 Opened July 1852 and now known as the San Quentin Rehabilitation Centre

1173 Paytress

1174 Paytress

1175 Paytress

1176 Oscar Wilde novel published in April 1891 by Ward, Lock and Company. The novella-length version of which was published in the July 1890 issue of the American periodical 'Lippincott's Monthly Magazine'

1177 Paytress

1178 1982 undeclared war which lasted for eight weeks and 14 June 1982 between Argentina and the United Kingdom over two British dependent territories in the South Atlantic Ocean: the Falkland Islands and its territorial dependency, South Georgia and the South Sandwich Islands. The conflict started on 2 April 1982 and ended on 14 June 1982

1179 Paytress

1180 thebansheesandothercreatures.co.uk 'Through The Looking Glass' Interviews/Articles. Source: Melody Maker 'Flying Down To Rio' written by Chris Roberts, published Chris Roberts 10 January 1987

1181 Released as a stand-alone single on 13 July 1987 on Polydor (UK) and Geffen (US)

1182 Concert venue in Bonne North-Rhine Westphalia, Germany

1183 Born Robert Allen Zimmerman on May 24, 1941. Dylan is an American singer-songwriter and considered one of the best songwriters in history

1184 Danko was a Canadian musician, bassist, songwriter, and singer, 29 December 1943 to 10 December 1999, best known as a founding member of The Band, active 1967 to 1977 and 1983 to 1999

1185 Song originally recorded by Dylan and the Band during their 1967 sessions. Released 26 June 1975

1186 Convention centre located in Santana, São Paulo district, Brazil

1187 Concert venue at Hudson River Park, 555 12th Ave, New York

1188 Stade Francis-Le Blé Brest, Brest, Brittany, France

1189 World Of Music Arts And Dance festival founded in 1980 by Peter Gabriel and Thomas Brooman born 1 April 1954, Bob Hooton, Mark Kidel born 6 July 1947 Stephen Pritchard, Martin Elbourne born 19 January 1957 and Jonathan Arthur

1190 Paytress

1191 Paytress

1192 Composed by bass guitarist Jack Bruce 14 May 1943 to 25 October 2014, with lyrics by poet Pete Brown 25 December 1940 to 19 May 2023 and released as a single in September 1968 (US single) and January 1969 (UK)

1193 Seventh studio (covers) album by David Bowie, released on 19 October 1973 RCA Records

1194 T. Rex song, written by Marc Bolan, released as a stand-alone single on 2 March 1973 T.REX label (UK), covered by the Banshees on the B Side of 'The Staircase (Mystery)', released 23 March 1979 on Polydor Records

1195 English duo formed in Kingston upon Hull in 1982, consisting of Tracey Thorn, lead singer, songwriter, composer and guitarist and Ben Watt, guitarist, keyboardist, songwriter, composer, producer and singer

1196 English musician and composer best known for playing keyboards and trombone for the band Landscape, active 1975 to 1983

1197 Work incudes The Anti-Heroin Project, The Bat Horns, The Noise Boyz and The Starcoast Orchestra

1198 Session musician for The Eurythmics, Toyah, Al Kooper, Siouxsie and The Banshees, Gil Evans, Topper Headon and Shakespears Sister among others

1199 Also credited with playing on the Manic Street Preachers album *Everything Must Go*, released 20 May 1996 on the Epic Label

1200 'Through the Looking-Glass', and 'What Alice Found There', otherwise known as *Alice Through the Looking-Glass* or *Through the Looking-Glass* is a Lewis Carroll penned novel published by Macmillan on 27 December 1871

1201 Paytress

1202 American pop and rock duo formed by brothers Ron Mael, born 5 October 1948 and Russell Mael born 12 August 1945, in Los Angeles, 1971

1203 American Western film directed by John P. McCarthy 17 March 1884 to 4 September 1962, released 16 September 1932

1204 English bass guitar, double bass, and piano player, born 3 May 1954

1205 Electric bass that was manufactured by Rickenbacker 1961 to 1981, 1980 to present (4003 model)

1206 British songwriter and record producer, born 15 June 1943

1207 Debut single released in January 1974 on Polydor Records by The Rubettes 1974 to 1980, 1982 to 1999, 2000 to present

1208 Third Sparks studio album, released on 1 May 1974, Island Records

1209 Broadcast on Children's ITV, 3 May 1986 to 28 August 1988

1210 The performance features a post-John Valentine Carruthers, Banshees line up with guitarist Jon Klein and cellist and keyboard player Martin McCarrick

1211 Side one, track two on Kraftwerk's sixth studio album, recorded in 1976 in Düsseldorf, Germany, released in March 1977, on Kling Klang Records

1212 German composer, musician, lead singer and keyboardist of Kraftwerk, born 20 August 1946

1213 Music festival that took place between 10 and 11th July 1987 at the Berlin Waldbühne, an open-air theatre and part of the Olympic park in the Charlottenburg-Wilmersdorf district of Berlin and the Loreley open-air stage in St. Goarshausen

1214 Featured in *The Jungle Book* Walt Disney file, the song was sung by American actor Sterling Holloway, 14 January 1905 to 22 November 1992 playing the part of Kaa, the snake. The song was written by Disney songwriters Robert Sherman 19 December 1925 to 6 March 2012 and Richard Sherman, born 12 June 1928

1215 Walt Disney 1967 American animated musical comedy, loosely based on the 'Mowgli' stories from the 1894 Rudyard Kipling book of the same title
1216 thebansheesandothercreatures.co.uk 'Through The Looking Glass' Trivia Source: 'The File', Phase Five, Issue One and Two
1217 Fictional character and the main character of the 'Mowgli' stories highlighted among Rudyard Kipling's 'The Jungle Book' stories. Mowgli first appears in 'In the Rukh', one of the stories in Kipling's 'Many Inventions' compendium, published in 1893
1218 French singer, 19 December 1915 to 10 October 1963, most well-known for performing songs in both cabaret and modern chanson genres
1219 American singer and actress, 17 January 1927 to 25 December 2008
1220 English studio guitarist, born 14 May 1937 most well known for playing the guitar riff in the 'James Bond Theme', released 1962 on Liberty Records
1221 thebansheesandothercreatures.co.uk 'Through The Looking Glass' Trivia. Source: Rock World (International short-living monthly magazine, active 1992 to 1993) 1 October 1992
1222 Canadian-American rock band formed in Toronto, Ontario, in 1967. Years active 1967 to 1977 and 1983 to 1999
1223 Two-thirds of the album's twenty-four tracks feature Dylan on lead vocals, backed by The Band, and recorded in 1967. Released on 26 June 1975, by Columbia Records.
1224 Debut studio album by The Band, released 1 July 1968 on Capitol Records
1225 britannica.com 'ixion' Greek Mythology
1226 *King Lear*, Act 4, Scene 7 by William Shakespeare, thought to have been written between 1603 and 1606
1227 King James Bible, first published in 1611
1228 English singer and actress born 8 June 1947
1229 British band led by keyboardist Brian Auger, born 18 July 1939. His 'Wheel's On Fire' duet with Julie Driscoll was a number 5 hit on the 1968 UK Singles Chart
1230 thebansheesandothercreatures.co.uk 'Through The Looking Glass' Trivia. Source: Melody Maker 17 October 1992
1231 thebansheesandothercreatures.co.uk 'Through The Looking Glass' Trivia. Source: Record Hunter, a free weekly supplement with Vox magazine, in circulation from 1990 to 1998, December 1992
1232 Former film studios based in Greenford, Middlesex
1233 Fictional villain in British author Dodie Smith's 1956 novel *The Hundred and One Dalmatians*, first published in 1956 by Heinemann press and subsequently made into a Walt Disney animated film, released on 25 January 1961
1234 The names of the horses were 'Dumpty' and 'Cornet', scratched into the runout groove on the A Side of the single. Source: thebansheesandothercreatures.co.uk 'Through The Looking Glass Trivia'
1235 Broadcast by AVRO (Algemene Vereniging Radio Omroep), established 8 July 1923 and withdrawn on 7 September 2014, *TopPop*, based on *Top Of The Pops*, ran from 22 September 1970 to 27 June 1988
1236 Founded in 1963 by Bob Marley, 6 February 1945 to 11 May 1981, Bunny Wailer, 10 April 1947 to 2 March 2021 and Peter Tosh, 19 October 1944 to 11 September 1987
1237 Broadcast by Belgische Radio- en Televisieomroep (BRT), active 1960 to 1991
1238 Now defunct concert venue on Sunset Strip, Hollywood, California. Active 1994 to 2015
1239 thebansheesandothercreatures.co.uk 'Through The Looking Glass' Trivia
1240 1956 American film directed by Carol Reed 30 December 1906 to 25 April 1976, starring Burt Lancaster, Tony Curtis and Gina Lollobrigida
1241 Ribble is played by the actor Burt Lancaster, 2 November 1913 to 20 October 1994. Lancaster was actually a circus performer before sustaining an injury
1242 Orsini is played by actor Tony Curtis, 3 June 1925 to 29 September 29 2010
1243 Lola is played by actor, model and photojournalist Luigia 'Gina' Lollobrigida 4 July 1927 to 16 January 2023
1244 First track on Bowie's 1977 album *Heroes* and released as the second single from the album on 6 January 1978, peaking at number 39 on the UK Singles Chart RCA Records
1245 American animated sitcom produced by Hanna-Barbera Productions. Aired originally from 23 September 1962 until 17 March 1963 and then resurrected from 1985 to 1987 on the ABC network
1246 thebansheesandothercreatures.co.uk 'Through The Looking Glass' Trivia. Source: Source: 'The File', Phase Five, Issue One and Two
1247 Adapted from the poem 'Bitter Fruit', published in 1937 by Abel Meeropol, 10 February 1903 to 29 October 1986, American songwriter and poet whose works were published under the pseudonym Lewis Allan. Holiday's 'Strange Fruit' was released as a single in 1939 on the Commodore Record label
1248 Born Eleanora Fagan 7 April 1915 to 17 July 1959. American jazz and swing singer. Otherwise known as 'Lady Day', coined by tenor saxophonist Lester Young, 27 August 1909 to 15 March 1959
1249 Born Norma Deloris Egstrom 26 May 1920 to 21 January 2002) known professionally as Peggy Lee. American jazz and popular music singer, songwriter, actress and composer. 'Apples, Peaches and Cherries, Side A, Track four, is from Lee's 1954 album, *Songs In An Intimate Style*, released on Decca Records
1250 The title song is from a ten-minute 1945 Sinatra film of the same name, directed by Mervyn LeRoy 15 October 1900 13 September 13, 1987
1251 Two African-American boys who were slaughtered in a spectacle lynching by a Lynch mob on August 7, 1930, in Marion, Indiana, USA
1252 the guardian.com 'How white Americans used lynchings to terrorize and control black people', written by Jamiles Lartey and Sam Morris, published 26 April 2018
1253 the guardian.com 'How white Americans used lynchings to terrorize and control black people', written by Jamiles Lartey and Sam Morris, published 26 April 2018
1254 American singer who appeared on stage in the 1930s and 1940s.
1255 the guardian.com 'Strange Fruit: the first great protest song' written by Dorian Lynskey 16 February 2011
1256 City located along the Mississippi River, in the southeastern region of the USA state of Louisiana
1257 thebansheesandothercreatures.co.uk 'Through The Looking Glass' Trivia. Source: 'The File', Phase Five, Issue One and Two
1258 Lubahn 20 December 1947 to 20 November 2019 played bass guitar on three of The Doors' albums, *Strange Days*, *Waiting For The Sun*, released 3 July 1968, Elektra Records and *The Soft Parade*, released 18 July 1969, Elektra Records
1259 Transistorised organ, manufactured between 1962 and 1971 by Vox
1260 Paul Allen Rothschild, 18 April 1935 to 30 March 1995, was an American producer during the 1960s and 1970s
1261 agapeta.art 'Poets and Lovers' 'You're Lost Little Girl', by The Doors'
1262 waiting-for-the-sun.net 'Song Notes: You're Lost Little Girl' written by Chuck Crisafulli/Waiting-forthe-Sun.net

1263 Twenty six poems which formed the second part of 'Songs of Innocence and of Experience', published in 1794
1264 thebansheesandothercreatures.co.uk 'Through The Looking Glass' Trivia. Source: Smash Hits 27 October 1983
1265 Also known as a harpsipiano, jangle piano, honky tonk piano and junk piano is a modified version of a straightforward piano, in which objects such as nails or thumb 'tacks' are placed on the felt-padded hammers of the instrument
1266 Four Tops recording, distributed as a single in 1966 from their fourth studio album, 'Reach Out', released in 1967 on the Motown label
1267 Scene wherein the 'Stupid Little Boys' are exiled and succumb to being firstly metaphorical and then literal jackasses
1268 American animated films produced by Walt Disney and released by RKO Radio Pictures
1269 Animatronic, laughing character that was built to attract carnival and amusement park visitors to funhouses and dark rides throughout the United States, developed in 1936
1270 Released by Iggy Pop on the *Lust for Life* album, 9 September 1977. It was initially the B Side of 'Success', a single released in October 1977, RCA Records
1271 Scottish guitarist and composer 31 August 1948 to 13 May 2022
1272 American rock band formed in Ann Arbor, Michigan in 1967 by singer Iggy Pop, guitarist Ron Asheton, 17 July 1948 to 6 January 2009, drummer Scott Asheton 16 August 1949 to 15 March 2014, and bassist Dave Alexander, 3 June 1947 to 10 February 1975. The band were otherwise known as the Psychedelic Stooges and Iggy and The Stooges
1273 Opened in 1961, consisting of The UCLA Neuropsychiatric Institute (NPI) and the UCLA Neuropsychiatric Hospital (NPH)
1274 Tour in support of the album *Station to Station*, released 23 January 1976, RCA records. The tour took place between 2 February 1976 and 18 May 1976
1275 Third Stooges studio album, credited as Iggy and the Stooges, released on 7 February 1973, on Columbia Records.
1276 Debut Iggy Pop studio album, released on 18 March 18, 1977, RCA Records
1277 Second Iggy Pop studio album, released on September 9, 1977, RCA Records
1278 faroutmagazine.co.uk 'Playlist: Every song Iggy Pop and David Bowie collaborated on' written by Jordan Potter, published 27 August 2023
1279 Originally published as two separate volumes of poetry in 1969, 'The Lords and the New Creatures: Poems' was collated and published by Simon & Schuster on 15 Oct 1971
1280 musicradar.com "'David Bowie said, 'Have you got anything?' Then I remembered these chords": Ricky Gardiner on co-writing Iggy Pop's 'The Passenger' written by Matt Frost, published 17 August 2022
1281 Recorded in a couple of sessions with the band as a three piece, along with another new song. 'Peek-A-Boo', which would subsequently appear on the band's *Peepshow* album, released 5 September 1988
1282 Fictional setting of the 1960s UK television series *The Prisoner*
1283 Paytress
1284 Paytress
1285 Paytress
1286 American actress, singer, choreographer and dancer, born 12 March 1946. Minnelli played Sally Bowles in the 1972 film *Cabaret*, directed by Bob Fosse 23 June 1927 to 23 September 1987
1287 British hairstylist 17 January 1928 to 9 May 2012
1288 thebansheesandothercreatures.co.uk 'Through The Looking Glass' Trivia. Source: The File, Phase Four, Issue Four
1289 Otherwise known as a wood scraper block, it is an idiophone percussion instrument
1290 thebansheesandothercreatures.co.uk 'Through The Looking Glass' Trivia
1291 Side Two, track 3, The only instrumental piece on 'Low'
1292 thebansheesandothercreatures.co.uk 'Through The Looking Glass' Trivia
1293 Cycle of frescoes completed by Italian artist Giotto di Bondone 1267 to 8 January 1337, in just two years, between 1303 and 1305
1294 Landlocked country in East Asia, bordered by China to the South and Russia to the to the north
1295 Located off the northern coasts of Russia and Norway
1296 The Nautilus Shell contains a series of unbroken perfect circles, an example of a 'golden spiral' in nature. In geometry and mathematics, this is known as The Golden Ratio, Golden Proportion or Fibonacci Pattern, and is the foundation for most sacred geometry, a ratio between two numbers that equals approximately 1.618
1297 In the late 1920s and throughout the 1930s and 1940s elaborate hood ornaments were very popular with automotive designers. Subject matter such as winged goddesses, graceful birds, and intricate animal designs were proliferate, with some ornaments used for branding the car manufacturer
1298 Photograph taken by Joelle Depont
1299 thebansheesandothercreatures.co.uk 'Through The Looking Glass' Trivia
1300 Fourth John Cale (born 9 March 1942) studio album, released on 1 October 1974 'Gun' appears on Side two, track one
1301 Bonnie Elizabeth Parker, 1 October 1910 to 23 May 23 1934) and Clyde Chestnut "Champion" Barrow, 24 March 1909 to May 1934) were two American bandits and serial murderers who travelled around the Central United States with their gang during the Great Depression, 1929 to 1939
1302 Appears as the main murderous character in Wes Craven's *Nightmare On Elm Street* franchise
1303 Born Phillip Geoffrey Targett-Adams on 31 January 1951, Manzanera is an English musician, songwriter and record producer, best known for his work as lead guitarist in Roxy Music
1304 Side Two, track one from the band's second album, 'White Light/White Heat', released 30 January 1968, Verve Records
1305 One of the earliest forms of rock 'n' roll music, dating back to the 1950s in the USA
1306 Paytress
1307 Paytress
1308 Electro-mechanical piano built by Hohner
1309 Oboe and saxophone player and founder member of Roxy Music, born 23 July 1946
1310 Roxy Music drummer, born 13 May 1951
1311 Founding member and bass guitarist of Roxy Music, 13 October 1943 to 17 April 2012
1312 thebansheesandothercreatures.co.uk 'Through The Looking Glass' Interviews/Articles. Source: Record Mirror, article written by Nancy Culp, 1987
1313 thebansheesandothercreatures.co.uk 'Through The Looking Glass' Trivia. Source: *NME* 1990
1314 Ralph Vaughan Williams was an English composer, 12 October 1872 to 26 August 1958
1315 First released as a 45rpm single in 1975 on Ork Records, named after the band's manager, William Terry Ork
1316 Recorded on 29 June 1978 at the Old Waldorf, San Francisco. Released 2003, on the Rhino Handmade label
1317 Thomas Joseph Miller, 13 December 1949 to 28 January 2023 and known as Tom Verlaine. American singer, guitarist, and songwriter and frontman of Television

1318 American guitarist, songwriter and founder member of Television. Born 25 October 1951

1319 American drummer and founder member of Television and The Waitresses, born 15 February 1950

1320 American bass guitarist, best known for his work with Television. Born 10 April 1948

1321 thebansheesandothercreatures.co.uk 'Through The Looking Glass' Trivia. Source: *NME* 23 July 1987

1322 The Modern Lovers' debut album, released August 1976, although the tracks had been recorded in 1971 and 1972, Beserkley Records

1323 The Stooges debut single from the 1969 self-titled debut album, released July 1969

1324 Only single from the Velvet Underground's 1969 eponymous third album, released March 1969, MGM label

1325 Released in January 1981 as a single from the band's fourth album *Remain In Light*, 8 October 1980, Sire Records

1326 Initiated by Clive Selwood and John Peel in 1986, Strange fruit was the primary distributor of BBC recordings, including Peel Sessions

1327 Paytress

1328 Paytress

1329 Paytress

1330 Paytress

1331 McCarrick worked with Almond initially on Marc And The Mambas' 'Torment In Toreros', released in 1983 on the Some Bizarre label, as well as a Willing Sinner on 'Vermin in Ermine', Some Bizarre/ Phonogram/ Vertigo labels, released October 1984, 'Stories Of Johnny', Some Bizarre/ Virgin label, released in September 1985 and 'Mother Fist and Her Five Daughters', Some Bizarre/ Virgin label, released 6 April 1987

1332 Paytress

1333 Paytress

1334 Guitarist of the British band Japan from 1975 to 1981, subsequently a professional illustrator. Born 23 April 1955

1335 altpress.com '10 bands who led the very grisly idea of goth-punk across history' written by Tim Stegall, 17 March, 2021

1336 1973 musical with music, lyrics and book by Richard O'Brien, born 25 March 1942, subsequently turned into 'The Rocky Horror Picture Show' musical film released in 1975

1337 1982 Ridley Scott directed science fiction film

1338 Released in 1983, London Records

1339 Released 28 October 1983, London Records

1340 Released 1985 on the Trust record label

1341 The UK Independent Singles Chart represents the best-selling independent singles and in the United Kingdom, for recording artists not attached to major recording labels. Established in January 1980

1342 Paytress

1343 Paytress

1344 American record label, founded in 1966, owned by Warner Music Group and distributed by Warner Records

1345 Paytress

1346 Released on 13 July 1987 on Polydor (UK) and Geffen (US)

1347 Paytress

1348 American tabloid newspaper. Founded in 1926

1349 Debut Wire studio album, released December 1977 on the Harvest label

1350 Second Wire studio album, released 8 September 1978

1351 Third Wire studio album, released September 1979

1352 Paytress

1353 Another song, 'Star Crossed Lovers', also with lyrics penned by Severin, and released on the 2009 remastered CD reissue, could be considered as part of a trilogy of songs about lovers meeting under cover of darkness under the stars with crashing waves etc.

1354 British counter-culture nightclub in London in the 1960s. In the basement of 31 Tottenham Court Road, underneath the Gala Berkeley Cinema, it ran for nine months, from December 1966 to August 1967

1355 'Song From The Edge Of The World' was part of the four song live recording with John Valentine Carruthers playing guitar on the BBC Radio 2 Janice Long Show, recorded 11 January 1987 and subsequently transmitted on 2 February 1987

1356 thenbansheesandothercreatures.co.uk 'Peepshow' Trivia. Source: The File, Phase Five, Issue One and Two

1357 American tabloid newspaper established in 1926

1358 The festival was at the amphitheatre venue located on top of the Lorelei rock in St. Goarshausen, Germany

1359 Paytress

1360 Paytress

1361 Paytress

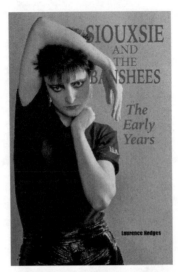

Siouxsie and the Banshees - The Early Years
ISBN: 978-1-915246-24-0

Monday 20th September 1976 saw one of the most unexpected moments in music history when what was to become one of the most iconic, important and mimicked bands of the 1970s, 1980s and 1990s took to the stage at The 100 Club in Oxford Street, London. A last-minute addition to the '100 Club Punk Special' that included The Clash, Sex Pistols, Buzzcocks and The Damned, an unknown Siouxsie and The Banshees, comprising Sid Vicious, Steve Severin, Marco Pirroni and Siouxsie Sioux, unleashed twenty minutes of 'performance art' improvisation, featuring fragments of 'Deutschland, Deutschland, Über Alles', 'Twist And Shout' and 'Satisfaction'.

'The Lord's Prayer', which was to become a staple of Siouxsie and The Banshees' early live repertoire, was a white-noise assault on the senses and a barometer of the alienation many teenagers felt from the bloated nature of mid-1970s 'arena rock'. Several line-up changes later, in 1978, Siouxsie and The Banshees were propelled into the pop stratosphere. Signed to a major record label, the band released 'Hong Kong Garden' and wrote one of the most influential post-punk albums of all time, The Scream, a savage critique of curtain-twitching suburbia, the cheap titillation of the tabloids, and the dangers of believing and following any one doctrine.

1979's Join Hands, influenced by the political landscape in Britain and further afield, and the catastrophic loss of life in World War One, was a milestone of the band's increasing maturity. After a tour fraught with fractiousness, a new line up with Slits' drummer Budgie and Magazine guitarist John McGeoch, together with Siouxsie Sioux and Steve Severin, released the band's most experimental album, Kaleidoscope, which was a heady mix of psychedelia and sonorous adventures including the singles 'Happy House' and 'Christine'.

Siouxsie and The Banshees The Early Years explores the adventures, trials and tribulations of a band defying categorisation. Their uncompromising brilliance is exemplified by three unique albums, which are chronicled in the pages of this authoritative survey.